PRAISE FOR MARIAN LANOUETTE'S JAKE CARRINGTON THRILLERS

ALL THE DEADLY LIES

"*All the Deadly Lies* is a rawly rendered thriller that toes the line between feisty and fierce without ever losing its underlying sense of fun."
—*Criminal Elements*

ALL THE PRETTY BRIDES

"Tense and authentic—a suspenseful page-turner!"
—Leo J. Maloney, bestselling author of the Dan Morgan thriller series

Books by Marian Lanouette

Jake Carrington Thrillers
All the Deadly Lies
All the Hidden Sins
All the Pretty Brides
All the Dirty Secrets

All the Dirty Secrets

A Jake Carrington Thriller

Marian Lanouette

LYRICAL UNDERGROUND
Kensington Publishing Corp.
www.kensingtonbooks.com

LYRICAL UNDERGROUND BOOKS are published by

Kensington Publishing Corp.
119 West 40th Street
New York, NY 10018

All Kensington titles, imprints, and distributed lines are available at special quantity discounts for bulk purchases for sales promotion, premiums, fund-raising, educational, or institutional use.

Special book excerpts or customized printings can also be created to fit specific needs. For details, write or phone the office of the Kensington Sales Manager: Kensington Publishing Corp., 119 West 40th Street, New York, NY 10018. Attn. Sales Department. Phone: 1-800-221-2647.

Lyrical Underground and Lyrical Underground logo Reg. US Pat. & TM Off.

First Electronic Edition: May 2019
ISBN-13: 978-1-5161-0481-9 (ebook)
ISBN-10: 1-5161-0481-1 (ebook)

First Print Edition: May 2019
ISBN-13: 978-1-5161-0482-6
ISBN-10: 1-5161-0482-X

Printed in the United States of America

This book is dedicated to my "From the Cradle to the Grave" friends, Dorothy Gregory Rigano, Maureen Geronimo, and Kathy Monahan Hyams. We've known each other since birth and have been there for each other through thick and thin. I cherish our friendship.

Chapter 1

Sergeant Louie Romanelli donned a second pair of gloves before he dared touch anything in the rent-by-the-hour room. Squeaky beds and low moans from the adjoining rooms bled through the walls, even on a Sunday morning. Someone was getting it, but not him. He'd been called from home on his day off as a special favor for Commissioner Todd Blake. Sophia hadn't been a happy camper when he told her he had to report in. His wife had planned a family outing for the day and now he had ruined the whole thing—yet again. *The job is the job*, he thought.

No, instead he'd get to spend his day in a diseased, bug-infested room, standing over the half-nude body of the commissioner's lovely wife splayed on the bed. He had seen her only the night before, at a local charity ball she had organized. Her brilliant blue eyes had been alive then, vibrant, but had now started to fade as Callie Blake stared up at the ceiling with a vacant death gaze. Not for the first time, he wondered why this classy lady had been in this fleabag motel dressed like a hooker.

Louie turned, then strolled toward the door when a car screeched to a stop at the curb. The low murmur of the crowd that had gathered outside the scene grew louder. A mixture of pimps, hookers, and local residents with their cell phones at the ready waited to learn what had happened in room 142. Not that it was uncommon for a death to occur here. Most residents at the motel were druggies and many had overdosed inside their rooms.

He handed the evidence bag to the uniform next to him. He'd recognized the captain's car. Louie waited for his passenger to step from the car. He swore under his breath when Commissioner Todd Blake climbed out. *Why the hell did the captain bring him to the crime scene?* Blake was a suspect, for God's sake. The media vultures hovered outside the police lines, shouting questions at the captain and Blake. *For pity's sake, it's going to be all over the news tonight that the police commissioner received special treatment.*

Blake ignored the screaming media as if they weren't there. Gwenn Langley, the reporter from Channel 5, stood off to the side, away from the herd. Gwenn placed her hand on Blake's elbow and leaned close to whisper into his ear. From his place in the doorway of the crime scene, Louie rushed toward the pair to shelter Blake from her.

"Step back or I'll have you removed from the scene. Gwenn, show a little respect. This isn't the time or the place to approach the commissioner," Louie warned.

"Louie, she's fine, leave her alone," Blake said.

Louie stared Langley down before shifting his gaze to Captain Shamus McGuire, who shrugged at the unasked question.

Louie cleared his throat before he spoke in a soft voice for Blake's ears only. "Commissioner, I can't let you on the crime scene."

"That's my wife in there, Sergeant. I'm going in come hell or high water. Now get the hell out of my way if you want to keep your job," Todd shot back. The veins in his temples looked as if they were about to burst from his skin.

Louie was afraid the commissioner would have a stroke and become his next casualty. As if a pack of lions, the media moved in closer, hoping for a sound bite for tonight's news.

"Captain…" Louie turned to Shamus, a plea in his eyes.

Commissioner Blake was his boss, but he couldn't allow him to muddy up the evidence. If it came to trial, Blake's lawyers would have a field day. They'd almost be guaranteed a dismissal based on compromised evidence.

Shamus grasped Blake's arm, and whispered something to him. Louie leaned in, trying to hear, but Blake pinned Louie with a glare.

"Callie needs me, Shamus. I have to go in," Blake said.

"I'll walk you in…" Louie said, conceding to his captain's judgment, but was cut off before he could finish his warning to Blake. He understood Blake's need. He'd want to see the body and crime scene if his wife, Sophia, lay dead in there instead of Callie Blake. The thought frightened Louie, and he blessed himself to banish it.

Shamus said, "Louie, step aside. Todd's going in for a minute, but you have to promise, Todd, afterward you'll wait for me in the car."

"Shamus…"

"Todd, I can't compromise the scene. If you don't agree to not touch anything, I'll have to have an officer escort you from the scene."

Blake's eyes narrowed as he stared down Shamus. Louie watched McGuire count down the seconds before Blake agreed.

Shamus led Todd Blake from the curb, up the path lined with the shouting media, to room 142. When Louie, his captain, and the commissioner stepped into the crime scene, Louie's team stopped what they were doing and came to attention. Blake approached his dead wife. Louie caught a few exchanging looks and behind Blake's back, he waved off the team. *At least they have the grace to drop their eyes*, Louie thought. *God, this is a mess.* It was painful to watch when Blake dropped to his knees by Callie's corpse. Sobs racked his body.

"Who could do this to her?"

Blake went to wipe her hair from her eyes. Louie started toward the commissioner, but Shamus pushed him away and grabbed Blake by his arm before Blake could touch Callie's body, which was dressed in black fishnet stockings and a black see-through bustier that fit a bit loose for Callie Blake's slender figure. There was a rip in the fabric, torn by the bullet that had entered her heart. To Louie, the crime scene seemed staged.

"I need you to go to the car, Todd," Shamus whispered to Blake.

It pained Louie to see the commissioner this way. Blake pushed off his knees, his fists curled by his sides. He hesitated, twisting back to look one more time at his wife. Blake then squared his shoulders and left the room. Louie pointed to a uniform to escort the commissioner to Shamus's vehicle and instructed him to keep the press out of his face. It didn't stop the media from shouting questions at the commissioner. Louie stayed in the doorway until Blake climbed into the car.

"Do you think he'll stay in the car?" Louie asked.

"Yes. What have you got?"

"A single bullet wound directly into the heart, but it looks like she fought before she was shot. Her knuckles are scraped up a bit. One shot, and I'd bet she died instantly, but we'll wait for Dr. Lang to verify the cause before we give that to Blake and the press. Shamus…"

"Just tell me, Louie."

"There are pictures by the body, of Mrs. Blake in stages of undress, posing with a man. His back's to the camera, so it will be hard to identify him. It appears she had been carrying on with him. From what I know of Mrs. Blake, she wasn't that type of woman, was she?" Louie asked. "Oh, and here's the clincher. There are also a couple of nude photos of her alone."

"No, she wasn't that type of woman. I was afraid something like this would happen. I need to be up front with you, Louie. When we were at the gala last night, Todd told me Callie had received a blackmail letter with some pictures. The letter demanded twenty-five thousand dollars, and said they'd contact her soon."

"Why the hell...I'm sorry, Cap, why didn't you tell me and Jake this last night? We could've jumped right on it."

"Todd wanted to wait until today. He didn't want to ruin the gala for Callie." Shamus pinched his nose as he evaluated the crime scene.

"Have you considered he needed time to plan this out?"

"Louie, I've known the man for over twenty-five years. He didn't kill his wife. He adored her."

"Even if she had an affair?" *Playing the devil's advocate is never a popular role*, Louie thought.

"She didn't, I know it...but I'll keep as open a mind as I can. Don't you worry about it."

Christ, if I nail the commissioner for this, there goes my career.

* * * *

Lieutenant Jake Carrington had been looking forward to his trip to Vermont with his girlfriend, Mia, while out on medical leave. He'd promised her that nothing and nobody would interrupt them. In the townhouse he'd rented on the mountain, a stone fireplace dominated the great room, which blended into the kitchen, and the stairs to the right wound in a wide spiral. Jake climbed them, Mia followed behind. Together they checked out the king-size bed. He lowered his body to the bed, ignoring the shooting pain in his gut, and flashed her his biggest grin. How fast could they mess it up?

"It's all I need, how about you?" He patted the place beside him.

"I love a fireplace in the bedroom," Mia said. "I'll light the fire and take the chill out of the air while you get the bags and we unpack."

Jake took the cue and went down to the car. Five minutes later he returned with their bags, to the pleasing smell of wood burning in the fireplace.

"You're pretty good with fire." He locked eyes with her as she turned from the fireplace. "I'll have to watch myself," Jake said.

Mia pushed up from her place in front of the hearth. Jake dropped her bags on the luggage rack and placed his single bag on the desk. Sunlight played off the floral wallpaper, putting half the room in shadows. It illuminated the bed, inviting them in. She had started to unzip her suitcase and put clothes in the dresser drawers. Jake admired the back view but wanted to hold her. He came up from behind and wrapped his arms around her waist, and then nibbled on her neck.

She tilted her head to the left as she sank into him.

"I've thought of this all week," he whispered into her ear, finding the sweet spot where her pulse throbbed in her neck. "I was so afraid something or someone would sabotage this—your deadline or my job. I'm glad it didn't."

He turned her around to face him. Jake gently bit her lower lip and snuggled her closer to him. "I want you."

Jake danced her to the bed as he unbuttoned her blouse and kissed his way down her neck. "My Mia," he whispered as he fell onto the bed with her and started working off her jeans.

His breath caught in his throat when he shucked his shirt and his cell phone tumbled from the pocket. He ignored the jabbing pain from the knife wound he'd received on his last case and bent to retrieve his phone before slamming it on the nightstand, and continued to undress Mia, never taking his eyes off her.

Mia's eyes darkened to midnight blue. He loved the change—no matter if it was with passion or anger—the color always drew him in. He started to slide her jeans from her hips when his cell phone started vibrating on the nightstand. He ignored it.

"Aren't you going to check to see who's calling?" Mia pushed up on her elbows.

Jake stretched his six-foot frame beside her and curled a strand of her silky black hair around his finger while leaning on an elbow. Though both had Irish ancestry, their coloring differed. Mia's pale white skin against her black hair and blue eyes engaged him every time he looked at her.

"No. You're all that matters in this moment."

"Jake, everyone knows not to bother you unless it's important. At least see who it is."

Whoever it is, is a dead man.

He sat up, threw his legs over the edge of the bed. Only then did he pick up his phone and check the caller ID.

Damn it! Louie.

Before he'd left Wilkesbury, Connecticut, he'd stressed that no one should bother him unless someone was dying or dead.

Jake answered.

"This had better be damn good, like you need a kidney or something in the next couple of hours," Jake snapped.

"I'm sorry to do this to you, but the commissioner wants to speak with you personally. I'll conference him in."

The fact that Louie didn't joke or jabber told Jake whatever had happened was big. Louie had been too formal. Half dressed, Mia sat up and leaned into Jake's back, her head close to the phone to eavesdrop. He didn't bother to untangle himself—she had a right to know what was going on. This would affect her vacation as well.

"Jake, it's Blake." The Wilkesbury police commissioner cleared his throat. In all the time he'd known the guy, Blake had never allowed an emotion to filter through. "My wife, Callie..."

"Commissioner, will it be easier for you if Louie fills me in?" *Something was definitely wrong.*

"No, no. Callie's been murdered." The commissioner coughed into the phone. "I need a personal favor from you and Louie. You're the only two I trust to handle this. I want the both of you working Callie's case."

"I'm so sorry for your loss, Commissioner," Jake said, squeezing his eyes shut. *I just saw her last night at the gala. What happened? Did the commissioner kill her? No, it couldn't be.* "Commissioner, I haven't been cleared for duty." Jake's hand automatically rested over the healing knife wound.

"I'll override it. I need you and Louie on this," Blake said.

Jake went immediately into cop mode. There was no question about what had to be done. He mimed writing on a piece of paper to Mia, hoping she understood. She jumped off the bed and shuffled through the desk drawer until she found paper and a pencil. She handed them to him. Jake took notes while Mia knelt close to his phone to listen in.

"I'm in Vermont. It will take me two hours or more to get home and another hour to drop off Mia. In the meantime, there's no one better than Louie to process the scene."

"I know that. But I want the both of you working it. It's delicate. There were photos found with her body..." The commissioner's voice faded.

"Jake, I'll fill you in when I'm through with the commissioner," Louie said.

Jake hung up and sat there for a second before turning to Mia. "I'm sorry. You know I need to handle this one."

"My God, Jake, I met her last night. I liked her. What happened?"

"Louie couldn't say with the commissioner there, but Blake said she was murdered."

"We better get going. We'll do this some other time," Mia said, pushing off the bed. She'd started to adjust her clothes, then emptied the drawers, putting her clothes back in the suitcase.

"Let me make a call to the rental agency."

Jake canceled the weekend and got stuck with the two-night minimum charge. They started the long drive home. He'd have to wait for Louie's return call to learn the facts of the case.

Jake pushed the speed limit when he hit I-91 south. Twenty-five minutes after getting on the highway in Vermont he approached exit 26 in Greenfield, Massachusetts. He put on his signal and veered off the highway. They'd have lunch here. When he'd have time for another meal, he didn't know. Jake threw the shifter into park as his phone started vibrating in his pocket.

"About damn time. What took you so long?"

"I questioned Blake, but we need to do a more in-depth one-on-one when you arrive. Shamus interviewed him with me. Lord, he tiptoed around the questions. It took twice as long as it should've."

"What happened?"

"The manager of the dive on Foundry Lane found her a little after two when he did his daily check of the rent-by-the-hour guests."

"Not Wilson's Motel?"

"Yep, the one and only. She was shot through the heart and one of her stockings was tied around her neck in a bow. The knuckles on her right hand were scraped. It tells me she fought back, trying to defend herself. Beside the body we found a picture of her in the arms of a man. His back was to the camera, but it was obvious it wasn't the commissioner. Not a pretty sight. In another photo, she was alone wearing one of those sexy bustiers with a garter belt and nothing else...as in no underwear. And there are some nude photos of her alone."

"Was she the one who rented the room?"

Jake couldn't find a valid reason Callie Blake would go to a motel, not to mention the Wilson. He'd known the Blakes for a good many years, and Callie cheating didn't add up. He'd have bet his house on her fidelity. What about her children? Did they know their mother had been murdered?

"Yes, she paid cash for it. The manager said it wasn't her first time there either."

"You sure he's not lying? And did the clerk see who went in with her?"

"Jake, I know how to do my job."

"Sorry, it's hard not being there. Do you know why she was there?" He'd run his own background check on the clerk when he got home. He had to be lying.

"Your guess is as good as mine. I'd say she'd been cheating on the commissioner, but he denies it. He insists she wouldn't do that."

"Ah." He understood what Louie wasn't saying. "Does he understand that we'll find the truth? No matter what he tries to hide, it will come out during the investigation."

How many times in his career had he been surprised by a friend caught in a bad situation—*Too many to count*, he thought. But with Callie Blake it really did seem unlikely.

"He's counting on it. And of course, the press is already here."

Jake groaned, rubbing his face. "We're going to stop for lunch now, then I'll be back on the road. I'm about an hour and a half out. Anything else I should know?" *Damn, I knew this getaway was a mistake.*

"No, let me finish processing the scene. If anything turns up, I'll call you back," Louie said.

Jake liked to assess the scene and the body himself, but by the time they got home, the body would be at the morgue.

"Louie, do me a favor and leave it exactly how you found it until I get there. No crime techs, please. You know I like to walk the scene even without the body."

"I figured you'd want a run at it. I'll keep a guard posted there until you arrive. In the meantime, I'll send you the pictures of how she was found."

"Who's posting?"

"Doc Lang."

"Good, she got the best."

"Blake requested him."

He hung up with Louie and he and Mia went inside the restaurant. The slow service had him cranky. Jake ate a sandwich but he didn't taste it, his mind already working the case. He took his ever-ready notepad from his pocket and started scribbling down his questions. His cell phone pinged. He opened up the attachment and studied the scene.

"That's disgusting, Jake. What a lovely lunch companion you make," Mia said, leaning over to view the photos and almost losing her stomach contents. "I can't wrap my mind around her death. It's like there's two sides to her," she said, pointing to his phone.

Was Mia correct? Did Callie Blake have a secret life?

Chapter 2

Melinda scanned the crowd from the right side of the reception area. She searched out an opportunity for the most-drunken-guest photo of shame. Sunday afternoon weddings were usually more sedate than evening ones. She hadn't had much luck in the first hour of the reception. She needed someone to bump into her hard to explain away the black eye once she removed the makeup. Melinda couldn't concentrate on the wedding, and her camera and light meter weighed on her. She wouldn't be in this situation if she hadn't been desperate for money. Why the hell had she listened to Sal in the first place? Last night's gig at the gala had worn her out. The mother of the bride beckoned her over again, directing Melinda to take this one or that one's picture, like she didn't know how to do her damn job.

"I'd like a family picture of me and my brothers. Then one with our spouses in it."

"Why don't you all come outside and we'll do it by the trellises?"

She lined up the siblings, set the speed and exposure on her camera, and almost swore out loud when she brought the camera up to her eye. The area around the left eye hurt like a bitch and had her wondering how Sal's job had gone today. *It'd been hard to believe that skinny stick of a woman had it in her, until her fist landed in my face.* Well, anyway, she'd covered it up with some makeup. Today, she'd be alibied up the ying-yang. Melinda inhaled and wished she'd never met Sal. This was all his fault. Yes, she needed money. Her husband, Tony, had left her deep in debt to the tune of five hundred thousand dollars when he died in the car accident. But there had to be a better way.

"Okay, everyone, big smiles—that's it." She clicked the button. "One more, then the spouses will line up, wives in the front, husbands in the back."

When she snapped the last shot, she decided this would be a good time for a quick break. She turned off the camera on the tripod and checked the smaller ones draped around her neck.

"Don't go anywhere, Melinda. Mom, I want a picture with all of you." The bride cocked her finger at her. Melinda wanted to bite it off. What a waste. Weddings like this were all show and money—the price tag on this one had to cost the parents well over forty grand. It would've made a nice down payment on a house. Yet, they'd fought her tooth and nail on her prices. A long time ago she'd learned not to cave in to the pressure. It'd taken her many long hours and functions to prove she was the best, and for that they had to pay her price or they could get someone else.

After she finished with them, Melinda went outside for some fresh air and to check her phone. The freaking thing had been buzzing nonstop in her pocket. It was distracting.

Eight calls from Sal had her worried. What was that about? Melinda reached for the callback button, but her finger never connected. Her break was over before it even began. Another guest wanted a picture with the bride. She'd call him back after the reception.

She put her phone on silent and continued to work the wedding. Three hours in she found her drunken target. *Oh yeah! He'll make the perfect patsy.* Melinda snapped pictures as she made her way around the room. She knelt, snapped, stood, snapped, and then spun around with her camera up around her face, and right on cue the drunken groomsman lost his balance and mowed into her, jamming her camera into her face. If anyone asked tomorrow, this would explain away her black eye, and she'd not have to wear makeup to hide it.

"Ouch!" Melinda said as she swooned. It hurt more than she had anticipated.

The bride and some of her guests rushed over to Melinda. She even let a couple women usher her into the ladies' room. She sat on the velvet chair. A waitress brought in a baggie with some ice in it for her eye.

"Here, sweetie, it's starting to bruise," the waitress said. "Oh no, there's a little scratch on your cheek too.

It dawned on Melinda the concealer might've worn thin.

After twenty minutes, she decided she was good. "Thank you so much for your help, ladies. I'm fine now. I'm going to use the restroom before I rejoin the party."

When she was certain all the helpful guests had left and she was alone in the bathroom, Melinda wet a paper towel and lightly rubbed the area around her eye to remove some more of the makeup to reveal more of the bruising.

Melinda rejoined the wedding and continued taking pictures of the guests as they danced or posed, and every once in a while she'd go to the ladies' room and wash off some more makeup. By the end of the night she sported a full black eye and had gained everyone's sympathy.

My cards should read "I'll do anything for my craft," she thought, and laughed.

* * * *

The noise and questions from the shouting press filled the car when Shamus climbed in to join Todd Blake. Todd sat in the passenger's seat, his posture ramrod straight. He ignored Shamus, who was racking his brain for the right words.

"I don't believe you killed her, Todd, but you have to understand why you couldn't stay on the scene. Please don't take it out on Louie for doing his job."

"Whatever happened to trust or a little courtesy? That's my wife in there, Shamus," Todd said, still staring straight ahead.

"I'll take you home. The kids need to know what happened. I'll be happy to speak to them for you." He wasn't going to restate the obvious. Investigations had to be clean to get a conviction. Once Todd settled down, he'd understand. At least Shamus hoped Todd would.

"No, I'll tell them. They should hear it from their father. God, I hope the media hasn't broadcasted her name yet. Hurry," Todd said, an urgency to his tone.

Shamus pulled out of the motel parking lot and maneuvered around patrol cars, the meat wagon, the media vans, and wires. He'd never given a thought to the media. *Lord, what if Darcy has already heard?* He extracted his cell phone from the inside pocket of this jacket. Eight missed calls from her. *I should've called her right away.* He'd hear about it when he got home, but Todd had been his only concern once he'd been notified of the death. He and Todd had been meeting to figure out how to trap the blackmailer when the call had come in.

Fifteen minutes later, Shamus clicked on his right turn-signal and drove onto Blake's street. The block was lined with media vans and TV personnel invading the quiet of Todd's ritzy neighborhood. *Shit, what is wrong with me today?* The front door opened as he drove into the Blakes' driveway. The Blakes' oldest son, Todd Jr., rushed to the car.

Todd jumped out of the passenger's side, ran to him and closed his arms around Todd Jr., rushing him back into the house before the young man could say a word. The agility with which Todd handled his son impressed Shamus. *At least one of us is thinking.* Squaring his shoulders, Shamus strode to the curb and addressed the press.

"There'll be no statements at this time. I ask that you give the family some privacy." He turned to walk away and then turned back. "I hope you're all proud of yourselves for broadcasting the victim's name before the family, especially her children, could be notified. I don't know how you live with yourselves."

He shouldn't have said anything. It's wrong to engage the press, but a quiet fell over the media. Shamus marched toward the Blakes' house.

* * * *

At 4:39 Jake stood in the doorway of room 142 at the Wilson Motel. He couldn't picture the commissioner's wife resting her body on that dirty bed. The motel rented by the hour or week. Most customers used the place for drugs or hooking or both. *What the hell was Callie Blake doing down here?*

The STD environment scuzzed Jake out as he and Louie cast black lights over the bed, walls, rugs, and furniture. How the hell did a person get bodily fluids on the curtains?

He'd known her for years. Callie Blake had been a lady in every sense of the word. She was a devoted mother and wife, yet all the evidence pointed to her being an adulteress. A word he'd never have associated with her. Not once in all the time he'd known her had there been a hint of a scandal. *Goes to show we don't know people as well as we think we do. Still...*

"Something's off," Jake said.

"Yeah, I got the same vibe," Louie agreed.

"I can't put my finger on it. There's no forced entry. She had to have let her killer in."

"Exactly. What I wanted to ask the commissioner, but couldn't in front of his kids, was did he and his wife do romantic weekends or role play."

"You think this is a role-play situation?"

"I don't know. The whole scene seemed staged. You'll see what I'm talking about when you view the crime scene photos."

"We'll get him alone and ask." Jake dropped an evidence marker by a cigarette butt and another one by a syringe. "Is Lang doing a blood workup?"

"Yes." Louie crossed the room and marked a blackened butter knife. Jake leaned over his shoulder.

"Have the lab rush the blood work. I want to check for drugs. Lang give you any idea what caliber gun was used?"

"No, he said the prelim would be ready by six tonight."

Jake took his own pictures of the scene. He was ready to start talking to people. "Call in the techs. Let's drop your car off. I want a go at the commissioner."

"You're not looking at him for this, are you?"

"Not yet. Knowing the guy, I'd say he didn't kill his wife."

Did he really know the guy? What he didn't want to say aloud was that he could see Todd killing anyone who touched his family. But would Todd Blake kill a cheating wife? For the time being, Jake decided to hold that one close to the vest.

* * * *

Louie dropped off his car at the police garage and climbed into Jake's police-issued sedan. "How'd Mia take it when you told her you needed to come back early?"

"Well, you called at the most inopportune moment. And remind me that I owe you one for that."

Louie studied Jake's irritated profile, and then it clicked. He started laughing. "You had to have just arrived, for God's sake."

"Is nothing exciting happening in your own life? Leave it be, Louie. She understood why we had to come home."

Louie noted the annoyance in Jake's voice as he continued, "I like it unexciting, especially after the last case."

Louie understood Jake was shutting down.

* * * *

Jake parked in front of Blake's house and together they studied the large structure.

"I'll let you question the commissioner. I've had my pass at him," Louie said before Jake opened the driver's door.

"You think he's holding back?" Jake asked.

"Yep, the place where Callie was found didn't seem to surprise him. Maybe I'm reading too much into it. He was cryptic in a few of his answers. I suggested the kids leave the room, but he wouldn't let them."

Louie jumped out of the passenger side of the car. "How're you going to handle him?" he asked as he and Jake made their way to the front door.

"Like any other suspect."

Louie turned, studied the large, rambling colonial house. The first time here his nerves wreaked havoc, forcing him to concentrate on the miserable task at hand. Now he estimated the square-footage before he knocked. He liked to know what he was dealing with and how many exits, if it played into a search. Not that he thought Blake would try to run from him.

Louie's fist had barely touched the door when it opened. The commissioner focused his gaze on Jake first, then him. It didn't get past Louie that Blake seemed ten years older since he'd seen him at the motel. A gray pallor emphasized his devastated eyes. Grief hung on Blake in ways Louie understood for the first time in his life. When he'd almost lost Sophia... he wasn't going there. He cleared his throat.

"Jake, Louie, come in," Blake said. "Jake, are you going to be okay coming back this soon from sick leave?"

"I'm ready, Todd. Don't worry about me," Jake said.

"Are Todd Jr. and Mary still here, sir?" Louie asked.

"No, I sent the children to Callie's sister. I knew you'd be back when Jake arrived. You guys want anything to drink?"

"No, sir," Jake answered. "We don't want to bother you for long. I have a couple of questions."

Louie took a seat on the red and yellow floral couch. Jake took the solid blue armchair. Todd Blake sank into the other armchair. When the commissioner nodded, Jake continued. "Was this a role-playing game gone wrong?"

Blake's eyebrows shot into his thinning hairline. A sad smile jerked at the corner of his lip. "Where the hell did that come from?"

"It needed to be asked."

"Did you know about the pictures?" Louie asked.

"You're both quite good." Blake examined his hands. "Yes, Callie showed them to me last night, along with the nude ones and the blackmail letter demanding twenty-five thousand dollars."

"Why didn't you have the department intervene on your behalf?" Jake said.

"I confided in Shamus last night. And this morning we were meeting to discuss how to handle it. If it was your wife, Jake, would you take anyone but Louie into your confidence?" Todd pushed up off the chair and paced the room. "No, you wouldn't. Callie and I both knew not to pay. It would never end. She told me that she didn't cheat, and I believe her. For our anniversary she went to a professional photographer and had what's called boudoir pictures taken for me. She explained the photographer had a male model there to spice up the pictures. You have to understand Callie is, I mean was, a very trusting woman. The photographer told her only the back of the man would show. And for God's sake, I don't understand why she'd think that would turn me on. I thought it was disrespectful, her standing around in her underwear with a stranger."

"How'd she react to your comments?"

"She started crying, begged forgiveness. Said she only wanted to spice up our marriage. So you see I'm partly to blame for all this if she felt it needed to be spiced up." Blake hung his head in his hands. "You understand, Louie, that I didn't want to say anything in front of the officers on scene or here with the children."

"Yes," Louie said.

Jake waited for Blake to lift his head before asking, "Commissioner, did you murder your wife?"

"God, Jake, no, I've loved Callie since I was fourteen. We would've gotten through it if there was a scandal. Anyone who knew her knew she wouldn't cheat. I think you should be questioning that damn photographer."

"Who was that?"

"Hold on, I'll get the card."

Louie shrugged as he tried to gauge Jake's take on the situation. Tonight, he'd make sure to have a discussion with Sophia about boudoir photos. Not that he thought she'd do them, but he'd have thought the same of Callie Blake. How did this photographer talk her into posing with a man?

The commissioner handed the card to Jake. *Damn, the expression that passed over Jake's face spelled trouble.*

"Commissioner, I'll tell you right up front, Louie and I know this woman. Her late husband was a school friend of ours. I also dated her for a brief period in high school right before my sister's death. We're not close, but you need to know all of this up front. I did notice her taking pictures at the gala last night. You believe she's connected, Todd?" Jake switched to the commissioner's first name. Louie understood the tactic. He'd used it many times himself. It made it personal, and Jake hoped he'd get more out of Blake.

Chapter 3

Darcy McGuire turned on the television for noise now that the kids were grown and out of the house. It had surprised her how much she missed their arguing and their company. Shamus rarely worked Sundays, but he said he had something urgent to attend to this morning. She'd long ago stopped asking about the job. When he could, he'd discuss a case with her. She grabbed the paperwork for the stockholders' meeting from her desk, and settled into the sofa in her home office to review the proposed takeover of Daton's Industries. Darcy tweaked a sentence here, added more info there. In midsentence her pen halted, the air thickened and the oxygen whooshed from her lungs as the news anchor announced her friend Callie's name in the same sentence as murder.

Her heart shattered into a million pieces. Her best friend, one of the few people who she could truly be herself with…murdered. *No, no, it's not true.* Darcy jumped up, her papers scattering to the floor as she grabbed her cell phone from her desk and pressed one, to speed dial Shamus while pacing the floor.

It rang three times and then dropped her call into voicemail. She hung up and dialed his office, his direct line—again it went to voicemail. Why the hell hadn't he called her? Was this why he went into the office today?

Last night at the gala when she'd come back to the table from the ladies' room, Shamus had seemed off. She'd brushed it away. She dialed Shamus again—still no answer. *What the hell's going on?* She dialed Callie's number. *Damn it, voicemail. Didn't anyone answer their freakin' phones anymore? Shamus is a goner, if Callie is dead. Why hadn't he called?*

She dialed Todd Blake and got another voicemail. Darcy's stomach quivered as she grabbed the remote and started channel surfing. Each channel shared the same details. They had only a name, not the circumstances. Callie, always so full of life, so beautiful, and so stressed over perfecting every detail for last night's ball, dead—no, she wouldn't accept that. Not her one true friend, whom she loved and had shared her most intimate secrets with since grade school.

Darcy collapsed into a ball on the floor, hugging her arms around herself as she rocked back and forth, her head ready to explode, unable to accept the reports. Shamus's job was never supposed to touch their lives.

Visions of Callie in grade school as the lead in the school play, Callie as prom queen in high school, and Callie, the most beautiful bride on her wedding day, filled Darcy's head. Their European trip in college, just the two them before Callie took the plunge and married Todd, her high school sweetheart, that fall.

Darcy looked around the room as if for the first time. Everything started to fade away except memory after memory tumbling around inside her head. The mini marble statue of Venus that Darcy had to have when the four of them had visited Paris, seemed trivial. The awards she'd received from various organizations and charities hanging on her home office walls, her pictures with several world leaders including the president of the United States, who had recommended her company's steel products to the military to use in their weapons, all meaningless now. Why hadn't she made it a priority to spend more time with Callie? Business, that's why. Her father taught her that business came first. And now she'd never get back the time she could've had with her friend. The world around her disappeared, leaving her empty, disoriented, and alone.

Time distorted. She didn't know if a minute or an hour had passed as she pushed herself up off the floor, her eyes stinging, her stomach upset. Darcy's nose ran as she hiccupped. If Shamus didn't call soon, she'd kill him.

* * * *

Though he'd seen her last night taking pictures at the gala, seeing Melinda's name tossed him right back there, to a time he'd rather not revisit.

Seventeen Years Ago
Jake mumbled under his breath. He tossed the bat behind him as he stomped over to the dugout. As his ass was about to hit the bench, he noticed the coach motioning him back to the plate, but not before the jerk Spaulding got in a few words.

"Hey, Jakey boy, you look distracted today," said his teammate George Spaulding, goading him. "I bet it's Melinda Blair sitting up there in the bleachers doing it to you. The girl gets around. She's had that effect on all of us." Spaulding winked at him.

Jake balled his fist at his side, itching to plant it in Spaulding's smug face. He needed to hold it together. If he didn't, he'd be thrown out of Saturday's game—it was something he couldn't afford if he wanted the scholarship. But afterward...he'd teach that asswad jerk a lesson. No one spoke about his girl that way. Jake started to walk away, changed his mind and turned back. He pinned George with his father's cop stare. "As captain of the team, let me remind you that sportsmanlike behavior is expected from all team members. If you can't comply, you'll be removed from the roster, George." Not that he had the power to do it, but hell...it sounded good.

He walked over to the coach, who stood at home plate. Jake put George out of his mind and listened to the coach's tips. Roberts was a miracle worker. Within a half hour Jake had corrected the problems with his stance and his swing. He'd swing, he'd hit the ball. It was well worth getting up at seven a.m. on his day off to work with the coach.

Though George's words jumped around in his head, Jake refused to allow them to distract him. He wasn't aware that Melinda had dated other team members, except for Mike Doyle. Maybe when they hit the showers, he'd pick Mike's brain about her. Jake had been dating her for only a week, but her pushiness was getting to him. Before he'd made his move, Melinda would beat him to the kiss. Bullocks to that, he thought, as he used his father's favorite expression. A man wanted to be in charge, and he'd tell her that when he saw her.

* * * *

He'd missed Mike Doyle after practice. Jake had stayed out on the field longer than his teammates while he continued to work with the coach. Jake understood there'd be scouts at Saturday's game. The coach had let it slip as he trained him. After his shower, he shoved his cleats, bat, and glove in his locker. He then stuffed his uniform in his gym bag with his other dirty clothes. Someone called out to him as he emerged from the players' tunnel to the parking lot.

"Hey, Jake, you almost walked by me," Melinda Blair said with a hand on her hip.

Jake refocused his mind onto her instead of the game. "Sorry, Melinda, I didn't see you."

"What time are you coming over tonight?"

"I can't make it tonight, I've got a family thing going on," Jake lied. Spaulding's words were deterring him. And how stupid was he? Any other guy would be jumping at the chance.

"Why don't you come over afterward?"

"I can't. Do you want to see a movie tomorrow?" Jake asked.

"Yeah, what time?"

"I figure I'll pick you up at 1:30 and we can see a movie at two? We can get a bite afterward," Jake said.

When Melinda drove away he'd given some thought to ending things with her tomorrow to keep his mind locked on the game. The more time he spent with her, the more he'd started to dislike her. If only he found the courage to tell her.

Chapter 4

Where the hell is she? Sal took a hard slug from the bottle. *Christ Jesus, this wasn't supposed to happen.* He paced, hitting *send* for the ninth time.

Bitch better answer. I'm not leaving another voicemail.

Sal threw the phone across the room. *I better not be tagged for this.* Quick money, that's what this was all about.

Where did the money go? Who took it, damn it?

It had creeped him out, the Blake woman lying there dead as he searched the room for the money. *Grotesque.* Her dead eyes stared at the ceiling and her body sagged in death, emphasizing her age. He wasn't going down for the murder. It was pretty clever of him to leave the pictures next to the body. But who the hell had killed her? Nothing would lead back to him. If anything, Melinda would be questioned.

What he needed to do was find out who took his money. He'd kill the bastard for stealing it from him. The scheme had been his brainchild, his money, his powers of persuasion that had convinced Melinda to play along. Then some asshole shows up and gets rich. He'd kill him when he found him. Had it been the motel clerk who took it?

Boudoir shots—how ridiculous these women were to trust a stranger. But he had to hand it to Melinda. She'd made them all look acceptable if not pretty. Some of them, even in their twenties, weren't anything he'd get involved with unless there was money involved. Moola washed away a lot of sins. Clever Melinda had taken legitimate photos, and then changed the backgrounds of each so they were perfect for blackmail and the location couldn't be identified.

The freakin' plan should've worked. He'd done the research and picked the targets from the social pages of the paper. If they were open to it, he'd seduce them, or Melinda would suggest they pose with him to spice up the shoot. Most said no to posing with him, but it hadn't mattered. Melinda worked her magic on their targets and melded him into their pictures. It was supposed to be fast money in his pocket. After ten women he'd have been pretty well off. Now the first one was dead, he had no money, his plan was shot to hell, and he was locked in a cheap motel room, nervous as a mouse.

This wouldn't do. Sal took another slug of whiskey. What he needed was another plan, an escape plan. Maybe he'd try down South this time. These Northeast bitches expected too much from him. The more he thought of the coming winter the more the idea of going south pleased him. But first he wanted to make sure Melinda got on board with his plans. If not…

* * * *

Jake leaned forward, rested his hands on his knees. The commissioner's living room in bright red, yellow, and blue, along with the fine art, presented a relaxed, easy atmosphere. One shattered today by murder.

"When's the last time you had contact with Melinda Mastrianni?" the commissioner asked.

"Outside of last night at the gala, I saw her three years ago at her husband Tony's funeral," Jake said.

Jake handed Melinda's business card to Louie. He thought of Tony Mastrianni, a teammate and friend from his high school days. Melinda had hooked up with Tony when Jake stopped dating her. Tony had been a laid-back kind of guy with no ambition. It had seemed an odd match to him back then.

"Then I don't think it will interfere with the investigation, do you?"

"No."

"Todd, do you know who'd want to kill your wife?" Jake asked.

"No, and before you ask, she didn't tell me she was going to meet this bastard. I had told her I'd handle it."

"Is there any money missing from your accounts?" Jake asked.

"No, she wouldn't have paid him off. We agreed to that."

"Are you sure she wouldn't have done it to protect you?"

"Jake, for Pete's sake, she was an intelligent woman. We agreed that once you paid a blackmailer, they'd keep coming back. Callie would never have gone there alone. She'd have asked me to go with her. And let me repeat, I didn't kill my wife."

"Commissioner, can you check your accounts online?"

"Jake."

"Please, we need to rule out the possibility that she went behind your back."

"This is damn intrusive." Blake stood without another word and left the room.

Louie handed him back the card. "Do you think Melinda's a part of this?"

"It's been many years since I've seen her. I don't know who or what she's become."

The commissioner returned with his laptop and a small notebook and sat in the armchair. After he logged in, he turned the screen to Jake.

"See, there's nothing withdrawn since August, when I made the payment to St. Lucien's for Todd Jr.'s tuition."

"Is this your only account?" Jake asked, taking the computer from Blake.

"No, they're all linked right here. Our retirement accounts are the only accounts not listed in the summary. And Callie has a trust fund. I don't have the statements for it. You'll need to get it from the bank."

Under the commissioner's gaze, Jake invaded Blake's privacy. No large amounts of money were withdrawn from any of the accounts except the tuition payment.

"Commissioner, I'm going to need you to log in to your retirement accounts and Callie's trust fund too."

"For the love of God, I didn't kill my wife, Jake. I don't have access to her trust fund either." Disgusted, Blake grabbed the computer back and typed furiously.

There weren't any large withdrawals. Jake let out a sigh of relief.

The commissioner had no more to offer. Blake's palpable grief had started to attach itself to Jake. He needed to distance himself from it to clear his head. They left Blake to grieve alone.

"What do you think?" Jake asked. Outside, he narrowed his eyes at the press still hanging around. "Let's get in the car before you answer."

"I don't think he did it," Louie said.

"Me either, but then who? We need to track down Melinda."

And won't that be fun. Every time he'd run into her since high school, she'd treated him as if he was diseased. Jake climbed into the driver's seat and started the car. He wondered how interviewing Melinda would go. Would she still be bitchy or had time mellowed her?

* * * *

At the station, Jake did a search on Melinda Blair Mastrianni. Her studio and home address popped up first. Melinda had sterling reviews on her business website. In high school she'd been the official school photographer for events. The portraits on her website showed a vast improvement in her skills.

He buzzed Louie. "What have you turned up?"

"I'll be right in."

A few moments later movement at his door had him raising his eyes. Louie's six-two frame filled the doorway to his office. "Take a seat," Jake said.

"Melinda's in debt up to her neck. When Tony died, his business was practically in bankruptcy. She signed a personal guarantee on all his business loans. Melinda had to assume them after he died. Her business has recently started to show a profit. It's taken a while for her to get it up and running, but most of her money goes to the payments," Louie said and settled into one of the seats in front of Jake's desk. "If she'd been smart she'd've filed for a business bankruptcy to get rid of his debt after he died, then she'd only have had to work at reducing the personal debt."

"I read that."

"You see here." Louie gave Jake a statement and pointed to a line on it. "She's current on her payments, but the principal on the debt has hardly come down in the last three years."

"Do you have her home number?"

"Yes," Louie said.

Jake turned his wrist to check the time. *Shit, it's after eight on a Sunday night.* "Let's try the home."

Louie placed the call on his cell phone but got her answering machine. "No dice. I'll call her business just in case she's working today." Again Louie her got her voicemail system and left an urgent message there for a callback in the morning.

"We're not going to get any lab results until the morning. Let's meet back here at seven," Jake said.

* * * *

Exhausted, Melinda hit the sack the minute she got home and didn't bother lowering the shades or listening to her messages. Six hours later, sunlight blinded her as she sat up in bed, rubbing the sleep from her eyes, and winced.

"Damn, I forgot that the drunken idiot bumped into me."

She got out of bed and made a beeline to the mirror. The scratch on her cheek glowed red. She tapped her finger on the mark, hoping it wouldn't scar. The black eye reminded her of the dog in the commercials for that big box store. *Aren't I attractive?*

It'd been a long wedding, not ending until well after eleven. She'd gotten home around midnight. Damn, she'd forgotten to call Sal back.

Another wedding—each one reminded her of her loss and tore at her heart. She loved photography, but it killed her to capture other people's moments. It made her puke, all these happy couples—most would be divorced before the ink dried on the marriage licenses. All that money wasted on a single day. Oh, what she could do with that kind of money. At first she'd learned to love Tony. They'd been happy until his spending got out of control, and his gambling got worse. Nowadays she wondered what she ever saw in him every time she had to write a check to the bank to cover his debt.

Tony...God, when he had been alive things seemed good, but now every pore of her being clogged with anger. He'd left her in debt to the tune of five hundred grand. The fool used loans to gamble. And he'd had the nerve to borrow against his life insurance policy, which she'd discovered the week after he died. If the drunk driver hadn't killed him she most likely would've.

Their happy life together had been a farce with all his lies piled on top of each other. Dead in his thirties—he left her all alone to deal with his mess. How she wished she'd been with him in the car on that fateful day.

Melinda trudged across the kitchen, switched on the small television, and started the coffee brewing. She hit the play button on the answering machine—several messages from Sal filled the air, each one getting more demanding that she return his calls. Before she faced him and what they'd done, she wanted to be fully awake. The morning news show droned on in the background. She reached into the cabinet for a cup while Sal's voice continued to fill the air. The coffee's aroma almost had her begging. She poured the hot liquid into her mug, steam warming her face as she lifted it to her lips. Before she could taste it, the reporter on the television caught her attention. Melinda grabbed the remote and raised the volume.

"This morning my sources stated that Wilkesbury Police Commissioner Todd Blake's wife, Callie Blake, has been found murdered in the Wilson Motel on Foundry Lane yesterday. The police neither confirm nor deny the allegations or the cause of death at this time. Please stay tuned for updates."

Melinda fell into the chair, sweat began to bead on her brow. She punched in Sal's cell phone number.

"What the hell happened?" she shouted into the phone.

"Calm down. I didn't kill her. She was dead when I got there," Sal said.

"Are you sure?"

"Of course I'm sure. Don't worry. Nothing can lead back to us."

Something in his voice set off alarms. "Who killed her?"

"I don't know. And we didn't get the damn money either. The bastard who killed her took it," Sal complained.

"Where are you?" She pushed from the chair and paced around the small kitchen.

She'd gotten involved in his scheme in the first place because she was tired of living like a pauper. He convinced her the commissioner had political ambitions and he wouldn't let the photos come to light. But she hadn't signed up for murder. Now they'd have the whole police force down on them and for what, twenty-five grand?

"I'm not home. I think it's best if we lie low for a while and not do the other women right away."

She needed time to think. "I agree, but I want you to make sure the other women aren't married to cops." Silence lingered on the other end. "Sal, they're not, are they?"

"Well—the CEO lady we're gonna hit for the one hundred grand is married to one, but don't worry, the others aren't. It'll be fine, Melinda. Don't contact me for a couple of days. I'll call you when I'm ready to start up again. Stay calm and act natural. Our lives depend on it. Someone knew what we were up to and played us," Sal said. "Hang loose, and I'll talk to you soon."

After Sal hung up, his answers spun around inside her head. Had he set her up? Gulping, she tried to force air into her lungs.

Cold seeped into her body and bile flooded her throat. Then it all came back to her—the conversations, the dead woman, the money.

Oh God! Oh God!

She pulled herself up with the help of the counter and noticed the answering machine still blinked with messages. She swiped the hair from her eyes as she hit the play button with her other hand. The first one froze her in place.

"Melinda, I don't know if you remember me. This is Lieutenant Jake Carrington from the WPD. Please return this call as soon as possible." He left a number she didn't bother to write down. *As if I'd forget him. The idiot left his title along with his full name.*

The last time she'd gotten a call like that, Tony had died. Who was it this time—one of her parents, her sister, or her brother? No way was she up to doing the identification again. *Or does it have something to do with... no, there's no way it led back to me this soon...did it?*

* * * *

After a quick shower, Melinda dressed, then loaded her equipment into the car and drove to the studio to process last night's wedding and Saturday's event. Normal. Sal said to keep a normal routine. For now she'd listen. She processed most of the digital and the larger format film for the sixteen-by-twenty portraits she hoped the couple would order. The larger format was where she made most of the money.

A thought slammed into her brain. The SD card—she'd need to wipe it clean from Callie's shoot. No, no, she'd keep the glamour shots. Those were legit. All she needed to destroy were the ones she'd doctored, where she added in Sal's apartment as background, the motel, and the nude body, which she'd cleverly attached to Callie Blake's head. It had taken some finesse to find the right shape to match hers. Melinda poured liquid antacid down her throat and hoped it stayed down.

She jammed the memory stick into the digital camera. As she surveyed the pictures, she hit *delete* whenever a shot showed Callie Blake in a compromising situation. Most only showed the back of Sal's head. But Melinda was smart. She'd kept her security cameras on, which showed Sal's face and actions. The ones with his face she'd keep for insurance.

She made a list of the things that could incriminate her. Sittings, photos— no, not photos, she didn't use the paper with her name imprinted on the back. Thank God she used the commercial photo paper she'd gotten at the local office supply store. Fingerprints? No, she'd worn gloves at Sal's urging. It had made the processing more difficult but would probably save her ass.

The precautions were taken to ensure the police commissioner's wife couldn't come back at them. She'd never have known about Callie Blake if it hadn't been for the reporter Lily Monroe, who'd recommended Melinda to Callie Blake to photograph the gala. Once Melinda had gotten to know Callie, she'd pegged her as an easy target.

All day long Melinda tuned into the television. She'd never been a news junkie, but today she couldn't get enough. The stupid stations kept repeating the same sound bite. She had to know what was going on. Though her studio fridge was loaded with food, she went to the diner for lunch.

Gossip flew in every corner of the place. The only subject today was the murder. Was it a career criminal who killed her, or had it been a crime of opportunity? Was Callie Blake a loose woman? Did she deserve what she got? On and on it went as each thought and accusation bumped around inside her head. Melinda had to pay her bill and leave before the waitress noticed she'd been sitting there too long.

* * * *

Monday midmorning, after reviewing Lang's preliminary autopsy reports and the lab results, Jake put another call in to Melinda Mastrianni. He didn't waste time on pleasantries.

"Melinda, it's Jake Carrington from the WPD. I—"

"Well, well, well. Need your picture taken, Jake?"

"I need to meet with you today about a case I'm working on, Melinda. When's a good time?"

"I'm processing photos from a wedding I shot yesterday. Can we meet later at my studio? Or do you want to meet me at home after work? What case are you investigating?"

"I'll see you at the studio at two," Jake said.

Her place of business will keep this meeting professional. I don't want her to start reminiscing about the past. It's the last thing I need at the moment. His mind screwed with him at will. This time Melinda's voice had triggered the memories of the fateful day. A day he'd fought every single hour of every single day to bury for the last seventeen years. *Damn,* he had no control over when they blasted through him. His brow broke out in a sweat.

* * * *

Seventeen Years Ago

Dinner at the Carringtons' was a ritual. They'd all gather to talk about their day, even when their father had pulled the night shift. He would take his dinner break and come home to join them. As families went, Jake's was a good one, he thought. Though his younger sister Eva loved to bust his chops, he gave it right back to her.

"How'd practice go today?" James Carrington asked over dinner.

"The coach gave me some pointers that fixed my batting problem. I think I'm golden for Saturday's game."

"What's bothering you?" James asked.

"Jake, eat," his mother, Maddie Carrington, said in her heavy brogue—hers much thicker than his father's.

"It's Spaulding. He's a pain in my butt. We went at it again today," Jake said, pushing his food around his plate.

"Keep your temper to yourself, Jake. You don't want to be thrown out of Saturday's game. This one is important."

"I've got a grip on it. Hey, can I talk to you after dinner?"

James studied his son. "Sure."

"Can't speak in front of us womenfolk," Eva teased, scrunching up her freckled nose. Eva was a carbon copy of their mother except she had their father's blue eyes and sharp tongue.

"It's none of your business, nosy," Jake said, tapping her on the nose. Eva pushed his hand away.

"Idiot."

When dinner ended, Eva got up to help their mother clear the table. Behind their mother's back Eva stuck her tongue out at him. Jake returned the gesture before leaping up and rubbing her on the head, something she hated. Eva couldn't swat his hand away this time with her hands loaded with dirty dishes.

Jake let Eva go and followed his father into his office and shut the door behind him. The walnut wall panels gave the room a sober feel. His dad's many awards and medals for bravery sat on the bookcase to the side of his large cherry desk. The green drapes behind the desk were opened, offering the only light. James went to the desk and switched on the lamp.

"What's on your mind?" James asked, pouring four fingers of Irish whiskey into a glass.

Jake studied the brown liquid before he found his words. He'd have talked to Louie if he had any experience, but he knew Louie and Sophia hadn't done it yet. It was embarrassing to speak with his father about it, but damn, he needed some advice. His father pointed to the chair with his glass.

"Spaulding is becoming a real problem. Today he said Melinda...you know, the girl who stopped by yesterday?" His father nodded. "George told me she'd dated the whole team." Jake stared down at his feet.

"Do you think he meant she slept around?" James asked.

"I don't know, but that's where my mind's gone."

"It's hard to be a teenager, Jake. The guys are going to rib you one way or another. You'll have to learn to wear a tough skin against it, especially in the clubhouse. Is it true what he said?"

"I'm not sure."

"And if it is, it would bother you?"

"Yes."

"Why?"

Jake watched his father sip his drink.

"I don't know. I can't explain it."

"Well, you have a moral dilemma going on. One only you can figure out. But I wouldn't judge the reputation of the girl on one spiteful comment. If it bothers you that much, find out the truth."

"She's pushy and showed up at practice today without being invited."

His feelings for her had cooled, but not because of Spaulding.

"You're a smart boy, Jake, but don't let your hormones lead you astray. You've been working hard on your game and she'd be a distraction. You need to determine where you'll spend your time and energy—will it be on the game, to reach your goal of playing professional ball, or seeing a girl you don't seem to like very much?"

"That's it? You're not going to tell me to drop her?"

"No. As I said, you're a smart boy, you'll figure it out," James said.

* * * *

It was his lucky day. Jake found a space on the street outside of Melinda's studio and parked the car. Prime real estate, he noted. It had to cost her a fortune to rent here. The old pink brick, four-story Scovill factory building sat on the Wilkesbury River. In its day most of America's kitchen appliances had been manufactured there. The bridge connecting both sides of the factory protected workers from going outside in inclement weather. For years it had sat empty, deteriorating, as the city's fathers fought over what to do with the atrocity. The clean up to rid the building of asbestos and the heavy oil odors seemed daunting and expensive.

An enterprising local businessman bought it, cleaned it up, and retooled it into smaller businesses, thus saving another landmark in Wilkesbury's history.

He and Louie climbed out of the car and studied the building. Melinda's studio entrance faced the street. Large colorful photos of happy people graced the windows as he approached the door. A tile and carpet store had the place to the right of her business and occupied two floors. To her left, a small manufacturer occupied four floors. Other businesses scattered throughout the building drew customers in with their unique items.

Would the girl he had dated briefly many years ago resort to crime to succeed? Unfortunately, he believed she would. Had she gotten meaner since school? Did the death of a spouse push a person over the edge?

Jake took off his sunglasses as a memory nearly tore his heart out. He'd been at Melinda's house on the day his sister Eva had been killed. Melinda had been the reason he'd turned Eva down for the ride she'd requested. With his nerves shooting in every direction, his anticipation for his evening with Melinda had made him selfish. But it hadn't been Melinda's fault Eva had died. It was all on him. He never called Melinda after that day or saw Eva alive again.

He couldn't help but connect the two incidents. A lengthy investigation pursued. Weeks after the murder, George Spaulding had been arrested for it. And it hadn't ended there. The trial kept the horror alive in the newspapers and nightly news for another year while Spaulding was tried and convicted. Jake couldn't go there today. Or think about the DNA test results or the possibility of a new trial.

When they stepped into the studio a loud bell over the door announced them. With cop eyes, Jake scanned the room and noted its contents. Louie did the same before he stepped to Jake's right. Jake said a prayer of thanks he didn't have to face Melinda alone—Louie always had his back. Two beige chairs in the far corner graced either end of a coffee table, and a green floral couch was positioned behind it. Melinda stood in the doorway of what he assumed was an office. She sported a black eye and held his gaze and attention. She wiped her hands on a towel when he stuck out his hand.

Melinda was a testament to her mixed heritage—fair skin surrounded by dark curly hair and hazel eyes. Her half-Italian, half-Irish ancestry came with, if he remembered correctly, a wild temper. And he didn't need her spiteful tongue when he wasn't up to par.

She raised her eyes and grinned. "Jake Carrington, as I live and breathe. To what do I owe the pleasure of your company, and your sidekick's?"

"Hi, Melinda. How'd you get the shiner and scratches?" Jake's gaze lingered on her left eye before dropping to her bruised cheek and hands. Melinda folded and unfolded her hands. *She's clearly nervous to see me*, he thought.

"Some drunken idiot at the wedding I was working yesterday fell into me, jamming my camera in my face."

"Hello, Melinda," Louie said.

"Louie, I see you two are still connected at the hip." She walked farther into the room and threw the towel on the counter and pulled up a chair.

Ballbuster, yep, it was all coming back to him. "We're here about a case. I understand you took pictures of this woman." Jake showed her a recent head shot of Callie.

Melinda studied Callie's picture. "Yes, I did glamour shots of her for her anniversary. Is there a problem?"

"Why would a woman pose this way?" Jake ignored her question and placed the next picture on her counter.

"Boudoir shots make a woman feel sexy and appealing. It builds their self-confidence. It's my job to make them relax in front of the camera. There are some sleazy photographers out there who exploit women. I don't."

"You were switching between glamour and boudoir—is there a difference?"

"It's the tone of the picture. Boudoir shots are less about a woman's overall sexuality and more about her feminine sensual side, and appeal to the woman to boost her confidence. Glamour photos are designed to appeal to men."

"What would you call this one?" Louie asked, holding up a shot of Callie with the unidentified male, which Jake had placed on the counter.

"That's a boudoir picture. Look at her expression. It states 'I'm in charge.'"

That's not how Jake interpreted it. To him it was a sad attempt by a woman trying to recapture her youth. *I wonder what Todd Blake thought when Callie gave them to him. I'll have to ask, and won't that be fun.*

"Why all the questions? What's up?"

"Did you set her up with this model?"

"Give me a break. She brought her own model with her. I took the pictures she requested. Why?"

"Where did the photo session take place?" Jake asked.

"Here in the studio."

"Nowhere else?"

"No."

He didn't miss the nervous pitch in Melinda's voice. Or her sideward glance to Louie. "Was the sitting the only time you've met with Mrs. Blake?"

"Yes, for her pictures, but she contacted me to photograph the charity ball. Why?"

"Mrs. Blake was murdered yesterday. It's been all over the news. The killer put the glamour shots beside her body. Is this your work?" He handed her a copy of one of the photos left on the scene.

She turned it over. "No, mine have my name imprinted on them."

"Can we see a sample?"

"I'll be right back."

Jake scanned the sample photos displayed on the wall in expensive frames as he waited for Melinda to return with the paper. He admired Melinda's eye and how she captured her subjects. From young to old, each person in the photo drew you to their smiles or eyes and told a story. She'd come a long way since she worked as the school photographer.

"Melinda, do you use film or digital?" he called out.

"Both—for the photo albums I use digital and for the large pictures you see on the walls I use the large-format film and camera, for a tighter grain and more vivid details."

"We'll need to see the computer you process the pictures on," he said, walking toward the back room. He pushed aside the curtain and held it open for Louie.

"I first show the customer what I shoot on my computer in the office. If they have a hard time choosing one, I give them a flash drive to review the photos in the privacy of their own homes. But the trouble doing it that way is I can't show them how I can smooth out their lines and wrinkles and soften the overall atmosphere," she said, turning and almost bumping into him. "No one is allowed back here unless invited. My office is out front. It's the door on the left of the curtain." Melinda moved back to where they had come from a minute ago.

"I thought the photographer owned the images."

"We do, but some clients are more comfortable taking the files away with them. If it means a booking or not, I give them the drive."

Jake didn't believe her. Melinda continued to move out front. "We'll need to search your computer."

Melinda looked from Jake to Louie. "I have nothing to hide, but you need to get a warrant. There are a lot of women who do the boudoir pictures for a loved one, who would be appalled to know someone else was pawing over them."

"You could save us time. If not, we'll be back within a few hours with a warrant. How about it, Melinda?" Jake asked.

"Sorry, once you have it, I'll let you view my files."

Shit, she'll have time to erase them before we get back.

Chapter 5

Though he'd tried to push away the memory, his mind took control and sent him back to hell.

Seventeen Years Ago

Jake stalled and decided he'd shower at home instead of hanging around. This way he'd have a couple hours before he had to pick up Melinda. For some reason she thought they'd hang together right after practice. He chose one thirty. It gave them plenty of time to get to the theater and buy some snacks to hold them over until dinner.

Jake stepped out of the shower, grabbed a towel, dried off and then wrapped the towel around his waist. He lathered up his chin, stopped, and stared in the mirror. Sometime during his shower, he had realized he was being stupid and decided to enjoy his date with Melinda and see how far they went. When he got home tonight, he'd need to do some research on the scouts to see who they'd signed in the past. With downward strokes he ran the razor over his chin.

"Ouch." Jake reached for a wad of toilet paper to staunch the bleeding.

With his chin twisted to the side, Jake swiped the razor over his other cheek. His eyes watered up when he splashed aftershave on his face. The cuts stung. He figured with the movie and dinner he'd be home by nine. He threw on broken-in jeans with a green collared shirt and his boots. No need to get fancy.

Whistling, Jake stepped into the kitchen. His mother stood at the stove and Eva sat at the table drumming her fingers. Wasn't today his mother's bridge day?

"Gee, Jake, I waited like forever for you. How long does a shower take? I need a ride over to Maureen's house," Eva said, pushing red bangs out of her eyes. She rounded the table and faced him down, her lips snarled. He always thought Eva had a lot of spunk for such a tiny thing.

Eva was small like his mother. At six feet, Jake towered over her five feet five inches. He tugged on a strand of her red ponytail.

"No can do, sis, I've got plans. I don't have the time to go out of my way."

"Jake, your sister asked for a ride. Five minutes isn't a big deal," said his mother.

"Mom, are you telling me that I have to take her to her friend's?"

"No, I'm asking you to do the right thing." His mother quirked her head toward him, her red curls sticking up in all directions.

"Any other time, Mom, I would. But I promised Melinda I wouldn't be late. A promise is a promise. You don't want me to break it, do you? We're going to the two o'clock show."

"Well, it's up to you, Jake."

He understood what his mother was trying to do. Maddie Carrington was good at dishing out the guilt—but not today, he had other plans. He wished his mother would get her license. He was tired of chauffeuring Eva around. Jake stuck his tongue out at his sister as he grabbed his car keys off the board by the door and left.

He drove down his block and waved to a few friends. He passed Chase Park. The green hills rolled every which way as kids kicked a soccer ball around and another group tossed Frisbees to each other. Halfway to Melinda's house it hit him. Why hadn't he tried to sneak a bottle of his father's whiskey out of the house to calm his nerves?

* * * *

Melinda had insisted on eating before the movie, and they'd missed the show time. Instead they wound up hanging out at her house and planned to attend the later showing. For a while they listened to music, then the next thing he knew, they were making out and Melinda was on top of him. He was to blame. He should've stuck to his guns and insisted they go to the early show.

A few hours later, Mrs. Blair knocked on the door.

When he came over, Mrs. Blair normally left them alone. Something had to be up for her to come into Melinda's room. His ears reddened as Mrs. Blair stared at him, then at Melinda, with an expression that broadcasted her displeasure. He figured she had to have seen their wrinkled clothing. He hated his damn skin as it lit up like a red light.

"Jake, your father's on the telephone," Mrs. Blair said, never taking her eyes off of Melinda.

Melinda got up to go after him, but Mrs. Blair told her to stay put. Jake walked into the kitchen and picked up the receiver. He couldn't figure out for the life of him why his father would be calling him there. He wasn't expected home until eleven.

"Hi, Dad, what's up?"

"Jake, I need you to come home immediately," said James Carrington, his tone off.

"Why?"

"No questions, Jake, just get home," ordered James Carrington.

His father had never used that tone with him before. Jake stared at the phone for several seconds after his father hung up. He placed the receiver on the hook and scratched his head. A noise behind him had him swinging around. Melinda and her mother watched him from in the kitchen entrance.

"Jake, Melinda is punished for the next month. Please don't come back," said Mrs. Blair. He didn't know if that meant for the month or forever.

"Mom…"

"Back to your room, missy."

Jake didn't hear the rest of the conversation as he rushed out the door. Later, he'd give Melinda a call. He hoped she didn't get into trouble. They hadn't even done anything.

* * * *

"Not my baby," screamed Maddie Carrington as Jake walked in the front door ten minutes later.

His mother's wails pierced his ears.

"Dad, what's wrong with Mom?" Jake said as he shuffled over and knelt in front of his mother, taking her freckled hands in his.

His father held her snug to his body. Her screeches dug deep craters into his soul. Did his grandparents die? Jake stiffened as he searched his father's teary eyes for an answer. James Carrington never cried. That's what scared him the most.

"Jake, sit down," James said, his voice cracking.

"Is Mom okay?" Jake let go of Maddie's hands.

"Jake…" The tears poured from James Carrington's eyes. Dumbfounded, Jake glanced from his father to his mother.

Jake noticed for the first time that his sister wasn't in the room. "Where's Eva?"

James tried to talk again. He barely got the words out. "Jake, Eva's been killed."

"Eva…"

His body went lax. Numb from head to toe, the room disappeared around him as he folded himself onto the floor. It could've been minutes or hours, time didn't register until his father wrapped his arm around his shoulders. Jake stared into his father's shattered eyes. Disbelief, then understanding encompassed him. Not his baby sister. He saw her only hours ago, before he'd gone to Melinda's…Oh God, he stuck his tongue out at her. His head swirled away from his father as he stared at his distraught mother, curled into a corner of the couch.

"Are you sure?"

"I know the cop who called. He was sure, but I'm heading out to identify her before she's transported to Farmington."

He wished with all his heart for it to be a bad joke, pulled by one of Dad's officers.

"I'm going with you, Dad."

"No, I need you to stay with your mother." James knuckled away a tear.

"I'm going with you, Dad. I'll get Mrs. O'Hare to stay with Mom."

"Jake, you don't want to see this, believe me," said James in a husky voice.

"I'm coming, Dad."

No one was going to stop him from seeing this victim. He'd prove them all wrong. It couldn't be Eva in the morgue.

Dear God, please not Eva.

* * * *

At the counter in her studio Melinda continued to stare out the window after Jake and Louie left her studio to apply for their warrants. Did Jake have enough evidence to get one? Did the courts override legalities when the victim was prominent in the community?

Melinda had to think fast if she wanted to unwind herself from this situation. Still, she had nothing to hide. Her business had been legit from the moment she conceived it. Her taxes were filed quarterly, and her reports annually, which kept everything in good standing with the secretary of state. After listening to Louie's message this morning, she'd run a virus scan on the computer in the studio, then a deeper search to make sure she hadn't been hacked. Down the road it might help her alibi.

She played with the thumb drive in her pocket. The one she used to copy the files that were none of the WPD's business. It was only one file, but she didn't want Carrington to open that can of worms. The ones they'd used for Sal's scheme she'd kept on her home unit, not here.

Which raised the question, how the hell did Jake Carrington get a copy of one of the blackmail pictures? Did Sal panic and leave it at the motel? Callie's instructions were to bring all of them with her.

Melinda hadn't budged from the counter. The jazz music playing softly in the background filled the studio with sad music. How appropriate, she thought, while drumming her fingers on the studio countertop as she tried to get inside Jake's head and his investigation. Was he still the self-involved asshole he was in high school? He'd dumped her in the hallway in front of the whole school two weeks after his sister's murder. She could've helped him. She thought back on the circumstances that had crushed her when Jake made it clear they were no longer an item.

Seventeen Years Ago

The wake had been horrible. The whole school had turned out for it—the girls in tears, even the ones who didn't know Eva. The boys milled around with their hands in their pockets, staring off into space. None of them knew what to do, or how to act. From her spot in line she studied Jake. The guy was catatonic. After waiting in line for over an hour, she approached Mrs. Carrington. She and Jake wore the same stoic expression. Melinda moved to Mr. Carrington, who at least had the manners to thank her for coming. Jake held himself erect, not acknowledging anyone. She reached her arms up to hug him. He stiffened, shifted his eyes down and stared through her before returning his gaze to the coffin. What the hell? Like his mother, Jake said nothing. Boy, wouldn't Lucille Watts give it to her after how she'd bragged that Jake had turned to her in his hour of need. He didn't even bother to acknowledge her.

She quickly moved past the humiliation, and didn't bother to talk to Louie or Sophia.

Melinda decided to attend the service. Maybe Jake would come around by then. The family had gone for a full mass that dragged on and on. Melinda stood, kneeled, sat, and did it all over again. She debated if she should go to the cemetery or not. In the end, she thought it best to finish out the day. She hoped at some point she'd get food. She was starving.

At the graveside after the service concluded, she tried several times to approach Jake, but Louie and Sophia always closed ranks and shielded him from the crowds, and her.

The undertaker invited all guests to join the family for lunch at the Ancient Order of Hibernians following the service. She'd decided to forego it. The last thing she needed was more rituals, or prayers.

Two weeks after Eva died, Jake came back to class. He was different. His teasing nature ceased, his easygoing smile had faded, but it was more than that. He seemed older and weary beyond his years.

Up until that moment, she'd really liked him. Lucille walked with her to her next class, seeing they both were heading to calculus. It was her lucky day, or so she thought. There she found Jake reaching into his locker with his back to the hall.

"Give us a minute, Lucille," Melinda said, hoping Lucille would go into the classroom. But no, Lucille remained, eavesdropping from the sidelines. It was now or never. "Hi, Jake, I've been trying to reach you."

"I'm sorry, I haven't wanted to see anyone," Jake said, turning to face her.

"I understand. I'm here if you need me or just want to talk. Why don't you come to dinner tomorrow night?"

"I can't, Melinda."

She hadn't meant to force the issue, but it'd been over two weeks, and the least he could do was extend her some courtesy. "Why are you ignoring me?"

"Not everything is about you," Jake said, turning back to his locker to take a book out. He slammed his locker shut and started to walk away from her.

She clutched his arm to make him look at her. "I'm your girlfriend. The least you can do is acknowledge me and tell me what's going on." A crowd had started to gather, even after the bell had rung for class.

"Melinda, my life's changed. I'm sorry, it's over."

Her eyes popped wide open. How dare he? She chased him down the hall. "We're all sorry for what happened to your sister, but she's the one who died, not you. Get it together, you asshole." She practically ran down the hall and out of the building. How would she ever be able to show her face in school again? The bastard, he acted as if the world revolved around him.

She blinked her eyes clear. She hadn't spoken to him again until Tony's funeral fourteen years later. He'd been invited to their wedding, because Tony had considered Jake a friend, but she'd been happy when Jake declined the invitation.

God, she hated the conceited bastard. Her life had turned out as it had thanks to him. If she and Jake had stayed a couple, she would have never dated Tony. And she'd have made sure Jake stayed in sports. She'd be the wife of a sports star, not a gambler. She'd grown to love Tony somewhat, but he hadn't been the love of her life. Two years into the marriage, his gambling addiction had gotten worse, and she'd started to hate him right before he died. God, when he died she thought she'd be free from it all; instead she'd become a member of the living dead—work, sleep, and more work.

Chapter 6

Outside the studio Jake stood by his car and studied the area. Businesses occupied the street, not residential homes. It'd be quiet on a Sunday afternoon, he figured, drumming his fingers on the dashboard.

"What's eating at you, Jake?" Louie asked, his face scrunched up while gauging his partner's mood.

"She's off," Jake said. "The news of Callie's death was all over the news yesterday and today. Yet Melinda lied, said she hadn't heard."

"You two have never mixed well."

"No, it's more." Jake cocked his head to the side and stared at her, still sitting at the counter in her studio, before he shifted the car into drive and pulled away from the curb. He drove directly to the courthouse to get his warrant. The judge didn't keep them waiting, which told Jake the case had a number-one priority. He and Louie entered the judge's chamber and took a seat.

"Judge Eisenberg, how are you?" Jake asked.

Judge Eisenberg wore a suit today instead of his judicial robes. Eisenberg's five-foot-nine-inch frame appeared large when seated. He sported a bald spot in the middle of his head that glistened when the harsh overhead lights glared off of it.

"You're handling the Blake murder, aren't you?" Eisenberg asked without ceremony.

"Yes, it's why we're here. Callie Blake had her portrait and what's called glamour shots done by Melinda Mastrianni Photography Studio. The owner, who I dated in high school, is insisting I get a warrant if I want to see her files. She claims the photograph with the body wasn't one of hers."

"You don't believe her?" Eisenberg asked.

"It's not a question of belief…I think she's holding up the investigation to bust my balls."

"And why would she do that?"

"It goes back to the time around my sister's death, but that's not the point. And it's personal, Judge Eisenberg." Jake hoped the judge didn't push the issue. "Callie had her pictures taken by Melinda. I need to see who else did, in case the blackmailer targets them," Jake said.

"You'll have your warrant…but first."

Jake raised his eyes from his notebook when the judge hesitated. "Yes?" Jake exchanged a look with Louie.

"You're going to find my wife's photo is in there. I'm going to ask that you both use discretion when you question her and not put them in your files."

What? Has the whole town gone crazy? "I will, sir. We're not out to destroy anyone or share what we find. As long as they aren't targeted by the blackmailer or killer, it's their business what they do."

"Do you know why they'd target cops' and judges' wives?" Judge Eisenberg asked.

"Not a clue, sir, but whoever the blackmailer is, he doesn't understand what he brought down upon his head," Jake said with conviction.

Judge Eisenberg locked eyes with him, then with Louie. "The warrant should come through within the hour."

Jake left the office deep in thought. What he said in the judge's office he believed. The blackmailer had to have reasons for targeting these women. Find the why, find the killer. Had Melinda run special ads for these kinds of pictures to entice women to pose? If she had, where did she advertise? It was an angle to search. He'd hand off the search for the ads to Kirk Brown, one of his junior detectives and an ace with online research. It would clear Jake's plate to move forward into his background checks on the Blakes after he executed his warrant for Melinda's place. He had to question the Blakes' neighbors and friends to get a feel for the couple. He was acquainted with some of them from picnics at the Blakes', and wasn't that going to be fun.

* * * *

Neither of them missed the expression on Melinda's face when Jake handed her the warrant two hours later. He nodded to Louie as he followed her to the back of the studio. Louie searched the front of the studio.

Upset he hadn't approached her the first time with a warrant, Jake hoped she hadn't wiped the computer drive clean after their visit.

"I need the password," Jake said, taking a seat at her computer.

Melinda leaned in over his shoulder and typed in the password before stepping back. Jake clicked on file after file. If he couldn't find anything, he'd bring the station's computer whiz here to search.

"Which photos were taken this year?" He wanted to narrow down the task.

"All files have a two-number extension at the end, with the year."

Jake searched the year, then the name. Christ, Melinda's business seemed to be doing well this year. She'd photographed over thirty women.

He clicked on a few files, then stopped. "Is there a way to cull through the boudoir pictures only, instead of the portraits and weddings?" Jake asked.

"A lot of the brides pose for the glamour shots as a special gift for their future husbands on their wedding night," Melinda said.

"Do you have a list of the ones that did both?"

"I need to sit back down at my computer."

Jake swirled the chair in Melinda's direction and stood. Melinda sat down in the black leather chair Jake had vacated and typed furiously. After a few keystrokes she opened a document. She rose and gave him the chair back. He bit back a remark as he viewed the list. If she'd given him this list to begin with…no, he wasn't going to go there.

"Can you print a copy of this document for me?"

"Jake, this is my customer list, and it is heavily guarded. If one of my competitors ever got hold of it, I'd be out of business."

"I'm going to have to insist. No one but Louie and I will see the file."

Even with the list, it took two hours to go through her records. Midway through he'd come upon Callie's shoot. He continued clicking through the pictures, finding pictures of other prominent women who had also posed for the same kind of shots.

"Do you have the addresses and phone numbers for each?"

"Good Lord, Jake, do you want me to do your job for you? Yes, I have the information that was current at the time of the photo session. Get your ass out of my chair."

She pushed him aside and sat down again. After bringing up another program, she printed out the file. "I'll sue you and the department if my client list is made public."

"Got it, and thanks for your time."

Louie wrote up a receipt for the printouts and handed it to Melinda. Jake didn't care how much he'd insulted her today. The last thing he needed was another body turning up—assuming the photos were the connection to Callie's murder.

"Thanks. If we need anything else, we'll give you a call." Jake tucked his notepad into his pocket and followed Louie out. Louie had remained quiet throughout Jake's questioning.

"I'll wait with bated breath," Melinda said as the door swung closed.

"She didn't seem hinky or anything," Louie said when they climbed into the car. "She didn't exhibit any tells."

"No, but she was nervous from the minute we walked in the door, too much to put it down to seeing me again. I'm going to dig deeper into her background."

Jake took his notepad out and started writing. "Are you going to drive, or what?" Louie asked.

"I will as soon as I separate out some names I found in her files."

He handed his pad to Louie when he finished. A low whistle filled the car.

"All of them? These women have everything. Why would they pose for something so stupid?" Louie asked.

"I haven't the foggiest idea, Louie."

"You got to see them? How come I get all the shit jobs?"

"A comedian you are. It wasn't pleasant. I'll never be able to look the lot of them in the eyes again without remembering their pictures."

"Do you think the captain knows Darcy is one of them?"

"He will after we tell him."

"Well, I didn't see them, so that task falls to you."

"Coward."

"Oh, you bet. I treasure my career." Louie's lips curved up.

* * * *

Jake pulled into the underground garage at headquarters, placed the stick shift into park, and drummed his fingers on the wheel as he ran through what he had to do. "I'm going to tell Shamus alone, to spare him the embarrassment."

Louie stepped into the elevator first, then pressed two. Jake pressed three. When the elevator stopped on two, Louie gave Jake a pat on the back before he stepped off. The short ride to the third floor had Jake dreading the meeting. Shamus's office was the first door on the right. He lifted his hand to knock on the partially open door when Shamus called out, "Come in."

"Shamus," Jake said as he closed the door.

"I've been waiting for you." Shamus stood behind his desk and threw a set of photos across it. "My wife gave me these this morning. And you need to know these were for my eyes only, Jake. I don't want them in the file. No one is going to ogle my wife. Am I clear?"

"Yes, sir."

"This is totally out of character for Darcy. And for my intelligent wife not only to have considered it, but to actually pose for them, is beyond my comprehension." Shamus's shoulders slumped. He sat in his chair but never took his eyes off Jake.

Jake didn't pick up the pictures. He left them where Shamus had tossed them. "I've already seen them."

"I figured. You and Louie work fast."

"If it makes you feel any better, I'm the only one who saw them, while Louie searched the front of the studio."

"No, it doesn't." Shamus picked up the photos and shoved them into his briefcase.

"I need to ask, did Darcy receive any threatening letters with copies of these, or any photos with a man in them?"

"Not that I'm aware of. These are the only ones she showed me."

Jake pulled out the picture of Callie Blake with the unidentified male. "I need to know."

McGuire grabbed his receiver and pressed in a number and got right to the point. "Did you pose with a male model?"

Jake noted the harsh tones in Shamus's voice. Shamus pushed out of his chair and stood. Jake noted Shamus's white knuckles gripping the phone.

Jake watched closely—he'd almost missed it. The surprise, then the disgust. Shamus's pasty skin reddened. "We'll talk when I get home. One more thing, it's very important. Did you get any kind of threatening letter?"

McGuire put down the receiver. He stared at it as if it would bite him. "Darcy didn't receive any kind of letter, but said a male model was suggested once she'd finished up with the agreed photos. It upset her and she refused the offer." Consternation dripped from his tone.

Jake had found pictures of Darcy with a man in a bedroom. It had surprised the heck out of him. He'd never have guessed it was her style or Callie's. "This is painful, Shamus. Do you believe your wife is faithful?"

"Without question, I know she is."

"Do you know who the man in Callie's picture is?"

"No."

"Can you let your wife know I'll be paying her a visit? I need to question her."

Shamus rubbed his chin, then slammed his hand down on his desk. "This will humiliate her."

"You know it can't be helped. I'll do it alone."

Jake understood from this day forward things would never be the same between him and Shamus.

* * * *

"I'm calling to let you know Jake Carrington has to interview you. He found and viewed your glamour shots in the photographer's files today. For God's sake, Darcy, Jake Carrington saw you in your underwear."

Darcy gulped. *How could I be so naïve? And how will I ever be able to look Jake Carrington in the eyes again?*

"Are there any more surprises that I should know about, Darcy?"

Shamus's controlled anger worried her, but she'd have to deal with it when they were both home, and not on the phone.

"No, Shamus. This was supposed to be for your eyes only as an anniversary gift. Though the photographer did offer an opportunity to pose with a male model, I turned her down. I thought it was rude, and invasive on her part to even offer such a thing."

Yesterday, she'd cried for three straight hours before her husband thought to give her a call and tell her the horrible news about her best friend. She replayed the conversation over in her head and how she'd tried to pin him with guilt for not calling her.

Her eyes stung as she forced them to focus on the vibrating phone in her hand. What could he say now? Callie's dead. I needed him hours ago.

"Shamus, tell me it isn't true." Her voice cracked.

"I wish I could, honey. I'm sorry I didn't get the chance to call you sooner. Todd has been with me since I got the call. Their kids learned about her death on the news."

"So did I, Shamus." The hurt in her tone was quite clear.

"I want to warn you, honey, there are pictures with the body that are pointing to an affair."

"No, Callie would never cheat on Todd," she said.

Yes, she was hurting, but she hadn't given him an ounce of understanding yesterday concerning the situation he'd been caught in with Todd. When she heard of the pictures found with the body, she tried to think if her shots compared. And would the blackmailer/killer target her?

"Darcy, if the blackmailer contacts you, you need to tell me immediately."

"I will, Shamus."

"I'm serious, and when I get home we're going to discuss this and your need to prance around in your underwear."

It was all innocent until the photographer suggested that slimy guy pose with her. Hindsight was great. She should've demanded the memory card be erased after she'd chosen her pictures. *Is this the end of my marriage?*

* * * *

Most days he liked working homicide. It gave the victim an identity and justice, which allowed him to handle the atrocities he witnessed each day. But on days like this, Jake hated his job. Not that he'd dealt with anything like this before. Having to question his captain's wife had him walking a tightrope. The door opened before he could raise his hand to knock. Darcy McGuire had always had his admiration and respect. And now it was his job to tear her down, to find the truth, and solve a murder and hopefully prevent another one.

"Come in and let's get this over with. I need to be back at my office by four," Darcy said. She was dressed in a tailored navy suit and pumps. Her brown hair was twisted back at the nape of her neck.

The busy CEO and successful businesswoman, Mrs. McGuire, ran a multimillion-dollar manufacturing company. She locked her sharp brown eyes on his. Not many could get him to look away first, but he did.

"Follow me." She marched away, leaving him to close the door behind him. "Take a seat." Darcy pointed to a muted beige wingback chair.

The living room with its couch and chairs at precise angles reminded him of the captain's office and the couple's military backgrounds. Not one knickknack out of place or a dust mote to be found. She favored blue and beige in her fabrics. Furniture, curtains, and the clothes she wore didn't vary from the theme.

There was no offer of coffee. The woman in front of him was used to being in control. "Mrs. McGuire—"

"It's always been Darcy, Jake."

"Darcy, this is embarrassing for both of us. In the course of my investigation into Callie Blake's death, I came across compromising pictures of you."

"Let's cut the bull, shall we? I posed for some racy pictures to present to my husband for our anniversary. If you'd been married as long as we have, you'd know that at times a little spice is needed to keep the spark alive. After the scheduled appointment I went to get dressed, and the photographer asked if I wanted to pose with a model. I didn't."

Another lie he'd caught Melinda in. He'd add it to his list of questions for his next interview with her.

"Why did you turn her down?"

"Well, for one, I felt this would be disrespectful to Shamus. But also… the model came down the stairs after I viewed the pictures Melinda shot of me. He made my skin crawl with the way he looked at me. I'm sure it was her boyfriend with how they interacted with each other. A real sleaze, if you ask me."

"What makes you think they were dating?"

"It was the way Melinda looked at him and touched him. And after years of reading people, he sent my antenna waving, so I declined. Blackmail never crossed my mind."

"Did you pose anywhere other than the studio?"

"No, why would I? I will tell you, Melinda told me the blue background I posed in front of allowed her to change the scenery. Oh, what a fool I've been. Jake, I never thought…"

"The pictures I viewed today showed you and a man in a bedroom." Jake watched her face carefully.

Fear, shame, and anger crossed her features in a matter of seconds. "Are you telling me Melinda doctored the pictures?"

"If you're telling me you didn't pose anywhere else but at Melinda's studio, yes. You'll need to tell your husband in case they get out."

"I swear to God, I didn't pose with anyone. Is there a way for your forensics team to see if the man was cut into the picture?"

"It's an avenue I'm pursuing, Darcy." Jake took her hand. "You have to promise me if you hear from blackmailers you'll contact me personally before you let Shamus know. Do not pay if they request money. I'll give you my cell phone number."

"I'm not stupid, Jake. Well, most times anyway. But if something like this got out, it could ruin both Shamus's and my careers."

"One other thing—what was his name?"

"Sal."

"You don't have a last name?"

"No."

"I need this guy's face. Can you work with a police artist? It will help me to identify him."

"Yes."

For the first time since he'd known her, Darcy broke down. Tears washed away the makeup. The sunlight shining through the living room window wasn't flattering as it landed on her face. It highlighted every wrinkle, aging her as he watched her try to compose herself.

"I'll let myself out." He could offer no comfort.

He passed the mailman on his way to the car.

Chapter 7

Edwina Dunstan sat across from her husband, Cedric, in the formal dining room, a ritual she'd grown up with and kept when she had gotten married. Her maid, Benita, placed the salads in front of each of them. Cedric, at the other end of the table, seemed preoccupied.

What had she seen in him all those years ago? *Ah, but he was a handsome young man filled with ideas on how he'd conquer the world.* Edy remembered it well, the night of the big dance, the bonfires, the excitement bubbling up inside her, and then she spotted Cedric across the blazing fire pit. She and her friend Margaret had been plotting their next move on Travis Dresser, the captain of the football team. But when she locked eyes with Cedric she'd fallen instantly in love with him. Cedric's green eyes and his cocky smile, his flirting nature enticed her in ways she'd never considered before.

Later she'd learn his name was Cedric Dunstan, a boy from Bridgeport, who lived in the projects. It hadn't mattered to her they came from different worlds. At home she relaxed in her bedroom after the game and doodled his name with hers on her notebook. His name went well with hers. He was the boy from the wrong side of the tracks who hated to be reminded of it. He'd won the prize when he caught Edy's eye. Her father had warned her about him, but no, she had made up her mind that he was the one.

She'd been a fool to feel anything for such a louse. When she'd fallen in love with him, she had given him only one rule—Don't Cheat. She asked nothing more of him. They'd married the summer she graduated from college. At least, at her father's insistence, she was smart enough to get an ironclad prenup. If he broke her one rule, he got nothing.

Though her father didn't approve, he gave Cedric a job at the bank. Cedric worked hard, climbing the ladder. He thought he'd replace Edy's father someday as president and chairman of the board.

But could Cedric keep it in his pants? No, right after our second anniversary he took his secretary away for a weekend while I was tied up with some charity work.

Call her perverse, but for the last several years she'd enjoyed making his life hell, flaunting her lovers in his face. Not to mention how at every event or dinner with friends she'd make a reference to the purse strings, and how it all belonged to her. The power of revenge had given Edy both pleasure and an overwhelming sadness when she'd humiliate him in front of people. And since he worked for her father, he'd lose his cushy job as vice president of the Colonial New England Bank and walk away with nothing if she divorced him.

She'd bought her beloved teacup poodle, Noodles, to cuddle with instead of him. But the void inside her grew larger with each of his infidelities until she had no respect, no love, no anything for Cedric but a deep-seated hatred.

A one-ton concrete weight had crushed her heart when the private detective Jimmy Nelson told her that Cedric had set up his latest mistress in an apartment where he paid the bills using an account he'd opened at a competitor's bank. And the bastard did it all with her money, for God's sake. She crumbled the copy of the rent check Jimmy had given her, then tried to work the creases out of it.

Now look at me. I'm sitting here plotting his imaginary death. If I thought I'd get away with it, I'd kill him in a horrid, painful way as I dragged the blade through his gut and up to his cheating heart.

She wanted him to experience each and every slice of the knife. The same way he'd jabbed at her heart. And she'd do all this while he begged for forgiveness one last time. Only this time, instead of forgiving him, Edy would laugh as she extinguished his last breath. His gushing lies would be the perfect end to this farce they called a marriage.

She hadn't told Cedric she'd drawn up papers for the divorce. They sat on her lawyer's desk awaiting her signature. But first she had to make sure all the accounts were out of his name, then she'd slash him to pieces. All she had to do was get Linden Smith, her current boyfriend, to do her bidding. If Linden wouldn't get her what she wanted, she'd forge Cedric's name on a check and wipe him out. *Then let's see who'd want the penniless old man.* It astounded her to learn Cedric had saved over one hundred thousand dollars. There was probably more, but Jimmy hadn't found it yet.

Oh yes, your days are numbered, Cedric.

* * * *

The day had gotten away from them. Though they'd been in motion for most of it, Jake felt they hadn't accomplished much. His retinas burned with the images of all the women in Melinda's file. He lifted his wrist and checked the time. 7:10. Yep, he'd already been at it for twelve hours. The next item on his list included digging deeper into the Blakes' financials and habits. Jake opened up the police database and entered both Todd and Callie's names. After much consideration he added the children's names in case they had trust funds. Callie might have raided their accounts for the blackmail money.

He filled out the forms to gather the banking information and emailed them to the proper authorities with a copy of his second warrant, which Eisenberg had issued today. He didn't want to take any chances that the info could be leaked. He'd do the work instead of using one of his junior detectives. The material, sensitive in nature, remained for his and Louie's eyes only. With his hands full with analyzing Blake's info, and to speed up the information flow on the others, he'd need to trust Kirk Brown with the list of non-prominent women with money. Kirk could check in with them and find out if any of them had received a blackmail letter.

Jake rubbed his eyes to clear his vision as he read his emails. He opened Kirk Brown's email first and scanned through it. Melinda had advertised in all the major papers in Connecticut. Kirk had attached the ad copy used. Jake studied them. Most said the same thing. *Capture your beauty and confidence as a gift for your loved one.* That was the ad for Valentine's Day. The Christmas one read *Add a little glamour to your holiday.* Each ad had a twenty-something model with a perfect, scantily clad body smiling out at the viewer.

"There's not much more I can do here. I'm going to head home," Louie said from his doorway.

"Good idea, I'm getting punchy myself. Oh, how far did you get with your searches?"

"I got a couple of little bumps on the oldest child at college, but nothing major. He got picked up with a group of kids for drinking on campus. I know both of them personally and they're good kids, Jake."

"That's what people said about the Menendez brothers. Tomorrow I'm going to dig deeper into Melinda and her recent activities and known associates. Kirk's email stated he's halfway through the list I gave him on the other women in the file. None of the ones he's spoken to have received a letter."

"Good to know. After I finish up my stuff in the morning, I'll help him with the rest of it," Louie said.

"No, I want you on this list. And remember, it's for your eyes only."

"Good night."

Jake waved Louie off and returned his attention to his computer files. He wrote up his activity report for the day, then called it quits.

* * * *

Jake put his feet up on the coffee table when he got home. He also popped a couple of pain pills. Mia had decided to spend the night at her condo when he told her he wouldn't be home before eight or nine o'clock. It fit perfectly into his plan. He'd be damned if he'd let on how much pain he was in. The doctor had been right not to clear him for duty, but he wasn't given a choice with this case. Jake rested the file on his lap and closed his eyes for a minute.

Five hours later, Jake woke with a start when a scream pierced the night. He realized the scream had come from him. Part of the requirements he'd been putting off was to talk to the department shrink. It was standard after an incident of this magnitude. The doc had to clear him before he resumed his duties. Lucky for him this case had fallen into his lap.

The nightmares continued with the knife digging into his gut, the popping noise echoing louder than a balloon exploding overhead. In his dreams his vision faded and sometimes he met his maker waiting for his judgment. Sometimes Eva, along with his father, waited there to greet him. Before he reached either of them he'd wake, relieved and empty.

When this case is over, I'll see the shrink.

* * * *

Jake hated the antsy feelings the meds induced. Once he'd awakened, he hadn't been able to get back to sleep. With coffee in hand, he settled in at his home office and signed into the police database. He started his runs on Melinda Blair Mastrianni.

Melinda had claimed no one but her had access to her files. She'd suggested that she might've been hacked *but*...and that was a pretty big *but.* Who knew to hack the files, and specifically Callie's file? There had to be a reason that Callie Blake had been targeted. A dissatisfied lover? If Todd had one, Jake hadn't found her. Nor did he find a lover for Callie, but it was early into his investigation.

Money and sex, sex and money, which one played into this scenario? He drew a blank and changed tactics. With his pen poised over the paper, Jake combed his memory and jotted down the names of Melinda's friends from high school. As an afterthought, he wrote down Tony's name and the names of their other teammates and started a search on Tony's business associates as well as Melinda's. Tony had been one of the good guys on his ball team.

It saddened him what he'd uncovered about Tony. People change, but the Tony he knew in high school hadn't been a gambler—or had he? Jake scanned the collection notices in Tony and Melinda's name. The amount of debt Tony had left Melinda after his death staggered Jake. Though she was current with her payments, she lived close to the edge. He kept circling back to money as the motive, with a dash of mean added, as the reason for Callie's murder. *And mean fits in with the Melinda I remember.*

On the right side of his desk sat his father's old file on Eva's murder. Though his father had worked the case off the record, he never wavered in his belief that George Spaulding had killed Eva. Not only did Jake want to make sure Eva's killer stayed in jail, he believed to this day that his father's death at an early age had been a direct result of Eva's murder. Right now it was a wait-and-see game as the state dragged its feet on Spaulding's DNA results. Callie's case had brought it all to the forefront again. Would Spaulding be set free? Everyone knew each other in a small city, and cases like the Blakes' would unearth skeletons from everyone's closet. Which brought him back to Melinda—were she and Spaulding friends? And what difference did it make to Callie's case? To keep his sanity, Jake shoved Spaulding out of his head.

At six thirty, after sitting for a while, his body rebelled. Jake stood and stretched out the kinks before jumping in the shower. Dressed, he went to the kitchen and made breakfast. He sipped his coffee and checked his phone. One missed call last night from Mia. Damn, the pills had knocked him out. He'd call her back after nine.

* * * *

Louie greeted him as he made his way down the hallway leading to his office. "Hey, you look like hell."

"Thanks, and you're a shining beauty too," Jake said, not slowing his pace.

Louie followed him into his office. "I'm serious. You don't look too good, what's up?"

"I had a restless night, throwing scenarios around in my head." He'd be damned if he'd let Louie in on his nightmares.

"You shouldn't even be back at work. I tried to talk the commissioner out of using you."

"Louie, I don't need you nagging me. Now let's get to work. What do you have?"

"The final autopsy report came in and there were no surprises in it. No fluids, no fibers, except for ones found in the room. Lang confirmed it was a single .22 caliber in the heart that killed her."

"All we have to do is find the gun, find the killer. What else?"

"Lab reports on the room. And holy cow, we both should've gone into a contamination chamber after leaving the place. Fluids, fibers, and blood from various individuals might've been there for a while. Lang's going to enter them into CODIS to see if there's a match."

Jake shivered at the memory of the room. He'd been in worse, but at the moment he couldn't say where.

"All right, they're not going to help pinpoint a suspect unless there's a match. We'll keep it under our hat for now. I started my search on Melinda and Tony from home this morning. It's running in the background."

"Why Tony?" Louie asked.

"He had a business that was deep in debt and his gambling problems contributed to it. I'm checking for friends, enemies, relatives, anyone who had the knowledge or opportunity to access her files."

"I know the pictures connect her, but I can't see Melinda for it."

"Too early to say one way or another," he said, entertaining an idea. "I'm going to go back to interview her with more personal and direct questions about her private life. Darcy said the man was Melinda's boyfriend, though Melinda never let on. I'm hoping she'll give me his name."

"Good luck, she didn't seem cooperative yesterday. Oh, I have Darcy McGuire coming in around noon to work with the artist."

"Joel Bennett, I hope?" Jake asked.

"Yes. If she can give us a face, we can run it through the facial recognition database," Louie said.

"Why didn't you have Joel go to her?" Jake asked.

"I didn't think of it. Do you want me to change it up?"

"No, if she didn't squawk about it, let's leave it be."

Politics. Jake hated it, or having to give people special treatment, but in this case he'd better check, to cover his team's asses.

"I'm going to pay Shamus a visit and see how he wants it handled. Do you have a problem with that?"

"No, it takes the pressure off me."

Jake left his office to go the captain's. Shamus's secretary didn't come in until nine. He stood at the open door and cleared his throat.

"Shamus, do you have a minute?"

"Yes."

Jake stared at Shamus's desk. Never had he seen it in such disarray. Lines in Shamus's forehead, which weren't there yesterday, had materialized overnight.

"Darcy's due in at noon to work with Joel Bennett. I was wondering if it would be easier for her to work with him at home instead of here."

Shamus rubbed his hand over the back of his neck. "It would, but she can't be treated differently, and she understands that."

"It's not a problem."

"Jake, all of Joel's equipment is here. If he goes to the house, he'd have to do it all by hand. No, Darcy will report at noon. I'll ask a favor. Can you escort her to his office?"

"I'll make sure I'm back here by then."

On the way back to his office Jake punched in Mia's number. He never checked the time.

"Hello," Mia said in her sleepy voice.

"Sorry, honey, I didn't realize the time." He turned his wrist up and checked it.

"How'd you make out yesterday?"

Tell a lie or give her the truth? After caring for him for weeks, she deserved the truth. "By the end of the day I was exhausted."

"I figured. My publisher sent my edits for my novel back with a short turnaround date. I'll need to work from home for the next couple of days unless you need me."

"No, get your work done. You've been putting it on the back burner to care for me. It's time for us to get back to normal."

"Trying to get rid of me?"

"No."

"Call me when you get home tonight."

After he hung up with Mia, he thought of the turn in their relationship. Mia had fallen into the caregiver's role too easily. Where did that leave them, going forward?

* * * *

Melinda lived in the Fairlawn neighborhood, a close-knit community of people who watched out for each other. At nine thirty Jake drove into her driveway and parked in front of a detached single-car garage painted to match the small taupe Cape Cod–style home. The records he pulled off the town hall database dated the home to the 1940s. Besides the front entrance, the record listed one on the side of the house that faced the garage. The specs on the blueprints showed a full basement with a Bilco door leading out to the yard. He walked around, peeked over the fence, and scanned the overgrown backyard, which encompassed a small raised deck with a wooden picnic table. He couldn't spot the cellar door.

Jake made his way back to the front door, pushing overgrown bushes out of his way and rang the bell. Melinda answered, wearing jeans ripped at the knees and a large oversized green tunic hanging off one shoulder, her hair held back by a headband, her feet bare.

"What do you want?"

"I have a few more questions."

"Come in and let's get this over with," Melinda said, stepping back to let him in.

Jake entered an oblong living room with a single beige couch and a brown print chair. The television sat under the window on a stand surrounded by green plants. At the end of the room a large archway opened into the dining room done in peach tones and pale green. The low ceilings made him feel cramped.

"Come into the kitchen," she said, leading him from the room.

As he stepped through the archway into the kitchen–dining room combo, the nine-foot ceiling opened up the space. Jake felt less confined.

She pointed to a chair at the narrow table attached to the wall, next to the sink. The workable kitchen area carried the pale green of the dining room's tablecloth. He removed his notebook from his pocket, then sat on the hardwood chair, pushing the place mat out of the way.

Jake decided to set the tone. "It's come to my attention that you lied to me the last time we met. I can pull you in for obstructing justice. I need the name of the man in the picture."

"I told you, I didn't hire him."

"One of the women you photographed said at the end of her session you offered her a male model to pose with her. You asked if she wanted to spice up her pictures. Is that true?"

"Who told you that?"

"The who is not important—did you offer your clients a model?"

Melinda's left eye twitched. "Only if the customer requested one. They don't come cheap. Artistically, I find the photos with the women alone in them more seductive."

"The woman is credible. She had not requested one."

Melinda twisted her mouth to the side and bit down on her bottom lip. "The models I hire are legit. What's the problem if I might've offered a customer a chance to pose with one? Honestly, I don't recall doing that with my last few customers."

"She said the man you offered to pose with her was your boyfriend. What's his name?"

"I don't use family or friends in my business. Talk about a can of worms."

Jake tapped his pencil on the notebook as he stared her down. He locked down his frustration and remembered how Melinda had always loved to grandstand.

"A woman was killed, and the pictures left with her body are pictures you took, whether they're printed on your photo paper or not. I need a little help. What's your boyfriend's name?"

"He's not my boyfriend. We only dated a few times, and I never had him pose with Callie Blake or anyone else. He must've stolen them off my computer. In digital photography it's easy to manipulate an image. Am I in danger?" Melinda wrung her hands.

Jake placed his over hers. She pulled back.

"I'm not sure. Give me his name and address. If it's warranted I'll assign a uniform for your protection. How would a person add someone to a shot after the session is done?" Jake asked.

"Digital allows you to smooth out lines, fix color, and cut and paste an item or person into an image. But if you aren't meticulous, you'll see where they were added. Like anything else, Jake, it's an art."

He wondered if she knew she'd thrown herself under the bus with her statement. Even in their teens she was a cagey woman.

"His name's Sal Gallucci. I need to hunt up his exact address. But he lives in one of the condos on Oronoke Avenue, called Oronoke Ridge."

Jake wrote it down, raised his eyes to meet hers. "I'll check it out. You lie again, Melinda, and you'll give me no choice but to arrest you. Do I make myself clear?"

"Yes."

"Good. The police commissioner's wife has been murdered. The whole town is on edge. If you think of anything else, here's my card. Give me a call."

* * * *

Darcy had thrown yesterday's mail on the table by the door, along with the package. She had to get back to work to prepare for her afternoon meeting, but she couldn't concentrate on her work. She decided to comb through the mail, a distraction she sorely needed to take her mind off her upcoming appointment with the police artist. When the postman rang the doorbell yesterday, Darcy thought Jake had forgotten something. She'd opened the door, surprised to see the mailman instead of Jake.

"Good morning, Mrs. McGuire. It was terrible about the commissioner's wife, wasn't it?"

"It was," Darcy said. She wasn't going to talk about her friend's murder now or ever.

"I have a package that needs to be signed for."

She scribbled her name on the receipt without verifying the sender. "Thank you," she said to cut off any further conversation on her friend's death.

It surprised her that Shamus hadn't sorted through the mail last night. It wasn't like him to leave things around. It relaxed her to do something normal, a simple chore to even out the hell she'd been through. Bills, advertisements, and a plain white envelope with no return address. She ignored the package from her favorite online store. Darcy ripped into the letter, her heart skipping a beat. It wasn't signed.

Her hands quivered as the pictures spilled and fanned out at her feet. *Dear God, this will destroy us. The slimy bastard—I never posed with the creep.*

Darcy trudged into the living room and sat in the first beige chair she came to. She read and reread the letter. Shamus had told her the blackmailer had demanded twenty-five thousand from Callie. Her letter asked for one hundred thousand. There was a vague reference to Callie's murder, with a line saying the same could happen to her if she didn't pay up.

Why me? And why Callie? It doesn't make sense. They have to know our husbands will hunt them down to the ends of the earth. Or is it because not many people in Wilkesbury have family money? Either way, when I get my hands on the blackmailer, he's a dead man.

The embarrassment faded to anger. Her ears burned with fury as she thought about what she'd do to the bastard for what he'd done to Callie.

The irony of it all hadn't gotten by her. Yesterday Jake had passed the mailman on his way out. She'd have to call him back and hand over the pictures of herself half naked. But first, she had to tell her husband, something best done in person.

She packed up her briefcase, placed it by the door with her purse, the pictures inside, and slid into her coat. She'd be a half hour early for her appointment with the artist, but it gave her plenty of time to discuss the letter with Shamus. Though not too much time to argue. She set the alarm and left the house. A prayer on her lips, Darcy backed out of the driveway.

Chapter 8

Melinda sat at her desk in her sparsely furnished home office and fingered the card Jake had given her. How convenient. It had his cell phone number on it. She opened the spreadsheet she'd made with the loan balances she owed and added up the money she'd spent on interest, the balance never seeming to go down. One windfall and she'd be out from under it all.

Sal's insight into not going home had paid off for him, but what about her? It was stupid of her to go into business with Sal, especially when hers had only started to show a profit and she'd gotten name recognition.

Oh, don't act all high and mighty. It all came down to money. It always comes down to money. I had a weak "poor me" moment when I agreed to this deal.

After writing last month's checks to the bank, she hardly had any money left over for food. Sal had told her cops had more to hide than the criminals they locked up. *Damn it, and I bought into his bullshit.*

Melinda didn't have time to dally today. One of the state's richest women had an appointment today to get her portrait taken. Edwina Dunstan, or Edy, as she liked to be called, had contacted her last week to request a sitting. At the gala Saturday she'd noted Edy's coloring, height, weight, and style, and matched the background setting to the woman. If Edy used her photos for public appearances or articles, she'd have to give Melinda credit for the photos.

Edy Dunstan could be my money-making machine in referrals. Why couldn't I have met her before we set Sal's stupid plan in motion?

Noting the time, she popped up from the table and rushed into her bedroom to dress. She couldn't afford to be late for Edy Dunstan's sitting.

* * * *

Jake wrote down his impressions and added them to the facts before pulling out of Melinda's driveway. He tucked his notepad into his jacket's breast pocket. Hunger pains kicked in, but a quick check of his watch had him driving to the station instead of to lunch.

With one hand on the wheel he hit the speed-dial button. Shamus picked up immediately.

"Where am I meeting Darcy?" Jake asked.

"She's here in my office."

"I'm on my way." Jake disconnected his phone and tossed it on the seat.

Jake rolled Melinda's statement over in his head while he drove. There'd been no evidence of a cut-and-paste job on the compromising photo of Callie, but he hadn't been looking for one. When he finished up with Darcy, he'd blow up the picture. If his untrained eye wasn't able to detect a fudge, he'd ask Joel Bennett to view it. Damn, did he need permission from Shamus or Todd before he showed it to Bennett? It was hard working with his hands tied.

Todd was a suspect who had no business offering advice or approving anything within the investigation. And Shamus...did he belong on the suspect list with his wife now involved? Did Callie and Shamus have an affair? Or did Todd and Darcy? No, it didn't play out for him.

My answer with any other suspect would be a resounding yes, Jake thought as he sat in his car in the precinct's underground garage. *I'd've dug deep into their backgrounds, gathering the dirt, until their lives were turned upside down.* He'd been tiptoeing around with his captain and the commissioner.

Jake rode the elevator to the third floor. When he reached Shamus's office, he knocked and took the empty seat in front of his desk. Darcy had perched herself at Shamus's office window, her arms folded across her chest. "We're early, but I'm sure Joel will take us. I don't want to keep you waiting, Darcy," Jake said.

If Darcy's nervous, she doesn't show it outwardly, he thought. He couldn't read Shamus's thoughts either.

"We need to show you something first." Shamus handed him a letter. Jake's stomach dropped. *Damn, damn, damn.* He'd been expecting this, but had hoped against it.

Jake opened the letter, reading it first before he viewed the pictures. "Is this the photographer's boyfriend, Darcy?"

"Yes. As you can see, his face is not exposed. What I'd like to do, and Shamus agrees, is to copy the photo for Joel Bennett, with me cut out of it," Darcy said. She took the seat to his left and pointed to the man in the photo.

"That'll work. When the session's done, I'm going to escort you directly to your car to avoid running into anyone. Is that satisfactory?"

"Thank you, Jake. I understand you're interrupting your investigation to make this easier for me, and I appreciate it," Darcy said, not making eye contact with him.

Jake reached over and draped an arm around her shoulders, waiting for her to raise her eyes to him. "Darcy, this isn't your fault or Callie's. I promise I'm going to get this bastard with as little publicity as possible."

"I'll see you at home when you finish up," Shamus told Darcy. "Jake, I'd like to thank you too. It's not easy working around the commissioner, and now me."

A slight movement of his head acknowledged Shamus and his words. Jake didn't want to prolong this. He stood and offered Darcy his hand to help her from the chair.

"Darcy, before we head up, I want you to understand, Joel is not a freelance artist. He's a cop who specializes in sketching forensic renditions."

He hoped she got what he wasn't saying. Joel still answered to her husband, who was a captain in the department. Cops gossip. If she didn't want anything repeated, she'd need to keep it to herself.

"I'll answer the questions that pertain to the man in the picture, nothing more."

"Yes, the why isn't important—you got a glimpse of the suspect, period."

"Let's get it done," Darcy said and marched toward the door.

* * * *

By two o'clock Melinda had her studio set up for Edy's sitting. Per Edy's instructions, she wanted a formal picture to replace the five-year-old one she used for publicity. Edy rushed in the front door fifteen minutes late for her appointment.

"I'm running a bit behind, sorry," Edy said. A bundle of energy in her five-six frame, her blonde hair flying behind her.

"No problem, I'm ready when you are. Did you bring a couple of outfits to change into?" Melinda asked, evaluating Edy.

"I did. I also brought the gown from Saturday night."

"Where are they?"

"I need to run to the car for the outfits. I'll be right back."

Edy went back out to her car. When she reentered, Melinda showed her the studio first, then the dressing rooms.

She'd approved of how Edy wore her long blonde hair down. At the gala, with her updo, she had appeared unapproachable and snobbish. With it down, she looked younger.

God, she hated to photograph women wearing pantsuits. They crinkled in all the wrong places. She took a few shots in the pale blue one Edy wore before she suggested Edy change into a dress or the gown.

"I'll wear the gown next," Edy said.

Melinda adjusted her camera and lights to compliment the gold hue of Edy's gown. The bell over the front door rang out, announcing a visitor. *Oh freak, I forgot to put up the closed sign.*

"I'll be right back, Mrs. Dunstan, as soon as I get rid of whoever's out front. I'm sorry for the interruption."

"It might be my friend Linden. If it is, bring him back."

Linden? Isn't her husband's name Cedric? It's none of my business. As Melinda walked into the store she spotted the six-foot-tall man scrutinizing her work.

"Your work is exquisite."

"Ah, a man of distinguished taste. How can I help you?"

"Edy, I mean Edwina Dunstan, asked that I meet her here. I'm Linden Smith."

"I'm Melinda, follow me."

She normally didn't allow visitors while she worked, but Edy had money and could bring more to her if she played along.

"Oh, darling, you made it." Edy swept aside her gown and extended her cheek for a kiss.

Melinda bit back the smirk as Linden obliged Edy. He bent over and kissed her cheek. Smith had to be at least ten years younger than Dunstan and a foot taller.

"Did you bring your tux?" Edy asked.

"I did, but I don't understand why."

"Linden, Melinda is my photographer. We're going to get our pictures taken." Edy's voice, Melinda observed, had taken on the tone of an adult speaking to a child.

"Do you think it's wise?" Linden asked.

"Yes. Now go change while I still have the gown on."

Melinda worked with them for an hour. Around the halfway mark, Linden loosened up. For their last pose, Melinda made sure to put Linden in the same position Sal had posed in, in Callie's pictures. If she could pull this off the payday would be huge. It could be her ticket out of there for good and keep her away from Sal.

"Thanks, Melinda. I'll be right out to review the pictures."

Melinda hesitated but then decided to go for it. She pulled Edy aside. "I do boudoir photos, if that would interest you. And with Linden here…" She left it hanging.

"No, I'm good with what we have. But I'll keep it in mind for the future."

Edy picked out the ones she liked. Melinda gave her an eight-by-eleven to take with her. She set Saturday's date for the delivery of the rest of the photos.

"Can you make it Friday? I have a showing in mind for them this weekend," Edy said in a hushed voice, out of Linden's earshot.

"Sure. I'll have them delivered to your home."

"Excellent, only give them to me—or Benita, my maid. Understand? If neither of us are available, call me at this number." Edy slipped a card from her pocket.

"Yes." And she did understand. Edy didn't want her husband to know about them. It was none of her business what her customers did with the pictures after she processed them. Or in this case, who they did, Melinda thought with a smile.

* * * *

Jake stayed in the background and roamed Joel's spacious office as Joel worked with Darcy. Sketches of people and buildings, which Jake assumed Joel had created, lined the walls. Tonka trucks from the early eighties or older sat on his credenza. With half an ear he heard Joel ask general questions to begin the session, and every now and then he slipped one in asking what the guy he was drawing might've done. He had to give it to Darcy. She made diverting Joel and his questions an art. Darcy took her time when she answered, closing her eyes at times to visualize the person. Jake couldn't've asked for a better witness.

"Joel, can I use the computer over here?" Jake asked.

"Sure."

Jake signed onto the WPD database and entered Sal Gallucci's name. He got a hit immediately. A petty crook out of New Jersey, Sal hadn't done heavy time except for community service in his teens. In both instances

Sal had pleaded down. Jake studied the guy's picture, then walked over to Joel and looked over his shoulder.

Pretty close, he thought, but he'd let Darcy finish it out before he showed her Sal's mugshot. He wiped his search and shut down the computer, but not before sending it to his office printer.

Jake left the room to call Louie's cell. "Hey, I just printed something to my office printer. Don't let anyone else see it when you take it off the printer. I'll explain when I get back. Lock it up for me."

"You got my curiosity up. When will you be back?" Louie asked.

"It'll be another hour until Joel finishes his sketch. Put out feelers for the person in the printout. I want to know when he hit town, who he hung with, and who he dated. Thanks."

Jake returned to the room and sat down next to Darcy. Forty minutes later, Joel dismissed them in order to perfect the sketch after Darcy was satisfied he'd captured the guy. It was a match to the one Jake had printed out. Excitement built as a viable suspect came into focus. If he made Gallucci the number-one suspect, he'd be able to remove the commissioner from the list.

He escorted Darcy to her car and showed her the mug shot. "That's him," Darcy said.

"I'll follow you home."

"Jake, I'm a big girl. I'm sure Shamus is there waiting for me."

"Are you positive you don't want me to follow you?"

"Yes."

He waited until Darcy had pulled out of the garage before he rode the elevator up to two. His cell phone rang when the door opened on his floor.

"Carrington."

"Jake, it's Mayor D'Angelo."

"Good afternoon, Mayor. What can I do for you?"

"I'd like an update on the Blake case. The media's hounding me. When can you and Louie come to my office?"

"I'm in the middle of chasing down some leads. Can we do this tomorrow?"

"I wanted an update today," D'Angelo said.

"It's early in the investigation, Mayor. We have a handle on a couple of things that need further investigation before I update you."

"I was told it was an open-and-shut case. The commissioner killed his wife."

Whoa! Where the hell did that come from? "Mayor, no case is open-and-shut. The evidence does not point to the commissioner at this point. If it does, he'll be arrested."

"Be in my office in fifteen minutes."

It was a good thing the mayor hung up without another word. Jake's temper boiled over. He didn't work for the mayor, he worked for the city.

Jake walked through the bullpen and stopped at Louie's empty desk. "Kirk, where's Romanelli?"

"I think he went to your office," Kirk said, his lip curling up.

It had become a standing joke in homicide how Louie gave Jake a coffee machine as a gift more for himself than his friend.

"Louie, we have a command appearance in the mayor's office in fifteen," Jake said, stepping into his office.

Louie sat at Jake's desk with his feet up, a cup of coffee in his hand. Jake knocked his feet off the desk. "Did he say what he wanted?" Louie stood, placed his cup on the desk and straightened his tie then buttoned his jacket.

"An update." Jake had also wondered what the mayor wanted when he summoned them to city hall. Had they jumped out of the frying pan and into the fire with the new mayor? He'd give the guy a chance—for now.

Chapter 9

Jake parked in front of city hall in a no-parking zone, and stuck his on-duty sign in the front window. He and Louie approached the old stately red-and-white-brick building done in the Georgian Revival style. The historic landmark, which housed city hall and other town offices, had recently been refurbished. Wilkesbury Municipal Hall was the official title, but residents and politicians alike called it city hall. Inside, its marble floors and walls now sparkled, the stone polished to a gleam. The old regime had wanted to tear it down and build some modern structure in its place. Voters and organizations fought to have it repaired. At the time, Jake even volunteered to help out on a committee to raise money for the project.

The impoverished town had the highest unemployment rate in the state, with 25 percent of its citizens living under the poverty level. *It's a shame that the number has risen in the last few months*, Jake thought. The national average was 14 percent. If not the poorest city, with the highest unemployment Wilkesbury competed for the infamous title.

Jake believed in the need to renovate after years of disrepair, when leaks in the roof had destroyed valuable records that could never be replaced.

"Do you think the mayor will try to grandstand over our case?" Louie asked.

"I hope not, but we'll see what we see." Jake folded his lips over his teeth as he lined up his thoughts.

They took the sweeping staircase to the right, following the winding path until they reached the second floor.

"Shit," Jake whispered as he tried to get his wind back after climbing the shallow marble stairs. The damn wound pounded in his belly.

"Are you okay?" Louie asked, placing a hand on Jake's forearm.

"Yes, but it's frustrating that it's not healing faster." He sucked it in and started to move forward.

"Why don't you take another minute before we head into the mayor's chamber?"

Jake pushed Louie's hand off his arm. "I'm good, let's go."

Louie bunched his shoulders, dropped his hands to his sides, and walked away from him. Jake understood it killed Louie not to have the last word.

The mayor's secretary wasn't at her desk outside his office. Louie knocked.

A gruff voice beckoned them in. Jake noticed the outlay of paperwork. The previous mayor had always had a clear desk.

"Mayor, I'm Lieutenant Jake Carrington," he said, then pointed to Louie. "This is Sergeant Louie Romanelli."

"Lieutenant, Sergeant."

Jake and Louie towered over the man's rumpled five feet, ten inches. Jake focused his attention on the man's bald spot in the middle of his head and waited for the major to talk first. D'Angelo's paunchy belly was winning the battle against his shirt buttons.

"Take a seat." They did. D'Angelo remained standing. "Jake, I'm aware of yours and the sergeant's reputations. In fact, the two of you have been all I've read about for the last six months." The mayor stopped, looked at him over the rim of his glasses. "I'm not a politician. The reason I took this job was to set this city straight." D'Angelo sat. "There's been talk around town you're giving the commissioner special treatment. And I want to stress that this soon after the last incident, we can't have rumors of that nature flying around."

"No one is getting treated any differently. We're hardly two days into our investigation and need to gather the facts and evidence before we can pursue a suspect. I will tell you that I did look closely at Todd Blake and his finances. I have feelers out for information on their marriage and how well they got along. Another string we're pulling is to see if either one had a lover. As of today, both Todd and Callie Blake are coming back clean."

When D'Angelo won in the special mayoral election to fill the vacated position, Jake had decided to give the non-politician a chance as long as he stayed out of their cases.

"Go on."

"I don't discuss a case with anyone who is not involved in the investigation. I'll keep you informed, but the evidence and steps I follow are information you're not privy to."

D'Angelo folded his arms across his wide chest and stared at Jake, then at Louie.

"Sergeant, what do you have to say?"

"We can't have an investigation compromised, even with someone who has good intentions. I hope you're able to turn this city around, but a murder investigation, like the lieutenant said, is on a need-to-know basis."

"I was told you two were thick as thieves—"

"Mayor—"

"Relax, Jake. I've heard a lot of rumors about the two of you. I needed to see for myself how you work. Are you honestly apolitical?"

"When it comes to the job, yes," Jake said.

"Lucky you, I'd like to be kept in the loop. If it turns out that Blake killed his wife, we'll be in the middle of another scandal, and I'd like to have time to control what gets out to the press."

"I agree," Jake said.

"Thanks for stopping by."

Dismissed, he and Louie stood, as did D'Angelo. The mayor extended his hand to him and then to Louie.

"Jake, I understand you use Gwenn Langley from Channel 5 to drip information when needed. I'd like any information to come from this office on this particular case. I have no problem using her."

"Good to know. She's fair and will hold back items until she gets the go-ahead. She's also an excellent researcher," Jake said on his way out of the office.

Outside the building they halted in front of the marble fountain. Jake asked, "What do you think of him?"

"I heard he's fair. My parents were friendly with his parents, and they say he's a good boy." Louie grinned.

Jake could just imagine the four-foot-eleven-inch Rosalie Romanelli saying such a thing, with her heavy Italian accent and expressive hands.

"The rap sheet and mug shot you had me take off the printer, who was it?"

"Our suspect—that's the face of the man in the compromising pictures with Callie Blake. He's a minor hood from Jersey. Did your sources turn up anyone?"

"Gee, Jake, it's only been an hour since you instructed me to dig," Louie complained.

"I've got an address on him. Let's head across the street and see if we can snag Judge Eisenberg again."

They crossed from city hall to the Chase building, dodging speeding cars and buses as they jaywalked.

Without comment, Eisenberg gave him his warrant to search Gallucci's condo. Jake sent Louie out first, then turned to the judge and handed him the copies of his wife's suggestive photographs.

"Those are all she had in her files."

"I owe you one, Jake."

"No, you don't, Judge. Take care."

Louie leaned on Jake's car door when they stood in front of city hall. "Are we heading to the station or this jockamo's condo?"

"The condo first. If we're lucky, we'll catch him at home."

"Right—and money grows on trees," Louie said.

Jake parked in the visitor's spot on the side of the three-story brick building. They walked down a long hallway on the second floor before locating Gallucci's unit. No one answered when they knocked on unit 25B.

Jake sought out the building manager. "We only rent through our agent," a man in a sleeveless, dingy gray T-shirt said. The man sported a three-day growth on his face, and his sparse gray hair stuck up in every direction. In the background, sinister music followed by gunshots rang out from the television.

"I'm Lieutenant Carrington from the WPD. I need to get into unit 25B." He held up his warrant.

"What'd the guy do?"

"That's none of your concern," Jake said.

"I don't know if I can. I'll have to check."

"Sir, this warrant allows me to enter the premises defined as unit 25B. You can either let me in with your passkey or I'll have uniforms here within minutes to break down the door. It's your choice."

"You don't have to get pissy." The idiot grabbed his master key off a rack on the wall by the door. "Follow me."

The manager opened the door and stepped into the apartment. "Sir, you can leave now," Jake said. He hadn't bothered to get the man's name. He slipped on latex gloves. Louie did the same.

Mumbling under his breath, the manager left. Jake closed the door behind him and locked it. He didn't want any surprises in case Gallucci decided to come home.

The place had a staged, for-sale vibe. Except for a couple of dishes in the sink, it appeared as if no one lived there. Jake walked farther into the room and scanned the apartment for Gallucci. The kitchen to his right opened into a living/dining room with sliders leading onto a small deck that overlooked the gazebo in the center of the complex. Off to his left, a set of stairs. No pictures, no personal trinkets to identify the dweller.

Jake went up the stairs. He lingered at the door to what he supposed served as a guest room. The double bed was made, covered with a green-and-pink flowered comforter. Silk flowers sat in a vase on the table under the window. A generic print hung on the opposite pale green walls.

Jake moved on to the master bedroom and stopped in the doorway to survey the room: a king-size bed, red spread, black pillows, a tallboy dresser with a small box on top of it, one nightstand on the right side and a large painting with swirls of red, black, and white. The harsh colors gave him a headache. It would drive him nuts to have to sleep in the room.

Jake opened the top drawer. Inside sat a few pairs of men's silk underwear and undershirts. The next drawer held T-shirts on the left and a few button-down shirts on the right. The third and fourth drawers were empty. He continued his inspection and opened the closet. Four pairs of dress pants, a pair of jeans, and a few dress shirts also hung there. Gallucci's dress shoes were lined up on the floor under the shirts.

The place and its furnishing told him the man slept here and hadn't planned to settle in. The bathroom also had little clutter. Jake went downstairs to check in with Louie.

"Got anything?" Jake asked.

"No, the place reminds me of a hotel," Louie said.

"I got the same impression. Was there an office down here?"

"No."

"Gallucci lived paperless. There weren't files upstairs."

"Where do you figure he's hiding out?" Louie asked.

"I'd give odds Melinda has the location."

"Why would she hold back?"

"Now that's a question, isn't it?" Jake rubbed his stiff neck. "Gallucci's a ghost."

* * * *

Jake drove to the fast-food chicken restaurant Louie loved and hurried him along. *I need to do some ass-in-the-chair work, and damn, it's well after four.*

At the entrance to the bullpen, Jake said, "Why don't you contact your snitches and see if anyone has information on Sal."

"What are you going to do?"

"I'm going to start setting up the interviews with Todd's neighbors. Once they're set, I'll assign Al and Gunner to conduct them. They'll be able to knock it out quicker while we concentrate on the players."

A few of his detectives greeted Jake on his way to his office. His lanky junior detective, Kirk Brown, caught up to him at the threshold of his office and shuffled his feet to get Jake's attention.

"Lieutenant, did you get my email last night?" Brown asked. Brown's dark brows gathered in the middle of his forehead.

"Yes, thanks for getting right on it."

"That kind of advertisement cost big bucks. I'll email you the names of the other papers as soon as I get back to my desk. Is there anything else you'd like me to do?" Kirk asked.

"No, I'm all set for now. Good work." Jake sidestepped Kirk to get to his desk.

The discomfort was instant when he sat. The pain had been easy to ignore when he was in motion, but once he stopped it kicked in. The doctor had told him to stay ahead of the pain and take the pain pills as needed, but taking them at work wasn't smart. They threw him off his game and slowed his reflexes.

He dialed five people on Todd Blake's list of neighbors and reached three. The rest he'd leave for Al and Gunner to handle.

"Hey, one of my snitches told me Sal hangs with a local photographer, the last he heard," Louie said from the doorway. "I think it's time to get a warrant for Melinda's financials, to dig deeper. Have you done a run on her family?"

He didn't offer Louie a chair. "No, that's up next. I've set three appointments for tomorrow afternoon for Al and Gunner," Jake said. "Two didn't answer, I left messages, the others I'll contact directly."

"What's that in your hand?" Louie asked.

Ace detective Louie missed nothing. Jake opened his fist, reluctantly revealing the pills.

"If you take them, I'll drive for the rest of the day." Louie frowned.

"I don't need them. It was something to play with while I worked out the situation in my head," Jake said, sticking the pills in his pocket. He leaned back in his chair. "I'm going to call around to the banks and see why I don't have the Blakes' information yet. Scram."

Louie stared at Jake but Jake ignored the unasked question. If Jake let him, Louie would mother him more than Mia, and that would be downright embarrassing.

Jake updated the murder book after Louie left his office. For this case he hadn't created a murder board for Callie Blake. The case was on a need-to-know basis. Murder books were a standard procedure, the board was not. Jake used the board to keep the facts from a case in front of his eyes at all times.

Todd Blake had called him six times yesterday, today none. Doctor Lang had released Callie's body late yesterday afternoon. He figured Blake needed time alone or was wrapped up in funeral preparations.

He picked up his phone, dialed McGuire's extension. "Shamus," he said, "have you heard when Callie will be waked?"

"I believe it will be Friday, with a Saturday burial, but Todd wasn't sure if that would work out with the funeral home. Why?"

"Curious. Who's in charge of the pallbearers and the timing of the force showing up?"

"His secretary is arranging all that. She'll notify me with the final details when things are all set."

He'd have to schedule a videographer to record the funeral and burial. Maybe the killer had the balls to participate.

His email notification popped up. The first one was from the CNEB bank. It listed Callie's trust fund account. Jake read down the report. It jibed with what Blake had told him.

He kept reading. At the end of the report he leaned into his chair and closed his eyes. The account in Callie's name went to Todd upon her death. It had a nice tidy sum in it. On the Saturday of the ball she had withdrawn twenty-five thousand dollars. Where was the money? He reached for the phone, changed his mind. He hated to do this to Todd, but he had to see his reaction when he hit him with the information.

He buzzed Louie. "Grab your coat and meet me at my car in ten."

Jake took his jacket off the back of his chair and walked up to Shamus's office.

He stepped in without knocking and jumped right into it. "Shamus, Callie had an account in her name only. Todd had told us about it but gave me the wrong balance. The balance is quite high, and on Saturday she withdrew twenty-five thousand dollars. I have a call into the branch manager to see how she took the money. Do you think Todd knew about it?"

"Hard to say, Jake, but according to Darcy, most married women keep an emergency fund."

"Well, Callie must have been expecting a big emergency."

"What was the balance?" Shamus asked.

Jake handed him the printout. Shamus let out a low whistle.

"Why don't you research where she got the bulk of it? Three hundred thousand dollars is a lot of money for a nonworking policeman's wife."

"I've already requested the information. A personal question, Shamus—would it piss you off to learn Darcy had those kinds of funds you couldn't access?"

"She does. When we got married, she was up front about her wealth. I guess in their money bracket it's standard for parents to open trust accounts for their kids. Darcy was able to access hers after the age of twenty-five. And Darcy's mother urged her to create what she calls the rainy-day fund. I'm listed as full beneficiary in case she dies. Also check the records to see if she gave him access by way of a debit card."

"I'm heading over there now with Louie to drop it on Todd. If he had access, he could've been the one to withdraw the money. I need to see his reaction."

"It can't wait until after the funeral?" Shamus rubbed his eyes.

"You know it can't."

Shamus gave a tense nod. "Get it done, Jake."

Chapter 10

Melinda decided to process Edy's pictures before she did the rest of the ones from Sunday's wedding and Saturday night's gala. She wondered how much the paper would pay for a shot of Edy with her lover. She knew the local paper's sales were down—they were desperate for some news to keep them afloat, even if it meant resorting to trashy tabloid topics. But she couldn't give them to the press. It would be shooting herself in the foot. She wanted referrals from Edy Dunstan. *If I get no referrals within three months, then I'll reconsider selling them to the highest bidder.* No, she had to stay on the straight and narrow with Jake lurking around. She stared down at her vibrating cell phone as it jumped around her desk.

She picked it up. "What do you want?"

"I heard the cops were at my place. Did you set them on me?" Sal Gallucci asked.

"No, one of the women, and the cop wouldn't say who, set him on me and you. She told the cop she didn't believe you were a model…but that you were my boyfriend. I tried brushing it off. I told him we broke up after a couple of dates. And how would I know where you hung out? Did you leave anything incriminating at the condo?"

"No, the place is clean. Listen, I'm going to take off for a few days until the heat lightens up," Sal said.

"Where are you going?"

"Not sure. Melinda, keep your cool around that cop you know. I checked around, he's one smart dude."

"I'm only acquainted with him," Melinda said.

"Right."

"I dated him in high school. It's ancient history."

"No shit! Did he cut you any slack?"

"He's a by-the-book kind of guy. Are you sure nothing led back to us in the motel room?"

"I'm sure. I was suited up. Any guesses on who left the pictures?"

"No, but I wouldn't put it past the blonde to have brought them with her. Sal, did you kill her?" She had to keep Sal off balance, keep him guessing until she was able to get out of town.

"Jesus, Melinda, of course I didn't. I'll call you once I land somewhere. Take care." He ended the call.

Melinda bit the inside of her lip. If Sal skipped town…she'd be left holding the bag. He'd promised her no one was going to get hurt. What was the big freaking deal if they forced a few dollars from the rich and powerful? *The Blake woman brought it on herself*, Melinda thought.

* * * *

It was dinnertime when Jake parked on the street in front of the Blakes' house. Several cars he didn't recognize sat in their driveway. A woman similar in coloring to Callie Blake opened the door. It seemed he had met her before, but couldn't place where.

"Is Todd in?"

"He's not up for visitors at this time. You're Jake Carrington, aren't you?"

"Yes, and this is Sergeant Romanelli. I'm sorry, you are?"

"I'm Katy-Lynn Melon, Callie's sister." The woman extended her hand.

"I'm sorry for your loss," Jake said.

"We got back only a few minutes ago from making her final arrangements. It was tough on all of us, Lieutenant. If you can come back some other time, we'd appreciate it."

"It's important, Katy-Lynn. I promise we'll only take up a few minutes of the commissioner's time." He felt like a heel, and glanced over at Louie, who hadn't said a word.

She walked away. "If we wait, we won't get him until next week," Louie whispered.

The commissioner entered the foyer carrying a glass filled with dark liquid.

"Commissioner, I'm sorry to bother you at this time. Is there a place we can speak in private?" Jake asked.

"Come into my office."

He and Louie followed Todd into a large windowed room. Dark panels lined one wall. The other wall consisted of a floor-to-ceiling bookcase.

Todd's wooden desk was more impressive than the one he had at the station. Two burgundy leather chairs placed in front of the desk looked comfortable, and matched the burgundy sofa to the right of them. A pair of overstuffed chairs in the left corner invited people to relax. The back left corner of the room was taken up with a bar that at first glance appeared well-stocked.

"Todd," Jake began as he took a seat. "Did you know the balance in Callie's account at CNEB has a few hundred thousand dollars?"

Todd's eyes widened. "What's the exact balance?" Todd sipped his drink.

"You're telling me you don't know?" Jake asked.

"Jake, it's Callie's trust fund, not mine. She recently tapped it for our son's college tuition."

"It's roughly three hundred thousand dollars, give or take a few," Jake said, watching for a reaction.

He got one. Todd spit the fluid out of his mouth. "Come again?"

"The balance as of her last statement is three hundred thousand and change. I verified with the bank today."

"Wow, I hadn't realized her investment had done so well. Check with her investment banker for details."

"I'm waiting on the bank for an answer. Can we ask Katy-Lynn to join us? If her parents opened one for Callie, they must've opened one for her."

"Go ahead," Blake said. Louie left the room to fetch Callie's sister. "The money came from a wrongful-death lawsuit when their grandparents were killed. She's had it since she was fifteen. She came into it at the age of thirty. I never was told, nor did I ask for the balance."

"While we wait for them to return, I want you to know I've assigned Al Burke and Gunner Kraus to interview your neighbors. They'll be asking questions about your and Callie's relationship. I'm sorry to have to put you through this, Todd, but you know it's standard procedure." It bothered Jake to hound a trusted ally and friend, but murder was murder. And everyone was capable of it, he'd learned over the years, even himself.

"No consideration for a friend or colleague?"

"No, I have to do my duty. At the moment I work for Callie, not you. And I trust Al and Gunner to handle it discreetly."

Louie returned with Katy-Lynn Melon. Like Callie, her sister had blonde hair and blue eyes. Though unlike Callie, her five-three stature had Jake looking down to speak with her.

"Katy-Lynn, the lieutenant has some questions about Callie's trust fund. Your parents opened one for you too, didn't they?" Todd asked before Jake could.

"Yes, my parents never wanted what they called blood money from my grandparents' wrongful-death suit."

"Callie's used hers over the years, mostly to get things for the children or for family vacations, Jake. After we married and I'd learned of it, I asked that we try to live off my salary. Callie agreed, but I know when things got tough she'd toss in a few bucks here and there." Todd's eyes lost their focus at the fond memory of his wife. Jake needed to pull him back.

"I know you wanted Todd Jr. to stay in-state, and you and Callie fought when she paid for his tuition to go to St. Lucien's," Katy-Lynn said.

"We saved for the in-state tuition, and UConn's a good school. She spoiled the children too much," Todd said, staring his sister-in-law down.

"Commissioner, there was tension between you and Callie over this?" Jake asked, taking back the conversation.

"Yes, for about a week, but I gave in. Callie had a way of getting what she wanted."

"And things were good after that?" Jake asked.

"Of course they were good. I'll tell you again, so you stop wasting precious time on me. I did not kill my wife. I don't know what we'll do without her. Now please just leave me to my grief." Todd got up from his chair and left the office.

"I didn't mean to imply Todd killed my sister, Lieutenant, Sergeant..." Katy-Lynn said, panicked. "He loves her."

"One more question, Katy-Lynn. Are your parents still alive?"

"No, my father passed away ten years ago, my mother five."

"Thank you for your time," Jake said.

In the car, Jake turned to face Louie. "What do you think?"

"I can't see him for this, Jake," Louie said, scratching his chin.

"Me either."

Louie's phone rang. Jake listened in as Louie spoke.

"Let's go to the motel by exit twenty-six. My source said Sal Gallucci's holed up there," Louie said, his voice filled with excitement.

* * * *

Sal Gallucci had rented room 211. Jake circled the building to check exits. Rooms facing the back were the only ones to have access to the stairs. There was no common hallway. Jake drove around and parked in front of 111. Louie walked to the farthest staircase while Jake started up the closest.

Jake stood to the left of the door, Louie to the right, their hands on their guns.

Jake knocked, then pounded his fist again against the door when Gallucci didn't answer. Jake called out, "Wilkesbury Police. Open up, Mr. Gallucci."

The door inched open. Jake shoved his badge in the man's face.

"What can I do for you?"

"Are you Sal Gallucci?

"Yes."

"May we come in?"

"Why?"

"We have a few questions for you. You can answer them here or downtown. Which will it be?"

"Here's good. Come in. What's this about?"

Jake entered the seedy beige and green room. A double bed took up most of the space. A narrow dresser held a twenty-inch television tuned to the local news. Gallucci's dark hair was slicked back. He wore black Dockers and a white T-shirt.

"Is someone in the bathroom?" Jake asked, pointing to it.

"No," Sal said. "Why?"

"The light's on. Do you mind if my partner checks it out?"

"I do, but if that will get you out of here faster, I'm all for it. I've nothing to hide. While he's checking out the john, you tell me what this is all about," Sal asked again.

A cool customer, Jake thought. "The murder of Callie Blake."

"Who's that?"

"The police commissioner's wife."

"Don't know the lady." Sal scratched his chest while yawning.

"You posed with her in some racy photographs," Jake said, watching Sal go to the nightstand to grab a cigarette from the pack sitting on it.

"I got paid a couple of bucks from the girl I was dating at the time to pose with several women. What's the big deal?"

"Mrs. Blake was murdered on Sunday, and the photo with you in it was left at the scene."

"Well, I didn't kill her."

"Mr. Gallucci, where were you Sunday between eleven a.m. and five p.m.?" Jake asked.

"Sunday, I was in Jersey visiting some friends."

"I'll need their names and numbers."

"Sure." Sal pulled out his phone and searched his contacts as Jake observed over Gallucci's shoulder. Sal wrote down the information on a pad by the bed.

"I need your cell phone number," Louie said.

"Why?"

"To clear you, we need to see if Callie Blake spoke to you directly," Louie lied, coming into the room from the john.

"Here's my number, but I know you can't look at my calls without a warrant," Sal said, visibly shaken.

"At this time we're eliminating people and their numbers from our list. If yours doesn't appear on her recent call list, you're all set," Louie said. Gallucci rattled off his number. "Sorry, I didn't get the whole thing, please repeat it."

"Thanks for your cooperation," Jake said. "Oh, by the way, how long have you been dating Melinda?"

"Dated, not dating. A couple of weeks is all. Why?" Sal's answers matched Melinda's. Jake wondered if they'd rehearsed it.

"How come you're staying in a motel instead of at your condo?" Louie asked.

Sal pursed his lips. "I had the place sprayed after I found a roach. I can't stomach bugs. The thought of going back there makes my skin crawl."

Hmmm! It's highly probable this room's loaded with more bugs, Jake thought but didn't voice his opinion.

Outside the motel Jake scanned the area before going to the car. "What did you think?"

"He's involved, we just need to figure out how," Louie said.

* * * *

On his office computer Jake ran the names Sal had given him. All the people on Sal's list had sheets for various crimes, mostly for larceny. Jake dialed the first number on his list to verify Sal's alibi. On the third ring Lorenzo Rigano answered.

"Mr. Rigano, I'm Lieutenant Jake Carrington from the Wilkesbury Police Department in Wilkesbury, Connecticut. Do you have a few minutes?"

"What's this about?"

"I'm trying to verify Sal Gallucci's whereabouts on Sunday afternoon," Jake said.

"This past Sunday?" Lorenzo asked.

"Yes, specifically between ten in the morning and five o'clock in the afternoon."

"Why?"

"I can't say," Jake said, his stomach growling. A quick check of his watch explained why. It was after eight and he'd missed dinner.

"He was here playing cards. The guy lost his shirt and made me a happy man."

"And where is here?" Jake asked.

"Jersey City. Come on, you're not going to give me anything on this? What did Sal do this time?"

"Thanks for your time, Mr. Rigano."

Jake hung up, dialed the rest of the people on Gallucci's list, and got the same story—perfect, concise, and fabricated. Sal's friends weren't great character witnesses, but witnesses nevertheless. He'd have to break Sal's alibi if he wanted to prove Sal murdered Callie.

He dialed Melinda next. "Melinda, Jake Carrington."

"What do you want now?"

"I need the name of the bride and groom from Sunday's wedding."

"Why?" Her annoyance bled through the phone—was it at him personally or professionally?

"I have to verify where all the players were on Sunday."

"I'm not a player. Do you understand how hard it is for me to get paid after an event? If you scare my customers away and they don't pay for their photos, I'll sue you and your department."

"I need to speak with them," Jake insisted.

"Why? Weren't the photos enough? You won't be able to reach the couple. They're on their honeymoon in Barbados for another week and a half."

"Then I'll need their parents' numbers."

"What the…are you trying to ruin my business?" Melinda demanded in a loud voice.

He waited her out, let the silence fill the phone.

"I swear if you ruin my name, my reputation, you will rue the day you met me."

He wrote down the numbers she gave him, hung up, and then dialed the bride's mother and identified himself.

"Nothing's happened to the children, has it?" she asked worriedly.

"No, I'm validating the time your photographer was at the wedding."

"Give me your badge number, Lieutenant. I'll call you back once I check you out," Mrs. Ellison said.

Ten minutes later his office phone rang.

"Now what's this all about?" Mrs. Ellison asked.

"I'm not at liberty to say, except to stress that Melinda Mastrianni is not in trouble, but I need to confirm she worked your daughter's wedding, and when she started and finished up."

"Melinda got to the house around eleven. She photographed JoAnne and I, and then JoAnne's bridesmaids. Melinda was organized and she was here for an hour before she left and went to the groom's parents' house to photograph the groom and ushers. The ceremony was held at the hall. Melinda had arrived before us because she was standing by the curb taking pictures when we arrived at one. The wedding broke up around midnight. We got hit for extended hours at the place. Melinda was there all the time taking pictures. Who else are you asking these questions?"

"We're also talking to the groom's family. At no time did she leave the place for, let's say, a half hour or more?"

"No, I'm ashamed to say we didn't give her a chance. Are you sure Melinda's not in trouble? I'd hate to lose the pictures from my only daughter's wedding."

Jake heard the threat in the undertones of her voice. "Not at this time, Mrs. Ellison. Oh, one more thing. Did a guest bump into Melinda at the reception?"

"Yes, one of the groomsmen was a little inebriated and fell into her as she took some pictures of my daughter and her friends dancing. It had dazed her for a bit. She didn't file a complaint, did she?"

"No, nothing like that. Thanks for your time, Mrs. Ellison. Goodbye." He hung up.

The groom's mother also verified the times and the incident that gave Melinda a black eye and the scratch on her face. It explained away Melinda's bruised face. Not that he suspected Melinda of killing Callie, but it was a line he had to tug before he'd be able to cross her off the list.

He called it a day and packed up his briefcase. Right about a now a drink—with his feet up, and a friendly conversation with Mia—sounded better than a good night's sleep.

Chapter 11

First thing Wednesday morning after he got into the office, Jake opened his mail. He'd ignored it the last couple of days. A typed letter fell from the first envelope. There was no return address, and it had been mailed from downtown Wilkesbury. He scanned it, then reread it.

Dear Lieutenant,

I cannot come forward because I'm a neighbor of the Blakes. Everyone in our neighborhood is speaking of Callie's death and how wonderful the Blakes are. I'm telling you to look deeper into their marriage and Todd. I wouldn't put it past the domineering bastard to have killed his wife.

Truly,

A Concerned Citizen

Jake pulled out an evidence bag from his bottom drawer and slipped the letter into it. He hit the button for Louie's extension. When Louie came in he handed it to him.

"I don't know when this came in. Would you take this to the lab and stay with it until they can determine if there are any prints on it? Ask them if they can process it right way. I'm sure there aren't any on it, but we have to check."

Louie read the letter.

"Hmmm! It's a little hinky, don't you think?" Louie asked.

"I do, but we'll follow the steps. We also need to speed up the interviews with his neighbors. How are Burke and Kraus doing with them?"

"I spoke with Al. There's nothing there. A few said the Blakes are like any couple—they've had arguments, but nothing major. On the whole they're great neighbors and parents."

"On your way out, send Burke in, please. Oh, and can you make a copy of the letter for the murder book before you leave?" Jake asked.

"Yes, boss," Louie said, using his favorite line to bust Jake's ass.

Al Burke, a senior detective in Jake's division, walked in and settled his large girth in one of the chairs in front of his desk.

"You wanted to see me, Jake?"

"Yeah, how did you gauge the neighbors' attitudes toward the Blakes?"

"Nothing popped, if that's what you're asking. The Blakes are normal people who act like any married couple. They fight, they're a team, they're excellent parents, et cetera, and wonderful neighbors who give great parties."

Louie joined them and handed Jake the copy of the letter, which he passed to Al.

"Hmmm!" Al said, as he looked back up at Jake. "I'd say someone's playing games or has a grudge against the commissioner. What do you say?"

"The same, Al, but it's a time waster that has to be processed. Keep digging into the neighbors and their relationships with the Blakes and their kids."

After Al and Louie left the office, Jake reread the letter. He leaned back in his chair to give it some thought. It could be from their killer, to throw them off the trail. Callie and Darcy were the only women who had received blackmail letters. He didn't want another killing, but a lead would be nice before the trail went cold. To have the murder of the police commissioner's wife go unsolved would cause a scandal. Accusations would fly around this town faster than Michael Phelps swam across a pool. It'd be unacceptable and career suicide.

* * * *

It's time to put the game in motion. Edy dialed Linden's cell phone number while she relaxed on the pale peach chaise lounge in the corner of her bedroom by the window. He picked up on the second ring.

"Hello, darling. Let's meet for lunch," Edy said.

"Does this mean I'm forgiven?" Linden asked.

"Forgiven for what?" She played dumb.

The pair had had a fight during their last hotel excursion on Saturday. She understood Linden was wondering if they were still an item. And for now the answer was yes. She still needed him.

"Okay, at our usual spot?"

"No, I'm hungry today. Why don't we meet at Town Hall Café?"

"Do you think that's wise?" Linden asked.

"What does it matter? I'm not ashamed of you," Edy said.

"Edy, I think we should keep our relationship low-key. You were right to suggest that in the beginning."

"Never mind, I'll ask someone else to lunch today."

The bastard didn't want to be seen with her. Well, he would. If not today, then she'd meet him for drinks out of town some night. She'd pick the raunchiest place too, then she'd contact that annoying reporter for the paper—what was her name—Lily something-or-other? She'd look that up after she ended the call. Edy disconnected without another word. Her phone started ringing almost immediately.

Ah, I got ya. "What now, Linden?"

"I'm sorry, what time do you want to meet?"

"Noon."

"Can we make it twelve thirty?"

Perfect. She'd expected him to change the time to meet his usual schedule. "Yes, I'll see you then."

She hung up and searched her contacts for the name of the gossip reporter. Edy blocked her number and made an anonymous call to Lily Monroe at *Wilkesbury Daily News.* When she hung up, she went into her closet to hunt up her sexiest outfit, with a touch of slutty, enough that Lily wouldn't be able to resist photographing her for lunch, out on the town midweek with her lover.

Hello world, the picture would shout if it landed in the column. Would Cedric be stunned or embarrassed by it?

Edy sang as she stepped into the shower.

This is better than murdering the lying, cheating bastard, she mused.

* * * *

At precisely twelve thirty Edy stepped into the Town Hall Café and scanned the room. She spotted Lily first, then Linden sitting at the far corner table fidgeting with his fork. The hostess led her to the table. Linden in his nondescript blue suit, his brown hair combed back, rose from his chair to greet her and helped her off with her coat. Linden handed her coat to the hostess. Edy had to push up on her toes to kiss him on the lips. She took the seat next to Linden, not across from him. The waitress rearranged the place setting and handed Edy the menu.

She handed it back without looking at it and ordered the steak. Linden ordered the fish of the day. He refused a cocktail. He had to go back to work. She didn't.

"You seem cheerful today," Linden said.

"I am. What did you do all weekend?" Edy asked.

"Nothing. I missed you. What's going on, Edy?"

"What do you mean?"

"Saturday you left the hotel in a rage."

"I did not. I was annoyed, but a rage, Linden, don't be ridiculous. I understand where you stand in life. Women are secondary to you and your career. I thought…" She peered at him from under her lashes and continued. "I thought we had something special."

He continued to roll the fork in his hands. "We do, but you're married. When are you going to file for divorce so we can be together and announce our engagement?"

"Engagement? You're assuming a lot, Linden. I told you I'd need to line things up before we consider a future together. My situation is complicated because of my finances and position in the community." She hoped he bought it. To cement the explanation, she leaned in close to him and whispered in his ear. "I love you, only you, Linden. We'll be together, but you have to be patient."

She was sure their ten-year age difference didn't bother Linden. Not the way she looked today, but in fifteen years would he still be around? No, because she wouldn't give him the chance. He was a tool, nothing more.

"I'm tired of sneaking around."

"So am I, but we won't have to much longer." She scooted her chair closer to him. "After the divorce is settled, we'll discuss our futures. I need a little more time."

"All right." He leaned into her and kissed her on the left cheek.

It was exactly what she'd been hoping for. She spotted Lily when she lifted her phone to take their picture. With both their faces aimed at the camera it would make them easy to identify when Lily printed it in the paper. Inside Edy was giddy. Lily should thank her for the amount of notoriety she'd get for capturing that tender moment. She'd have to practice her outrage when it came out.

Edy angled away from Linden, her chest hitching. She had initiated the first step in her divorce, but not for Linden. *It's all for me.* A cold sweat ran over her body. After twenty years of humiliation she was dumping Cedric in style. Linden would be another bad chapter in her dating history she'd close. Her head felt light, her breathing short. She'd need to learn to cope with the start of the end of her marriage. No, not the start—Cedric had instigated that when he'd dated the first woman. Now that he had dozens of them behind him, she'd had enough. She'd conquer the world on her own. They hadn't been intimate in over a year. When Cedric tried to make love to her she pushed him away, his touch nauseating her, knowing where his hands had been earlier.

The waitress placed the steak in front of her. Edy stared at it, her appetite gone. There'd be no going back once the picture hit the paper. She'd have no choice but to divorce Cedric.

Oh God, it's over. The loss washed over her. She loved Cedric even with his indiscretions, but putting his current mistress up in an apartment had been the final straw. He killed what she'd felt for him all those years ago.

Linden leaned toward her. "What's wrong with your meal?"

"Nothing," she said in a monotone, angling away from him, cutting a minuscule piece of steak and placing it in her mouth. Bitterness stung her tongue, the meat flavorless.

* * * *

Back when Callie Blake had shown up for her appointment, Melinda had picked her brain. She'd followed Jake's career over the years for reasons she couldn't explain. It was stupid of him to give up a promising career as a ballplayer. Mrs. Blake held Jake in the highest regard. An idea had popped into her head when the commissioner's wife had praised him more than Melinda thought he deserved.

Alone in her shop after Mrs. Blake had left, Melinda drafted a letter to the corrections department, requesting an interview with Spaulding. She'd personally called to see if George would be game for an interview and some pictures. The warden replied with yes on the interview and no on the pictures at this time, per the prisoner's request. Once there, she thought she'd talk George into posing for her.

She wanted to do a shoot with Spaulding to display his story through a series of photos. She originally thought this would be a strong entry for a national professional photo contest in New York City. If she won first place, it would double her business and get her out of this hellhole town. Jake showing up at her studio had spiked her interest in another direction.

If she won the contest and got her pictures publicized, it might distract Jake enough to turn him in a new direction. *Even if I don't win, maybe someone will think it newsworthy. I can only hope.*

The hour drive to Osborn prison in Somers gave her time to line up her questions. To fit the dress code, she'd picked her most conservative suit in navy blue, which she reserved for clients like Edy Dunstan. She wasn't exactly a friend of George's, even back in their school days, but they were friendly enough.

When she'd called George, he hadn't been receptive about the pictures when she'd tried to convince him. He'd negotiated for cash to be deposited into his account before he granted her an audience. She'd almost hung up on him, but he was intuitive enough to pique her curiosity. After all these years, she'd get the deets on what happened to Eva Carrington, from the source.

In the prison parking lot, she locked her equipment in the trunk and clicked on the alarm. Inside, she stored her purse in a locker provided by the guard before continuing to the security scanners. It was similar to the procedure at the airports. She passed through and was led to a room after they'd assessed she wasn't a threat. It unnerved her when the guard unlocked the door and put her in the nine-by-nine room. Her heart hammered in her ears as the walls seemed to close in around her. She sucked the cloying air into her lungs while fighting her claustrophobia. It wouldn't do to show George her weaknesses.

"The prisoner will be here shortly. Remember the instructions. A guard will be monitoring the room, not your conversation. Do not give the prisoner anything and keep body contact to a fast hug or brief kiss." As if she'd kiss Spaulding. "Any unexpected movements from the prisoner and we will cut the visit short," the burly guard explained in an authoritative voice.

"Thanks." Her stomach jiggled as the lock clicked behind her.

Though minutes passed, it seemed like an hour. She jerked her head and got her first look at Spaulding as the guard escorted George into the room.

He'd aged. George's full head of brown hair sporting white at his temples emphasized his beak-like nose. He appeared older than his years. His thin lips curled in a natural smirk he'd fixed in place. Black eyes void of expression or humanity surveyed her from head to toe. She fought a shiver as he swept his gaze over her. He didn't do it on the sly; it was blatant and insulting. She felt like a piece of prime rib as those dead eyes memorized every inch of her. She itched, as if snakes crawled over her skin. Why had she forgotten the creep factor Spaulding had exuded? Her chest tightened. The guard shackled him to the floor, anchoring his legs in place.

Shit! What was I thinking? She should've brought her camera in with her. His face would make an interesting study. She'd name it "The man locked inside." As a subject, and shot at the right angles, he'd win her the top prize this year. She'd have to get his permission first, which he'd already denied, but in her head she'd lined up her shots. One with Spaulding by the bars in his cell, looking out, could clinch the coveted award. In another picture she'd show Spaulding on his bunk, his head in his hands, appearing lonely, lost, and remorseful. Even if he wasn't, it'd make a great shot.

"Hi, George," Melinda said.

"Why are you here?"

Well, that cut to the chase. "I want to photograph you. Do a story detailing your life in prison in a series of photos, as I explained over the phone. I'd show you as you were in your teens, at the time of your trial, and today, after being incarcerated for years."

"Why now?" George draped his left arm over the chair.

A cat ready to spring, she thought. *Christ, he's not making this easy.*

"I've recently had dealings with Jake Carrington and it reminded me of the incident."

"Thanks for sending the cash."

"You're welcome. They wouldn't let me bring even cigarettes."

"Rules are rules," he said in a flat voice. "Now tell me the real reason you're here." George pinned her with his ebony pools, dragging her deeper into his black soul.

"Carrington is busting my ass because one of my photos wound up at one of his murder scenes. He's asking questions of me and my clients as if I'd have anything to do with murdering my customer."

"And?"

"I hate Carrington's guts."

"I remember that about you. What is it you think I can do for you?"

"Maybe I can dredge up interest in your case with my photos, if I get permission from you and the warden. I've read that you've applied for new DNA testing. I want to send Jake into a tailspin. In order to do that, I'd need the whole story of what happened and why the investigation led to you."

"Assuming, of course, that I'm the real killer," George said, a feral grin playing on his lips.

"Yes."

She sat quietly and let his mind spin. George never took his eyes off her face. She almost squirmed. Almost, but she couldn't show George any sign of weakness. She had no doubt whatsoever he killed Eva Carrington. Today's visit confirmed it.

"I'll think about it." He signaled for the guard.

Freak! I didn't drive all the way up here to be put off. "George, it will take some time to get permission. I'll start the process, and you can let me know your answer when you decide."

"Part of the process is me requesting it, Melinda. You'll get nowhere until I do."

"I'll wait for your answer."

"It will come with a price tag, if and when I agree."

"Doesn't everything?" She stayed seated until the guard entered the room and allowed her to leave.

Back at her car, she glanced over her shoulder at the nondescript gray concrete building with its barred windows. How the hell had Spaulding lasted so long in there? *I can't wait for Jake to question me again and watch his reaction as I drop George Spaulding's name and send his regards. George hadn't, but what did it matter?*

* * * *

An air bubble burst inside Jake's head—the echo deafening. The sensation of floating filled his mind, his knees weakened and forced him to sit before he passed out. He didn't need this shit now.

The letter fell to his desk. On the eight-by-eleven sheet of paper there was one sentence in a weird font.

Soon Eva's story will go national, and the killer WILL GO free. What are you going to do about it?

"Nag" by the Halos played on his cell phone, announcing Louie as his caller. It hauled Jake back to the present. He dragged in air, let it out, and did it again before he was able to answer the phone.

"What've you got?" Jake asked.

"The concerned citizen letter pointing the finger at Blake had no prints on it. It's standard paper anyone can purchase at an office supply shop."

"I figured."

"What's wrong?" Louie asked.

Leave it to Louie to pick up on his nuances. "I've received a letter which doesn't pertain to the case. I'll show you when you get back, or are you heading home from there?"

"I planned on going home, but I'll meet you at the station."

"No, stop by my house," Jake said. From his bottom drawer he pulled out a paper evidence bag. With tweezers he carefully put the letter into it, and labeled and dated it, in case he wanted to pursue it legally.

Why George Spaulding? There's no sense to this, except to distract me from my current case. Melinda? No, she's not a real suspect. Or is she? Damn it!

Jake placed the letter into his briefcase, shut off the office lights, and walked to the bullpen. Most of the day shift had gone home, but Al Burke was still at his desk. Jake made his way over to him.

"Is there anything new since we last spoke?"

"No, I'll let you know if and when. Have a good night," Al said.

Jake waved to a few of the night-shift detectives on his way to the elevator.

* * * *

Jake slowed his car to avoid hitting his next-door neighbor, Mrs. Maher, crossing his driveway with her French poodle. Brigh jumped into his mind. He hadn't picked up his pooch from Louie's since he got home from Vermont. Louie's son LJ was dog sitting for him. Jake loved the dog he'd adopted the month before. He wasn't sure of her breed, though she looked part beagle and part Dalmatian. It's funny how fast Brigh had grown on him. He missed her.

He dialed Louie. "Hey, why don't you bring Brigh home when you come over?" Jake said before Louie said a word.

"I'm turning onto your street now. LJ will bring her over when he walks her."

"Good enough." His neighbor, Mrs. Maher, knocked on his window.

"Jake, I've wanted to ask you about poor Callie Blake. She was such a good girl. It's awful."

"It is. But I can't discuss an ongoing case, Mrs. Maher."

"Are you close to solving it?"

"We're getting there. I see Tiger's in an uproar," Jake said, pointing at her barking white French poodle. He'd known Tiger for eight years and the dog barked every time she spotted him.

"He wants all the attention. How's your little one doing?"

"Good. That's Louie pulling up. I need to go, take care." Jake drove into his garage to avoid further conversation.

"What'd Miss Nosy want?" Louie asked, tilting his head in the direction of Maher's house.

"The usual. Come in. Do you want coffee or a beer?"

"A beer's good."

Jake turned off his alarm and he and Louie walked straight to the kitchen. He set his briefcase on the table, then opened the refrigerator, moved some stuff around before he found the beer and grabbed two. Jake handed one to Louie, then twisted the cap off his own, raised it to his lips and tipped it back as he drew a long, thirst-quenching sip.

He placed the bottle on the table as he sat down. Jake slipped on a pair of gloves and opened his briefcase before snatching the letter from it. He glided it across the table to Louie and waited while Louie also donned a pair of gloves to read it.

"Got any ideas as to who sent it?" Louie asked taking a seat.

"Plenty, but they're all guesses."

"It'd be stupid if Spaulding sent it. It might come back and bite him in the ass with his petition for a new trial."

"I agree. It's strange it appeared now. I'm assuming it's someone involved in the Blake case trying to throw me off. Why else do it?"

"That doesn't make sense, Jake."

"Damn, I know it."

"We'll go through the steps again. I'll take it to the lab in the morning. In the meantime, you better buy a top-notch bottle of scotch for me to hand to Tom Jones when I go back tomorrow and beg him to rush it again. He did today's analysis on his own time," Louie said.

"Can you call your son and have him bring Brigh home?"

"Ah," Louie said, a small smile tugging free. "You got attached to the little devil, didn't you?"

He loved his rescue pup. It hadn't taken long for them to bond when he first laid his eyes on Brigh, shaking in the corner of the vet's office, afraid of the world as she scrunched down to make herself invisible. The first owner abused Brigh. She was scared of her own shadow and cowered every time someone came to the door. "Yep. Call LJ?"

"Hold on."

Jake nursed his beer. He rinsed out Louie's bottle in the sink while Louie made the call. "You want another?" he asked.

"No, I told Sophia I'd be home in five. She said LJ will bring Brigh over after dinner. See you in the morning."

Jake sat on the couch after Louie left. He reread the two-sentence letter in his hand while staring at it as if it'd yell out the sender's name. His phone vibrated in his pocket, jolting him back to the present.

"Hey," he said.

"Hey, are you coming over tonight?" Mia asked.

"I just walked in the door a few minutes ago. I'm waiting on LJ to bring Brigh home. You want me to bring her?"

"No. Why don't I come to you. I've hit a wall and need a break. You two are exactly what I need," she joked.

"Want me to order dinner?"

"Yep, I'll see you in an hour," Mia said.

He'd appreciate the distraction. Jake fingered the letter, hoping it was a one-time annoyance from a crackpot. But deep in his gut he knew it wasn't.

Chapter 12

Thursday, on a whim after her shopping spree, Edy popped into Cedric's office.

"Hi, Linda, is he in?"

His secretary rushed to block the door. "He's in a meeting. I can have him call you when he's done."

She gave Linda a gentle shove aside and opened Cedric's office door. Her cell phone in her hand, she hit the camera and shot away. The other woman wrapped in her husband arms looked so shocked it was comical. Edy kept snapping away, but the pictures weren't needed. Her PI, Jimmy Nelson, had documented the two together on many occasions. It would be a quick and dirty divorce when she took him to court. Positive the bastard would try to overturn the prenup, she wanted lots of pictures.

Tawdry little bitch, exactly how Cedric loves them.

Cedric roughly pushed the woman away as he wiped his mouth, her lipstick smearing his sleeve.

"Edy, what on earth are you doing here?" Cedric said, adjusting his shirt back into his pants.

"Obviously, catching my husband in the act with his little tramp," she crooned. *Yes, it's humiliating, but it is a scene his secretary will not soon forget, especially when I have her called into court to testify.* She'd need to start emptying out the joint account before he did.

Five days ago, Edy deposited a check from Cedric's account in the amount of one hundred thousand dollars into the one joint checking account she and Cedric shared. She'd forged Cedric's signature, as she had many times before. No one dared question her. After all, she was Edward Rockford's daughter, founder and CEO of CNEB, and a former commissioner of banking for Connecticut. When the check cleared, it would leave Cedric one hundred dollars to his name.

Edy left an angry Cedric in his office and locked herself in the car. She drove down the street before she allowed the tears to fall. When the tears stopped she drove to the lawyer's office. It's was a little after three o'clock. Her attorney, Randal Wellington, assured her they had plenty of time to file the petition for divorce today. Edy parked in the attorney's lot and dialed the preset number for Benita, and gave her instructions. All of Cedric's things were to be thrown out on the front lawn, except for his office papers. She wanted time to sort through those first. She also told Benita to call a locksmith and change all the locks immediately.

Free! She was free of the bastard at last, and it felt good until it didn't. She dialed Jimmy Nelson's number next.

"I filed a few minutes ago, Jimmy. I have Benita throwing his clothes out onto the lawn. She's also having the locks changed. I'm going to send you the picture I took at the bank today to add to your collection. He was screwing her in his freaking office." She stopped to slow the hitch in her voice before she continued. "I don't know how he'll react tonight when he gets home, if he even comes home. I was going to ask you to spend a few days at the house, but decided I can handle Cedric."

"Do you think it's wise? When cornered, people react funny," Jimmy said.

"I'm calling my father next. He'll put Cedric in his place. If I need you, Jimmy, I'll call."

"You're taking everything from him, Mrs. Dunstan. He may become dangerous."

"I can't see the wimp doing anything," Edy said.

"I'll at least have a twenty-four-seven patrol on the house. If for any reason you need me, call at any time of the day or night. Do you understand?"

"Yes. You're scaring me more than the thought of having an angry Cedric here."

"Good, it will keep you alive."

"Don't be ridiculous."

"I'm not," Jimmy said.

"I'll be home in an hour. I'm stopping at my father's first to fill him in on the situation."

"Take care, Mrs. Dunstan."

She thumbed off her phone with one hand and steered with the other.

How would her father react? She'd kept him in the loop the last couple of years. He hadn't made a judgment either way. Well, now was the time to choose sides—his bank's vice president or his daughter.

I guess I'll find out. She turned into her father's driveway two hours after she'd confronted Cedric in his office.

* * * *

Jake swung around to face his computer, frowning at the conversation he had had with Mia the night before when Louie entered his office, whistling.

"You have anything new?" Jake asked.

"No, but Tommy Jones said thanks for the scotch, it wasn't necessary," Louie said.

"Jones likes his gossip. How much info did you have to give him?"

"Not much. I told him someone decided to target you pertaining to your ongoing."

"I appreciate you taking care of it. It's a damn nuisance. While you were gone, I analyzed the neighbors' statements. Burke was right, there's nothing there, though the way the crime scene was staged still makes me think the murder was personal. I think the killer had a grudge against Callie or Todd. I can't put my finger on it, but something's off. While I work it, I'm going to have you process the rest of the mail, if you can."

A uniform walked in with today's mail and dropped it on the desk. Jake handed it all to Louie and swung his chair around to face his computer.

"Something else up?" Louie asked.

Jake rubbed his neck, glanced over his shoulder at Louie. "Mia suggested we move in together."

Louie let out a belly laugh. "Hot damn, and look at you all wound tight as a drum and running scared. I can see your freaking wheels rolling to come up with a reason not to. Right?"

"It came out of the blue and it's too soon."

"Did you give her an answer?"

"No. Can we get back to work?"

"Sure, but I'm not through," Louie said, rubbing his hands together.

"No shit."

Jake continued his work for the day. He opened the financial file on Melinda Mastrianni. The woman had no wiggle room in her budget, and minimum insurance if she was unable to work. Was she desperate enough to blackmail someone? Off the cuff he'd say no, but then a memory forced its way to the surface. Melinda had been the original mean girl. He remembered Dilly Emerson and her dress malfunction at the Harvest Ball. Melinda had taunted the girl to tears for weeks after the dance and got others to join in. Jake tossed off his grim musing and continued to dissect Melinda's business records.

What she'd recorded in them didn't point to a woman who had excess funds. He started to shut down the file when an account caught his eye. It was still listed in Tony and Melinda Mastrianni's names. Tony had been dead for over three years. Why keep his name on it? The more he dug into Melinda's background, the more cunning he found her. Tony, along with his social security number, was the primary on the account. Melinda was listed as only a signer. Hmmm! Had she underreported her income this way? It could be a tax violation, something he could use if he needed it to dig deeper into her background and finances.

He searched the file he'd requested on Sal Gallucci's bank records and hit a dead zone there. Gallucci had none. Was he a mattress stuffer? No, he'd never leave his condo if he hid it there. He rented, not owned, his place in the west end of town. Gallucci had no financial ties to the area. He fit Jake's profile for the blackmailer, though Jake didn't see him for the murder. Then who? The thought tripped around in his head.

Again, he had to consider Todd Blake. Why kill his wife? Money? He'd known about her inheritance for years, so why now? Sex? There'd been no evidence of an affair from either one of them. The commissioner's job was a political appointment, and most political appointees hadn't been cops. Todd had. He'd spent twenty years on the job before being picked for the position. Was it someone from the job with a vendetta against Todd? Jake had crossed that off the list, but kept coming back to it. As commissioner, Todd didn't touch many cases. He was administrative. Cops could be disgruntled that the raises had sucked this year, budget constraints the reason offered again, but he didn't see anyone killing over that.

The intercom buzzed. He flipped the switch. "Jake, come to my office, please," Shamus said. Not a command, but Shamus's voice was odd.

Shamus pointed to a seat in front of his desk when Jake walked into his office. Shamus's wife, Darcy, again leaned against the window sill. When Jake's rump hit the chair, Shamus handed him a letter in a clear folder.

"I received this in Tuesday's mail. I didn't open it until this morning," Darcy said, moving behind him.

It gave him the opportunity to stand.

"Sit down, Jake," Darcy said. "I've paced enough for the lot of us."

"Why didn't you call me immediately?" Jake sat back down next to Darcy.

"I spoke with your boss first," Darcy said, glancing over at her husband.

"Jake, it doesn't matter who she called first, it matters where it came from." Shamus pinched the bridge of his nose. Jake's gaze swept from husband to wife. Palpable tension extended from one to the other. *I'm a soldier trapped between two armies*, he thought.

"Darcy, you have to promise me you won't meet them on your own."

"I've been through it all with Shamus." Darcy sat in the chair to Jake's left. "What I want—and I can't convince Shamus it's for the best—I want him to use me to set up a sting operation. I want to nail the bastard who killed Callie."

"We can use a policewoman who resembles you. This way you're never put in danger. What do you think, Shamus?"

"As long as my wife is safe, I'm fine with it."

At last, something to work with, Jake thought. "Have you dusted for fingerprints?"

Shamus's sneer warmed his heart. "Not my first day on the job, Jake."

Darcy stepped behind the desk and put her hand on Shamus's shoulder. He reached up, covering her hand with his.

They're a unit, Jake reflected.

"I'll need the original for the murder book, and a copy to work with. Can I take this?"

"Yes, I don't want to see it again," Shamus said. Jake started out of the office. "Jake, look into Captain McGregor's background, and his feud with Todd Blake."

"What feud?"

"It's an ongoing thing. I'm not suggesting he had anything to do with Callie's death, but investigate it to cross it off your list."

"Why don't you interview him if you're familiar with the problem?"

"I want fresh eyes on it."

Jake mulled that over on his way back to his office.

* * * *

In his den, Edward Rockford tossed the *Wilkesbury Daily News* and the *Hartford Courant* across his desk at his daughter. "Are you proud of yourself?"

Edy studied the picture of her and Linden at lunch yesterday. Lily had captured them perfectly. Edy refused to cave in to her father's outrage. She handed her father her cell phone with it open to the pictures of Cedric and his mistress.

"That's what I walked into today in his office at the bank. About an hour and a half ago I filed for divorce. Last week I wiped out his account at the branch on North Main Street and deposited his funds into our joint account at your bank. It will be difficult for him to keep housing and supporting his mistress. I am not going to stand for the humiliation. And if I were you, Dad, I'd make sure to keep an eye on the bank funds once he learns I wiped him out. I wanted you to hear this from me." Why she'd thought he'd support her was beyond her.

"Edy, sit down, please. His secretary has been keeping me in the loop. The lawyers have been working on his dismissal for three months. What you did today…I don't know how that will affect it. He could claim discrimination now, based on family bias. I have to go into correction mode immediately. Why didn't you talk to me before you did this?"

"I didn't believe you'd support my decision," she said, her eyes on her hands, not him.

"Oh, sweetheart, I'm sorry. For over fifteen years I've wanted to fire the lying bastard. I didn't for your sake. Why have you stayed so long?"

"I can't explain it."

Edward Rockford's gray mane tickled her cheek when he came around the desk, pulled her into his arms, and tilted his head downward to kiss her on the cheek to comfort her. She barely came up to his chest. "We should've addressed this sooner."

"Hindsight," Edy said.

"Yes. Do you want to stay for dinner?"

"No, Benita has thrown all his possessions on the lawn. I better get home and deal with the aftermath."

"What have you done with his paperwork?"

She winked at her father. "I only had Benita throw out his clothes. I've kept everything else, including all the jewelry I've given him over the years."

"There's my girl," Edward said, and hugged her again.

Time to go home and face the music, she thought.

When she reached the door to her father's office, he called out, "I'm setting up security for you. They'll be a phone call away."

"I've done the same, Dad. Thanks."

* * * *

Edy drove into the driveway, laughing. The place looked like a dump with Cedric's possessions strewn about. *Boy, most of the women on this block, who acted as my friend to my face and who have screwed Cedric at one time or another, must be going crazy.* She flipped the switch on the garage and headed inside, then reprogrammed the code for the garage door opener.

Edy sat in the garage for a good ten minutes before she was able to get a grip on her emotions.

"Benita, I'm home," she called out, stepping into the long hallway off the garage.

She decided to hit the problem head-on and went to Cedric's office. She rummaged through his desk and papers. *I've been too complaisant over the years. Not anymore. I'm a strong, kickass woman, and the likes of Cedric can go to hell.*

"Mrs. Dunstan, Mr. Dunstan is pounding on the front door," Benita said from the doorway to Cedric's office.

"If he persists, call the police and have him removed from the property. It's my house, not his."

"Yes, ma'am."

Edy closed the top drawer of Cedric's desk. She swung the chair back and started out of the room with the intention of going upstairs. She changed her mind and walked to the front door. She pressed the intercom button on the surveillance system and watched him rant. It amazed her, the crimson color Cedric's face and neck had turned. It'd be nice if he blew a gasket and saved her from a ghastly divorce.

"Cedric, you're making an ass of yourself. Gather up your possessions and go to your little love nest you share with Rosie. Oh yes, I know about that too." His head jerked up to look directly into the camera. "It's over. Accept your responsibility in the demise of this farce we call a marriage."

"You cold, unfeeling bitch, you drove me away."

"Think what you want. It's over."

"It's not, and you'll find out soon enough."

"Goodbye, Cedric. If you're not off my property in fifteen minutes, Benita will call the police."

"You stuck up, conceited bitch. You'll regret the day you tangled with me."

"I have for years." She leaned her back against the door and fought the tears threatening to fall.

No, I'm stronger than this. She decided to follow it through. Edy locked her gaze on the screen, silently cursing him as Cedric tried his key in the front door again.

"The locks on all my houses were changed this morning, Cedric."

"Our houses," he screamed into the camera.

"No, mine. It was my money that bought all of them, and my money that maintained them. All of them, including this one, are in my name only. Your name doesn't appear on any of my assets or the deeds. You've wasted five minutes. Now you only have ten left before Benita calls the police. Oh, and Cedric, anything you leave here will be disposed of."

"I'm not through with you, you just wait."

It might've destroyed her to see him leave, but when he bent over to pick up his belongings, it lifted the big boulder off her heart. Point one for her, though she didn't feel like a winner.

"Mrs. Dunstan?" Benita hovered behind her.

Edy turned. Benita's arms were open, ready to comfort her as she had done over the years. *It would be nice to rest my head against the cushy pillow of Benita's breast, and inhale her vanilla cologne mingled with house cleaners, but it's about time I grew up*, Edy thought, and walked over to the staircase. "Yes?"

"Are you going to be okay?" Benita asked, dropping her arms.

"Yes, I have no choice. I'm going upstairs to rest for a while. Can you bring dinner up to me tonight?"

"Certainly. What time would you like to eat?"

She glanced at the watch on her wrist. "Seven," she said, tears in her voice, the weight of the world pressing down on her shoulders.

Chapter 13

Everywhere he went he heard rumors about Callie's virtue, her husband's affairs, and who each person thought had killed her. *They were all wrong,* Jake thought, sitting at the counter in the diner and wolfing down his BLT. In small cities, people fed on gossip. If they gossiped about someone else, it kept them out of the spotlight.

Gwenn Langley hounded him for sound bites when he landed a meaty case, but for Callie's case she'd kept her needling to a minimum. He dialed her cell before he went to Captain William McGregor's office to interview him.

"It's about time, Jake. What's going on with the Blake case?" Gwenn answered in her sultry voice.

"It's ongoing," he said, bringing a picture of Gwenn into focus in his mind, matching the voice to the woman.

He'd bet this week's salary the five-foot-nine-inch blonde had her pencil perched and ready to scribble down any news he gave her. Gwenn's eyes were a lighter shade of blue than Mia's but as sharp, and nothing got past her. Every time he spoke to her he kept that in mind.

"Funny. Is there anything new I can report?"

"I wish. We have a few leads, Gwenn, but nothing solid at this time."

"Would you tell me if you did?"

"I would if it helped my case. Have you learned anything?"

"No, the woman lived a saintly life. As does her husband. Somewhere, somehow, she met her killer and set him off. But where did she meet him?" Gwenn said.

"Welcome to my life. It's frustrating, isn't it?"

"Extremely—you seriously haven't found anything to nail this killer, Jake?" Gwenn's voice trailed off.

Gwenn cared for her story and career, but even more she cared about the victims. It made her an ace reporter. He thought back over the last case, which had lots of evidence, lots of bodies, and clues he'd eventually been able to hone to catch the murdering bastard. This time, outside of the picture left with the body, he had nothing.

"We're working on it."

"Can you give me a statement I can use on the six o'clock broadcast?"

"It's ongoing, and the team working the case is confident the killer will soon be behind bars."

"Thanks for nothing."

"You're welcome," he said with a smile. He hung up and strolled back to the station for his scheduled meeting.

Jake had dug into Captain William McGregor's background before the meeting. The captain ran illegals and a little shine had been knocked off him ten years ago, when his and Todd Blake's cases collided. Blake had tried to work with McGregor, who worked for glory and to further his career. His lack of cooperation with Blake cost them both their cases. A demerit was issued for McGregor's file. Ever since the incident, he'd blamed Todd for his failure to go any further in the department. The irony of it: Todd was now his boss. *It must stick in McGregor's gut.*

Jake sat across from the man whose desk was large, dark, and clear of paper. McGregor's girth filled his chair, and he wore his salt-and-pepper hair cropped close to his scalp. His brown eyes locked on Jake's as he waited him out.

"Thank you for seeing me, Captain," Jake said, his notebook ready in his hand.

"I've heard good things about you, Jake. Who pointed you in my direction?"

"It's a natural progression to interview anyone who has had a problem with a victim or their spouse. I've heard rumors over the years and thought I'd put them to bed."

McGregor folded his hands, resting them on his desk. "It was a petty argument the brass and a few officers blew out of proportion. Todd and I have made our peace over the years." McGregor squinted as he continued to size Jake up. "You're here to interview me based on an incident from ten years ago. And one you believe I'd kill Todd's wife over? Why? It had nothing to do with Callie."

"It's a string I have to pull."

"Which tells me you have nothing," McGregor said.

"You're correct."

"I will tell you I liked and respected Callie. She was a fine woman. One Todd didn't deserve. That said, he'd say the same about my wife. Is there anything else, Lieutenant?"

"No, sir, thank you for your time." Jake stood, as did McGregor. They shook hands, and he left. It had been another dead end. Nothing had been accomplished in the interview except to note McGregor still held a grudge against Blake, though Jake couldn't see him using Callie to get back at Todd. But he'd been wrong before.

* * * *

Melinda parked her car in her driveway after running her errands. She'd garage it later. She reached into the trunk for the groceries and started lifting them out as someone came up behind her.

"Jumping Jesus, you scared the shit out of me." Melinda dropped the bags and spilled the contents all over the trunk. "Don't sneak up on me like that," she said to Sal.

"I didn't. Christ, you're jumpy," Sal said. "When I realized you weren't home, I decided to hide out back in case the cops showed up. It's not good to be seen together."

"Then why are you here?" She squinted, trying to figure out his angle.

"I miss you. We need a plan in case this blows up in our faces. Whoever killed that poor woman understood what they were doing by pointing the cops in your direction. Have you been able to find someone with a grudge and computer knowledge to steal your photos?"

"No. And the last thing I planned on was Jake Carrington. Come inside before someone sees you."

Sal stuffed the spilled items back in the bags and carried them into the house. Melinda followed him but not before she glanced up and down the street, satisfied no one saw them.

"If the cops visited you last night, are you sure they don't have someone following you?"

"I made sure. After I checked out, I took a few detours to throw anyone off. I'm positive I wasn't followed."

If Sal's right, it would mean he's not a suspect. How about me? Am I? I think he's looking to throw me under the bus.

"Tell me exactly what you did this morning," Melinda said as she stored her groceries in the cabinets.

"I checked out at eleven. Acted casual and drove to Southington. I sat in the commuter lot for twenty minutes. No one got off the exit when I did or pulled into the lot. I hopped back on the highway going west toward Wilkesbury and drove here. I'm parked around the corner one street over. Listen, dodging cops isn't a big deal for me. It's child's play. My problem is I need money. If I get my hands on the bastard who took our money I'll...."

"It's a moot point. What we need to do is move on to the next one. I'm cash strapped and I've got my mortgage payment coming up." She almost laughed out loud. The blackmail money gave her a good cushion, but she needed more to get the hell out of this hick town. What Sal didn't know wouldn't hurt him. She bit down on her bottom lip to hide the smile.

"Are you sure hitting the next one this soon is smart?" Sal asked.

"We both need money. Do you think we have a choice? This time let's make them go out of town to drop the money off. It will put us out of Carrington's jurisdiction."

"I don't know..."

"Are you going to wimp out on me now? I thought you said you had no cash. Where are you going to go if you don't have any money?"

Sal paced the floor. Melinda let him work it out for himself. She'd give him no money. As it was she didn't have enough for herself. If he didn't come to her conclusion, well she'd have to...better not go there. She leaned against the kitchen cabinet.

He stepped in front of her, pinned her to the counter and wrapped his hands around her neck, a bit too tightly. "I'll do it for the money. If you cross me, Melinda, it'll be the end of you, do you understand?"

Hot lava burned her lungs, her eyes watered, as Sal squeezed his hands tighter around her neck. She wasn't in the mood for his sex games. But had Sal started to figure out who took the money? If he had, she'd need to throw him off the scent.

Melinda leaned into Sal, kissed him while she tried to figure a way out of sharing the blackmail money with him. He relaxed his grip around her throat as she danced their way out of the kitchen and into the bedroom.

* * * *

On a whim, on his way home Jake called Sal's poker buddy Lorenzo Rigano again.

He started right in when Rigano answered. "Mr. Rigano, Lieutenant Carrington from the WPD. I forgot to ask you the last time we spoke, what does Sal Gallucci do for a living?"

A chuckle, followed by silence. Jake waited him out for a few seconds. "Mr. Rigano?"

"Anything and everything that will line his pockets—let's say he's a freelancer."

Interesting, Jake thought. "Thanks, I hope not to bother you again."

"You're not going to give me a little tidbit I can use at the poker table this week to unnerve him?"

"It's an ongoing case. Sorry."

Jake hung up as he drove into his driveway. *Another day into the case and we're no closer to solving it than when I arrived on scene Sunday.* He sat in his car for a couple of minutes to regroup. Tired, he scrubbed his hands over his face to revive himself before he faced Mia and her question from last night about them selling their current homes and getting a place new to the both of them. Why not, since they were practically doing it now? But he couldn't sell the house. It would cut the last tie to Eva and his family if he did. Throughout the years he'd redecorated. Eva's room had been converted into a spare bedroom done in yellow and blue, the pink fluffy bedspread and curtains gone. His parents' room, now his, he'd redone in blues instead of burgundy. The house for him still held his family's essence. Fanciful, he understood, but it wasn't only his mother who couldn't let go...He had to make Mia understand his logic.

Ha! This week he'd bring Mia with him to the nursing home to meet his mother. A deterrent, maybe. He'd have to see how Mia handled facing Maddie, who lived in the past. She seemed to forget his mother used to have two children, not one.

Brigh jumped up on his leg as he walked in the door—her big brown eyes pleading for attention.

"How's my girl?" he said, bending down and rubbing her black, white, and brown spotted coat and head. "Did you miss me?" He kissed the top of Brigh's head.

Brigh licked his hand. "Go sit." Jake pointed to her bed in the corner of the foyer. He found Mia at the stove. *Sorry, stomach, we'll have to eat whatever it is.* His stomach growled at the memory of the burnt pork chops she'd made last week that were tougher than leather.

"Hi, babe." He leaned in and kissed her on the back of the neck.

"Hi, we're having pasta for dinner."

Excellent, it's hard to mess up pasta. "Smells delicious," he lied. The bubbling sauce smelled too spicy. He put his briefcase on the table.

"Oh, Jake, take it off the table." Mia pointed at his case.

He placed it on the floor and took the dishes from the cabinet to set the table. When the rolls were ready, they ate. He forked up the first peppery bite and prayed his stomach didn't rebel.

When they'd finished dinner, Jake cleaned up the kitchen before going to his office to dig into Sal Gallucci's work record. He'd been waffling back and forth on who the killer could be: Gallucci, the only suspect who made any sense to him—or Gallucci and Melinda. Blinders blocked him from getting inside the killer's head on this one. Out of Mia's ever-watchful eyes, he popped a pain pill to kill the constant agony in his gut. The spicy dinner hadn't helped any. Occupied with the case all day, he'd been able to stifle the jabbing sensation. With Brigh at his feet, he started his search as she stared up at him with her big chocolate eyes.

"Who are you to judge?" he asked the dog, and typed one-handed. "All right, I'll call the doctor tomorrow." He patted Brigh on the head while reading his screen. Something caught his eye and he backed up the cursor.

* * * *

"We do have chemistry, Melinda," Sal said, rolling over to grab a cigarette from the nightstand.

"We do. Let's plan the time and place to put the finger on the next victim. With how the newspaper is portraying Blake as a loose woman we can use that against the next victim. Fear is a great motivator. We need to time it down to the last minute. Nothing can go wrong this time," Melinda said.

"I still think the motel manager took the money."

"Why?"

"It's a feeling. Who else but him? He let me in the room," Sal said.

Melinda liked where Sal's mind ventured, as long as he strayed from her direction. She rolled from the bed, picked up her robe, slipped into it and tied the sash.

"I'm hungry, how about you?" Melinda asked.

"I could eat. Why don't you bring it in here along with the bottle of vodka and we'll make a night of it."

Melinda made baloney sandwiches with mustard. She had to drag a chair to the cabinet to get the vodka. She put the food and booze on a tray and started toward her bedroom. The carpet silenced her footsteps.

In the doorway she almost upended the tray. Sal was rifling through her closet. *Son of a bitch, he'll find the money if he hasn't yet.* Backing into the hallway, she retraced her steps to the kitchen, where she'd left her purse with the gun inside.

There's no way in hell I'm sharing the money with him. I did all the work.

With the gun cocked, she stuck it in her robe pocket, then lifted the tray to go back into the bedroom.

Sal charged into the kitchen with the bag of money in his hands.

"I'm starved," she said, setting the tray on the counter.

Melinda slipped her hand in her pocket, placed her finger on the trigger and waited.

"What the hell is this?" Sal asked, shaking the bag of money.

"What does it look like?" Melinda waited.

"You killed that poor woman. Why?"

"She fought me," Melinda said.

"You lied to me."

"Yeah." Melinda stared at Sal.

He started toward her, but she fired through her robe pocket, hitting him in the chest.

His eyes widened, his jaw dropped, he clutched his chest, his fingers covered in blood. Sal dropped to his knees, then his stomach.

Instead of calling 911, Melinda watched the life drain from Sal. Empty of feeling, light-headed, she huddled at the small, narrow table against the wall and rested her head on her arms.

What am I going to do with him? With her vision blurring, her head throbbing, she swore.

Damn it, not a migraine. I need a clear head to get rid of him, but where? It has to be someplace he won't be found right away. An area with known criminal activity would be best to convince Jake that Sal tangled with the wrong people. That's it. After a few days I'll disappear. Jake will think I'm another victim. Which I am, thanks to Sal.

After dark, she took a walk through the neighborhood and located Sal's car. With his keys in hand she drove it to her kitchen door and then dragged Sal down the steps wrapped in a blanket. Thankful for the muscles she'd developed from years of carrying around the heavy camera equipment, Melinda squatted then hefted Sal into the trunk of his car and drove him to the dump site.

Chapter 14

Last night, Jake uncovered some interesting info on Gallucci. He'd need to verify and re-question Sal. Jake got an early start and called Louie from his car. He engaged the engine and drove toward Louie's house, located one block over from his place.

"I'm going to reinterview Sal Gallucci today. Do you want to come along?" Jake asked.

"Sure, you got something hot?"

"No. The guy hasn't worked in years, but he rents an expensive condo, drives the latest-model cars, and hangs with money people wherever he goes. It's sending up flags."

"Okay, pick me up when you're ready," Louie said.

"I'm sitting outside your house."

"Gee, Jake, nothing like giving a guy a little notice. I'll be out," Louie said without telling him when.

Jake sat patiently for ten minutes before he climbed from the car and knocked on Louie's front door. "Hey, LJ, where's your father?" LJ, Louie's rangy teenage son, whose dark olive complexion and brown eyes looked like a replica of Louie, opened the door.

"Dad's in the shower. Want some coffee?"

"He's a piece of work," Jake mumbled, following LJ into the kitchen. "Hey, Sophia, LJ, here's the money for watching Brigh. Thanks again." Jake pulled some bills from his pocket.

"You don't have to pay me, Uncle Jake. I love that dog," LJ said, tucking the money into his jeans pocket, not giving Jake a chance to take it back.

"A deal's a deal, though she is a heartbreaker. Why are you up so early?"

"It's a school day," LJ said.

"Sophia, can you pour some coffee into my to-go cup?" Louie asked, ambling into the bright green kitchen, tucking his shirt into his pants, his briefcase under his arm.

"Here," Sophia said, handing Louie a cup. "Take care, boys."

Louie kissed Sophia goodbye, then chased Jake down the hall.

"Working banker's hours?" Jake said when Louie jumped in the car, tossing his briefcase in the back seat.

"It's barely seven, Jake, slow down," Louie said. "You seem antsy. What's up?"

"The case, my stomach, Mia, the taunting, I'm still trying to figure out the purpose of the letter and what it hoped to accomplish. The only good thing is the new information on Sal Gallucci."

"It's not healing?" Louie asked. Leave it to Louie to latch on to one thing. But it's the one thing Jake didn't want to discuss with Mia or Louie. He couldn't, really.

"It's nothing, the doc said I'd have pain. I do. Now do you want to listen to what I have on Gallucci or talk about our outfits?"

"Relax, Jake. You already explained it on the phone. Where are we going? The motel is in the other direction."

"I called ahead. The motel manager said Sal checked out yesterday. I want to do a run by his condo. If he's not there, we'll have Detectives Brown and Lanoue check the other motels in town and the surrounding area, while we check out Melinda's house to see if he stayed with her last night."

"You've been a busy little bee this morning. Didn't you sleep?"

"Some, but Brigh's been jumping up on the bed and waking me," Jake said, leaving out the part about how the dog kept landing on his gut.

The manager wasn't a happy camper when he saw them. "Do you know what freakin' time it is?"

"I do," Jake said. "It can't be helped."

The manager turned away. Jake didn't miss the raised eyebrow Louie shot him. He lifted his shoulders as he slid his hands into his pockets.

"Here's the key. Let yourself in, and slip it in my mail slot, and don't freakin' knock again before nine." The guy slammed the door in their faces.

"Let's get it done." Jake started up the stairs to Sal's unit.

"It's gonna be a long day," Louie muttered under his breath.

Jake knocked, several times. The next-door neighbor called out for them to shut up. He used the key to enter the unit. If they were asked, the manager had given permission, which covered their asses. They walked into the apartment. Nothing had been disturbed since their last visit. Again, the hotel atmosphere in the unit struck Jake. *Clean and impersonal, this is only a stopover for Sal*, Jake thought.

"It's got an empty feel to it. Gallucci hasn't been back," Jake said. "Think he rabbited?"

"Why? We didn't give him any cause to get nervous yesterday. Are we really going to visit Melinda's this early?" Louie squinted down at his watch.

"Yep. If Sal's there, we'll catch both him and Melinda off guard."

Jake drove across town and parked on the narrow street. If two cars tried to pass at the same time, it'd be hairy. Melinda's car sat in her driveway. Jake strode over to the garage and peeked inside.

"Sal's car isn't in there," Jake said.

The overgrown shrubs blocked his view of the front door. He led the way to the side door and knocked.

Over the half curtain on the door window, Jake watched Melinda tie the sash to her robe and push aside the window treatment.

"What the hell do you want at this hour?"

When the door swung open, a familiar odor assaulted his nose. Jake's eyes watered at the concentration of it. "I'm looking for Sal Gallucci. Do you know where he is?"

"No, why would I?"

Melinda's body blocked the doorway. "Can we come in?" Jake asked.

"No, you can't. Come back at a decent hour and I'll consider it. Now get out of here and let me get back to sleep. I got a job to shoot today."

Another door slammed in their faces. "Nobody likes you today," Louie said.

"I have a couple of people in New Jersey to tug on to see if Sal's gone back there. If not…"

"What?" Louie spun around to face Jake.

"Something's off. Is she still at the window?"

"Yeah."

"Did you smell the bleach?"

"Yeah, but women have been cleaning with it throughout the ages," Louie said.

"I've been inside. She's not that thorough of a housekeeper."

Jake drove around the block, then parked across the street from Melinda's house on the diagonal to keep both the front and side doors in his view. After twenty minutes of no movement at the windows, he drove to the station.

"Did you expect her to go to Sal?" Louie asked as they drove away.

He ignored Louie as he ran the sights, sounds, and smells through his mind.

* * * *

No one in Jersey had heard from Sal since Sunday. Jake leaned back in his chair and considered. Where'd Sal go if not to Melinda's or New Jersey? And why take off? He hoisted his desk phone to his ear, then, remembering Louie's words, checked the clock in front of him. Eight o'clock shouldn't be too early to get ahold of Darcy McGuire. She ran an international company. Didn't she have to connect with people in different time zones? *Hell.* He hesitated before he dialed her cell number.

"What can I do for you, Jake? I'm in a meeting," Darcy said in her no-nonsense tone.

"Can you call me back when you're done?"

"Give me two hours." Darcy hung up without waiting for his response.

Two hours to get his answers or he could call Judge Eisenberg's wife and question her. Did he also want to paint a target on his back with the judge? No, he'd wait and question Judy Eisenberg only as a last measure.

What he wanted to ask these women would insult them. Edy Dunstan popped into his head as he remembered a picture of her in yesterday's paper, with a man in a restaurant. Was it her lover or a friend? All the women thus far had been in attendance at the gala. Had Edwina been approached?

How do I broach the subject without giving away too much info on the murder? He dialed her home number.

"Mrs. Dunstan, it's Lieutenant Jake Carrington. I'd like to ask you a few questions about your picture in the paper. Was Melinda Mastrianni the photographer?"

"No, but I recently had her do some publicity shots for me. Why? What have my pictures to do with your case? From everything I read in the papers, I assume you're working Callie's murder?" Edy asked.

"Yes, I am. Is this morning or afternoon better for you?"

"Why don't you come around eleven? Do you have the address?"

"Yes, eleven's perfect. Thank you."

Jake hung up. Edy hadn't mentioned getting a blackmail letter. Pursuing Edy made more sense to him if someone had been blackmailing her for quick money. But what made the blackmailer target Callie? Had she been a test subject?

He picked up Todd Blake's credit card file, which someone had put on his desk. It was a complete file that went back one year. Jake highlighted the hotel charges, restaurants, and jewelry store purchases.

Todd had a twenty-five-thousand-dollar credit line, with an outstanding balance of eight thousand. Not ridiculous, but high if you added in his monthly mortgage payments of three thousand, tuition, food. clothing, tickets to the theater, and vacations. How much of their daily living expenses had Callie covered with her inheritance? Did it matter?

Jake pulled her account from a separate folder. He matched payments on the credit card to the withdrawal from her account. She'd paid part of the tuition as her sister had said, and she'd made monthly payments on their credit cards. He hated to do it, but he'd have to interview their kids. He pressed in Shamus's extension.

"Captain, do you have a few minutes?"

"Come up now," McGuire said.

Jake walked into McGuire's office and shut the door behind him. "I need to know what the commissioner's salary is."

"You have something?"

"A bump, nothing more," Jake said.

"Like what?"

Jake twisted his lip in thought.

"Jake?"

"They used her trust fund more than he disclosed. It's nothing major, but it was used not only for the kids but for clothing and vacations. Todd's tailor bills were paid from it. And she left him as the beneficiary with small endowments for the kids."

"Jake, as I told you before, my wife has an account in her name only. I can't tell you how much is in it. I don't touch it, even though she gave me a debit card for access. Does she have other accounts in her name only? Yes, and she also pays for my tailor bills and other things. I'm not, nor was Todd, married to the standard cop wife. We married rich women who maintain a certain position in the community. I've never asked to see a statement and yes, I'm the beneficiary. Because we're married doesn't mean we have complete knowledge of our spouses and their actions. Knowing Callie, she'd use it if she wanted something or she felt the need to help out with expenses. She was a generous woman. If you're leaning toward Todd again…."

"Shamus, I'm not leaning toward anyone but the male model. I haven't found anything that points to Todd, but I have to be thorough. The mayor's concerned Todd's getting special treatment. Between you and me, he is, but it won't stop me from doing my job, especially if he's guilty of killing his wife."

"I've known Todd for years. Do you want me to go with you to read him?" Shamus asked.

"No, not since Darcy received her letter. It makes her a victim. I can't have you there."

Jake left Shamus's office. On the way to his office, he called and scheduled a meeting at noon with Todd. His morning calendar had filled up. Spiders crawled up his skin at the thought that he wasn't further along on the case. Callie Blake deserved justice from him, from the department, and for her husband.

Who killed you, Callie?

He strolled into the bullpen and made a beeline to Louie's desk. He tapped on it and continued on to his office.

"What's up?" Louie asked, running after him.

"We're going to go at Todd again after we interview Edy Dunstan."

"Why the both of them?"

Jake filled Louie in, and then continued analyzing Todd's financials. The man loved his clothing. His suits were tailor-made by Mannie's, the best in town. Callie also preferred high-end designers. It seemed all this money had been spent on trivial items, but maybe in the commissioner's position it had been required to maintain a certain air.

Money, and people with loads of it, had him thinking about Mia and her wealth. Though she didn't flaunt it, as the relationship had gotten serious they'd spoken of Mia's family's money, her trust fund, her good investments, and her hard work—but she never told him her exact worth and he'd never asked. Another conversation pertaining to her wealth might be awkward, but did it open her up to be a blackmailer's target?

Chapter 15

Jake and Louie drove through the gates of the high-end division where the Dunstans lived in the west end of town. Edy lived at the end of the cul-de-sac in a large white house with black shutters. Two round pillars supported a black-roofed portico that extended to the walkway. The Dunstans' home, the highest valued in the area, kept their neighbors at bay with a large plot of land. It overlooked both Wilkesbury and Middlebury. A wide, sweeping lawn lined with mature trees on either side of the house ensured privacy.

It surprised him to find clothing littering the front lawn. He knocked as Louie gaped.

"Close your mouth there, buddy."

"Why would she allow this?" Louie spread his arms to encompass the mess.

Before Jake could comment, a maid dressed in a gray uniform, her black hair pinned in a neat bun, opened the door. With their badges at the ready, Jake introduced them.

"We're here to see Mrs. Dunstan. I'm Lieutenant Carrington and this is Sergeant Romanelli."

"Come in, please. Mrs. Dunstan is expecting you," the woman said, dropping vowels at the beginning of a few words, showing English wasn't her native tongue.

"I'm sorry. Do you know there's a bunch of clothing strewn all over your lawn?" Louie asked before Jake could put a lid on it.

"Yes, we do." The maid escorted them to a living room, without giving them an explanation. "Please take a seat while I announce you."

Jake chose to stand. The bright room done in burgundy and pink silk quietly showcased the owners' money.

Edy strolled into the room, a wide smile on her face.

"I threw my cheating husband out last night. Those are his things he left behind. A service will be by to clean it up. I'm baffled as to how I can help with your case."

Jake turned his attention from the room to Edy. She wore a pale blue raw silk blouse and matching slacks with beige spike heels. Her blonde hair had been drawn into a bun at the base of her neck, showcasing her fine bone structure and piercing blue eyes. Edy lasered her focus on him, not Louie.

"We're interviewing everyone who's recently been photographed by Melinda Mastrianni. Have you ever posed with this model?" Jake showed her a picture of Sal Gallucci and watched for a reaction.

"I brought my own sandwich to the banquet, Lieutenant." She giggled. "This is a sleazy one, isn't he?" she said, examining the picture. "Who is he?"

Jake wondered what her comment meant, but had a pretty good idea. "A model Melinda used sometimes in her boudoir photos," Louie said.

"Ah, why would a woman want to be photographed with him?"

"Different tastes, I suppose," Jake said.

"Well, not mine." Edy wrinkled her nose at the model in the photo.

"Were you offered a model when you posed for your portraits?"

"No. As I said, I brought along the man I'm sure you saw me with in yesterday's paper."

He decided the woman wasn't hiding anything. "Did you receive a blackmail letter threatening to expose you with the man?"

"Heavens no! Between you and me, I set me and my date up to have our picture taken, knowing it would it hit the papers. I did it to humiliate my husband. After years of dealing with his cheating and the scandals, I've had enough. He pushed me too hard this time."

"Thank you for your honesty, Mrs. Dunstan," Jake said.

"I'm taking back my maiden name, Rockford, once the divorce is final."

Out on the street Jake climbed into the driver's side, Louie the passenger's. "I'm glad I'm not married to her," Louie said.

"Why? I like her style." And he did. A strong woman who refused to be a victim had to be admired.

"You would," Louie said.

"Let's head over to Todd's. Give him a call. Tell him we've finished up early here," Jake said, pulling away from Edy's house.

* * * *

Todd's neighborhood was also located in the west end of town but attracted successful, middle-class, working families. He led the way to the door. He and Louie found Todd alone, his eyes red and roaming.

"Let's get this over with. I'm burying her tomorrow, Jake." Blake walked away from them, leaving Jake to close the door behind him.

"Todd, I'm sorry…"

"Cut it, Jake…I asked everyone to leave so I could mourn her alone. And again you're intruding."

"We have a few questions, and then I'll be out of your way," Jake said. Jake took the lead. He and Louie had decided beforehand that Todd responded better to him.

"Ask them, then get the hell out and leave me alone." Todd plopped down in the recliner.

"I reviewed your financials—and you've lived above your means for a long time. How did you not know that Callie was covering the expenses?"

Harrumph! "I knew. It was a game with me and Callie. She thought I had to present an image of success. In Callie's mind that meant dressing well. You're both young. In my day the woman took care of the house and its finances, and the man earned the money. I left it to Callie to use her judgment and her trust fund as she wished."

"You've spent a lot on not only tuition, Commissioner, but on clothing, theater tickets, travel, and more," Jake said.

"I told you before, Callie decided when and where to spend her money. Is that a crime, Jake? In the beginning I'd question an expense or a trip and insist she not use her funds, but she'd explain it away. She'd say she saved, or used the gift money her parents gave her while they were alive. I'm not stupid, I know she used her funds, but she was discreet and didn't flaunt it around, embarrassing me. As I said, it was a game we played."

"I'm sorry we took up your time. We'll see you tomorrow. We're honorary pallbearers. But if you'd rather not have us…"

"No, Jake, I requested you and Louie for the investigation and as pallbearers. There are no two people on the force I trust more. I didn't realize then how hard you'd come at me. Please believe me when I say, I did not kill Callie. No one loved her more." Todd picked up his whiskey glass on the end table by his recliner and drained it.

They left Todd to his grief and climbed into the department-issued car, but Jake didn't start it. "What do you think?"

"He's mourning his loss, though we both know abusers do," Louie said.

"Louie, he's not an abuser, for God's sake. And why didn't you jump in and ask if you thought he was?"

"I thought it better you handled the commissioner. We've both seen abusers kill a loved one then regret their actions. But I agree with you, I don't think he murdered Callie."

"Let's put an APB out on Sal Gallucci. I want to question him again, but this time in a formal interview at the station."

Louie issued the bulletin while Jake drove back to the station.

* * * *

"Mrs. Dunstan, Mr. Dunstan's on the phone," Benita said.

"Tell him to drop dead," Edy said over her shoulder as she stared out her bedroom window. "Never mind, I'll do it myself."

She sat in the peach wingback chair by the window and picked up the phone. "What do you want?"

"I'm sorry, really, Edy. If you'd let me explain..."

"There's nothing you can say that will change my mind, Cedric. You went too far when you set her up in an apartment."

"I had no choice. She's pregnant."

The phone dropped from her hand. Pregnant. After all the years they'd tried, he'd gone and gotten someone else knocked up. She'd have killed him if he stood in front of her.

She reached for the phone to hang it up and heard him calling to her. "You're a bastard," she said, then slammed down the phone. The house phone rang.

Benita knocked. "He's on the phone again. Do you want me to take care of it?"

Edy wiped her eyes, blew her nose. "No, I'll deal with him once and for all. Close the door, please."

She waited for Benita to leave, then lifted the phone to her ear. "You have five minutes."

"Edy, when I learned she was pregnant, I thought we'd take the child and pay her off. Isn't that what you've always wanted?"

He must think I'm an idiot. "No, it's not. I wanted our baby—not yours, but ours. Don't you get it?"

"This is an alternative."

A thought niggled at the back of her brain. She had to buy time. "It is. Let me think about it. I'll call you tomorrow or the next day." Edy hung up, closed her eyes, and fished for the elusive thought.

Ah, of course. Years ago, in heat of an argument, the bastard had claimed to have had a vasectomy to spite her. Did he? And if so, how could his latest mistress claim to be pregnant? Not that it mattered anymore; she was well past the age to conceive and Cedric was the last person on earth she'd want to have a baby with—things worked out for the best there. She dialed Jimmy Nelson, and started right in when he picked up. "Jimmy, I need you to get all of Cedric's medical records. What I'm looking for in particular is to verify whether he had a vasectomy. I'm not sure what year. How long will it take?"

"A day, a week, or even a month. Let me make a few calls and I'll get back to you."

She'd been through all the tests back then and couldn't conceive. Cedric had refused to undergo any test and blamed her. Even back then she'd had her doubts he really wanted a baby.

* * * *

Jake was pounding away on the keyboard to update his report for Shamus when a knock at his office door interrupted him.

"What've you got, Kirk?"

"I've finished up with your list. None of the other women who posed has gotten a blackmail letter. My call put some of them in a panic mode, but I reassured them it was nothing. Do you have anything else for me to do before I start in on another case?"

He went to dismiss Kirk when a thought slammed into his head. "Has anyone checked the area around the motel for security cameras?"

"I don't know. I'll ask the sergeant."

"Hold up," Jake said, dialing Louie's extension.

"Did you do a run on the area around the motel for security cameras?"

"No, damn it. When the commissioner came on scene, I lost my train of thought. I only checked the motel itself. There weren't any."

"I'll put Kirk on it now." Jake hung up. "Kirk, it's your lead. Run with it."

"Thanks. How's the commissioner holding up?" Kirk asked, his shirt tails sticking out the back of his pants. Though Brown was young, you could pick out the cop in his brown eyes.

"As you'd expect. Is everyone ready for tomorrow?"

"Yes, the captain sent the memo. It's full dress uniforms."

"Let me know if anything turns up on the cameras."

Jake listed on a sheet of paper everything he'd learned about the case since Sunday. In the left-hand column he listed Doctor Lang's findings, the lab reports, and the kind of gun that had been used to kill Callie—a .22, small enough to fit into a woman's hand or purse. With the smell of bleach still in his nostrils and mind, Jake wondered if he'd overlooked Melinda due to their past relationship. Or was it his old-fashioned notion that women were the gentler sex? Though, if the job had taught him anything, it was that women could sometimes be more vicious than men. Did Melinda kill Callie, and if so, why? It kept coming back to money for him. Murder, money, blackmail, marriage, pictures, who took the pictures—Melinda took the pictures—Melinda needed money—did that make her a murderer?

Round and round he went, only the pictures pointed to Sal and Melinda. Had the killer pulled off the perfect crime? No, there had to be evidence, something he'd missed.

"Louie," he said as his friend picked up on his call. "Get your coat. I want to go over the crime scene again, and re-canvass the motel employees and surrounding residents."

"I'll meet you at the elevator, Jake. Afterward we'll get something to eat," Louie said with longing in his voice.

He'd forgotten about food, but the mention of it had the hunger pangs screaming out. Jake found Louie standing by the elevator. When the doors opened, it was full.

"Let's take the stairs," Jake said with a file tucked under his arm. In the garage he regretted the decision as the right side of his stomach sung out from him bouncing down the concrete steps.

"Did something strike you?" Louie asked.

"Yes, your words came back at me."

"Which ones?"

"You said the commissioner being on scene disturbed your concentration and routine. Didn't you also say the reporters were there before you even got a chance to report the crime—someone dirtied up the scene and compromised evidence? I don't believe in the perfect crime, so we had to miss something. I want to go in and process it as if we're first eyes on the victim."

"It makes sense. Is that the whole file?"

"Yes."

When they reached the motel, Louie went into the office to get the keys to room 142. Back in the car he said, "The manager's bitching he's losing income with the room tied up. He wants to know when we're going to release it. I gave him the standard answer."

"Let's do this."

Louie unlocked the door and stepped back. Jake stood on the threshold, scanning the interior as he imagined the body where it had been found. After a couple of minutes they stepped in and closed the door.

Jake opened the file, placed it on the dusty dresser, and scattered crime photos over the area. He'd memorized them during the week. He hated that he hadn't been first on scene, but he'd been out of town and nothing would change the circumstances.

He read through Louie's report, the CSIs' reports, and the ME's. Something, something, wasn't there—was there—was out of place, but damn it, what?

"Read this and tell me what's missing," Jake said.

He waited while Louie studied the file. Louie glanced up at him. "I'm not sure."

"Me either. What were the contents the ME listed from Callie's person, purse and/or pockets? Can you read them aloud?"

"A mirror, two tubes of lipstick, tissues, a checkbook, various credit cards from the wallet, along with her debit cards, a mini address book, a comb, a brush, the program from the Palace Theater, a couple of safety pins, and a hair clip."

"Nothing else?"

"No."

"Where's her cell phone or the room key? Did you recover her wedding band and engagement ring?"

"We recorded the phone was missing on Sunday. No trace was found when we had the phone company ping it. She wasn't wearing any jewelry when she was found."

"The room key?"

"There wasn't one," Louie said, scratching his chin. "I'm ashamed to say I missed it. Why would someone take it?"

"The killer had his or her reason. Find the answer, we find the murderer."

"You verified she rented the room and paid cash, correct? Also let's check in with the pawn shops for the jewelry."

"Yes. It was her."

"Keep reading."

Nothing else popped out at them.

"Why don't you take this end of the street, I'll take the other end, and we'll meet in the middle. Kirk's researching security cameras, but keep your eyes open for some."

A half hour later, Jake drummed his fingers on the steering wheel and stared out the window as he waited for Louie to finish up his last interview.

Louie jumped into car. "I have something new. How about you?"

"Nope, give."

"The woman next door said she's a permanent resident of the motel. I think she works her tricks out of there and splits it with the manager. Anyway, she said two women went into the room at different times."

"Can she identify them?" Jake asked, excitement building within him.

"All she can say is one was blonde and the other a brunette. I asked her their ages and she said she didn't get a good look at either one of them. The woman's a stoner and wouldn't be a reliable witness."

"It's something. Callie was a blonde and Edy is one. Melinda's a brunette, but so is Darcy McGuire, and Judy Eisenberg, along with several other women who had Melinda take their pictures. Let's use it as an excuse to go back in and re-question Melinda."

"We'll stop by her house tomorrow morning."

Chapter 16

The next morning, Melinda's car was gone when they drove up to her house. Jake peeked into the garage window, but she hadn't parked it there either. He knocked on the side door. Melinda didn't answer. He tented his hands over his eyes and swept his gaze over the half curtain into the kitchen. He stepped back, almost knocking Louie off the bottom step as he drew his gun.

"What's going on?" Louie slid his weapon from the holster, following Jake's lead.

"Take a look over the curtain. Someone's ransacked the place." Jake called it in before he broke the glass in the door.

He went left, Louie went right. They cleared each room before holstering their weapons. "Whoever did this is long gone."

"Jake, check this out," Louie said.

Louie handed him Melinda's purse and wallet. The money and credit cards were gone, but her driver's license was there, along with her medical card. If Melinda went on the run was she stupid enough to use her credit cards? Why leave your driver's license? It looked like a grab. Why Melinda? What was she involved in for someone to snatch her? Was it Sal Gallucci? It didn't feel right to him. Could it be another staged scene?

"Louie, we have cause, call in the CSIs. I want this place searched, especially the kitchen. Something happened in there for it to smell of bleach. And issue an APB on Melinda in case she rabbited."

"Why do you think she ran and wasn't taken?" Louie asked.

"It's off, don't you feel it?"

Louie's normally the one to detect if a scene reeked. Maybe...it's my dislike of Melinda.

"No."

"Call it in anyway. We need to uncover if someone died here."

He stepped outside with Louie and waited for the crime scene techs to arrive. *What do we know about the crime? One, Melinda took the victims' pictures. Two, Sal's her boyfriend. Three, I smelled bleach. Four, Sal's disappeared along with Melinda. Are they partners in crime? Or are they my next victims?*

"Louie, call Al Burke and have him and Kraus initiate another search around the motel for the gun."

"What are you after?"

"Sal's our prime suspect. He disappears, now Melinda. It only makes sense if they're involved in some way."

"Yeah...the case is leaning toward him, but her? I'm not seeing it," Louie said.

"Melinda had motive. She's smothered in debt. But where's the money and the gun from Callie's killing? We didn't find it here or at Sal's condo."

"I see Sal Gallucci for it. Ask yourself, how did Melinda overpower Callie, who was a few inches taller than her?" Louie asked.

"I'm not saying I have all the answers worked out. If Melinda turns up dead, that'll clear her," Jake said, using cop humor, and tossed Louie a smirk over his shoulder.

"Where are we going after the team arrives?"

"Melinda's studio. It also has to be searched."

"I'll call the judge for a warrant," Louie said and stepped away to make the call.

* * * *

Jake paced in front of Melinda's studio while he waited for the crime scene techs to arrive. The sign on the front door said closed. He'd scanned the inside when they arrived and found nothing had been disturbed that he could see. If it was a grab, did the person find what they were looking for at her home? If not, why not search her business?

"We're not going to find anything here." Jake pursed his lips while scanning the street. A white van with WPD posted on its sides in bold black letters pulled to the curb.

"You think she messed up her home?" Louie asked.

The CSI team got out of the van. Jake and Louie followed them into Melinda's studio. "It's too convenient, don't you think?"

"Yeah, the odor of bleach is still bothering me, but…Melinda a killer? We went to school with her, Jake."

"We went to school with George Spaulding too and look at what he did. She's mixed up in this, Louie. Consider it. I'm not saying I'm locked on the idea, the whole situation is hinky, to use your own words." His cell phone rang. "Carrington."

"Lieutenant, it's Kylie Shaker. We got blood here. Lots of it."

He thanked his lucky stars to have drawn the head crime-scene technician for this. "How fast can you process it to give me a type?"

"I'll see how many cases are before yours and give you a call," Kylie said. "Oh, and Lieutenant, the amount of blood we found says we'll find a body. No one loses that much without dying."

"Thanks, Kylie." *Did another woman die in Melinda's kitchen? If so, then who and when did it happen?*

He updated Louie when he hung up and before he called the station for an update on the APB—neither Melinda nor Sal had turned up yet.

"Louie, dig deeper into Tony Mastrianni's background. Was his gambling debt owed to the mob, and if so how much was he into them for, and is Melinda stuck paying another debt that's not on the books?"

"Christ, Jake, where'd that come from?" Louie said, rubbing his chin.

"Nothing points in that direction, but at least it's an avenue to pursue."

"I'll check it out."

His cell phone rang again. "Carrington."

"Lieutenant, it's Edy Dunstan. I received a blackmail letter a few minutes ago demanding five hundred thousand dollars. It doesn't make sense," Edy said, her voice clearly strained.

"Are there pictures with the note?" *Damn!* He'd thought she'd be a target. The blackmailers had worked their way around to her. How many more? And with each woman, depending on their wealth and standing in the community, the blackmailer demanded more money.

"Yes, but I didn't pose for these. They were shot while I was dressing. I can't make out the background, but I'm sure they were taken in my own dressing room."

"I'm at a crime scene now. I'll swing by in about an hour to pick them up. Can you put it into a paper bag to preserve it for me?"

"Yes, I'll cancel my plans and wait for you."

He hung up, stuck the phone back in his pocket, and changed his mind. He walked up to Louie. "I'm going to leave you here. That was Edy Dunstan. She received a blackmail letter. I'm going over to her house to pick it up. Coincidence that it comes on the same day Melinda is missing?"

"It is. I'll call you if the team turns up anything here. Oh, and Al's going to jump right on the debt issue," Louie said.

* * * *

Edy roamed the living room. She tried to place where she'd worn the undergarments and the outfits in the pictures. The nude photo with the background blurred pissed her off. The only places she'd been nude had been here, the hotel with Linden, and her doctor's office, but there she'd donned a johnny coat.

This has the markings of Cedric. Linden doesn't have the balls to do something like this—or does he?

A sense of relief filled her when the bell sounded. She rushed to answer it instead of waiting for Benita.

"Lieutenant, come in," she said. "Benita, please serve coffee in the living room."

"It's not necessary, Mrs. Dunstan," Jake said.

"Nonsense. After you view the pictures we'll have no secrets. The least we can do is share a cup of coffee and be on a first-name basis."

She took the burgundy couch, a large yellow envelope in her hands. Jake took the floral chair.

"Here." She leaned forward and handed him the photos and watched him study each one as she twisted her hands. His expression never changed. It impressed her.

"Any idea who might've sent these to you?" Jake asked.

"This is mean enough for it to be my husband. Lieutenant, there are only three places a person could've gotten a picture of me naked. Here, the doctor's office, or in the hotel with Linden Smith. The background is blurred, and I believe it was done on purpose. I have my security team scouring through the upstairs rooms for any kind of surveillance equipment." She ran a finger through the pearls on her neck.

"Can I speak with them?"

"Sure, they're upstairs. Follow me."

Jake stood and followed Edy from the room to the staircase in the hall and went up after her.

Edy stopped at the entrance to her bedroom. "This is my room. The one next door was Cedric's. I haven't slept with him in over a year." She entered the room.

"Jimmy, this is Lieutenant Carrington from WPD."

"Hi, Jimmy," Jake said, extending his hand.

"Good to see you again, Jake," Jimmy said, lowering the meter in his hand and gripping Jake's. A wiry little man, Jimmy Nelson ran the top security company in town and Jake respected Jimmy's talents.

"You two are acquainted?"

"Yes, you have the best," Jake said. "Did you find anything, Jimmy?"

"Yes, I've placed it on the table over there and the dust tells me it's been there awhile. There's more. I've got a guy in the other rooms."

"How sophisticated is the equipment?" Jake asked.

"Very, and it's expensive. The thing is, it sent the pictures directly to a cell phone. I already put a trace on the number to try to locate it."

"Mrs. Dunstan, your letter is similar to the one Callie received, but not exact. The amount demanded from her was much smaller, though her letter didn't state she'd receive another letter with instructions as yours did," Jake said. "I'd like to put a tap on your phone in case they call you. Is that okay?"

"I have one set up already, Jake. Mrs. Dunstan asked me to. She wants all the calls from Cedric Dunstan recorded," Jimmy said.

"Mrs. Dunstan, can you draft a letter for my file, granting me access to Jimmy's tap?"

"Yes, I want to splay the bastard and peel his skin off his body," Edy said, her nostrils flaring.

"I'll take care of it. It was great seeing you again, Jimmy. Mrs. Dunstan, I'd like a look at your husband's bedroom, if you don't mind?" Jake asked.

"Go ahead," Edy said.

"My guy Steve is in there working. Go in and introduce yourself," Jimmy said.

"I'll let myself out when I'm done," Jake said. "Jimmy, give me a detailed report of the equipment and cell number you discover. I'm going to pay Cedric a visit."

"Lieutenant, if you could hold off, I'd like the opportunity to give this information to my lawyer to shut Cedric down," Edy said.

"I'll tell you from experience that's not wise. You can shut him down with the lawyer but I also recommend you let us shut him down. He had to be anticipating your actions to have planted these devices."

"I agree with the lieutenant, Mrs. Dunstan," Jimmy said.

"Can I call you in an hour with my answer? I want him out of my life one way or another," Edy said, frowning.

"Okay, but I'm taking the letter with me. Whoever sent it broke the law. Extortion is a felony. If his fingerprints are on it, I'll have him arrested."

* * * *

Back in his office Jake sat and turned to his computer. Before he could hit the power switch, Louie knocked on his door.

"Did you find anything?" Jake asked.

"No, the place was clean. No one bothered to toss it. What did you get from Edy Dunstan?"

Jake passed him the letter enclosed in an evidence bag. "Hmmm! It's a higher dollar value, which is more logical since the woman's loaded. Who does she think sent it?"

"She believes it's her soon-to-be ex-husband. Hey, Jimmy Nelson was there checking for cameras." Jake handed Louie the pictures.

"Did he find any?"

"Yes, in her bedroom and shower," Jake said.

"These are damn invasive. The background has been blurred out. Does she know where they were taken?"

"There are three possible sites. Tomorrow, we'll interview Linden Smith, Cedric Dunstan, and her physician, though I'd stake my reputation they were taken in her bedroom. What have you dug up on Tony Mastrianni? Also, did Joel Bennett send over the sketch?"

"Gee, Jake, I got back here the same time you did. Cut me some slack. Joel said the hooker never showed. The manager said she checked out. I'll need to hunt her down." Louie said, pulling on his bottom lip.

"We can hit the motel first thing tomorrow. I'm going to call Melinda's credit card companies to see if she's charged any hotel fees or fuel fill-ups in the last few hours. You keep digging on Tony. Let me know if you find anything."

Louie left his office; Jake flipped on his computer and opened a new file, labeled it *Edy Dunstan*, and started typing in his notes and impressions. Edy's note felt different than the ones Darcy and Callie had received. The sentence construction was different, as well as the wording. What did Cedric Dunstan get if Edy divorced him? He picked up his desk phone and dialed her.

"Mrs. Dunstan, it's Lieutenant Carrington. What does Cedric get if you divorce?"

"Nothing. He signed a prenup. And he broke the one condition laid out in it by cheating."

"Are any of the property or bank accounts in his name?"

"No, my father made me set things up this way to protect me."

"Does he have any money of his own?" Jake asked.

"No, he goes through his salary as if it were water. Why?"

"I'm curious. Does he know how much you're worth?"

"I'd say no, but he could've gone through my papers. I keep them in my desk in my room."

"Okay, thanks. I want to add all this to your file. Did Jimmy find anything else today?"

"Yes, a few cameras in the kitchen and living room with audio equipment. Jimmy's also taking the pictures to a computer expert to see if he can clear up the background some." Edy let out a heavy sigh.

Jake wished he could wipe away Edy's humiliation. Cedric Dunstan had committed the ultimate betrayal if it turned out to be him. "If I have any other questions, I'll give you a call. Oh, is Jimmy leaving some of his guys around there?"

"Yes, he and my father want to make sure Cedric doesn't come back around."

"Good, take care."

He sat back, put his feet up on his desk, closed his eyes, and played around with the possibility that Callie's and Edy's cases were not related. Edy's pictures had a meaner tone to them and weren't doctored. If Jimmy proved they had been taken in her home, it would suggest her husband, and not his current suspect Sal. Had Cedric Dunstan tried to make Edy's letter a copycat crime? Jake hadn't released the contents of the letter, but knew from experience that for the right price information leaked to the media all the time. The newspapers had speculated about it, which told him it came from a cop. Edy's and Callie's letters had discrepancies, but they were similar enough for them to have been sent by the same suspect. He'd keep an open mind and open suspect list until proven otherwise. He couldn't rule anyone out.

"Ya got me doing all the running around while you sleep?" Louie said, standing in his doorway with his arms crossed.

Jake opened one eye and peered at Louie. "Yep, it's one of the advantages of being the boss. What did you turn up?"

"Tony didn't owe the mob. He played in small games around the state and always paid his debts, not his bills."

"Okay, let's move on. It was a long shot anyway." Jake slumped back in his chair. His stomach shouted out for relief from the constant twisting and turning he'd put it through today.

Al Burke's Jupiter-sized belly preceded him into the room when he rushed into Jake's office. "Look what I've found." He held up a pink wallet.

"Where'd you find it?" Jake asked.

"I saw a kid playing with it two blocks from the crime scene as I drove by. I stopped and asked him where he got it."

"And..."

"It matches the commissioner's description of Callie Blake's wallet. The kid found this yesterday in the street by his house."

"Any identification or credit cards in it?" Jake asked.

"No, the kid said it was empty."

Damn, it was stupid and careless of the killer, but good for us. Hopefully we'll find fingerprints.

"Good. Send it down to the lab with a rush on it. Better yet, take it to the lab yourself, and offer up a bribe if you have to. I'll spring for a bottle or whatever is needed." Jake's mind spun in every direction. "Al, have them check the sewers around the crime scene for the gun."

"Won't the lab boys love me? This might cost you big," Al said.

"Try to keep the cost reasonable if you can. Now, get out of here and call me on my cell with the results as soon as you get them, Al."

Jake's email pinged. He opened it and read the update from the bank. Damn it, Melinda hadn't used her cards since Wednesday. If she did kill Callie, she had twenty-five thousand dollars with her to stay under the radar. Tomorrow he'd need to send out a BOLO to the tristate areas and hope something showed up.

Jake shut off his office lights. He called it a day, blackmail and murder gnawing at his mind.

Chapter 17

Jake snuggled into Mia as he eyed the clock. Soon he'd have to get up, get ready, and stand as an honorary pallbearer for Callie Blake. Due to his injury, he couldn't help lift the casket. Callie was a woman he'd respected, and whose company he enjoyed—now she was gone, taken in a flash by greedy hands. What ran through her head when the small piece of metal slammed into her body? Did she experience that moment of clarity, knowing that her life was over, the same way he had when the knife plunged into his gut?

It'd been eight days since the gala. A party Callie had worked hard to pull together. It saddened him that he'd known the victim. Callie, a wonderful, loving person, who had done nothing wrong to anyone, killed because she wanted to surprise her husband.

And today, with the whole department there, he'd have to face superiors, friends, and foes alike. He wouldn't be able to work the case, his attention divided, as he stayed on his guard and fielded questions about his health and the investigation. Moments like this with Mia balanced the scales and kept him on an even keel.

He swung his feet over the side of the bed. Brigh glanced up from her bed in the corner, her sad brown eyes searching his to see if food was in her future.

"Come on, I'll let you out." Jake stepped from the room, Brigh at his feet.

Jake opened the back door to let Brigh out to do her business, and allowed the early November chill to sweep over him. He backed into the kitchen and took out Brigh's bag of food, pouring some into her dish. At the sound of her food hitting the dish, Brigh ran into the house and nudged him aside.

"Ah, all you want me for is the food." Jake ran his hand over her coat. "Enjoy."

He obliged the pooch, put the coffee on and headed into the shower.

On his next visit to the doctor, he hoped he'd be able to do away with the waterproof bandage protecting the wound. He finished toweling off as Mia walked in.

"What time will we meet up?" she asked.

"Whenever the burial ends, I suppose. Do you want to head out together for the reception or do you want to meet at the AOH club?"

"Want to spell that one out?"

He forgot at times, Mia wasn't from the area. "Ancient Order of Hibernians, otherwise known as the Irish club."

"Good to know."

"You don't have to put yourself through this." Jake rubbed his hands up and down her arms.

"Jake, I met the woman and liked her. I'm also going for you. And remember, you promised not to help lift the casket."

"Mia, I'm not a kid. I understand my temporary limitations, so please back off on this issue. It's driving me nuts."

"I will, until I don't." With a flirtatious smile, she closed the door in his face.

* * * *

He reported to Sergeant Nickelson, who had coordinated the troops. There'd be three pallbearers on each side of the casket, and Jake in full dress uniform in front, escorting the body into the church and then again at the cemetery. Not only had all of Wilkesbury's finest turned out, so had many from all 169 communities throughout the state.

It'd been a while since he had to wear his uniform. The last time it had been to bury Officer Audrey Knowlton, who had been killed in the line of duty three years before, while protecting a clerk at a convenience store from a drugged-up shooter.

The noise level in the gymnasium at Crimson High School buzzed to deafening decibels as cops from all shifts caught up with friends and coworkers. Jake leaned on the wall, away from the crowd, to conserve his energy. Assignments had been handed out. He'd tucked his in his pocket while watching Louie work his way across the room.

"Several of the guys were asking for you," Louie said.

"I'm taking a quiet minute before it starts," Jake said. "When are we scheduled…"

"Attention everyone, the buses are outside to transport us to the church, and after the burial they will bring you back here to retrieve your cars. Please go to your assigned buses now. The honorary and regular pallbearers will ride in the limo and will be transported to the funeral home to accompany the hearse to the church. Any questions?" Sergeant Nickelson asked.

No one asked a question or made a comment.

"Okay, let's head out."

* * * *

The pallbearers wheeled the casket into the church through the double doors. Jake and the honor guards moved aside for the priest to greet the family and perform the introductory rites. The six pallbearers stood three on each side as Jake and Officer Fairway took up their positions in front of the coffin, behind the altar boy with the cross.

The priest walked behind the casket, sprinkling it with holy water during the procession to the altar. The family, wrapped in their grief, marched tearfully behind Father Nardonni, who'd officiate the requiem mass.

At the front of the altar the undertaker locked the wheels on the church truck supporting the casket. As instructed, each pallbearer found their seats in the left pews in the front row. The immediate family was helped into the front right-side pews. The rest of the mourners filed into the remaining rows on either side of the church.

With pomp and ceremony the mass progressed and the priest's words hummed on. Jake's mind wandered back in time to when the words had washed over him, and he questioned whether there was a God—one who allowed such atrocities to happen to innocent people. Deep down he understood what Todd probably felt today as the priest's words droned on. It took him years to understand the need for the mass, but in his teens it had torn at him during those three days of greeting people at the wake and then the funeral, and lastly the luncheon. Long days followed by months of quiet time, when everyone backed away to allow the family to grieve in private. As if they'd ever recover and life would go back to being normal ever again. It never had for him, since Eva's murder.

At the end of the mass and the blessing, the coffin came back down the aisle, to be loaded into the hearse and taken to the cemetery.

The final act of closure—only it never is.

* * * *

Jake ached to sit as the graveside service concluded. The doctor had mentioned on his last visit that he'd be starting physical therapy soon, but working this case had postponed it. People hung around talking, stalling, not wanting to be the first to arrive at the club for drinks and food. Jake pulled Mia aside.

"We have time, why don't we stop by the house and drop off one of the cars?"

"Good idea, and from the looks of it, you need some downtime," Mia said, taking his arm.

Mia drove him to the school parking lot where he had left his car earlier. He leaned over and kissed her. "I'll see you at the house."

He parked in his home garage fifteen minutes later and climbed out. Mia pulled in a few minutes later.

"I thought we'd take your car," Jake said.

"Why? You love to drive," she said.

"I'm going to pop a pill to be ahead of the pain. I'll be a minute."

In the bathroom he tilted the bottle. A couple of pills fell into his hand. Jake took one, placed it on his tongue and swallowed. It annoyed the hell out of him that he needed them in the first place. It wasn't like him to succumb to pain. He placed his hands on the counter and leaned toward the mirror, stared, and tried to figure out exactly when he'd become a pansy. He screwed the top back on the bottle, jiggled the pills for a second or two before he put the bottle into the medicine cabinet and rejoined Mia.

They drove to the Ancient Order of the Hibernians (AOH) and found all the good parking spaces gone. He directed Mia to the far corner of the lot. The whole department would be here, and by the end of the day, those not going on duty would be three sheets to the wind. Functions like this made him edgy. Idiots like Sergeant Miller and his cronies who, when liquored up, might sound off and try to pick a fight. It wasn't the time or place for his feud with Miller to come to a head and he'd do his best to fend him off. But it'd be coming to a head soon.

"So do me a favor. No matter what, stick by my side," Jake said.

"I have no plans to be anywhere else," Mia said as he helped her from the driver's seat.

At the entrance, he signed the guest book for both of them and scouted the crowd for Louie and Sophia.

"Looking for someone?" Louie tapped him on the shoulder from behind.

"You. Where're we sitting?" Jake and Mia followed Louie to the front of the room.

Their table sat a few feet away from the commissioner, his family, and the brass. Jake greeted Sophia with a kiss on the cheek. Mayor D'Angelo sat with Todd in a show of support. *Hypocrite*, Jake thought. Only a few days ago the mayor had hinted he wanted Jake to arrest Todd to shut down the media. He continued to scan the room. Shamus and Darcy also sat with the family. It made sense to him. Darcy and Callie had been best friends their whole lives.

"Do you want a drink?" Jake asked.

"I'll get them, you sit," Mia said.

"I think I can carry a couple of drinks, darling. You visit with Sophia." Jake's shoulders squared as he stepped away from the table.

"You didn't have to bite her head off," Louie said.

"I'm telling you, the woman's driving me nuts the way she hovers over me as if I'm on my last leg."

"She cares, Jake. You gave us all a scare. It was touch and go for three days there in the ICU. Let her fuss and stop picking on her."

Jake bellied up to the bar, ordered Mia's vodka and tonic, and a water for himself. As he moved aside to let the next person order, someone bumped him hard. He swung around, spilling some of the drinks he held, and came face-to-face with Sergeant Ralph Miller. Jake stared him in the eye for a second. They'd never be friends or respected colleagues after Jake had got Ralph's brother kicked off the force, but at some point he expected Ralph to move on.

"Close quarters, huh, Ralph?"

"A bit, but it's the stench that got to me," Ralph Miller said, grinning to his friends.

"Then you should change deodorant," Jake said with a feral grin as he turned away to pick up a few napkins.

"Jake..."

"Listen, Ralph, this isn't the time or the place. But it's coming..." Jake leaned in and whispered in Ralph's ear. "Show some respect to the commissioner and to the uniform. Not here, not now." The idiot had to have had a few drinks in him.

"Asshole," Ralph said loud enough for Jake to hear. Jake let it roll off as he stepped around Miller and walked away.

"For a second there, I thought you'd come to blows," Louie said.

"It's coming, but I'm not engaging until I'm up to full strength. And a funeral isn't the place to air personal grievances. I wish Ralph would give it up. Why doesn't he admit his brother screwed up?"

"If Roger was your brother, would you?" Louie asked.

"I guess not, but it's getting ridiculous." Jake stopped a few feet before he got to their table.

"What's ridiculous?"

He swore Mia's hearing had to be sharper than a bat's. "Nothing. I'm starving, how about you?" he asked, still standing with the drinks in his hands. "Let's get in line." He placed the drinks on the table.

Several hours later, Jake was ready to scream *hallelujah* when the function wound down. He and Mia said their goodbyes to the commissioner.

"What's the rush?" Louie asked.

"I'm tired," Jake said.

"Sophia wanted me to ask you and Mia over for drinks," Louie said.

"Some other time, Louie. You're welcome to come over to my house, but I need to put my feet up." Jake hated to admit it, but the day had worn on him.

Chapter 18

On Sunday morning the house phone woke her. Edy tried to untangle herself from the covers as she rolled over to answer it. "Hello."

"Please don't hang up. I'm not asking for another chance, I blew it this time. I know that. I'd like to meet with you and discuss whether you've given any thought to adopting the baby."

"We have nothing to discuss, Cedric. The child's yours, not mine. You've got to think me a fool if you imagined I'd take that slut's child, or yours. Don't call again."

"After twenty years of marriage, that's it? We need to discuss what you're going to give me to get rid of me."

"Exactly what you've given me—nothing," she said in a controlled tone, the lieutenant's warning holding her back from engaging him more.

"I'm going to drag this divorce out for years, Edy, if you think I'm walking away empty-handed. And when I'm done, you'll never be able to show your face anywhere. I'll get what's mine."

"You signed the prenup. And you're the one who couldn't keep it in his pants." *For too many years I've allowed my love for him to cloud my judgment. Well, not anymore.*

"You'll regret this."

Edy jerked the phone from her ear as he slammed his phone down. She checked the time. A little after eight on a Sunday morning was a little too early to call her dad. She'd wait until nine to call him to give him an update. Together they'd make Cedric's life a living hell.

She climbed out of bed, tugged her robe off the bedpost, and went downstairs for coffee. The purpose of Cedric's call baffled her.

"Good morning, Benita."

"Morning, ma'am. I'll pour." Benita pushed up from the kitchen chair, closing the newspaper.

"No, I'm good. Make sure all the doors are locked at all times, okay?"

"Yes. What would you like for breakfast?"

"Nothing. I'm going to go up and shower first. Are you going out today?"

"Yes, my sister and I are going shopping," Benita said.

"Well, enjoy yourself."

Halfway up the stairs, she realized Cedric had to have figured out that she had disabled the cameras yesterday. Had he been waiting for her to explode or mention the blackmail letter? *Lord, I should've worked in a vague reference to see how he'd react. Isn't it brilliant of me to think of it after the fact?*

She wondered what Cedric, a vindictive man, had cooked up for her. She'd have to wait and see. The sneaky little weasel didn't worry her. *I hold all the cards*, she thought, with a savage vengeance eating away at her heart. Then she paused. *Except for the photos.*

* * * *

Jake woke refreshed, stretched, then inched his hand to the other side of the bed, only to find it empty, the space cold. *Mia up before me?* Jake rolled toward the clock, stunned at the time. He got up and went down the hallway to the kitchen.

"Half the day is gone. Why didn't you wake me?"

"You needed the rest. What do you want to eat?" Mia asked.

"Why don't I treat you to breakfast or brunch? Where do you want to go?"

"Sit down. I can cook breakfast without screwing it up. This way you can read the paper and take some downtime today. We don't have to be anywhere. Isn't it glorious?"

"Mia, I have to go in and work. I lost a whole day yesterday. I thought before I went in we'd have a relaxing meal that neither one of us had to cook."

"I still want to cook. Sit." She placed a cup of coffee in front of him, turned and got busy at the stove, cooking.

"What's wrong?"

"Nothing…yesterday…I noticed you're taking more pain pills than you normally do. It's easy to get dependent on them. When's your next doctor visit?"

"Mia, it's been a tough week, but me hooked on prescription drugs? That's crazy."

"I didn't say hooked. I understand they ease the discomfort, but a stomach wound can get infected, and it's quite painful. I think it's prudent that you have the doctor examine it this week, especially since you returned to work without his clearance."

Every muscle in his body tightened, his fight-or-flight instinct kicking in. He didn't want to argue.

He took her hand in his, raised it to his lips. "I'm sorry. I'll call the doctor this week, I promise."

He shoveled in the eggs she'd cooked then headed to the shower. He got dressed and left for the station to put time in on his cases.

* * * *

Jake dropped down in his chair, turned on his computer and read his emails. According to the database, the only suspect with a record was Sal Gallucci. He kept coming back to Gallucci. If Gallucci wasn't the killer, he was involved. Jake's gut had told him from the beginning to dig deeper into Gallucci's background.

And he'd let Sal Gallucci slip through his fingers.

Damn, with Melinda gone, his two leads proved worthless. *Bingo, her mother*, he thought, and typed in Mrs. Blair's name and the old address. What was her first name? Did she still reside in town? He scrolled through the list of names and hit on the right address. Joanne Blair, according to the DMV database records, hadn't moved. He scribbled down her number and dialed.

"Hello?" A blast from his past sounded in his ear.

"Mrs. Blair, this is Jake Carrington. I don't know if you remember me."

"I remember, Jake. What do you want?"

Hmmm! She hadn't forgiven him for her daughter's transgression. He'd wondered what she thought she saw that day she burst into Melinda's room. Nothing happened, but he too wondered if Mrs. Blair hadn't come in at that moment if things would've gone any further. "I'm trying to locate Melinda. Her house has been ransacked, and I haven't been able to get in touch with her. Do you know where she is?"

"Ransacked? Is she okay?"

"I don't know, I haven't been able to contact her."

"The last I knew she had a fancy party and a wedding last weekend. Her normal routine after a job is to process the pictures right away. She doesn't like to be disturbed while she works. Have you checked her studio? She's most likely there."

"Yes, we checked. Do you know her boyfriend, Sal Gallucci?" Jake asked, switching subjects.

"I never heard her mention the name. What's really up, Jake?"

"Her house was broken into. I'm doing a wellness check. Do you want to go through it with me and see if anything is missing?"

"When can I meet you there?"

"Anytime. What's good for you, Mrs. Blair?"

"Now you've got me worried."

"Do you want me to pick you up?"

"No, I'm quite capable of driving myself," Mrs. Blair said. He hadn't missed the sarcasm in her voice.

Jake drove across town and sat out in front of Melinda's home while he waited for Mrs. Blair to arrive. A blue foreign compact car pulled into the driveway. Mrs. Blair stepped out. Her short salt-and-pepper hair blew in the light breeze. She had her wool coat buttoned up to her neckline.

"Do you have a set of keys?"

"Yes. How come the window in the door is boarded up?" Mrs. Blair asked as she walked up to examine it.

"I broke it yesterday when I spotted the mess in there and no one answered my knock."

"Why didn't you call then? Are you two dating again?"

"No, we're not. Mrs. Blair, there are procedures in place. I thought Melinda was in immediate danger when I peered over the curtain and saw the mess."

"I don't have the front door key. We'll need to get in the side door." She stopped and threw him a scorching glance over her shoulder. "But you're saying you *thought* she was in danger. But what you're not telling me—*is* she in danger?"

"I'm not sure. It's the reason I called you."

After she unlocked the door, Jake stepped in front of her and scanned the kitchen before he allowed her to enter. He surveyed the place and pressed a hand over Mrs. Blair's as she latched on to his arm. "This isn't Melinda's doing. My daughter is a neat woman. What's that stain on the floor by the refrigerator? It wasn't there last week."

How much did he tell her? "It tested positive for blood. I have the lab typing it now. What's Melinda's blood type?"

"She's O positive. You think it's hers?" Mrs. Blair whispered as she swayed.

Jake took hold of her arm and led her to a chair. "No, but I want to be sure. The lab promised to have the results by tomorrow at noon."

"And until then I'm supposed to do what? Pray my daughter's not hurt?"

"Mrs. Blair, the whole department is searching for her, though it appears one of her suitcases is gone. Do you know if she had a full set?"

"She did. I gave her a red plaid set for Christmas."

"What did it include?" Jake pressed.

"There are three, one large, one midsize, and an overnight case. Which one is missing?"

"The midsize one—I'm hoping she took it to go away for the weekend, and someone broke in and…" He didn't know how to finish the sentence.

"I know you're a homicide cop, Jake. What do you think happened to my daughter?"

"I don't have any idea. My goal is to verify she's okay after finding her place in disarray."

"You never said why you were here to begin with. What business did you have with Melinda?"

Ah, do I tell her she's a suspect in a murder? A victim? No. "She photographed the woman who was murdered last week."

"For God's sake, you think she killed the woman?" Mrs. Blair screeched.

"No, I don't. The woman who was killed was found with pictures of her posing with a man, who I later learned was Melinda's boyfriend. I need to find him."

"Melinda doesn't have a boyfriend. She dates, mostly her models, but since Tony died she has no desire or need for another man. She's never been good at picking the right kind of guy."

He took the veiled insult and pushed on. "She did verify she had dated the man in the picture, but broke it off. He's disappeared, and now Melinda has too. I need to find her to make sure she's all right."

Mrs. Blair slowly pushed her body from the chair and walked through the rest of the house. She found some of Melinda's clothes and jewelry missing, but nothing else.

When they returned to the kitchen, Jake said, "One more thing, Mrs. Blair. Do you have a list of Melinda's friends?"

"You're worrying me, Jake. I don't have a list of them but there's her address book on the counter," Mrs. Blair said, pointing to the countertop. "I'm giving you permission to take it. Make sure you find my daughter alive and healthy."

"I hope to, and thank you for the book. Here's a receipt for it." Jake handed her his scribbled note. There was nothing else he could accomplish here. He escorted Mrs. Blair to her car after she locked up the house.

"Call me as soon as you have a match on the blood-type. I'm not going to be able to sleep tonight worrying about her."

"I will."

He sat in his car as Joanne Blair drove away.

* * * *

She'd go crazy if she had to hang out in the house all day. Edy picked up her cell phone, fingered down to Linden's number. She put the phone back on the table and grabbed the remote but didn't switch on the television.

"What the hell? I need a distraction." A little after eleven she plucked the phone back up and dialed Linden without hesitation.

"Hi," Linden said in a faraway voice.

"Am I interrupting anything?"

"No, I'm surprised you called on a Sunday."

"I'm legally separated now, so weekends aren't a problem anymore." Edy stared out the front window at an unfamiliar black car parked across the street. Probably the security company or a visitor, she concluded. She brought her attention back to Linden and didn't give it another thought. "I called to see if you were free to do something today."

"I'm sorry, I have plans. In fact, I'm out with friends. We can get together tomorrow for lunch."

"Tomorrow's not good. Enjoy yourself," she said, ready to hang up.

"Edy, if you'd called earlier I could've canceled."

"Linden, it's fine, I'm fine, it's not a big deal. Take care." She ended the call without waiting for his reply.

A flush crept up her neck, to her cheeks. She must have sounded desperate for him to have apologized. Once there was a time she'd had to fight off her suitors. When had that changed, and since when had she had to chase down people to socialize with on a Sunday afternoon?

Lunch sounded good, even if she had to eat alone. Where to go was the question. She didn't want to run into any acquaintances this afternoon. How pathetic she'd look alone, after filing for divorce. She didn't know if word had gotten out about it, but people might assume she'd been the one dumped.

Edy stepped away from the window, her phone still clutched in her hand. A drink was in order. After mixing a scotch and water, she took it upstairs to dress, still undecided where she'd go, but she had to get out of the house. The walls were closing in on her.

Chapter 19

Jake put the car in gear, then jammed on the brakes when his cell phone started vibrating on the passenger seat.

"Lieutenant Carrington," he said without looking at the caller ID.

"Lieutenant, it's Dispatch. There's a body in a parked car on Industrial Lane behind the abandoned glass factory."

Damn it, and on my day off. "Male or female?" He checked his watch: two fifteen. He made a note of it on the notepad resting on the seat.

"The reporting officer didn't say."

"I'm in the east end. My ETA is ten minutes. Give Sergeant Romanelli a call."

Jake stuck the bubble on the top of his car and hit the sirens. He drove toward the crime scene. He crossed under the I-84 bridge before he spotted the flashing lights a quarter mile past the entrance ramp. The cruiser had blocked the road to civilians. He parked beside a patrol car and climbed out with his notebook in hand. He hadn't realized how long he'd been with Mrs. Blair.

"Hey, Murphy, where's the body?"

"It's down the side street under the overpass, Lieutenant," Officer Murphy said, pointing to a burned-out car as they hoofed it toward the crime scene.

"Damn it, no one said it was a crisper." Jake clenched his jaw.

"It's not. Someone tried to make it one, but the fire died out and left the body intact for the most part."

At least something was on his side. Jake leaned into the car and took a whiff. The accelerant used was gasoline, he guessed. Jake tapped his finger on his notebook, taking in the body. There went his case against

Sal Gallucci. The poor bastard was deader than a doorknob—and slightly charred. Did Melinda kill him or was she his next victim?

He dialed Louie. "How long before you get here? I've got a dead body," Jake said before Louie greeted him. "It's Sal Gallucci. I'm on Industrial Lane."

"I've been notified. I just got on the highway. Give me about ten minutes with all these Sunday drivers dragging their feet."

Jake hung up and faced the assistant ME. "Hey, Tim."

"I thought you were tied up on the Blake case," Assistant Medical Examiner Dr. Tim McCoy said tugging his coat across his pot belly.

"I am. He's my main suspect."

"Ah, well, a fly in the ointment, is he?" McCoy scratched his chest. He stood five ten, his middle-age paunch hanging over his belt, but he looked shorter standing next to Jake. McCoy's thin brown hair barely covered his head. Jake wanted only Lang, the head ME, or McCoy, the assistant ME, working his scenes.

"Yep."

Jake observed the crime scene from all angles while McCoy examined the body and his assistants removed Sal Gallucci from the car.

Why kill Gallucci? What did he know? Did he and his accomplice have a fight? Was Gallucci going to rat him out? Around and around his thoughts went. Jake's mind spun toward Melinda as the killer, not a victim, unless, of course, her body turned up. Killing Gallucci made no sense. He'd have to go back to the beginning to see what he'd missed. *Damn it, what was it?*

Deep in thought, he didn't hear Louie walk up behind him. "Fill me in," Louie said.

Jake glanced down at the body on the stretcher. "Someone unsuccessfully tried to torch the car. As far as I can see there are no cameras in this area, not even on the building over there. Traffic cams are aimed only toward the highway. It's a good dump site. That tells me someone's familiar with the area to have dumped him here."

"Anyone who lives in town knows the area," Louie said.

"Exactly my point, and it's not too far to walk to catch a bus or walk home."

"Jake, the man wasn't killed here. He lost a tremendous amount of blood," McCoy said.

"Thanks, Doc. How'd he die? Can you type him right away? We might already have the crime scene," Jake said.

"The wound's been compromised. I'll determine the cause back at the morgue. The area's charred, but my first guess is he took a bullet to the chest. I'll know more once I post him," McCoy said, packing up his medical bag.

"If the bullet is still in him, will you be able to determine if it's the same type of bullet that killed Callie Blake?"

"We'll see if it's still in him, and what condition it's in," McCoy said, not committing one way or another. "Give me a couple of hours."

Louie had waited McCoy out. "You're back to Melinda?"

"Seems like it. If the killer killed Sal and not Melinda, where is she?" Jake asked.

"I'll check but last I did there wasn't anything on the BOLO," Louie said.

"We need to start a search of surrounding states. If I'm not mistaken, Melinda skipped."

Jake was more convinced than ever Melinda was his killer. But how was she able to shoot the victims without a fight? He'd need to ask Dr. Lang if the gunshot had an upward trajectory on Callie Blake.

"Jake, check this out," Louie said from behind Gallucci's car.

He walked to the area where Louie stood. Louie pointed to a briefcase the other CSI tech, Willie Phelps, held in his gloved hands.

"Has it been dusted yet?" Jake asked.

"Yes. Do you want it opened?" Willie asked.

"Please," Jake said.

Willie lifted the case onto the trunk of the car and worked the lock until it popped open. He took out photograph after photograph of the city's most prominent women.

Louie let out a low whistle. "Damn, Jake. He could've only gotten these from one place or person."

"I'm already leaning that way," Jake said, staring at the photographs. "We're going to have to go back and interview every single wedding guest and see if anyone noticed if Melinda had the bruised eye before the incident with the drunk."

"I'll start Al and Kraus on that," Louie said. "You have any idea where she'd go? A place she has a fondness for?"

"I'm racking my brain, but so far I haven't come up with anything." Jake's chest tightened as he searched his mind for a memory, or a tidbit of information to track her down. *I'm a freaking idiot. I let her slip through my fingers.*

"Give it a rest, it will come to you," Louie said as if reading his mind.

"You do the search for next of kin, I'll talk to his New Jersey buddies again in the hopes that Sal talked about Melinda."

There went his Sunday. Before he got too involved, he dialed Mia's cell phone number. "Hi, hon, I'm going to be more than a couple of hours," he said as Mia answered the call.

"Who died?"

"My prime suspect in the Callie Blake murder case." He walked to his car, sat with his legs hanging out, his body facing the crime scene. It bothered him. Why kill Gallucci? What purpose did it serve? Keep him quiet, and keep more money for yourself, or had that been the plan all along?

"Ouch, where does that leave you?" Mia asked.

"It leads back to my gut instinct, which I should've followed in the first place." Jake rubbed the back of his neck.

"Monday morning quarterbacking is great. Don't beat yourself up. Follow the trail," Mia said. "Who killed him?"

"I believe it's the same person who killed Callie Blake, but I ignored my gut because I didn't think the culprit could be a woman. I have to get going. I'll see you when I see you."

Two hours later, after exhausting his search of the area, Jake drove to the station to start the calls. He parked in his reserved spot in the garage, a perk of his position. Detective Burke waited at the elevator, repeatedly slamming the up button.

"It doesn't make it go any faster, Al." Jake slipped his hands into his pockets.

"But it makes me feel better. I heard you lost your suspect," Al said. "Tough luck, huh?"

Jake gave Al a sideward glance but didn't respond. The elevator doors slid open. Together they stepped into the empty space.

"Have you started on the list?"

"LT, you're killing me, I only got off the phone with the sergeant a few minutes ago. I have seventy-five percent of the neighborhood interviews done. Kraus has been running names and addresses from home. We're working our way through the wedding guests. It will be a few hours or days before we have anything for you," Al said with a pained expression. "Kraus will be joining me in a half hour, when his wife gets home from work. It should go faster with him here."

"Okay, I'll be in my office. When I finish my calls, I'll grab a few names to help out," Jake said.

They parted ways in the bullpen. Al went to his desk, Jake to his office. He didn't jump right in. Instead he gazed out his window at nothing in particular. The hair on the back of his neck lifted, sending a sense of doom into the air. Would there be a third body? He whirled from the window, searched his notes for Darcy and Edy's numbers.

He dialed the McGuire home first. "Captain, has Darcy received any more letters?"

"No, why?"

He explained Gallucci's death and his current theory.

"I'll make sure she's safe, you check in with Edy," McGuire said.

Jake dialed Edy Dunstan next. The home phone rang and rang, and went to voicemail. It surprised him that the housekeeper hadn't picked up.

He tried her cell phone number, got voicemail again. "Mrs. Dunstan, this is Lieutenant Carrington. Please return my call as soon as you retrieve your messages."

Now he'd wait.

Logic brought him back to the money. Who needed it the most? Melinda. How much did she have left from the original twenty-five thousand dollars? Would Melinda go for the one-hundred-thousand-dollar payday or the five-hundred-thousand—who made the easier target? And would he be able to use the drop-off to trap the killer?

"Yes?" he said, looking up from his report.

"I notified his mother. Mrs. Gallucci said she felt it in her bones when he hadn't called her in days," Louie said.

"How many days?"

"She said three. And Sal never went more than two without checking up on her."

"Kraus arrive yet?"

"No."

"Why don't you pitch in and take a few of the wedding-guest interviews from Al. I'll join you after I connect with Edy Dunstan and Sal's friends."

"Why Edy?" Louie asked.

"I checked up on Darcy, and now I want to check in with Edy and make sure she's okay. Twenty-five thousand dollars doesn't hit me as enough money for Melinda to vanish. The killer would need more."

"If the killer is Melinda," Louie said.

"No, any killer. I'm not drawing the net in yet. Melinda could still be a victim or the top suspect. Until we find her we won't know. We need to keep searching."

Al Burke burst into Jake's office. "Hey, I got one."

"Who?"

"A friend of the bride's said the photographer was in the ladies' room applying concealer over concealer before the bride and groom showed up for the nuptials. When the friend commented, the photographer said she'd worked late the night before the wedding and wanted to hide her black circles."

"Did she remember which eye she was applying it to?"

"No, but she said she'd think about it and call me back," Al said.

"You think she killed Callie before the wedding?" Louie asked.

"I do. She had plenty of time to go between the bride's mother's house and groom's mother's house to take pictures before she was due at the place where the ceremony and reception were held."

"Humph! If another body turns up, I'm betting it's going to be Melinda," Louie said.

Jake and Louie most times were on the same page when it came to an investigation.

"Why?" Jake asked.

"Well, the blood at her house. The motive—money is too obvious, it's as if someone had set her up. And if you timed her movements from the bride's house to the groom's, there's no room for error," Louie said.

"We'll need to drive it. How long does it take to photograph the bride, then the groom before a wedding?"

"I'll give Sophia a call and ask her." Louie pulled his cell phone from his jacket pocket.

Jake listened in as Louie talked to his wife. *Who's right, him or me?*

"Sophia said it depends." Louie tossed him a smirk.

"Well, that clears that up," Jake said.

"It can take up to an hour, but no more than two at the bride's house, before a photographer either goes to the church or groom's house to photograph him."

"Hmmm! Three hours or less, that's plenty of time. We need to check in with the mothers again, they'd know."

"I'll handle it," Louie said as he left the office.

He hoped Louie'd been right about Melinda's innocence, but it didn't look that way to him.

Chapter 20

Edy picked the corner table with a view of the whole room at the restaurant in Wansley Park in West Hartford. The park had been decorated with autumn plants in reds and oranges to brighten up the grounds since the trees had lost their colorful leaves. She entertained herself by eavesdropping on conversations at the surrounding tables. She'd planned to shop until she realized the mall closed early on Sunday. If she had planned it better, she'd be in New York at a play or something. The city never closed as Connecticut did on Sundays. Here the pickings were slim. Home didn't entice her. Who could she drop in on? No, she'd go to a movie. She hadn't been in years.

She lingered over dessert, ignoring the guests staring her way who were waiting for tables. Edy motioned to the waitress when she'd drained her second cup of coffee, and paid her bill. Outside the restaurant she walked among the flowers before going to her car. Halfway to the spot where she had parked she spotted a black car parked along the path. She stopped, startled, frozen. *Don't be ridiculous. It can't be the same one. There are a lot of black cars in the world.*

Nevertheless, she picked up the pace, her hand shaking as she stuck her key between her fingers and made a fist. It hadn't seemed that far away when she'd parked earlier. Footsteps behind her had her heart racing in her chest and her steps quickening. She nearly dropped her keys as her hand trembled when she clicked the fob. She hit the alarm instead of the unlock key. She tried again, then climbed into the car and threw her purse across the seat, locked the doors, and shifted the car into gear. Edy drove the speed limit exiting the park, but every few seconds she checked her rearview mirror, her stomach clenched, until she reached the entrance to the highway. Relief flooded her body.

"You're a fool," she said, exhaling. She hadn't noticed any car following from the park.

Forty minutes later she hit the Wilkesbury mall and parked in front of the movie theater's entrance. With no preconceived notion of what she wanted to see, Edy picked one at random that didn't sound like a kids' movie.

The movie she chose hadn't drawn a crowd. Edy sat in the center row in the middle seat.

Halfway through the action movie she got up and started to walk out. When she pushed open the door she ran smack into Cedric and his tart.

"Well, look who's out and about," Cedric said with his arm around his date.

"Step aside," Edy ordered.

"We aren't allowed to be civil?"

"I was." She didn't budge.

"Let me introduce..."

"No need, I'm aware of who the slut is," Edy said as she spun away from him.

Cedric tugged his date to the side and continued into the theater without another word. In all the years she'd lived with the man, he'd never mentioned he liked going to the movies. *Who cares anyway*, she thought.

It took her fifteen minutes to get home. The grandfather clock in the foyer chimed five as she walked in the door. The aged heirloom clock had been her great-grandmother's treasured antique. Their familiar chimes usually comforted her, but tonight they grated on her nerves. Water whooshed through the heating system, clanging through the radiators when the heat built up. The house settled, its bones creaking. She made a mental note to have the heat system bled to get the air out. The silence echoed through her head, reminding her of her solitary life. Not much had changed. Cedric had hardly ever been home when he did live here. The long night ahead forced her to revisit her mistakes.

Charity work and volunteering hadn't made a life she loved or friends she'd cherished since she lost Margaret to cancer several years ago. Loneliness slammed into her. She and Margaret had been friends from childhood, her confidant, her rock.

Everyone she'd met wanted a piece of her, or at least her money. Edy roamed from room to room before settling in the library with a book, but her mind grasped nothing she'd read and her eyes started to droop.

A loud, crashing metallic sound filled the halls. She woke with a start, her heart racing. Cripes, she'd fallen asleep. It took her a second to clear her foggy mind and get her bearings. She overreached for the lamp switch and almost knocked it off the table, but caught it before it crashed to the floor. She felt around for the drawer in the table and grabbed for the flashlight. She located her cell phone and pressed in the lieutenant's number but held off hitting the send button. Instead, she made her way to the kitchen window to survey the area out back. She'd look ridiculous if it had been a raccoon instead of a burglar.

All the garbage cans had been upended, their contents spread around the backyard. Edy went to the door, her finger on the lock as movement caught her eye. She switched off the flashlight and listened. She squinted out into the darkness. Nothing moved. Why hadn't the light sensor switched on?

She thumbed the send button.

"Lieutenant Carrington."

"Lieutenant, it's Edy Dunstan. I don't want to appear skittish but someone just turned over all the garbage cans and it's not animals, I'm sure of it," she whispered into the phone.

"I'm at the station. I can be there in less than ten minutes. Don't answer your door until I get there."

Edy left the lights off as she waited in the dark living room by the window. A streetlight reflected off an inky-colored, slow-moving vehicle as it drove down the street with its lights off. Red brake lights lit up the end of the street for a second before it disappeared.

Edy dialed her security team to find out why they hadn't heard the commotion. She started right in before the person on duty could say a word. "Are you on the street in a dark car?"

"Mrs. Dunstan, we're a street over. I heard the noise, we're investigating. There's been no action on your block."

"No action? This afternoon, there was a black car I didn't recognize on the other side of the street directly across from my house. Now another dark car drove down the street with their lights off. And you're telling me your team observed nothing either time? What good are you?"

"There has been no report file for such," the man said stiffly. "Their job is to patrol your block, not sit in one spot all night. The black car might've entered while the team was on their rounds."

"Excuses. You have Jimmy Nelson call me right away, and I mean within two minutes."

Headlights caught her eye. "I have to go, the police are here. I called them."

She hung up and waited before heading to the door to make sure it was Carrington and another man.

She answered the door when he knocked. "Lieutenant, come in."

"This is Sergeant Romanelli. If I'm ever not available, call him and he'll come right away."

"Sergeant, Lieutenant, can I get either one of you a drink?"

"No, thank you, Mrs. Dunstan, just tell us what happened," Jake said.

She relayed the facts and stuck in the tidbit about running into Cedric and his mistress at the movies. She wasn't taking any chances, in case the bastard had started to play games.

"I can't believe security didn't pick up on anything." She paced the living room. "I have the guard putting in a call to Jimmy Nelson to explain it. A black car in the middle of the day parked on the road should be a flag. I also thought I saw one in West Hartford when I was lunching there, but I'm not sure."

"Let's see what Jimmy has to say when he calls you back," Jake said. "In the meantime, we'll look out back, and check all the windows and doors before we leave. Where's Benita?"

"She spends Sundays at her sister's."

"She won't be home until tomorrow? Is that her routine?" Louie asked.

"Yes, she's had Sundays off for as long as she's worked for me."

* * * *

Jake and Louie went outside and walked the back perimeter. The garbage cans had been knocked down. They'd been upended, not by animals but a human. All the contents were spread over the backyard.

"Petty divorce bullshit?" Louie asked, picking up the garbage and placing it back in the cans.

"Might be, might not," Jake said, checking the back gate. It swung open as he touched it. "The lock's broken. I'm going back in to talk to her. Leave the trash, Louie."

"I can't. The place is too nice, and she'll get a bunch of critters if it's left as is," Louie said.

Louie, the Good Samaritan. Jake helped him clean up the garbage before going in to question Edy some more. Sometimes Louie put him to shame.

Inside, he settled into the chair to Edy's left, Louie took the other to her right. "Mrs. Dunstan, it was a person you heard. I'm glad you didn't go out. Now about the black car you saw today, you didn't recognize it or the driver?"

"I noticed it in passing before I went out, and figured they were visiting someone on the street."

"Next time, snap a picture with your cell and zoom in on the license plate if possible. Can your phone record the date and time on a picture?" Jake said.

"You're scaring me, Lieutenant. You don't think kids did this?"

"No, I don't. If you get a feeling you're being followed or watched, call it in. After receiving the blackmail letter, you don't want to take chances." Jake stood. Louie followed.

"I'll see you out," Edy said, rising also.

"There's one more thing. Do you always keep the gate locked out back?" Jake asked.

"Yes."

"Is there anyone you can call to spend the night with you?" Louie asked.

"No, Sergeant, there isn't. I might call my father and go over there."

"Why don't you pack a bag and give him a call. We'll follow you over there," Jake said.

She stared first at Louie then Jake, picked up her cell phone and pressed in a number as she climbed the stairs.

"Overkill?" Louie asked.

"No, someone is trying hard to scare her, or give her a warning. It could be the blackmailer trying to get their money faster, or the ex, but let's be prudent either way."

* * * *

Edy roamed her father's living room for a couple of hours after she'd been spooked. "Will you please sit down? Pacing never solved anything," Ed Rockford said. "Jimmy Nelson will be here shortly, and we'll get to the bottom of this."

"Why didn't his men see anything?"

"I'm going to find out," Ed said.

As if on cue, the front doorbell chimed. Mildred, the Dunstans' maid, answered it and escorted a contrite Jimmy Nelson into the room.

"Mr. Rockford, Mrs. Dunstan, I checked the neighborhood myself, and questioned your neighbors. No one had a visitor who drove a black car. And they thought it was animals knocking over the trash cans. It's the reason no one bothered to come out and help," Jimmy said as he waited for an invitation to sit.

"How could your men not see the car?" Edy asked before her father had a chance.

"I'm looking into the whereabouts of the two who were on duty at the time. I'll get to the bottom of it," Jimmy said.

"Sit," Rockford barked. "It's not acceptable. We're talking about my daughter's safety. I want whoever was on duty today and tonight fired. I'm not risking Edy's life."

"I understand. I'll reassign them, but they've been with me for a long time and are good people."

"Well I sure haven't witnessed that. Your men never see a thing. Where are they when my daughter needs them?" Ed Rockford went to the bar. From a crystal decanter he filled a tall glass with ice and poured scotch into it.

"I have two men assigned to patrol the neighborhood. Do you want me to do something different?" Nelson asked, his jaw tight.

"Yes, I want one in the house with her…"

"Dad, I'm not having anyone live with me. I want my privacy. They should be able to handle it from the outside," Edy said.

"Are you staying here tonight, Mrs. Dunstan?"

"I was, but I've decided to go home. No one is going to force me from my home."

"Edy, darling, it's not smart to leave now, it's after eight. Let Nelson set up his new team first, and then tomorrow you can go home. Please stay," Ed said.

Whoever had done this had to be laughing, forcing her from her home. All the nerves in her body grated against each other. "Jimmy, your team is still watching the house, correct?" she asked.

"Yes. Why?"

"I'm wondering if forcing me out was a ploy to break in and take what they wanted, which leads me back to Cedric."

"I'll inform the team. Can I put someone on the inside tonight?"

"Not unless I'm there," Edy said.

"You're not being reasonable, Edy," Rockford said.

She lifted a blonde eyebrow at her father. He, of all people? Mr. I-don't-negotiate, it's-my-way-or-no-way should understand. Her lips slanted down into a pout, something she'd done to annoy him since childhood. There was nothing he hated more than when she wrapped herself in misery. Named for him, though she'd never liked her name, she secretly thanked him for all the life lessons he'd taught her. He'd have to trust her judgment. Cedric had disrupted her life enough.

"Dad, I'm going back. Do you want Cedric to drive me from my home?"

"No, I can stay the night," he conceded.

"If you'd like. I'd enjoy having you," Edy said.

Her bags were parked by the door. She hadn't let Mildred, her father's housekeeper, bring them upstairs. She exhaled and walked to her luggage.

Her short-lived freedom hadn't had time to settle in. Her father placed his drink on the bar before he rang for Mildred.

Mildred glided into the room as if a ghost. In the best of times it unnerved Edy, but tonight it spooked her.

"Please pack an overnight bag for me," he said.

"Yes, sir."

"I'm leaving now. I'll fix up the guest room before you get there," Edy said as she opened the front door.

"I'll carry out your bags, Mrs. Dunstan," Jimmy Nelson said. "And I'll follow you home."

"Thanks. How long will I have to put up with this nonsense?"

No one had an answer for her. She'd be a prisoner in her own home. The lieutenant or Nelson better find the blackmailer fast or she'd go stark raving nuts.

My sanity's on a short tether as it is.

* * * *

Somehow, his couple of hours turned into many. He'd have to make it up to Mia. Jake put his personal life aside and started the murder book on Sal Gallucci. He filled in all the information they had. A blank page stared back at him. He organized the facts on the case and the cause of death as he understood them. He compared Callie's case to Gallucci's for similarities and differences pertaining to both.

Two things bothered him. First, the letter about Eva which caused busywork, then Gallucci's death. It seemed like overkill. If Sal hadn't killed Callie why not leave him alive to take the blame? As far as he could see Sal, Callie, Edy, and Darcy—they all had only one thing in common— Melinda. Damn, he might as well add himself to the list. No matter how he lined it up, he kept circling back to Melinda as the killer. How had she lifted Gallucci into the car? Gallucci had been killed elsewhere. Had it been his blood in Melinda's kitchen? Was there another person backing up Melinda, and if yes, then who? He'd found no other person with close ties to her except her mother. And Jake didn't consider Mrs. Blair a suspect.

Round and round he went, but no matter how he looked at it, the page remained blank. Jake picked up Callie's crime scene photos and placed them beside Gallucci's. The lab hadn't sent over their results. With a skeleton crew on Sundays, the lab probably hadn't had time to process the crime scene. Jake drummed his fingers on his desk. Ready to put the pictures back in their case folders, something in Gallucci's death pictures caught his eye. He took a magnifying glass from his middle desk drawer. A small metallic object, partially hidden by Gallucci's right foot, caught his eye. What was it? He hit the intercom.

"Louie, come in here," Jake said.

"What?" Louie rushed into his office.

"Look at the object in the lower right-hand section of this photo. Can you make out what it is?"

"No, give me the glass."

Louie studied it as Jake looked over his shoulder. "First thing tomorrow, I'll check in with Willie Phelps and find out what items he recovered from Gallucci's car. Can you make anything out?"

"It's a chain of some kind, but I'm not sure," Louie said.

Interesting. It couldn't be, could it? He'd have to wait until tomorrow.

Jake checked his watch. "We've done all we can today, let's go home. It's after seven." He dropped the pictures in the proper files, his magnifier into his middle drawer, and the murder book in his bottom right-hand one. He slid some documents into his briefcase, then shut down his computer, his mind, and his body for today.

In the past, he would have stayed well into the night, but now he had to consider Mia, and the life they were making together.

It's not all about the job anymore.

Chapter 21

Edy took off without waiting for Jimmy Nelson to get into his car. The drive was her last fling with freedom for a while. God, she needed the time to think. She hit the dark stretch of road she used as a shortcut from her father's to her house. Tonight, it gave her the willies. She checked her rearview mirror. No lights. What was taking Jimmy so long to catch up? Did he take a different route? This was the quickest way to her house. Hadn't he known that?

Bright lights flooded her rearview mirror, blinding her. She adjusted the mirror, switching it to the nighttime setting to cut down on the glare. Her mind and eyes on the mirror, she hadn't seen the car pull out of the side street until it was too late. Edy swerved to avoid it, but the car never slowed down and sideswiped her. Her neck snapped back, her breath whooshed out of her as the airbag exploded and slammed into her chest. Everything happened in slow motion. Something smashed in her window, then someone opened her door. Hands tugged on her.

"I didn't see you, I'm so sorry...What the..." Something stung her arm—a needle?

Dizzy, her mind cloudy, she shut her eyes to clear her vision, then opened them. Everything blurred around the edges. She couldn't make out the person's features, her stomach heaved in her throat, and her world spun away from her. She tried to lean out the door as her lunch exploded from her mouth.

"Shit, you bitch, you'll pay for that," a woman said.

The voice sounded far away, but familiar. Edy couldn't place it and continued to throw up. The dry heaves came next. After a few minutes it slowed and she tried to clear her head. Edy swallowed the next burst when a cloth bag dropped over her head. She reached out, clawing at anything in front of her and hit her mark. At least she'd gotten a piece of them.

"The bitch scratched me. I'm telling you, I'm gonna kill her myself."

She screamed at the top of her lungs while hands jerked her from the car.

Calm down, remember everything, it's important, Edy. They tossed her into a car. A waft of perfume hit her. Edy inhaled to identify the brand. Cheap, it was cheap perfume or cologne. Her kidnappers pushed her down to the floor behind the front seats. Roses, musk, and wood filled her nostrils, mixed in with the scent of new car while the hump in the floor wedged into her back.

Who had gotten a new car recently? Damn it, Edy, think, she chided, her thoughts tumbling one after another. Short, uneven breaths had her fighting for air under the hood. A rank smell caused her to gag. She realized it was the stench of her own fear. *A woman, it was a woman who spoke, but who else was with her? Cedric? The blackmailer? Who? Oh, God, please get me out of this. And where the hell is Jimmy Nelson? Is he part of this?*

She gathered her strength and fought to keep the panic at bay and tried to stay conscious. It was hard to think with her head pounding like a bass drum.

The car pulled out, tires squealed. Edy struggled, turning every which way. She felt every bump and pothole the car hit. It tossed her up against the driver's seat, then the back seat. A deep soul digging eeriness encompassed her, pricking every nerve in her body, while her abductors remained silent. With each mile her fear increased until she couldn't grasp a single molecule of air. Why? Did she know at least one of them? The moving car made it hard for her to keep track of time. No sounds of passing traffic, ambulances screeching or dogs barking reached her in the darkness.

Where the hell is Jimmy? Does he think I pulled a hissy fit? Why didn't I stay at my father's?

Tears dripped from her eyes, mucus from her nose. Each musty breath jabbed her chest. She sank into the floor of the car, making herself as small as possible.

It can't be Cedric. He'd never treat me this way. Who then? Come on, Edy, think. She tried to wipe her eyes, realized her hands were tied. She must've passed out. She'd no recollection of being tied up. She inched over the hump in the middle of the car, her back aching as she worked her way across the floor. Even with her hands tied, Edy hoped she'd have enough strength to get the jump on her abductors if she got the chance.

The car slowed as it turned left onto a rutted road. Her head hit the back seat, wedging her on her side. *It must be a dirt road. How long have they been driving? My God, I don't know. Where am I?*

A scream escaped her lips.

"I told you we should've gagged her," the woman said.

Whoever her accomplice was, he still hadn't spoken. Well, she assumed it had to be a man. Could a woman lift her as easily as the person who had placed her in the car?

The car stopped and the back door opened, the night air sweeping over her body chilled her skin. Her legs were useless since the last jolt had pinned her on her side. Edy sniffed in the scents around her. Something sharp punctured her skin. The scent of decaying leaves faded along with her thoughts as they merged into darkness. Her battle to remain conscious was lost, and the floating sensation overtook her body and mind.

* * * *

When he got home, Jake found Mia fast asleep on the couch. Brigh lay beside her, and the television was tuned to a cooking show. Brigh lifted her head, stared at him for a second, then went back to sleep. He took the blanket off the back of the sofa and covered Mia.

"I'm awake," Mia said. She rolled toward him, displacing Brigh.

"You always watch TV with your eyes closed?" He kissed her on the forehead.

"What time is it?"

"Around eight. Are you hungry?"

"Let's stay in, you cook," Mia said.

"I can do that."

Brigh followed him into the kitchen. Jake filled her dish with food and freshened up her water. He pulled out a skillet, a wooden spoon, the garlic grater, and measuring cups. As he reached into the refrigerator his cell phone rang.

"Oh, for the love of God," he muttered, reading the caller ID.

He listened to Dispatch, closed his eyes, and wished he'd given Edy Dunstan some protection. "Call Sergeant Romanelli and tell him I'll pick him up in five." Jake stuck his phone in his pocket. Mia ambled into the kitchen and sat at the table.

He took the seat beside her. "I'm sorry. I have to go back out. Edy Dunstan went missing on her way home from her father's tonight."

"Is she going to be okay?"

"I don't know. All the victims so far have the photographer in common and loads of money. I hope she'll be all right, but I'm not sure. This feels off. Callie met with her blackmailers and brought the money with her. Edy was on her way home from her father's, where I left her to spend the night. I don't understand why she didn't stay there," Jake said, his thoughts already at the scene.

He kissed Mia goodbye and drove to Louie's. On the way he called Shamus on his cell.

"Shamus, Edy Dunstan's gone missing. I'm going to assume she's been kidnapped and work it from that angle. Did Darcy receive any more letters?"

"No."

"Good. Tell her to use extreme caution. It doesn't feel like Callie's murder, but I won't be sure until I get to the scene."

"I'll warn her. Call me when you're done at the scene," McGuire said.

"It might be late," Jake said.

"I don't care, call." Shamus hung up.

Louie was standing at the curb in front of his house when Jake drove up.

"Why was she out after we dropped her off at her father's?" Louie asked, jumping into the car.

"I wasn't given any information except that her car was left running and abandoned."

"Of all the stupid things," Louie said.

It took them less than five minutes to get to the scene. "Yep," Jake said, cutting off the rest of the conversation as he eased closer to the blocked-off area.

He hung back and evaluated the scene before talking to anyone. The right side of Edy's car had been crushed inward, skid marks ran along the lane for about five feet, the driver's side window had been smashed, and the seat belt hanging out the door had been cut.

"Has anyone checked the hospitals in case a Good Samaritan took her to one?" Jake asked.

"I've checked them and all the ambulance services. No one fitting her description has been admitted, and no one requested a wagon either," Officer Jones said.

He'd worked with Tara Jones before and appreciated her professionalism, and he respected her. Her investigations and crime scenes were kept pristine for the detectives. Jones's cap sat on her head at a precise angle, her black hair neatly pinned up under it. In the overhead light her mahogany skin glowed.

"Good to see you, Jones. Give me your report," Jake said.

Jones recited the facts, concluding with how she found Mrs. Dunstan's purse and cell phone on the floor of the car.

"A woman doesn't leave her purse in the car if she left of her own accord, sir," Tara Jones said.

"What's in the back seat and the trunk?"

"Jake, her luggage is back here," Louie said from under the lid of the trunk. "And the usual items one keeps in the trunk. A spare tire, tools to change it. Otherwise it's clean."

"Okay, Jones, give me your take of the scene," Jake said.

"Sir, there's a dent in the back fender. It looks like a person hit her from behind as someone cut her off from the front."

"Noted, please stand by."

Jake walked the scene. This section of road had no street lights, no houses except off the side street that intersected with the road a few yards back. The skid marks, along with the car's crushed right side, said Edy tried to avoid a car pulling out of the side street. *A crime of opportunity? No, someone familiar with Edy knew she took this way back and forth from her home to her father's and planned this. It points to her husband or a friend.*

"Officer Jones, get me the phone number and address for Rosie Riverton, and if you can, get me the cell number for Cedric Dunstan," Jake said. "For his number you can check with the officer who is on duty at her father's place. His name is John Kennedy."

"I'll get right on it, sir." Jones approached her cruiser, its lights still flashing.

Willie Phelps strolled up to him. "Next time, Jake, can you have your crimes happen on someone else's shift?" Willie said, rolling his eyes. The CSI tech carried his bag to Edy's car to start his investigation.

Jake watched Willie slide on his gloves, then pull out his flashlight. He'd need to get to Cedric Dunstan before he heard anything on the news. He signaled for Louie.

"What?"

"I'm going to Dunstan's mistress's place in Middlebury. You stay here and finish processing the scene. If you're finished when I'm done, I'll come by and pick you up, then we'll interview her father together."

"Are you going to notify Middlebury?" Louie asked.

"Yes, after I interview Cedric," Jake said, tossing Louie a smirk over his shoulder.

"It was damn stupid of her to leave her father's in the first place," Louie said, stating the obvious again.

* * * *

Shamus hung up with Jake and paced his home office while rubbing his throbbing temples. Darcy had to be informed of the latest development, but things had been tense between them since she'd received the letter with the nude photos.

It's now or never. He walked to the living room and pulled up short at the entrance. Darcy sat on the couch with papers spread out on her lap and the seat. Tears ran down her face while she stared at the wall. It undid him. A strong woman, Darcy never cried, but since Callie's murder she'd cried a lifetime of tears.

"Darcy." Going to her, he pushed the papers out of the way and sat beside her.

She brushed the back of her hand over her face. "I miss her."

"It's only natural, honey." Shamus draped his arm around her shoulders and drew her close to him.

"Is Jake any closer to solving the case?" Darcy asked.

"Edy Dunstan was kidnapped a little while ago. Have you gotten any other letters?"

"Shamus, I'm not stupid. Had I gotten any I would've told you. Is she going to…"

Shamus understood the unfinished thought. Neither wanted to believe Edy might be the next victim. It'd be a mistake to give her his wait-and-see speech.

"Jake and Louie are on it. He wants you to use extreme caution whenever you're alone. I'd prefer if you used a car service instead of driving anywhere. I can assign a uniform to you."

"I'll use the car service, Shamus. If you want to assign one of your men as the driver, he'll have to be in plainclothes. A uniformed officer would open up a line of questioning at work I'd rather not have to address."

He'd expected that reply, but it didn't make him happy. "Have you called Todd this week?"

"No, we saw him yesterday at the funeral, and besides, I wasn't up to it. Selfish isn't it?" She blew her nose in a tissue she'd produced from her pocket.

"I'll give him a call tomorrow," Shamus said, kissing her forehead.

* * * *

Jake programmed Cedric's new address into his GPS and drove away from the scene. He'd have to stow his anger before he got to Dunstan's place, otherwise he might do something stupid.

Sex and money—most times murder came down to those two things. Sometimes the murderer proclaimed it was done out of love for the victim— if they couldn't have them, no one would. In this case it'd be one or both. From the first caveman knocking the second over the head for his food or woman, man had taken what he wanted with force, not caring what the consequences might be. Greed, a formidable bitch, blinded many in their quest to acquire wealth.

Greed, murder and stupidity ensured he had a job.

Jake parked in the Middlebury Tower's parking lot. It was a five-story apartment complex that sat on the Wilkesbury-Middlebury line along I-84. It charged its residents high rent for the privilege of dwelling there. Jake wondered how Cedric would meet the obligation after Edy cut him off. It made for a good motive for blackmail—if the blackmailer turned out to be Cedric.

He knocked on the door to unit 5C and waited. Cedric came to the door wearing a gray hooded sweat suit. It seemed out of place on Cedric and a far cry from his thousand-dollar business suits. Cedric's wet brown hair had been slicked back, his cheeks flushed.

"Cedric Dunstan, I'm Lieutenant Jake Carrington from the Wilkesbury Police Department. May I come in?"

"I remember you from the gala. What do you want?"

"I'd like to come in and discuss it with you. Is your girlfriend home?"

"Why?"

"Mr. Dunstan, we can do this here or at the station. What's your choice?"

Dunstan opened the door wider and stepped back. "Now tell me what all this is about."

"Is Rosie Riverton home?" Jake asked, ignoring the demand.

Jake did a quick scan of the apartment. Minimal furnishings looked lost in the big room. Blinds covered the large picture window, and an area rug filled the space between one blue chair and the yellow-and-blue sofa. He noted the kitchen to his left as he passed by it to go into the half-furnished living room. From his vantage point, Jake didn't spot another exit.

"She's out with her girlfriends tonight. Why?"

"I'll need their names."

"Not until you tell me what this is all about." Cedric stood in the middle of the room, his shoulders squared, his spine stiff.

"Someone kidnapped Edy tonight on her way home from her father's house. I'm questioning everyone who had contact with her, or knowledge of her."

"You think I did it? You're crazy. I was home all night," Cedric said.

"When's the last time you saw or spoke with Mrs. Dunstan?"

"I spoke with her today at the movie theater. She was quite rude to me and Rosie."

"Did you expect her and your mistress to become friends?" Jake sneered. *It takes all kinds.*

"No, I expected common decency on her part."

"I need your exact movements this evening. If you were home, what did you watch on television? Who did you speak with? And leave nothing out."

"I was home working on papers. Edy's father has served me notice of termination. Tonight my lawyer emailed me the paperwork I need to review. I've been combing through it. After reviewing the papers, I made notes for my attorney. I'm going to sue that obnoxious bastard for wrongful termination. If he and his stuck-up daughter think they can destroy me and my reputation, they're messing with the wrong guy."

"You're angry. Are you angry enough to blackmail Edy?" Jake watched for a reaction, got none.

"Why would I? I'm suing her too. She forged my name on a check and emptied out my account. I can prove it. She's been sleeping with the VP at the bank where I kept my individual account. I'm going to own her after the divorce. No, I'd never physically hurt her. Someone like her, you have to hit in the pocketbook, and I'm going to do just that."

"Where is Rosie Riverton tonight?" Jake asked again. "And what kind of car does she drive?"

"I told you she's out with friends."

"Out where?"

"I think they went to dinner at Tiramisu's restaurant on East Main Street."

"I'll check it out with the owner. Why's your hair wet?"

"I took a shower."

"What kind of car do you drive, and Rosie?"

"I drive a black Lexus. Rosie drives a gray Hyundai."

"Is her car light or dark gray?"

"Light, more silver than gray."

"Thanks for your time, and oh, one more thing. I need the license plate numbers for each vehicle."

"Why?" Cedric asked, clearly losing his patience.

Jake wanted to push him.

Cedric stared him down before giving up and grabbing a pad to write down both numbers.

"Thanks," Jake said, sticking the paper into his pocket. He turned away from Cedric, then turned back. "A black car was sitting outside Edy's house all afternoon. Was it you?"

"No. Why would I waste my time like that?"

"Beats me," Jake said, his shoulders hitching up, then down. He moved toward the door. "I'm sure I'll have more questions as we proceed with the investigation. So please stay available, Mr. Dunstan."

"I had nothing to do with this. I'm calling my lawyer. The next time you want to speak to me, you call him," Cedric said, his face flushing red.

"Here's my card. Have Rosie call me when she gets home. I need to speak with her tonight. If she doesn't call, I'll be back here knocking on your door at an ungodly hour, understand?"

"Yes."

Downstairs in the parking lot, Jake searched out Cedric's car. He placed his hand on the hood. Warm, not hot, but the car had been used tonight, which made Cedric a liar. Back in his car, Jake jotted down his notes and impressions as well as the time. Car still warm at ten p.m. told him Cedric had jumped up the list to be his prime suspect.

* * * *

"Are you all set with the crime scene?" Jake asked Louie when he answered the phone.

"Yes."

"I'm on my way to you. I'll be there in ten." Jake hung up, then tossed his cell onto the passenger's seat.

Louie jumped in his car the minute Jake pulled up. "What did Dunstan have to say?"

"That he was home all night. The hood of his car was warm, and he had gotten out of the shower minutes before I arrived."

"And his girlfriend?" Louie asked.

"She wasn't home." Jake glanced at Louie as he drove away from the crime scene.

"Ah, and your conclusion?" Louie said, curling his lip to the side.

"The same as yours."

"How do you want to handle Rockford?"

"He's not a suspect," Jake said. "You might want to play the father angle if you see it's needed."

"Okay, maybe he's had enough of his daughter's antics," Louie said.

"Louie, would you kill Marisa for making bad choices?"

"I wouldn't kill her even if she killed a person. She's my little girl."

"Exactly. I don't think Rockford would commit filicide," Jake said.

Chapter 22

Jake noticed Jimmy Nelson's car parked in front of Rockford's house as he pulled into the driveway and climbed out. He wouldn't want to be in Jimmy's shoes tonight. Louie knocked.

Mildred, Rockford's housekeeper, answered and showed them into the living room. Jimmy, his body coiled to spring, stood by the window, his back to the room. Rockford hung out behind the bar, rattling the ice in his glass. Tension thick as fog sucked all the air from the room. Jake waited for the sparks to ignite as he glanced from Rockford to Nelson.

"Mr. Rockford, we have some questions for you first. Jimmy, Louie will take you in the kitchen and question you. I also want to talk to your men who were stationed here and at Edy's house tonight."

Nelson's eyes pleaded with him to understand, but Jake ignored him. "Mr. Rockford, please join me over here," Jake said as he took a seat in the overstuffed gray chair by the window.

In the few hours since he'd last seen Rockford, the vigorous, commanding man was gone, replaced by a haggard old one. His gray mane was mussed, his eyes empty, and his shoulders sagged.

Ed Rockford sank onto the other chair with his glass in hand. "What are the chances she's still alive?"

"I don't know," Jake said, deciding honesty was best.

"I'll pay anything to get her back, Lieutenant. And I'll even go on television to plead for her return."

"It's not wise to pay a blackmailer, and we're not sure it's the blackmailer who snatched her. How many people knew she was heading home?"

"Mildred, Nelson, and me. I'm not sure Nelson contacted the men at her house to tell them she was headed home. She called no one."

"Did she tell you she ran into Cedric and his girlfriend today?"

"No, she didn't. I begged her to stay, but she's stubborn."

"Whose bags are those?" Jake pointed to the ones by the front door.

"They're mine. I was going to spend the night at her place. She said she'd head home to make up the guest room for me. I should've made her wait until I was ready. I sent Jimmy Nelson to follow her home."

"Hindsight is great, Mr. Rockford. Don't beat yourself up. Jimmy Nelson didn't see what happened?"

"No, Edy took off before Jimmy got in his car. He said he spotted her but then he got caught at a light. He's the one who found the empty car," Rockford said, rubbing his chin. "Do you think he had anything to do with this?"

"I don't think anything yet. But most likely no, Jimmy's a good guy." Still, it bothered Jake how Jimmy could've lost sight of Edy on the short trip to her house. "I'm going to do everything in my power to find her, Mr. Rockford."

"I understand, but don't risk her safety to catch the people who did this. Edy home and well is all that counts, Lieutenant."

"I agree. If you'll excuse me, I want to ask Jimmy a few questions."

Jake left Rockford sitting on the chair staring into his drink. Jake hadn't missed the tear spilling down his cheek.

He approached the kitchen and stood at the entrance and gauged Jimmy's demeanor and answers to Louie's questions. Louie lifted his head and locked eyes with him.

"Jake, can I speak with you for moment?" Louie asked.

He stepped into the hallway, and Louie followed.

"What's up?"

"He's beating himself up over this," Louie said.

"I understand, but how do you lose someone you're tailing on such a short trip? And who the hell stops for a red light while on the job?" Anger oozed from Jake's pores. "Who else did he tell?"

"He called his men stationed at her house and told them to watch out for her."

"I want background checks on all of them, including Jimmy. I also want financial checks on each one. Who besides Cedric would gain from her disappearance?"

"I'll get right on it," Louie said.

"I know you questioned him, but I have a few questions I'd like to ask," Jake said.

"Go at it." Louie walked farther into the hallway with his phone out.

Jake stepped into the kitchen. "Jimmy, I need your personnel records for the employees you told about Mrs. Dunstan's movements tonight. How the hell did you lose sight of her?"

"Jake, she took off before I got in my car. When I started to catch up to her, she rushed through the light. I stopped."

"Why would you stop?"

"I can't answer that. I've been asking myself the same question for over an hour," Jimmy said, dropping his head into his hands.

"It makes you look guilty, as if you were involved in her disappearance."

"Don't you think I understand that? For God's sake, I'm sick over this, Jake, you have to believe me. For the record, I had nothing to do with Edy Dunstan's kidnapping. I'll do everything within my power to help you find her."

"I can't use you, Jimmy. You and your men are suspects. Stay available."

"Jake, you know me…I'd never go against the law!" Jimmy shouted. "My clients depend on me. I take my responsibilities seriously. You've got to understand."

"Right now all I understand is a woman is missing, frightened, and needs my help to stay alive. Nothing or nobody else matters, including you, Jimmy." Jake stormed from the room.

"Jake, I've got Al and Kraus working the background checks. Who's next on the list?" Louie said.

"I need a picture of Rosie Riverton. Call Al back and ask him to search for one and send it to our phones. Once we receive it I want to head over to Tiramisu's restaurant and see if she dined there tonight, and what time she left. Do a search for their hours of operation."

"It's closed on Sundays," Louie said, looking up from his cell phone.

"Another lie. We're heading back to Middlebury. I want Rosie Riverton's whereabouts. If Cedric doesn't supply it, he's going into lockup for the night."

* * * *

In the parking lot of the apartment building where Cedric and Rosie lived Jake parked next to Rosie's gray car after matching her license plate number to the one Cedric had given him earlier. He nodded to Louie as he got out. Louie placed his hand on the hood.

"It's hot," Louie said, taking his pad from his jacket pocket and noting the time, 10:50 p.m.

"Is there a dent in front?"

"No."

"I forgot to check Cedric's car to see if there's a dent in it."

"There isn't," Louie said after inspecting both cars.

Shit, did they use a different car? If not, who else was out to get Edy? Melinda? No, it didn't make sense, unless Edy had the money with her for the blackmailer. For the second time tonight, Jake knocked on the door to 5C. Louie stood off to his left. Cedric answered in the same sweat suit, his hair dry.

"What do you want?"

"Rosie didn't call," Jake said, the underlying threat in his words clear.

"She got home five minutes ago. Besides, she's too drunk to talk to anyone."

"Are you going to invite us in?"

"No."

"Hands behind your back, I'm taking you in."

"You can't do that," Dunstan said, trying to shove the door closed. Jake pushed against it.

"The Supreme Court says I can. Cedric Dunstan, you're under suspicion for the kidnapping of Edwina Dunstan. "You are entitled to a lawyer..." Jake continued to read the Miranda rights to Dunstan until the graveness of the situation sunk into his head.

"For the love of God, I didn't do anything," Cedric Dunstan said.

"Don't test me, Mr. Dunstan. Here or downtown?" Jake stared Dunstan down until he called for Rosie.

"Rosie, come out here," Cedric said, blocking the doorway.

"What?"

Jake got his first look at Cedric's mistress. She wasn't anything he'd turn Edy in for.

"Rosie Riverton, I'm Lieutenant Carrington from the WPD. Where were you tonight?" Jake filed away Riverton's stats—five five, a hundred and thirty pounds, brown teased-out hair and brown eyes.

"I was out with friends." Rosie constantly blinked her eyes. He couldn't help but stare at her purple-eyeshadowed lids.

"Where?"

"I don't have to answer you," she said, her words tumbling from thin red lips. She slurred her words as she spoke. It hit Jake wrong. *She's acting. She's not drunk. Boy, what a far cry from Edy.* He noted the jut of her pointed chin as she defied him.

"You answer here or downtown at the station, either way I don't care," Jake said, taking on a bored tone.

"I had dinner at Tiramisu's with two girlfriends."

"Do you have a receipt?" Jake's eyebrow quirked.

"No, I didn't know I'd needed one."

"What did you eat?"

"Why all the questions?" Rosie asked, looking at Cedric, not Jake.

"What did you eat?"

"Chicken parm. I'm not answering any more of your questions unless you explain why you're here."

"Don't play dumb, Rosie. I'm sure Cedric told you that Edy has been kidnapped. Let's stop playing games."

"We had nothing to do with her disappearance. This is harassment."

"Tiramisu's is closed on Sundays. Where were you tonight?" Jake repeated.

"Yeah, where were you?" Dunstan asked, his brows pinched together.

"I want a lawyer," Rosie said.

"You can call one from the station, where we'll continue our questioning. Rosie Riverton, you are the prime suspect in the disappearance of Edy Dunstan. Anything you say…"

"I didn't do it, you can't arrest me!" Rosie shouted at the top of her lungs as she lunged at him.

"You're not under arrest. I'm only holding you for questioning." Jake slipped the bracelets on her. "You are being handcuffed because you charged at me. This is for both of our safety."

"This is ridiculous," Riverton said, her speech clear.

He found it interesting how Dunstan never came to Riverton's defense. "Do you have anything to add, Mr. Dunstan?"

"No." Dunstan jammed his hands into his pockets.

"Mr. Dunstan, you can come quietly, or I can also handcuff you. What's your choice?"

"I'll come, but you've got this wrong. I want to call my lawyer."

"You'll be able to call one from the station."

"Why can't we drive ourselves there?" Cedric asked.

"You're being treated as hostile witnesses at this time," Jake said.

Louie walked Cedric out, and Jake led Rosie by the arm.

* * * *

Jake put Cedric Dunstan and Rosie Riverton in separate interview rooms. "Why can't we be together?" Rosie asked in a whiny voice.

"It's standard procedure," Jake said. "Do you want something to drink?"

"No, I want to get this over with so I can go home."

"I'll be back in a few minutes," Jake said, leaving a female officer in the room.

He scanned the half empty bullpen for Al Burke and found him at his desk.

"Jimmy Nelson sent over the personnel records," Al reported. "I'm still digging on the financials. Kraus is on the rest of it."

"Here are two more names to run. Can you put them at the top of your list? I have them in interview now."

"Sure, I'll get right on it," Al said.

Jake took Jimmy's personnel records into his office while he waited for the information on Dunstan and Riverton. Out of the six pairs of guards assigned to watch Edy's house, one guard's record caught his eye. He'd been disciplined several times for leaving his post without explanation. Next to Ronald Hooper's name Al had made notes and attached the public records and social media accounts he'd dug up on the guy. A steep mortgage, five kids, and a stay-at-home wife must add to the financial pressure on Ron. Next to Al's notes, Jake wrote a note: *Al, pull Hooper in, then check to see if he was open to bribes or willing to look the other way. Then question the others in turn.*

Jake stopped writing as he thought through the steps. If Al or Kraus got anything in their interview with Hooper, Jake would dig deeper into his financials.

"Jake, I have something," Al said stepping into the office.

"On who?"

"Cedric Dunstan took out a personal loan from his own bank in the amount of two hundred and fifty thousand dollars two months ago. The cosigner was Edy Dunstan."

"She never mentioned it. I think if she had signed for one she would've told me," Jake said, his line of questioning changing with the information. "Thanks. Good work, Al. Oh, I was writing you a note." Jake handed it to Al. "Follow up on Ronald Hooper."

"We aim to please, though I'm not coming up with anything on Riverton. But I'll keep digging," Al said on his way out of the office.

Jake pressed the button on his intercom for Louie. "Are you ready?"

"Yes, who are we questioning first?"

"I want a go at Cedric." Jake filled in Louie, then picked up his file and left. He dismissed the officer on duty inside Cedric's interview room. "Why the hell have you kept me waiting? I'm going to report you to your superiors," Dunstan said.

Jake ignored him and read the pertinent information into the record and took a seat. Louie remained by the door with his arms folded across his chest, his expression grave.

"Mr. Dunstan, where is your lawyer?"

"He's out of town. I'll need a public defender until mine shows up."

"Okay, you'll be put back into holding until one arrives."

"I'm not going back there." Dunstan pushed up from his seat.

"We can't conduct this interview until your lawyer arrives," Jake said.

"Forget it, ask your questions."

"For the record, you want to continue this interview without your lawyer?" Jake asked.

"Yes."

'I'd like to start with the loan of two hundred and fifty thousand dollars you financed two months ago."

Dunstan pushed out of his chair, his eyes wide. "Where'd you get that information? It's confidential."

"Sit down, Mr. Dunstan. You'd be surprised the information we have at our fingertips."

"What I do and don't do is none of your damn business!" Cedric shouted.

"Your wife, I mean your soon-to-be ex-wife, is missing. I see from these documents that she cosigned the loan?"

"Yes, she did," Cedric said in a quieter voice, sweat forming on his brow.

"Is that a fact? In my interview with Mrs. Dunstan earlier about the blackmail letter she'd received, I asked if she could get the money, if needed. She said yes. And when asked if she'd need a loan, she said no, she had the funds and had no outstanding loans," Jake lied.

He wondered if Ed Rockford had got his hands on this information, and if it'd been the reason for the termination proceedings.

"Well, she must've forgotten this one," Cedric said.

"If you'll excuse me, I want to send this document over to Ed Rockford for him to verify his daughter's signature. I'll be a moment." Jake stared into Dunstan's eyes.

"There's no reason for you to do that. I'd never hurt her. I want her and her father out of my life."

"Killing her would certainly achieve your wish, wouldn't it?" Jake pushed out of his chair and waved the papers at Dunstan.

"I didn't kill her or abduct her."

"I'll be right back."

Jake made it to the door before Dunstan spoke up. "That's not her signature. I signed for her. Husbands and wives have been doing that for centuries. It's not sinister or anything."

Jake sat again. Louie glided behind Dunstan and lingered against the wall.

"Funny use of the word—two months after you forged your wife's signature on a large loan document, and now she's gone missing. Where is Edy, Cedric?"

"I have no idea where she is. How could I?"

"Mr. Dunstan, you lied about being home all evening. When I left your place I checked the hood of your car, and it was still hot. Where were you all night?" Jake asked, leaning in closer to Cedric.

"That's it. I'm done until my lawyer gets here."

"Louie, can you take Mr. Dunstan back to holding? I'll be in with Miss Riverton. Please join me after you turn him over to a uniform."

Louie took Dunstan by the arm and escorted him around the cramped space. At the door he stopped, tossing Jake a lopsided grin behind Dunstan's back.

Jake stood by the water cooler, downing cup after cup before he geared up to question Rosie Riverton. He figured Louie had had enough time to catch up with him as he entered interview room B. He kept the female officer in the room until Louie could join him.

He read in the pertinent facts as he waited for a reaction from Riverton. She didn't disappoint.

"I'm not a criminal. Why are you treating me like one?"

"I'm not, Miss Riverton, I'm protecting both you and me by recording our session. I'll state once again that you have the right to an attorney during these proceedings."

"I have nothing to hide. I want to go home." She leaned forward, arms resting on the table as she slouched.

She whines like a nine-year-old. "We all do, Miss Riverton. The sooner you answer my questions and stop stalling, the sooner we'll be done. You'll be dismissed then," Jake said.

He failed to tell her that she could be remanded into custody if he felt it was warranted. "Let's get started. Where were you tonight?"

"I was out with friends."

"Where?"

"Why does it matter?"

Jake inhaled to control his mounting impatience. He sat staring at her for a few seconds before he spoke. "Telling me is the difference between you spending the night in a cell or at home. Let's try this again. Where were you tonight, Miss Riverton?"

"Fine. I went out to dinner with Kathy Fasano and Diane Gaston. We ate at some Italian place. We tried Tiramisu's first, but as you said they were closed. I wasn't driving and didn't pay attention."

"You weren't driving?"

"I left my car at Kathy's. We all met there and she drove. If you let me call her, I'll get the name of the restaurant."

"Rosie, did you pay cash for your dinner or did you charge it?"

Louie slipped into the room and took up a position by the door and dismissed the uniform. She took up her post outside the door.

"I charg…" She realized her mistake and stopped speaking.

"May I see the charge slip?" Jake asked.

"I gave it to Cedric."

"You were home less than five minutes and you dug the receipt out of your large purse and gave it to Cedric, is that correct?"

"Yes."

"And he'll confirm it?"

"I don't know." She sat back in her seat, spine straight, her eyes roaming the room.

"You're lying, Miss Riverton. Please hand me the receipt."

She dug around in her purse, then started plucking items from it, dropping them on the scarred wooden table. "See, it's not there."

"Please check your wallet," Jake said, surveying the mess she had pulled from her purse.

Rosie picked up her green wallet, opened it, and searched the billfold. She retrieved three receipts and handed them to him. Jake reviewed each one. Two were dated midweek, the time stamp around noon for each. He figured them for her lunch receipts. The third, dated today, had a time stamp of six forty-five from the Sunset Korean Restaurant on Meriden Road, not to be mistaken for Tiramisu's or any other Italian restaurant.

"What did you and your friends do after dinner?"

"Afterward, I went home."

"You finished up dinner at a quarter to seven and didn't get home until after ten? Where were you in the time between finishing dinner and arriving home?"

"I think I want a lawyer now," Rosie said, biting her nails.

"I'll have an officer take you to a phone, but remember, if you know anything about Edy Dunstan's disappearance, now's the time to tell me. I might be able to offer you a deal."

"I want the lawyer." Rosie crossed her arms over her chest as she bit down on her bottom lip.

"Noting this interview has ended at 11:55 p.m." Jake continued reading the rest of the information into the recorder. Louie handed Rosie to the female officer. Jake stayed seated and checked his watch. Edy had been missing for three and a half hours. With each hour that passed, her chance of survival lessened.

He wouldn't be able to cope with another death on his watch.

Chapter 23

Jake dragged his tired, sore body to bed after one. Mia stirred, then rolled to her side.

Cedric and Rosie had used the same lawyer. Attorney Thomas Kincaid had made it back from his trip. Dunstan had dismissed his public defender. Kincaid hadn't allowed them to answer most of Jake's questions. He had no more information at the end of the session with the damn attorney than he'd had before it.

Jake could only imagine what thoughts were going through Edy's head as she sat alone. Had they blindfolded her, tied her up? Where were they holding her? Rosie had had plenty of time to stash her away before she'd gotten home. And Cedric, why the shower? Did he have blood on him—Edy's blood? Jake pushed the disturbing image from his head. Until he found Edy, or her body, he'd keep her alive in his mind, and the pressure on to recover her.

"Jake, you need rest," Mia said, yawning.

"Sorry, I can't shut it off."

"You're not going to help Edy if you're not up to snuff."

"Go back to sleep. I'll go out on the couch," Jake said, rolling to his side of the bed.

"No, stay right here." Mia stretched an arm across his chest, snuggled in close to him.

He slipped into sleep somewhere around three a.m. and woke in a fog when his alarm went off at five thirty. Jake tucked the covers around Mia before he went into the shower. Brigh lifted her head, stared at him with her big brown eyes, circled her bed, and went back to sleep. He was glad someone was able to rest.

The hot water hit his stomach before he realized he hadn't waterproofed the bandage. For crying out loud, it wasn't as if he still needed it. He ripped off the tape and examined the wound. A red ring circled the scab and it itched like crazy, though he didn't dare scratch it. *I better make time for the doctor this week.*

Twenty minutes later, showered and dressed, he went into the kitchen to brew a cup of coffee and toast a bagel to bring with him to the station. He filled Brigh's dish with food, topped off her water bowl, and through it all Mia hadn't budged.

* * * *

Louie was sitting at his desk, his phone stuck to his ear, when Jake arrived. Jake tapped on the desk, pointed to his office, and continued walking.

"Get anything new on the case?" Jake asked when Louie joined him.

"I got the owner of the restaurant where Riverton and her friends ate. Ji-woong, the owner, said after they paid their bill she and her two girlfriends didn't linger."

"What time did he close?"

"Around eight, but he said they were gone long before he shut the place down."

"Okay, call her attorney. I want the names and numbers of her girlfriends. If he gives you any lip, get a warrant to search their places, and make sure their cars are included in it."

"I've already requested one from Judge Eisenberg. He's one of the few who gets to his chambers this early. Plus, he's personal friends with Ed Rockford. He didn't bother to give me any guff about calling."

"Good thinking. How long have you been here?"

"A while," Louie said, slipping a cup under the spout of the Keurig. The strong scent of coffee filled the air. Jake lifted his cup off his desk and waited for his turn at his own coffee machine.

"Did Officer Kramer report in?"

"Yes, Dunstan and Riverton never left the apartment after they got home from here last night."

"Who else could've taken her? I'm not leaning toward Melinda for Edy's kidnapping." Jake stared out his window into the darkness. It'd be another hour before the sun rose.

"Could it be one of Jimmy's men?" Louie said.

"I have Al checking out Ronald Hooper."

"It's a longshot I'm throwing out there. The more we look into Dunstan, Riverton, Melinda, and Jimmy's guys, the more I see people desperate for funds. Most of them are living above their means." Louie sipped his coffee.

"We all can't be a magic man with money like you are," Jake said, running Louie's last statement through his brain.

Edy's disappearance bore no resemblance to Callie's murder. It appeared he had two suspects for two separate, unrelated crimes to hunt down. Did he have a copycat crime?

"Lieutenant, this came in the mail on Saturday and got routed to the wrong desk," interrupted Officer Trudy Callahan from the mailroom. "I'm sorry for the misdirection."

"No problem, Trudy. Thanks."

Jake accepted the large yellow envelope from her. He carefully slipped his letter opener through the space at the top and tilted the envelope to empty the contents onto his desk. Pictures of George Spaulding dressed in prison garb and a typewritten letter stared Jake in the face. He pulled latex gloves from his middle drawer and donned them before he touched the contents. Louie did the same.

Jake read the letter first.

Dear Jake,

I spoke with my mother. Mom said you needed to speak with me. I'm sorry I missed you. I've been up at the Osborn state prison in Somers, interviewing Spaulding for my next assignment. I've enclosed some photos for you, to see if you have any comments I can add to my article on Spaulding and his request for new DNA testing. And if you still believe he's the killer. I'll contact you when I'm back in town. In the meantime, here's my cell phone number. 555-2355.

Best,

Melinda

Jake handed the letter to Louie. He lifted the pictures up by the left-hand corner. A gaunt George Spaulding stared back at him. Who hired Melinda to photograph George? Or was it a ploy to distract him? Take him off Callie's case.

"What do you think?" Jake asked.

"Are you okay?"

Louie understands more than any other person how Eva's death has affected me. But this...no...I'm not all right, this is a stupid move on Melinda's part to mess with me. "I'm fine. It's not going to slow me down, if that's what you're asking. Right now Edy Dunstan is our priority. Callie's dead. We still have a chance of finding Edy alive."

"Agreed. Where do we go from here?"

"You log the letter and pictures into evidence and create a file." Jake reached into his top right-hand drawer, drew out a file with the other letter he'd received earlier in the week, and handed it to Louie. "From now on, each time she contacts us this way, we keep track of it. Dust it for prints."

"It's not my first rodeo, Jake." Louie's eyebrows knitted together as he glanced down at the pictures. "He's gotten meaner looking."

"It's as if he knew these shots were coming to me. I wonder if it's a line worth tugging, though I'd send someone else out there to interview Spaulding."

"Maybe he did know these pictures were for you. I wouldn't put it past Melinda to play this sort of game. I'd go and face the bastard down," Louie said.

"I'm not going to play her game or his. If and when it comes to that, it definitely will not be you or me. Give me a call when the warrant comes through." Jake popped a couple of antacids.

Louie took the file. "Jake, you're not in this alone. Don't do anything unless you run it by me. Together we'll go after her or George, if need be."

Words stuck in Jake's throat. He offered Louie a tight smile. He waved his hand to clear Louie out of his office before he lost it. Jake sat, opened a file on his computer, and typed in the information about the letter. A loud clang echoed inside his skull. Without looking at the time he grabbed his phone and dialed the nursing home his mother resided in.

"This is Lieutenant Jake Carrington from the WPD," he told the woman who answered. "I need to speak with the administrator."

"He doesn't come on duty until eight a.m., Lieutenant. Can I give you to the night supervisor, Mrs. Athens?"

"Yes, I'll speak with her."

He waited five minutes for the woman to pick up as he drummed his fingers on the desk. He started right in on her after identifying himself.

"There's a woman who might try to see my mother or send her a package. I want to be sure you check her mail for pictures or letters pertaining to my sister's killer. Someone is sending them to me. Please verify my mother hasn't received any. It'll send her over the edge. The administrator also needs to be informed of this development."

"I'll make sure, Lieutenant. Why would someone want to hurt her?"

"I don't know. I hope whoever sent them keeps me as their target. I'll be sending over two pictures. One is of the woman, and the other will be of the killer."

He planned on sending over Spaulding's picture too, in case Melinda was in the process of helping George to escape. Jake wouldn't put it past either one of them. On the pad in front of him, he wrote a note to check in with the prison to verify Spaulding was still there. "For no reason whatsoever are they allowed to visit with my mother. Understand?"

"Yes, I'll spread the word. Is she, or anyone here, in danger?" Mrs. Athens asked.

"I don't believe anyone is at this time, though if and when the circumstances change, you'll be notified."

Jake hung up. He rolled a package of antacids in his hand. *God forgive me, but I hate Melinda and George more than anything on this green planet. It never ends.* Strange, he'd clumped them together. He'd have to dig deeper into their past and current relationships. First and foremost, finding Edy alive took precedence over everything else.

He dialed the cell number for Ed Rockford. "Mr. Rockford, can you give me a list of properties Edy owns, and which ones are her favorite places to get away for a weekend or vacation?"

"Lieutenant, she owns a beachfront property in Saybrook, one in Rhode Island, a ski house in Vermont, and a hunting lodge in the Litchfield Hills, which was primarily used by Cedric, not Edy."

"Fax over the addresses and how long she's owned them, and any other place she might take off to for solitude," Jake said.

"She didn't take off," Ed Rockford protested, his voice rising in Jake's ear.

"I'm sure she didn't, sir. But someone might use one of her locations. Or use her credit cards to check into a hotel. I need to be sure we leave no stone unturned."

"Sorry, Lieutenant, it's just…I had a bad night wondering if she's unharmed."

"I understand, and will do my best to find her," Jake said, not confident at all that he would. "Do you have a set of keys to her places?"

"I do. I have three meetings this morning, but I'll leave the keys with Mildred, my housekeeper."

"Thank you, Mr. Rockford."

Louie stood in his doorway and waited for him to finish up his call. "I sent the pictures and envelope over to the lab by courier and gave Tom Jones a heads-up on it," Louie said as Jake put his phone down on his desk.

"Why him and not Willie?"

"Willie's working the case, and Tom ran the other photos for you last week, remember?"

"No, it seems ages ago. Ed Rockford is sending over a list of properties Edy owns. We'll hit those that are in the state and have the respective departments in Rhode Island and Vermont check out the properties there. I want to go to her hunting lodge up in the Litchfield Hills first. Ed said Cedric used it the most. Afterward, we'll check out the beach property."

"Why not have Al and Kraus check out Saybrook and save us some time?" Louie scratched his chin.

"I want to see each property and gauge the last time each was used."

"Why aren't you considering Melinda for this?"

"Louie, you waffle more than a waffle iron. First you think Melinda's innocent, now you think she's guilty. What gives?" Jake asked.

"I'm not locked in to her guilt or innocence. If the kidnapping is for money, and so was the murder, Melinda is the one who's in the most debt."

"You forgot the two-hundred-and-fifty-thousand-dollar loan Cedric took out?"

"No, I didn't."

A uniformed officer knocked on his door. "Lieutenant, this arrived for you," Officer McDonald said.

"Thanks." Jake grabbed the fax, ran his eyes down the page, stood, and lifted his jacket off the back of his chair. "Let's go out to the hunting property in Goshen. It's not a bad ride. What else are you waiting on?"

"The background and financials for Rosie Riverton and Ronald Hooper," Louie said.

"Hand them off to Al and Kraus."

Jake stopped at Rockford's house first for the keys. It was on the way. It took him forty-five minutes on the back roads to reach Goshen, a rural community of farmers and, in recent years, winemakers. Light traffic along Route 63 made for a pleasant trip. Though it was November, some trees clung to a few of their burnt orange and red leaves. Forty-five minutes after leaving Wilkesbury, Jake found the turnoff to Route 4 and took a left.

Jake drove six miles on Route 4 before he turned right onto an unpaved road. The car bumped along the dirt road, jostling his queasy stomach. A few miles in, a log cabin appeared in the middle of nowhere. If he had to hide a person or body, Edy's secluded lodge provided the perfect place, with no neighbors for miles and miles. A person could scream their lungs out before another human being heard them.

Jake parked and climbed out and stretched his legs. Louie did the same. From its size most people would consider this a full-time home. He guessed the rich needed their comforts no matter where they hung out. He and Louie drew theirs guns from their holsters. He took the right side of the building while Louie checked out the left side. They met in front of it. A wall of windows looked out upon the small lake, as did the wraparound porch. It'd make a perfect place to weigh down a body, which might stay hidden for years.

"There aren't any recent footprints. How about you? Notice any?" Jake asked.

"No, the leaves seemed undisturbed."

Jake peeked into one of the windows. Sheets covered the furniture and a thick layer of dust streaked the table under the window. He unlocked the door with Rockford's keys and searched the place anyway before they locked it back up and headed to the shoreline.

"Why is nothing easy?" Louie asked, patting dust off his pants.

"Because this isn't the movies. Let's move out. We have a lot to cover today."

He sat in the car and stared out over the lake before he put the car into reverse and started to back up, his mind calculating the odds. He braked to follow a thought.

"Let's walk the driveway and the area on each side for a bit before we leave."

"You see something?" Louie scanned the woods.

"No, I want to make sure there's not a hidden building or tracks other than ours here," Jake said climbing from the car.

"There go my shoes." Dry leaves crunched under Louie's feet as he stepped out from the passenger's side.

Jake held back his comment as he watched Louie make his way gingerly through the woods. He rested his gun against his leg and listened. Nothing out of the ordinary sounded. Twigs snapping to his left had him pulling up short.

"Freaking woods," Louie mumbled when he stepped in front of Jake.

"Anything?"

"No, except bear shit." Louie stared down at his shoes.

"Let's keep walking for a bit longer. It seems odd this is the only house around the lake."

"It's not a lake. It's a pond, Jake." Louie leaned against a short tree, tore off some leaves, and started wiping the bear scat off his shoes.

"And you know this because…" Jake twisted his mouth to the side.

"It's not on the map. I want to get the hell out of here. You should've sent Al and Kraus to check this out."

Jake left Louie to clean his shoes and walked deeper into the woods. He circled back fifteen minutes later to find Louie in the car with his cell phone in his hand, waving it in all directions. Jake kicked his shoe against the outside of the car before he got behind the wheel. He repeated it with the other foot.

"If he took her, Cedric's smart enough to know we'd check out all the properties," Jake said. "Make a note in case we don't find her to recheck this place in a few days."

"I'll put Al on it."

Louie had never been much of an outdoorsman.

It took Jake forty-five minutes to reach the highway. All the while, Louie used his bottle of water and the paper towels Jake kept in the car to polish his shoes.

"You understand we're heading to the beach next. There's sand there," Jake said, slipping a sideward glance Louie's way.

"The next time we go on an outing we'll take my car. I have boots in the trunk for this sort of thing."

Chapter 24

Edy stirred, fighting to clear her hazy head, but only bits and pieces came through the foggy mist as she struggled to open her eyes. Something blocked them. *Oh God, they've blindfolded me, but why?* Gritty sand rubbed against her eyeballs and burned as if they'd been set on fire. She couldn't rub them because her hands were bound behind her. Pins and needles raced up her arms while she grappled with the rope to try to loosen it and free her hands. *I'm so thirsty.*

Her swollen tongue ached, clogging her throat as she begged through the gag for water. No one responded. *Dear God, help me,* she prayed. Simple childhood prayers she hadn't said in years. *I have to get myself out of this, and when I do I'll kill both of those cretins.*

She had to make sense of what had happened, try to remember everything if she was to get out of this alive. Had the lieutenant been notified of her kidnapping? If so, had he gone after Cedric and his bitch? It took a while for the haze to clear. Once it had, Edy categorized everything she'd been able to recall.

Was it an hour ago, or yesterday?

A setup? How'd they know I'd take that route home? It had to be someone who knows me and understands I wouldn't cower to their demands. She remembered swerving to avoid the car head-on, but it had driven straight into her door.

It dazed me. How long before they pulled me from the car? Wait, my doors were locked, how'd they get in? Edy inhaled through her nose as she dug into her memory for more details. *A key? No, they broke my window, the glass shooting at me as I shaded my eyes. Cedric had a key to my car.*

Why not use it, unless it wasn't him? No one else had anything to gain. The blackmailer? But why? They haven't given me a drop location yet.

Footsteps off to her left had bile bubbling up from the pit of her stomach. A roaring fire burning in her belly worked its way up into her chest before expelling into her mouth. It hit a wall of cloth, forcing her to swallow the bile as it cooked her throat. The muscles closed, her air cut off. She coughed hard and rolled around on the hard surface as she continued to choke. Large hands grabbed her by the shoulders and lifted her to a sitting position as a hand whacked her on the back a bit too hard. The more she tried to get air in the more she hyperventilated.

Was he here all along?

Someone ripped the gag from her mouth and grasped her by the hair, tilting her head back. He poured water down her throat as she struggled to swallow to keep from choking. Edy gulped and gulped, but the water flooded her esophagus as it choked her, the excess streaming from her mouth, soaking her in front and back.

"If I hear one word out of your mouth, I'll put you back to sleep, understand?"

Edy tried to nod, but the man still had a tight grip on her hair. She hadn't recognized the distorted voice. How much was he being paid? She'd beat the offer. She opened her mouth, hoping for more water.

"Say one word…"

He let his voice trail off. She rolled her lips over her teeth as she wet them with her tongue. *I need more water, can't he read the sign?* She moistened her lips again in case he'd missed it.

"Good girl." He ran his calloused hand over her cheek. Edy flinched. "Now if you want the blindfold removed and your hands untied, you'll sit perfectly still until I tell you that you can move, understand?"

The man thinks I'm mentally challenged. I'll do anything to see. She tried to tilt her head up and down.

He undid the blindfold first. Bright lights blinded her, forcing her to close them. She lifted her lids a few millimeters at a time to grow accustomed to the light. A looming black silhouette came into focus. She squinted, her breathing uneven—seeing made it worse. He was dressed in all black, his face covered in a hood. Edy shivered, unable to control the tremors running through her as she struggled to quiet her thoughts.

"You're a smart one. If you make any attempt to get out of here, I'll shoot you. Understand?"

Edy nodded.

He cut her hands free. She went to rub her aching wrists when he jerked her left hand back and snapped one side of a pair of handcuffs to her left wrist, cuffing the other side to a metal railing running along the bed. Without thinking, she tugged her hand hard, the metal cutting into her sore arm.

"Why are you doing this? What have I ever done to you?" Edy hated the whine in her voice.

"Lady, I told you, no talking or I'll gag and bind you again. Do you understand?"

In the little time she'd been with him, she'd come to hate the word *understand*. Once she was freed she'd shove the freaking word down his damn throat. He turned off the light and left the room as quietly as he'd entered it. A metallic door slammed shut, a deadbolt thrown in place, flinging her into darkness. Before the light faded she had committed to memory the room, the door, and the window. The size of the window told her she was in a basement. She'd never fit through it. A sheet of metal blocked her only escape.

She replayed the conversation with him, noting the nuances of his speech, his size in the shadows, and the calluses on his hands. He'd spoken in a Wilkesbury accent, reducing the r's in his words and dropping the h's. If he was local, Cedric had hired him. He met all kinds of people in his job.

Who are the woman and the man who feed me? If it's Cedric, did he participate in the actual abduction? It had to be Cedric, otherwise why hadn't he spoken when they snatched me? A puzzle she had to figure out in order to escape.

Last night only the woman spoke, but I'm sure there was a man there. And there was something familiar about his scent—but what?

Large hands had held her down and jabbed her with the needle. *The scent—think, Edy, you know it.*

She leaned back against the concrete wall, exhaustion overtaking her, her tired, scratchy eyes begging for relief. A few seconds later she bolted upright. A spicy smell of musk and lime along with a floral feminine perfume confused her senses. It was hard to define but it'd come to her.

Though Edy was no longer gagged, her breathing constricted when she inhaled, forcing her to take small breaths—in through the nose, out through the mouth—after five minutes of breathing yoga style, her heart rate returned to normal. As it slowed, her senses started to work. The musty scent of rotting leaves filled her nostrils. The damp cold air washed over her skin, sending a chill through her. Off in the distance she heard a car—several cars. No birds sang, no dogs barked, no familiar sounds for

her to identify. *Where am I—the city, woods, or a house?* Cold seeped
into every bone.
Will this be where I die?

* * * *

Melinda stretched before climbing out of bed. Her back ached from
the lumpy mattress. She focused her mind and body on the location. She'd
spent the last couple of days photographing Spaulding for her fictitious
article and hoped the letter she'd sent to Jake threw him a curve. She'd
use anything at her disposal to get him off her back. Spaulding had cost
her plenty before he agreed to let her photograph him.

Her mother's message on her voicemail had sent Melinda running.
What had Jake found at her house for him to bring her mother into all this?

She pulled the curtain aside. The water rushed to the shore as she
contemplated her next move. When Melinda needed a break from work
and all the debt, she'd borrow this place from her college friend Lisa,
who lived in Jersey. Lisa only used it in the summer. Melinda came here
for a week or more during the off-season and helped maintain the place.
She'd never brought anyone with her or told anyone where she went when
she disappeared. This time of year the beach was deserted. She couldn't
afford to take a chance she'd be found. She'd brought her groceries with
her from Connecticut.

Melinda dropped the curtain and wrapped her arms around herself as
she planned her next move. She'd have to hit up Darcy McGuire or Edy
Dunstan for cash before she'd be able to vanish. Dunstan would be the
bigger payday, but McGuire was also worth big bucks, though dealing with
a cop's wife again might not be smart. It came down to who'd be able to
get the money the fastest.

Who should she do—the banker's daughter or the CEO, a cop's wife? She
turned on the television to the news, giving it half an ear as she continued
to figure out who she'd target next. Dunstan's name caught her ear. She
turned and listened. *The bitch got herself kidnapped. Whoever did this
is a dead man. She's mine. Well, it's risky, but Darcy McGuire wins by
default. I'll have to settle for one hundred thousand instead of five hundred
thousand. How far away can I get on one hundred grand? The islands?*

With the decision of who to blackmail next out of the way, she'd have to
figure out the where. She'd pick a place in the other direction, away from
Wilkesbury. An internet search on her phone gave her the Royal Arms in

Southbury, one exit away from where McGuire worked. It'd be convenient, and out of Jake's jurisdiction—a win-win situation all around.

The papers she'd collected all week sat on top of the desk. Melinda donned a pair of surgical gloves, cut out words in various fonts and pasted them to a sheet of paper, then stuck it in an envelope and sealed it. This time she'd send it to Darcy's job, not her home. Everything would take place outside of Wilkesbury. She'd need to chance a ride into Connecticut to mail it.

* * * *

With one hand on the steering wheel, Jake turned his in-car computer toward Louie. "Do a search of the area for rentals, in case we come up empty-handed again."

"What are you looking for?" Louie asked while Jake navigated the curvy road.

"Two things. One is Edy, but I also want to make sure Melinda's not in the area. I remembered last night how much she loved the beach," Jake said.

As they had driven through the neighborhood on their way to Edy's, Jake had been on the lookout for Melinda's car. So far, he hadn't seen it.

"You think she's dumb enough to hang around here?"

"No, but I'm not going to take a chance that she isn't. If we get nothing, we'll contact the beach areas out of state."

"Most of the rentals are seasonal," Louie said.

"After we check Edy's place, let's walk the beach."

"Damn, you really are bent on ruining my shoes today." Louie continued to type on the computer as he complained. Jake ignored him.

In the last two days he'd been to a funeral, another murder scene, and a kidnapping. He'd all but dropped the ball on finding Melinda. He'd have to decide if splitting up the investigations between him and Louie would be a benefit.

"Here's the turn," Jake said, taking a left onto Ocean Boulevard. Louie scanned the house numbers as Jake slowed the car. At the end of the boulevard, on a curve that extended over the water, rose a huge white home with black shutters and many balconies.

Louie let out a low whistle.

Jake stopped the car in front of Edy's cottage and studied the house. Edy Dunstan was indeed loaded. Her beach house was bigger than his and Louie's homes combined. Wooden shutters were fixed in place around windows and doors. They got out of the car and walked the property before testing the carved doors with stained-glass side panels.

"I'm going to go to the car for the toolbox," Jake said. "You keep looking for another way in."

From his toolbox he pulled a crowbar, a hammer, some nails, and the keys to Edy's place. He returned with the crowbar resting against his shoulder.

"What are you two doing over there?" a man said, his collar turned up against the wind. Jake estimated the man to be in his late seventies.

"Sir, we're authorized to be here." Jake showed his badge. "And you are?"

"I'm Trent Stevens. I live next door all year around and keep an eye on the place for Mrs. Dunstan."

"Have you seen anyone going in and out of the house in the last week?"

"No one's been here since summer. Edy always has someone close the place up after Labor Day."

"It's important, Mr. Stevens. Are you sure?" Jake asked.

"Yes. Tell me what's going on."

It'd been on the news. Hadn't Stevens heard?

"Edy's been kidnapped. Her father sent us to check out her properties," Jake said.

"If she disappeared, it's her no-good husband, if you ask me," Stevens said, biting his lip.

"Why?"

"She argued with Cedric all the time. And during the week he'd bring his girlfriends down here. He's a scuzzy one."

"Thanks, Mr. Stevens, I'll take it under advisement. We'll be going in, but I'll nail it back up when we're through. Oh, one more thing. Has anyone new been around, renting one of the homes on the beach?"

"No, there are only a few of us full-time residents. I'd know if someone rented a place."

Jake pried the wood off the door. He and Louie lifted it and placed it on the ground. He used the keys Rockford gave him, trying each in turn until one opened the door. A quick search turned up nothing. It was another dead end. The house hadn't been used since it was closed up. He nailed the plywood back in place and they climbed into his car.

Jake still hadn't seen Melinda's car. Stevens struck him as a nosy neighbor and would've told them if someone new had rented a house out of season.

Jake placed a call to the locals in Rhode Island and found out Edy's property there had been locked up and not disturbed.

Jake's cell phone vibrated in his pocket. He didn't recognize the number but answered anyway.

"Carrington."

"Lieutenant, it's Linden Smith. Your office gave me this number. I've just heard about Edy. I've been dating her for two months. Is she okay?"

"We hope so. When's the last time you saw her or spoke to her?"

"I saw her last week for lunch and spoke with her yesterday around noon. She called, but I already had plans. Now I wish I'd canceled."

"Do you have time to come into the station later today and give me a statement?" Jake asked while balancing his phone between his left ear and shoulder, his other hand on his keys, ready to start the car.

"Anything that will help get her back. What time?" Linden asked.

He started the car and checked the dashboard clock. "Give me two hours. If I'm not there when you arrive, ask for Detective Burke. He'll take your statement."

"I'll see you in two hours, Lieutenant."

Jake hung up. "Well, he saved me a call."

"Who?" Louie asked.

"Linden Smith. He sounded genuinely concerned for her."

"And still, love can kill," Louie said.

"So they claim." Jake shifted into drive and pulled out of Edy's Saybrook driveway.

Chapter 25

Construction along Route 9 impeded Jake and Louie's trip back to Wilkesbury and the station. An hour and ten minutes later they pulled into the garage under the building. The squad secretary handed him a message as he stepped into Homicide. Jake glanced at it and continued on to his office.

"What's the frown for?" Louie asked, stepping in behind him.

"The mayor wants to meet again. I'm going to call him instead. We don't have the time for politics."

"Why don't you do that while I see if Linden Smith has arrived?"

"Thanks."

Jake dialed the mayor's office after Louie left. "May I speak with the mayor, it's Lieutenant Carrington returning his call."

"Lieutenant, he cleared time to see you this afternoon," the mayor's secretary said.

"I'd appreciate a few minutes of his time now," Jake said, standing firm.

"Hold please. I'll check."

Flowery music filled his ears.

"Jake, I've a busy day," Mayor D'Angelo said, coming on the line.

"I do too, Mayor. It's the reason for the call. I'm about to go into an interview now on the Edy Dunstan case, which might lead back to Callie Blake's murder."

"I haven't heard about Dunstan. Is she dead too?"

"No, sir, someone kidnapped her last night. She has also received a blackmail letter. The main suspect in Blake's murder has been killed. His body was discovered yesterday. I've new leads that Sergeant Romanelli and I are following. I'm pressed for time in the kidnapping if we hope to find her alive."

Jake threw the ball to D'Angelo—if he decided to make Jake go out of his way for a meet, and Edy was found dead, the media would have a field day with his career, as would Rockford. Jake counted on D'Angelo making the right decision.

"Keep me updated, and put me on your calendar for noon tomorrow," D'Angelo said in a sharp tone. "Here."

"Yes, sir."

When he hung up, Jake pushed the mayor to the back of his mind. Louie had texted him that Smith had arrived and he'd put him in room 4.

Louie noted Jake's arrival for the tape when he stepped into the interview room.

"Mr. Smith, thank you for coming in. Did the sergeant read you your rights?"

"My rights? What for?"

"This is for your protection and ours, and it's standard procedure," Jake said, taking the seat across from Linden and next to Louie.

Linden's cell phone rang. He looked down at the caller ID, frowned, then pressed a button before he slipped it into his jacket pocket.

"Do you need to take that, Mr. Smith?" Jake asked.

"No."

Jake read Smith's Miranda rights into the recorder. "Let's get started. What can you tell me about Edy's mood yesterday?"

"She seemed upset when she called and found out I was busy."

"Why, because you made plans?"

"No, I never saw her on the weekends. We only met during the week on my lunch hour."

"Where did you normally meet?"

Linden stared at Jake for a second, dropped his gaze to his hands.

"Mr. Smith, I'm trying to find her before the kidnapper kills her. Your answers are important," Jake said.

Smith raised his eyes to Louie, and then to Jake. "We mostly met at the Eaton Hotel on the outskirts of town."

"You weren't dating, but only having an affair?" Louie asked, distracting Smith.

"In the beginning, yes, but I fell in love with her. She's the one who didn't want to be seen around town until she filed for divorce from her husband."

Smith's phone sounded in his pocket. He took it out and pressed a button and returned it to his pocket.

"Are you sure you don't need to take that?"

"I'm good, it's nothing important," Linden said.

"Let's get back to this. Your picture with Edy at the Town Hall Café last week didn't bother you?" Jake asked.

"No, it meant she was ready to take our relationship to the next level."

"Which was?" Jake asked.

"I want to marry her."

"And she was on board with your plans?" Louie asked.

"She didn't commit to anything. Edy said she had to concentrate on the divorce before she'd consider her future."

"I bet that made you mad," Jake said.

"It annoyed me, but I understood." Smith's shoulders stiffened. He adjusted his position. "You're wasting precious time with me if you think I'd hurt Edy. I love her. It's that asshole of a husband who did this."

"What makes you say that?" Louie asked.

"He hates her, cheats, lies, and steals from her. What more do you need?" Linden asked, disgust dripping from each word.

"What do you gain by marrying her?" Jake asked, keeping Smith off balance.

"I'd assume nothing. She'd probably have me sign a prenup." Smith drummed his fingers on the table.

"And you're okay with that?" Jake asked.

"Yes, I have my own money. I'd never use her like Cedric does."

Jake wanted to believe him. "Stay available, Mr. Smith." Jake said, feigning an end to the interview, hoping to give the man a false sense of security. "But if you were to kidnap her, where would you hide her?"

Smith's mouth fell open. His eyes roamed from Louie's to Jake. "I'd never take her. I don't know. Have you checked her other properties?"

"We'll be in touch, Mr. Smith. Thank you for coming in."

Louie ushered Smith out into the corridor. Jake sat there reviewing his answers. He'd gotten nothing from Smith except to learn that he knew about Edy's properties. Minutes later Louie walked back into the room.

"You get anything?" Jake asked.

"Smith only showed nerves on the last question, but I'm still leaning toward Cedric," Louie said.

"Me too. We have to find her alive."

"I agree. What's next?"

"Why don't you check in again with the police in Vermont and Rhode Island? I've got another angle I want to consider."

Jake hoped all the strings he pulled got him closer to saving Edy.

* * * *

A knock on her closed door had Darcy adjusting her suit jacket before taking her seat.

"Come in."

"Mrs. McGuire, I found this on my desk. It must've come while I was on break," Jen, her secretary, said.

Darcy took the large manila envelope. No return address. It had a Hartford postmark, and large red letters scrawled across it: DO NOT BEND.

Darcy tapped her fingers on the clasp. She debated whether to open it. She'd promised Shamus she'd tell him if the blackmailer contacted her again, but first she needed to see what the envelope contained.

"Thank you, Jen, please close the door behind you." Darcy sat and stared at the envelope.

It's now or never.

She slipped the letter opener from her top drawer, tucked it under the fold, and slit the envelope inch by inch. She slid the contents of the envelope onto her desk. A folded letter and nude pictures of her fanned out. She shuffled through each one, disgusted. Her mind twirled in every direction as dizziness overtook her.

Dear Darcy,

It's time to pay up for your indiscretions. You and Lieutenant Carrington look ravishing together, don't you think?

Meet me at the Royal Arms in Middlebury at five p.m. and remember to come alone and bring the money, or these pictures will hit the newspapers and the evening news today.

I can just see the headlines now, can't you? "Cop busy with boss's wife leaves no time for him to solve a murder."

Delicious, isn't it?

Until we meet.

No signature, no scent, no anything to distinguish the author. She tucked the letter back in the envelope with the pictures of her and Jake Carrington. Pictures she'd not posed for. The nude ones she went to tuck into her purse, but instead she took out her magnifying glass and studied them. It wasn't her body, but who would believe her? *The timing sucks on this with the big vote for the board coming up. Would they vote me back in if they saw these pictures?* She'd make damn sure no one saw them. Darcy rubbed her temple as she tried to come up with ways to beat Melinda at her own game. It had to be Melinda. She could think of only one other person than the photographer who would do this—Grant P. Stevens. *Stevens wants my job. As if he could run my family company better than me.*

Darcy stood at the window in her penthouse office surveying the parking lot as she forced down the nausea. Work called to her, but her energies had taken a nosedive. How had the photographer placed Jake Carrington beside her in the picture with her wearing the red bustier? Something was off, but she hadn't been able to pinpoint it. Even with a magnifying glass she hadn't figured out how the photographer had blended him in. She'd done a superb job. Darcy had never seen him with his shirt off. But Mia had.

Her attention since receiving the blackmail letter had been split. How could one simple event ripple through so many lives? *First Callie, then Edy...and now me.* Why? She'd come at the problem as she did with all problems. She'd analyze, dissect, and try to find a solution. Though she hated to admit it, she'd racked her brain since yesterday and hadn't come up with a fix yet.

Would Shamus believe I posed with Jake? And dear God, what will the children think if this hits the paper? And the board of trustees, would this end my career? And will Shamus and I survive the scandal, and put this behind us? I'm an old fool who tried to look young.

She'd meet this greedy bitch in person and drop down to her level, but she wasn't stupid enough to bring the money with her. If the person was that desperate, it'd buy her time. She'd call Shamus after she arrived at the hotel. This way she'd have time to confront the blackmailer on her terms before Shamus arrested the woman. No one messed with Darcy or the people she loved. *I'm not as naïve as Callie*, she thought, loading her gun. Darcy fingered the safety into place before she put it in the outside pocket of her purse. *Just in case*, she thought. Shamus had made sure she knew how to defend herself when they'd been stationed in the Middle East. She loved her trusty .22.

Darcy pressed the intercom button. "Jen, would you please come in?"

"Yes, Mrs. McGuire." She entered Darcy's office.

"In a half hour please call Shamus and give him this message," Darcy said, her eyes fixed on Jen's. After she had received the first set of pictures, she'd clued Jen in on what was taking place. She trusted her. Jen had been with her for fifteen years. Jen never bothered to dye her brown hair. It had grayed this past year and her short haircut fit her personality and flattered her face and matronly figure.

How far should I take Jen into my confidence? Should I show her the disgusting pictures? In today's environment people react to rumors before anyone verifies them. I can't trust that anyone will take the time to authenticate the validity of these pictures. Not with the board meeting and the vote so close. Whoever was at the hotel was going to get it—for both her and Callie. With an election for the board coming up, she could be voted out, whether they proved real or not. After all, they'd always been a family-values company.

"Why don't I call him right away?" Jen asked, clasping her hands together.

"Jen, please, I know what I'm doing. Call in a half hour, no sooner."

She handed Jen an envelope. "These are copies of the pictures and letters I just received. Lock them in my safe, and give them only to Shamus or Lieutenant Jake Carrington if I don't return. Understand?"

"Yes, but I think you shouldn't go anywhere alone." Jen tugged on the chain around her neck.

"Don't worry, I can handle myself. One half hour, Jen, not a minute before." Darcy left her office without another word.

* * * *

Jake stopped in his office doorway after interviewing Smith. He studied the back of his visitor. The mayor's department-store suit rode up his back, static causing the polyester to cling to his wide ass and stretch as it tugged across his back. D'Angelo's brown hair was tufted up in back, as if he constantly pushed on it. The mayor had his hands locked behind his back and faced the street. D'Angelo certainly had made himself at home in Jake's office. Jake cleared his throat.

"Mayor, I thought we were meeting tomorrow?"

"What I have to say is important and couldn't wait." D'Angelo turned to face Jake, thrusting papers at him. "This was sent to me this morning. Hayes over at the newspaper is going to run with this story in the morning unless I can assure him that the police, you in particular, are not shielding Blake from prosecution."

"Mayor"—Jake took the paper and glanced at the headline—"Hayes and I have come into conflict before. He tries innocent people in the press all the time, with no thought to the consequences. I've explained the evidence does not point to Todd Blake. My only suspect is in the morgue, and his partner is still out there lining up more women. I don't want to say who I suspect for the murder, but I'm leaning toward a woman. As for Edy Dunstan, I'm ninety-nine percent sure it's her husband and his current girlfriend who snatched her last night."

"You don't believe it's the same person for both crimes?"

"It appears to be a copycat on the blackmail but not the kidnapping. Please take a seat." Jake pointed to one of the chairs in front of his desk and walked around to sit at his desk.

"I'm not going to be long, I'll stand," D'Angelo said. It changed the dynamics of the meeting, with the mayor now towering over him.

"First, kidnapping Edy Dunstan is a scare tactic. It smells of intimidation to me. Callie's murder was downright mean. We're sure she had the money with her when she met her killer. All the person had to do was hide their identity, collect the ransom, and take off. Why kill her? Todd's devastated at her death. I'd bet my career it's not him."

"You might be doing just that. I still want you to pull him in for a formal interview to stifle the rumors he's getting special treatment. I can't order you to do it, Jake, but I can make your life a living hell. Is that what you want?"

Jake didn't want to start out on the wrong foot with D'Angelo, but he'd played this game before and won. The victims had to stay the focus of his cases, not politics.

"No, sir, what I want is to catch a killer and a kidnapper. I think wasting my time with Blake narrows the chances of me finding Edy Dunstan before she's killed. I don't want you as an enemy, Mayor, but I have to do the job before politics."

"Politics is an important part of the job as you climb higher in the ranks. I like Todd Blake and don't want to cause him any more pain than he's already in, but you have to follow a straight line when handling this case. We're both under the microscope on this one."

"I understand."

"I hope you do, Jake. Follow the line." D'Angelo left him to consider his words.

Jake reached for his desk phone, then changed his mind. *Not here*, he thought, and strolled up to the third floor to McGuire's office. McGuire's door was half closed. He knocked.

"Shamus, you got a minute?"

"Come in."

Jake shut the door behind him. Stress lines had appeared around Shamus's gray eyes. Jake was sorry for his part in causing them. *Weary*, he thought. *Shamus looks defeated.* Jake wished he could unsee Darcy's photos, but he and Shamus both knew he couldn't. In a few words he explained the mayor's visit.

"What do you need from me?"

"Can you speak to Todd, and have him come in this afternoon, to keep up appearances?"

"I'll try, but he's not been answering his phone. Both Darcy and I have tried to get in contact with him."

"Why don't you do a wellness check on him?" Jake asked.

"I can do that, and work it in," Shamus said. "I'll keep you informed. Keep going on the kidnapping before she's our next victim."

"Thanks," Jake said as he left McGuire's office.

Jake went straight to Louie's desk when he got back to Homicide. "Pack it in, I want another go at Cedric Dunstan." He checked his watch. "Dunstan should be at work. Let's stop in and embarrass him."

"I thought Rockford fired him," Louie said.

"No, he's in the process of building his termination file. Rockford's covering his ass against lawsuits."

"Why visit Dunstan before Riverton?" Louie asked. "She's the weak link."

"Agreed, but his place of business closes in half an hour, hers doesn't."

Louie tucked an arm in his jacket sleeve as he downed his coffee and joined Jake at the elevator.

* * * *

Jake parked at the curb in the no-parking zone in front of the main branch of the Colonial New England Bank. He placed his "on-duty" sign in the front window to avoid a ticket.

"When we get into Cedric's office, if things don't strike us right, you go out and call Rockford in. He can search the office without a warrant. I'll stall until he gets there, okay?"

"Yes. What are you looking for?" Louie asked.

"The loan papers he forged. I let it slip last night. He's had time to think about it and do something with it. We only have a warrant for his computer and cell phone for the pictures, but I want the original loan papers."

"Got ya," Louie said.

Jake went straight to Cedric's secretary's desk. "Remember me?" he asked, palming his badge. Louie showed his too.

"Yes. Mr. Dunstan asked not to be disturbed today. Can I help you with anything?"

"Yes. Leave your desk, for plausible deniability. I'm going in either way."

Jake stared her down. She reached into her bottom drawer for her purse, stood, flung it over her shoulder and stalked away without a word.

Interesting. The woman doesn't like her boss.

"I told you I don't want to be interrupted, what don't you understand?" Cedric said without looking up.

Jake spied loan papers and a ledger Cedric had been working on. "Your secretary wasn't at her desk. We let ourselves in."

Jake caught the panic in Cedric's eyes when he raised his head. He scrambled to cover the papers on his desk with one of the ledger books.

Louie's cell phone rang. "Excuse me, I need to take this call," Louie said, stepping out of the office.

"I'm a busy man, stop wasting my time. I didn't do anything wrong," Cedric said.

"Mr. Dunstan, I have some follow-up questions and a warrant to confiscate your cell phone and computer."

"I told you last night to talk to my lawyer," Dunstan said, staring down at his desk.

"I will. Give him a call. I'll wait."

"This is harassment." Cedric lifted the receiver off the base, then made no move to press in a number.

"We can do it here or at the station, your choice," Jake said. "Oh, while we wait, do you know anything about these photos?"

Jake handed Cedric two of the many photos of Edy in various stages of undress.

"No, why would I? Who took these?" Jake was impressed by Cedric's acting skills, his range of outrage which never quite touched his eyes.

"You," Jake said, waiting, watching, and judging each of Cedric's nuances.

"You've got to be out of your mind. I didn't take these."

"Mr. Dunstan, I've got a warrant for your phone and computer here and at home." Jake reached into his pocket and extracted the paper.

"You can't do this."

"I can. The cameras in Edy's bedroom could've only been placed there by you. She's had no service people in the house in ages. Benita will attest to it."

"Those bitches stick together. I'm not handing anything over until my lawyer gets here."

"Fine, then have a seat," Jake said.

"No, I've got a business to run." Cedric started around his desk after grabbing up the papers from under the book. Jake stepped in front of him.

"You'll have a seat and place those papers back on the desk. And together we'll wait for your attorney."

"I will not," Cedric said, his voice indignant.

"Louie, handcuffs please," Jake said. The corner of his mouth turned up as Louie stepped back into the office.

"You wouldn't dare."

"Wanna bet?" Jake never broke eye contact with Dunstan. "Your wife is missing. She's my concern, not you."

"If you embarrass me, I'll sue you."

"At least wait until I arrest you for hampering a kidnapping investigation, Mr. Dunstan." Jake accepted the handcuffs from Louie and dangled them in front of Dunstan.

"Here, take them." Cedric threw the papers at Jake. They spilled all over the floor. "Pick them up."

Without a warrant, Jake and Louie didn't move toward the papers. They kept their hands in their pockets.

"Well, what are you waiting for?" Dunstan asked.

"I'd assume the lieutenant and sergeant are waiting for me, Cedric," Ed Rockford said as he stepped into Dunstan's office.

Chapter 26

"Mr. Rockford, as president and chairman of the board, do you give me your permission to retrieve the confidential documents on the floor? And please be aware that I'm recording this," Jake said, eyeing Cedric.

"You do, but I'd like to review them with you."

"Thank you."

Dunstan's expression was all the reward Jake needed as he knelt on the floor to gather the documents, while Louie moved in behind Dunstan.

"What are these, Mr. Rockford?" Jake asked, handing Rockford the papers.

"They're loan papers in my daughter's name. Do you have the signature page?"

Jake continued to search. No signature page. "Mr. Dunstan, please stand aside."

"It's my desk, you can't touch it."

"It's the property of this bank. I give you permission to go through any and all papers you deem necessary to your case involving my daughter's kidnapping, Lieutenant," Rockford said, studying his son-in-law.

Jake moved aside the book where Dunstan had first hidden the papers and retrieved a sheet of paper—the page with Edy's signature.

"Is this your daughter's signature, Mr. Rockford?"

"It's close. We'll need to do a comparison. She never told me she was taking out a loan, and one this large should've had my approval, not Dunstan's. What do you have to say, Cedric?"

"Husbands and wives forge their spouses' signatures all the time. You know that, Ed," Cedric said.

"You made this a practice at my bank? Opening us up to lawsuits?" Rockford asked.

"No…" Dunstan clammed up.

Rockford stepped from the room and scanned the lobby for Linda, Dunstan's admin. Once he spotted her, he signaled for her to come back to her desk.

"Yes, Mr. Rockford?"

"Linda, you process the paperwork for Mr. Dunstan. Is it normal practice to allow a spouse to sign for the other when they're not there?"

"Oh no, sir, the person is instructed to bring their spouse in for a signature. We don't even allow them to take the paperwork home with them."

"Thank you, Linda, you're dismissed."

Rockford waited for Linda to leave. "Well, Cedric, by the end of the day we'll know if you forged Edy's signature and stole two hundred fifty thousand dollars from this bank in her name. You are now relieved of your position."

"You bastard, you'll pay for this. You all will pay for this. I'm going to sue your ass from here to hell until I own every last one of your dollars and Edy's."

Cedric stormed out.

"Aren't you going to arrest him?" Rockford asked.

"No, I have nothing yet, but this should put him into action if he's the one who grabbed her. Excuse me. I have to make a call," Jake said.

He pressed five on his cell phone. "Burke, have you got him?"

"Yes, Jake. I'll keep an eye on him," Detective Burke said.

"Remember to check in every hour."

"Will do."

He ended his call with Burke and addressed Rockford. "Have you locked down his accounts?"

"His ones here, I have. I've also found out Edy deposited a check last week for a hundred thousand from Cedric's account from another bank. He must've spread it around. I'll give the other banks a call."

"No, Mr. Rockford, I'll do that, and follow the proper channels. I hope it was a joint account."

Rockford shrugged. "I can get the info quicker for you, and no one will be the wiser," he said, with a predatory grin and his hands folded behind his back.

"Thanks, but no," Jake said. "May I take these documents?"

"Yes, and I'll get our lawyer to send over other documents I've witnessed Edy sign, for comparison."

"Have you thought of any other places he'd keep her?"

"No," Rockford said, his shoulders slumping. Today the man looked his seventy years.

Linda knocked on the door. She stood there with a large white envelope in her hand. "I overheard you're taking the papers with you, Lieutenant, so here's something to put them in."

"No love lost, miss?"

"It's Linda Eaton, and no. Dunstan's not a nice man once you turn down his advances." Linda handed him the envelope and started out of the office.

"I might need to interview you down the road. Will that be a problem?"

"You believe he's involved with Mrs. Dunstan's disappearance?"

"I can't comment on an ongoing investigation," Jake said, and hoped Linda read between the lines.

"I'll make sure I'm available."

He thanked Rockford and started back to the car. Once inside he made notes. Louie did the same before they ran their impressions by each other. Jake's cell phone vibrated in his jacket pocket. He checked the caller ID before answering.

"What's up, Shamus?"

"Todd Blake will be here in fifteen minutes. How soon can you and Louie be here?"

"We're five minutes away."

"Good, I'll book the interview room."

* * * *

"I'm going to be in the room when you question Todd," Shamus said.

"Shamus, do you think it's wise?" Jake asked.

"Yes, he's my friend and colleague. He didn't kill his wife."

At five o'clock they stepped into interview room 2 together. Jake observed Todd before saying anything. The man's hollowed-out eyes ringed with deep, dark circles expressed his grief. Jake hated his part in adding to his misery.

"Commissioner—"

Shamus's cell phone rang, interrupting his greeting. Jake glanced over at Shamus.

"Hello, Jen, what's up?" Shamus asked.

Before his eyes Shamus fell apart.

"I'll be right there, call the Middlebury Police and get them there immediately!" Shamus shouted into the phone, and every nerve in Jake's body shot to the edge.

What happens if I'm too late? Dear God, please keep her safe, Shamus prayed. "Todd, I'm sorry to leave you, I'm taking Jake and Louie with me. Darcy's gone after the blackmailer on her own."

"Shamus, fill me in," Jake said, dialing Louie. "Louie, get my car, I'll meet you down there in a few minutes and fill you in," Jake said to Louie when he answered his extension.

"She's at the Royal Arms off of exit 16 on I-84."

"I'm going too," Todd Blake said, his jaw set.

"No, I can't have that." Jake shook his head at the commissioner.

"Listen, Callie was my wife. I want—no, I need—a chance to face him down."

"He's coming, Jake. Todd, you'll ride with me," Shamus said.

In the underground parking garage, Louie leaned on the car, with Jake's keys and jacket in his hands. They got in the vehicle and Jake filled him in on what had happened as he drove.

"Let's make sure we get there before Shamus and Todd. Who knows what they'll do if they get there first."

With his sirens blasting, Jake sped up the street, swerving around cars, driving into oncoming traffic. Jake made it to the highway entrance ramp in record time, and continued running hot until he pulled off the highway in Middlebury.

He prayed if Shamus got there first he'd leave the blackmailer alive. Otherwise he'd complicate both their lives.

* * * *

Rain drenched the windshield, the wipers working at the fastest speed to clear it. Heavy rush hour traffic slowed down her drive, but Darcy had no intention of rushing into a situation. If she timed this right, Shamus would show up a few minutes after she arrived. She'd played it this way to get a bit of time alone with Callie's killer, to inflict pain on her for all the suffering she'd caused.

Halfway there she started to question her own judgment—an unfamiliar experience for her. No, she had to run this as she did all her meetings. She'd not allow some two-bit thug to push her around. Darcy drove around the hotel several times, examining cars and license plates for any familiar ones. Nothing popped out at her. She parked in the last row by the road. It'd be easier for Shamus to pick it out when he arrived. She reached for the switch to open the trunk. She'd cashed in one hundred thousand dollars' worth of bearer bonds before she got here. Her finger hovered over the button. *No, I'll check out the situation first*, she thought. *I'm not handing over a hundred grand that easy.*

She popped an antacid into her mouth to quiet her queasy stomach. Darcy stepped from the car, inhaled, squared her shoulders and marched into the hotel lobby. A few businessmen and women dressed in suits sat on couches with papers on their laps and computers on the coffee tables. She recognized no one as she scanned their faces.

To her right, she spotted the registration desk. "I'm Darcy McGuire. Is there a message for me?"

"I'll check," the clerk said, reaching behind her. "Yes, here it is."

Darcy took the folded paper, walked to the bank of elevators, and opened it. Whoever it was wanted her in room 327. Before stepping into the elevator she typed in the room number and hit send on her cell phone. And hoped Shamus got here in time.

She knocked firmly on the door, her purse slung over her right shoulder, her hand in the side pocket of her purse, fingers gripping the gun as she flipped off the safety with her thumb. Darcy braced as the door inched open and she got her first glimpse of the occupant. Melinda. She'd have bet her pay on it.

"Come in, Mrs. McGuire, unless you want to conduct our business in the hallway."

Melinda had her gun in her right hand. She waved Darcy in and then aimed it at her stomach.

Darcy identified the .22 in Melinda's hand and understood it could do some damage. Darcy pulled the twin to Melinda's gun and pointed it at her. "No, we'll do it inside. Before we start, let's get one thing straight. I didn't bring the money up with me. I want insurance that I'll leave here alive."

"That wasn't the deal."

"I'm aware." Darcy surveyed the room in hopes of finding something heavy to whack Melinda with in case they came to blows. She didn't want to have to use her gun unless absolutely necessary.

"Where's my freaking money?"

"It's my money and it's in my car. Once I'm comfortable with the way our conversation goes, you'll accompany me there and I'll give it to you," Darcy said.

Quick as a snake, Melinda swung her left fist into Darcy's face. Darcy ducked, but caught the blow on the right side of the jaw close to her ear. It rang her bell and sent her crashing into the door. In the few seconds it took for Darcy to refocus, Melinda knocked Darcy's gun from her hand with her own gun. Darcy rolled her bottom lip, tasting the blood dripping down her face, and thought of Callie. *If this is how the bitch wants to play, I'm up for it.*

Darcy ducked the next punch, kicked off her heels, and leaped on Melinda, knocking her to the floor and sending her gun skittering across the rug. Darcy pounded her fists into Melinda's face. Melinda raked her nails down Darcy's face. Waves of grief and anger, bottled inside her along with the hate for this woman who had killed her best friend, washed over Darcy.

"You're a stupid twit if you think I'm going to give you the money. I would've if you hadn't killed my friend," Darcy said, taking a hard left in the stomach. Winded, Melinda got the advantage and rolled, pinning Darcy under her as she slammed her fist into Darcy's face again. Darcy used the pain and bucked, bunching up Melinda's shirt in her left fist. She'd gotten enough leverage to throw Melinda off balance. Switching up their positions again, she swung her right fist into Melinda's face, then kneed her stomach and knocked the air from her. Darcy wasn't going to give her a break after what she'd done to Callie. She wrapped her hands around Melinda's throat and squeezed.

"You killed the wrong person, you bitch. Now I'm going to kill you," Darcy said, sweat pouring down her face. Darcy ignored Melinda's gasps for air and her fingernails digging into Darcy's hands as Melinda tried to loosen Darcy's fingers from around her throat.

* * * *

Tears threatened to fall as Edy huddled in the dark, a crack of sunlight peeking through a small pinhole in the cardboard blocking the window. It helped her keep track of time.

Is anyone looking for me? Yes, of course they are. Aren't they?

Her father wouldn't give up. She had to stay positive or she'd never get out of this mess. Every time doubt bubbled up inside her, Edy shoved it down or at least tried to. Otherwise, if they sat outside her door they'd hear her screams pierce the quiet. Would they rush to shut her up? Was Carrington as good as his reputation? It'd be up to him to find her. Or would it? He was homicide, not missing persons. Did she have to die first before he got involved? No, the blackmail letter and Callie's death already had him involved.

The thought of Callie Blake's death quashed her spirits. Was she next? But why had they not waited until they got the money? The letter never stated when or where, only that she'd be contacted.

Despite herself she started to shiver, her lips trembled with thoughts of dying—and for what—money? Had life lost its value, only to be replaced by life-or-death choices?

If she got out of this alive she'd skin Cedric from the belly button down in long, slow cuts, while he screamed for forgiveness. She had none for the loser, the cheat, the bastard. She had to keep thinking these thoughts to survive or she'd lose it, and God knew that wouldn't help.

When a key turned in the door, Edy tried to back into the corner. She'd have jumped on the man when he fed her, but her handcuffed wrist locked her in place. The door opened, bleeding light into the opening, silhouetting the person, hiding his features as she squinted at him, searching for a thread of recognition.

"Here's some food and water," the same man from before said in his tinny voice.

He placed the tray on the bed and backed up toward the door. Despite her fear and her longing for freedom, her hunger swamped her. Stale bread never tasted as good as it did at the moment. She shoved it into her mouth, washing it down with the glass of tepid water. It was hard to make out what else was on the plate. She placed her hand on it and pulled it back. Meat chopped into small bits and potatoes, she thought, all lukewarm, but she didn't care. Edy had to keep up her strength for when an opportunity presented itself.

The greasy meat turned her stomach as she ate but she continued to shovel it down with zeal, not knowing if and when her next meal would show up.

"Ha, he was wrong. He said you'd be all high and mighty. You're no better than a trapped animal. Welcome to the lower class, Mrs. Dunstan," the man said in disdain.

The ice in his voice chilled her bones, her heart, and her mind.

Dear God, I'm not getting out of this alive, am I?

The food she'd eaten gushed up her throat and shot out of her mouth as it dawned on her. She'd been kept alive for something—the only thing she had to offer was money. How much would it cost to buy her freedom?

"That's disgusting. Now you'll have to sleep in it," the man said.

"How much is he paying you?"

"Why?"

"I'll double whatever it is," Edy said.

"He said you'd say that. But he also told me you're a liar and not to trust you." He started to close the door.

"He's the liar and the cheat. I bet you don't get a dime from him. What's he got on you?"

"Lady, you're barking up the wrong tree. Stay put," he said, slamming the door shut, cutting off her light.

Edy wallowed in her vomit, the stench penetrating her nostrils and sinking into her throat, triggering her reflexes until she vomited again. She inched away from the mess, the tears flooding down her face, the hard metal of the cuff slicing into her wrist.

Humiliation before they kill me, that's what this is about. A hiccup stuck in her throat as she fought the tears. *But what the hell does it matter? If anyone was going to rescue me they'd have showed up by now. It's up to me to get out of this mess.*

Chapter 27

Jake parked in front of the entrance to the Royal Arms. He'd left his lights flashing as he and Louie ran into the hotel.

"What's the fastest way to room 327?" Shamus had texted him the room number a few minutes ago. "And have you seen this woman?" Jake flashed a picture of Darcy at the clerk at the front desk.

"Yes, she got here fifteen minutes ago."

"Get us a key," Jake demanded.

"You need a warrant. Don't you?"

"That's my police captain's wife up there in danger. She's locked in a room with a killer. Now give me the key or I'll jump over the counter and get it myself," Jake said.

"Here." The clerk must have seen something in his eyes. He handed Jake the key, his hands shaking. "Take the stairs behind the front desk."

Jake took off with Louie not far behind him. They raced up to the third floor and got there as Shamus drew his gun, Blake standing off to his right, his back against the wall.

"Shamus," Jake said above a whisper. "I go in first." He shoved Shamus aside, not waiting for him to acknowledge him. He didn't care that it was his captain he was ordering around. He'd face the music later.

Louie pushed in beside him, and together they blocked Shamus and Todd. Jake raised his hand to knock when a loud crashing sound echoed through the door, followed by a scream. The hotel manager raced down the hallway.

"What's going on? I want an explanation. My clerk said you demanded a key."

"Step back. We're going in. If you interfere you'll be arrested." With the key card in hand, Jake reached for the door and waited for Shamus's go-ahead.

"I'm going to sue your department."

"Good. Now get the hell out of his way," Shamus said, grabbing the man by the shirt and slamming him up against the wall.

"Or what?" the arrogant manager asked.

"Or I'll shoot you where you stand. That's my wife in there with a killer." Jake watched as the man stared into Shamus's gray eyes. The manager tugged his shirt from Shamus's hands and ran away down the hall. The stairwell door opened and Middlebury police officers rushed the hallway. After a quick word to them Jake turned toward Shamus.

"Shamus," Jake said with his palm out. A second or two passed before Shamus turned toward him.

"Do it," Shamus said.

Jake slipped the keycard into the lock. It went green. He opened the door and rushed in with his gun drawn and the others following behind him. Middlebury had supplied several uniform officers to assist. Darcy sat on top of Melinda, her hands wrapped around Melinda's throat, choking her. He said a prayer, asking for a miracle that Darcy hadn't killed Melinda.

"Darcy, get off of Melinda," Jake said, aiming his gun at the floor.

Melinda's face was bloodied, her eyes bulging from their sockets as Darcy's hands tightened around her throat.

"She killed Callie," Darcy said, breathing heavily.

Jake approached the women and put himself in Darcy's line of sight. He bent down and put a hand on Darcy's to work her fingers off Melinda's neck, while Shamus tried to talk her down.

"Honey, listen to Jake. He and Louie will take her into custody," Shamus pleaded. Jake waited for Shamus's voice to penetrate Darcy's mind as Shamus continued to coax her. "Darcy…please…this won't help Callie."

In a second Jake would have to forcibly pull Darcy off Melinda. Darcy stared up at him before she loosened her fingers from around Melinda's neck. Jake slipped off his sports coat and wrapped it around Darcy's shoulders. Shamus rushed to Darcy, lifting her into his arms.

"That bitch almost killed me. I want her arrested," Melinda said in a hoarse voice as she lay on the floor, struggling to breathe. "You could've pulled her off of me sooner. I'm going to make sure my lawyer hears about how slowly you acted, Jake."

Jake ignored her and handed Melinda off to Louie.

"I almost killed her," Darcy whispered to her husband.

Jake heard every word. Shamus steered her to the bed and sat with her on the orange and brown spread. Jake left them alone for the moment. He sketched the room on his notepad, noting the pictures, desk, window, bathroom door, dressers and the closet. No suitcases in sight.

"You were defending yourself. Make sure you put it exactly that way in your statement," Shamus whispered into Darcy's ear.

Jake approved. It meant he'd not have to lead her in the right direction.

"One more thing, Jake. Spaulding is going to come after you once he's exonerated. I made sure of it," Melinda screamed from the hallway outside the door, where Louie had stationed her.

Jake listened in as Louie cuffed Melinda and read her the Miranda rights. Louie leaned Melinda up against the wall, an officer at her side while he called for the medics. Jake wanted Melinda checked out and her injuries listed before he took her into custody. He also wanted the medics to catalog Darcy's injuries. Darcy's face had fared worse than Melinda's, which would add credence to her self-defense statement. The Middlebury police, who Louie had called en route to the hotel and apprised of the situation, had stayed in the background. There to help only if needed. Jake owed them one, but it was worth it.

"Lieutenant, I'm Lieutenant Carrington." Jake extended his hand.

"I'm Harry Goodman, nice to meet you. Is your captain's wife okay?"

"I called for a medic to be sure. To cover our asses, I also want them to examine the suspect and catalog her injuries before you transport her. And to show she received them in a fight before we broke it up. Do you have a female officer in the area?"

"Officer Steward is on her way," Lieutenant Goodman said.

"Thank you, Harry. Anytime you need anything, please don't hesitate to give me a call," Jake said.

"My pleasure," Goodman said as he left the room.

Jake turned toward the McGuires and focused his attention on them. "Shamus, I have to interview Darcy."

"I'm staying," Shamus said.

"Shamus, let Jake do his job. I'm fine, really." Darcy pulled Jake's jacket tighter around her torn clothing.

McGuire glanced from his wife to Jake, opened his mouth, then shut it and walked to the window. He kept his back to them.

He's close enough to hear, far enough away for show, Jake thought.

"It's as far as he's going to go," Darcy said, studying her husband's rigid shoulders and back.

"It's okay. Can you tell me what happened? I want you to start with when you read the letter and decided to come here and not call me."

"Jake, Shamus already reprimanded me as if I was ten. I don't need it from you too. I'm used to handling problems and troublemakers."

"You promised me, Darcy. And this was a little more than a troublemaker. Melinda might've killed you."

"I understand now and I understood when I decided to confront her. She killed my best friend. I wanted to take her down, and bad. That's why I didn't call. I had my secretary wait a few minutes before she contacted Shamus."

"We're not on record yet. You'll want to clean up your statement and leave out the revenge part."

"I never said it was revenge." Darcy stared at him.

"You did in not so many words. Review your statement before we go on record," Jake said. "What happened when you received the letter?"

"The letter came with pictures…"

"It's going to be all right." Jake held eye contact with Darcy.

"Pictures of you and me…"

"Can this get any worse than it is—"

Jake cut off Shamus's outburst. "Go ahead, Darcy," he said, taking her hand.

"It was hard to determine how she cut your image into the photos. I'm not sure it's even you. She threatened to release them to the press. And there were nudes of me too. But I studied the body and it's not mine."

Damn it, no matter how I deal with this, it's going to backfire on me. The department will go ballistic with me being involved in another scandal.

"We'll send someone to the paper to retrieve them, in case she did. Give me a minute." Jake walked out to Louie and explained the latest development "Since you've dealt with Wilson at the paper before, you go over and speak with him. See if Melinda sent the photos. If he has them, tell him the photos are doctored and will be proven and exposed as fakes, and everyone involved will sue the paper. See if you can convince him not to print them even if you have to promise him some deets on the investigation and killer. Got it?"

"Yes. I'll turn the prisoner over to Middlebury, you can collect her when you're ready," Louie said.

"Thanks." Jake spun away from Louie when a hand landed on his sleeve.

"I want to thank you for not succumbing to pressure and for catching Callie's killer," Commissioner Todd Blake said, clearly shaken.

"If it's worth anything, I never believed you killed her," Jake said.

"It means a lot. When something like this happens, you find out fast who your friends are, and more importantly who your enemies are," Blake said.

They left it there. Jake went back into the room. He took a seat next to Darcy and barely gave Shamus a nod before he continued to interview Darcy. "Go on."

"I was aware of who I was meeting. I left the money in the car to ensure I got out of the room alive."

"You never told me you withdrew the money—" Shamus said, cutting off the rest of Darcy's statement.

"Shamus, please—Darcy, go on."

"When Melinda learned I didn't have it with me she lunged at me. I had my hands on my gun, but she knocked it to the floor. Before I knew it, I was in the fight of my life, and I was determined I'd be the one coming out alive."

Jake bit his lip to hide the smile. Darcy did the same. "Okay, continue."

"She had me pinned on my back. I bucked and bucked until she lost her balance and I flipped our positions. I got a knee into her stomach and knocked the wind out of her. That's when she ran her nails down my face. I blindly threw a punch and dazed her, then I grabbed her by the neck to stop the assault."

"And..."

"You and Louie burst through the door, end of story." Darcy folded her hands in her lap, squared her shoulders, and tilted her head toward Shamus.

The medics came into the room and Jake turned Darcy over to them for an evaluation.

"Shamus, I never posed with your wife," Jake said when McGuire started to leave the room.

"I'm aware, but more importantly, I trust my wife. If she says she didn't, she didn't."

Shamus locked eyes with Jake. If he was guilty he'd have flinched and backed away from his captain.

"But there will be fallout from them. We'll both have to stand firm and take it, or someone will try to use the photos to force us both out. Since the last incident with dirty cops, the WPD has been trying to clean up its act. Let's hope the new mayor doesn't succumb to pressure. I will use all my power to make sure it doesn't happen, but who knows," Shamus said, shrugging his shoulders.

"I agree. Louie's on his way to the paper. He's persuasive. If anyone can talk them out of printing them, he can," Jake said.

"In case he can't, you better give Mia a call," Shamus said.

"Good call," Jake said, stepping from the room. He walked to the end of the hallway and pressed one on his speed-dial list. When Mia answered he updated her on the latest developments in the case from hell.

Mia had mentioned his injury, and right on cue the damn pain kicked in when he hung up from her. His side hadn't bothered him today, until now. He'd been too busy to think about it. A pill now would dull his senses, and he'd need all of them to deal with Melinda. There were things he still had to process before he collected his prisoner and questioned her.

At the door to room 327, Jake stopped and observed his captain consoling his wife. He understood better than anyone that even when the killer had been caught, it never lessened the grief or loss. The loved one forever a memory, a hole in your heart nothing or no one could replace.

"Shamus, why don't you take Darcy and Todd home? I'll finish up here. I'm not going to question Melinda for a couple of hours yet," Jake said.

"Give me a call when you're ready to take her. I want to observe the interview," Shamus said.

What secrets will Melinda dish out with the brass listening in? Jake wondered. *It doesn't matter. She can't hurt me.*

Chapter 28

Isolated, she felt the growl churn deep in her throat. A sound she barely recognized as her own. Hope lost, the darkness encompassed her. The constant scratching in the far corner had Edy withering into a smaller ball. *Rats! Please, Lord, no rats*, she begged. The little buggers creeped her out and might break her spirit.

Had an hour passed, or maybe two? With no way of telling, she pinned her eyes on the light coming through the minute hole in the cardboard and then searched the wall for its position. It wouldn't tell her the time, but it'd give her a measure of its passing. She scratched her head, pushing the dirty, matted blonde hair out of her eyes. Her finger landed on one of the bobby pins she'd used to twist her hair up today—or was it yesterday? It didn't matter.

Is it possible to pick the lock with it? She tried to remember the show she'd watched that demonstrated the trick. Edy closed her eyes and concentrated. Had they used the open end of the pin or the looped end? What if she got lucky and freed herself? What next? The man had to be over six feet tall, or had the light played tricks on her? At one hundred and twenty pounds she'd need an advantage to overpower him or outsmart him. Outsmarting him, she decided, gave her the only chance to get out of there.

Edy inched her way down the bed and pressed her fist against her mouth to stifle the scream as she jerked her right hand up after it had landed in the vomit.

"Damn it, damn it, damn it," she shouted.

She'd dropped the bobby pin in the mess. Eyes closed, she inhaled… exhaled…then shoved down the revulsion. She ran her hand through the mess until she found the bobby pin. A quick wipe on her pants took off most of the liquid, though her fingers were sticky.

Forget it, keep going. She cringed as she knelt in it.

She gripped the end of the pin and groped around for the handcuff lock's opening. When she found it, she inserted the hairpin. The pin went in deep, too deep to do any good. She drew it back and spread it open, then stuck in one end and jiggled it around. Nothing, the lock hadn't opened. Edy played with it for a while, before she stopped to rest. *There's no way I'm going to open this thing.* Clutching the pin in her hand, she reached forward and placed it at the top of the bed.

Edy stretched her back and neck, despair digging its fingers into her throat, choking her. How could she fight back if she had nothing to use against the man? A quick jerk of her wrist slammed her new reality into her. Being handcuffed to the bed rendered her useless. She'd have to try to dislodge the railing.

She placed her right hand on the railing and got a good grip, then angled the cuffed wrist up as her fingertips tried to cushion the rusted edges from digging into her skin. Edy tugged with all her might. The railing rattled. Again, she tried to gain traction as she strained against the pain in her wrist and yanked the rail toward her. It produced noise, cut hard into her wrist, stinging her skin, but she hadn't loosened it one bit.

With trepidation she slowly placed her feet on the floor and twisted under the handcuffed arm ignoring the shooting pain traveling up her shoulder as she positioned herself to face the bed. She envisioned the rats rushing her as their scratching grew louder. Her lips trembling, the veins in her temples throbbing, she stamped her feet hoping to scare the rats away. After she'd positioned herself in front of the rail, Edy locked her knees and wrenched the bar. This time the bed moved, but not the rail.

If I get out of this—no, when I get out of this, I'll boil the bastard in oil.

To sustain herself while struggling to keep the panic at bay, she embraced the image in her mind of Cedric being lowered into hot, bubbling oil in a large pot on an outdoor fire.

Edy continued to tug, yank, and scream until her aggrieved handcuffed wrist begged for mercy. The metallic smell and pain told her she'd only accomplished drawing blood—the rail, the lone victor.

Disarmed of strength and the will to fight, she sank to the floor, warm blood running down her wrist.

* * * *

Jake plotted out his strategy for his interview with Melinda as he drove back to the station. Years ago he'd realized dating her had been a mistake and he had thought he'd corrected the error. Melinda, like a bad penny, turned up again, disrupting not only his life but the lives of many others in the direst of ways. How appropriate that they'd come full circle on a dismal day to close it out once and for all.

With Louie tied up at the paper, he'd have to go into the interview alone, then he'd head back to the scene in Middlebury. On second thought, he'd bring Al Burke and Stella Fisher into the interview. He'd cover his bases with Melinda and not give her a reason to yell foul.

Jake walked to Burke's desk before going to his office. "Al, come with me, please."

"What's up, Jake?"

He held his response until they reached his office. "Close the door."

"Am I in trouble?" Al asked.

"Should you be?" Jake pointed to the chair in front of his desk.

"No."

"Louie's tied up. I want you and a female officer in the interview with me. I've requested Stella Fisher."

"You think the suspect will cry wolf?"

"I'm not going to give her a chance. We have a history." He figured with Al parenting five kids, he'd pull off the fatherly bit well, if needed. "I want you all fatherly with her, while I attack. Got it?"

"Yes. Considering your history with her, shouldn't someone else conduct the interview?"

"Al, the captain will be behind the glass, and I'm sure the commissioner will be there as well. I'm covered." Jake pressed his intercom button. "Gunner, come into my office."

"You want him in there too?" Burke asked.

"No, I want him to keep on the Dunstan kidnapping. Time is running out for her."

"Yes, Lieutenant?" Gunner Kraus stepped into the office. Kraus's tall, muscular frame displayed well in his suits, and his brown hair and blue eyes caught the ladies' attention. Something the married Kraus was proud of and took advantage of, much to Jake's chagrin.

"Here's my file on the Edy Dunstan kidnapping. In it you'll find what Louie and I have covered today and my notes on what needs to be done. Find her, Gunner. After each item is ticked off my list, call me with your findings and take Kirk Brown with you."

"Do you think she's still alive?" Gunner asked.

"I think she is. There's been no demand for ransom yet. It's a good sign," Jake said. "Ready, Al?"

"Yep."

Jake walked out with Al and Kraus. He and Al headed to interview room 2. Kraus split off from them in the bullpen. When Jake walked around the corner, he spotted Officer Stella Fisher standing at the door to the interview room. Fisher, a ten-year veteran of the force, came to attention, her five-foot-nine-inch height setting her off from most. With green eyes and blonde hair she was pretty, but no one messed with her. On the job she was a consummate professional.

"Glad to see you're available," Jake said.

Jake looked through the window on the door to the interview room and noted Melinda's attorney pacing the small room. She appeared young and wasn't one he'd had dealings with in the past. The attorney wore her long, brown, streaked hair loose around her shoulders. A red suit and three-inch heels emphasized her figure.

"The suspect's been fidgety and her attorney's gnawing at the bit for whoever's in charge," Fisher said.

"Good, let's go in," Jake said.

"Oh, Lieutenant, after this is done, may I have a few minutes of your time?" Fisher asked.

"Sure, Stella."

At seven thirty p.m., Burke read in the pertinent information for the voice recorder. Fisher stayed at attention inside the room by the door. Al sat to Jake's left and Melinda and her attorney across from them.

"Melinda, Detective Burke will reread you your rights," Jake said. He placed his hands on the table and folded them, never taking his eyes off of Melinda. Melinda's usual cocky expression was gone, replaced by worry lines on her forehead and at the corners of her eyes.

"We'll stipulate to them," Attorney Carissa Gantry said. "What are the charges?"

"Melinda Mastrianni has been arrested for the murders of Callie Blake and Sal Gallucci. She's also been arrested for blackmailing Mrs. Blake and Darcy McGuire and assault with a deadly weapon on Mrs. McGuire. As the investigation continues, there may be more charges levied on Ms. Mastrianni."

Gantry put her hand on Melinda's sleeve as Melinda opened her mouth to speak. "What evidence do you have?"

"Ms. Gantry, we confiscated a gun from Melinda in Middlebury, where she fought with her victim. Ballistics is running it against other crimes as we speak. As soon as I have the results we'll know if it's the weapon used to kill Callie Blake and Sal Gallucci. We've found a large amount of blood in Melinda's kitchen, which is not hers."

"They can't go into my home, can they?" Melinda asked her attorney. The lawyer leaned in and whispered. Melinda shut up.

"Did you have a warrant when you entered her home?"

"The first time I entered under exigent circumstances," Jake said. "We believed Melinda had been injured after viewing her ransacked kitchen through the window. The second time her mother let me in when Melinda went missing. The third time I got a warrant for her home and business when she went from victim to suspect."

"I'll need a copy of the warrant and its scope. Until you have the results from ballistics on the gun you confiscated from my client, you have nothing to hold her on," Gantry said.

"Nice try. Melinda is being held for blackmail, and for holding Mrs. McGuire against her will, and let's not forget the assault with a deadly weapon."

"My client was protecting herself. Have you noticed the marks around her neck? She will be countering with a complaint against Darcy McGuire. Did you find any of this supposed blackmail money on her person or in her room?"

Jake ignored the question. "You can stall for as long as you like, Ms. Gantry. I have all night. Mrs. McGuire was lured to the hotel with threats from your client. She threatened to publish doctored photos of Mrs. McGuire and me in stages of undress. Our lab is also working on proving they were doctored."

He stared the lawyer down. She blinked first. "Melinda," he asked, "what happened between you and Sal Gallucci?"

Melinda leaned into her attorney, whispered into her ear. Jake waited. After a few seconds of back-and-forth, Melinda faced him.

"We dated for a while."

"And?"

"He worked for me for a short while."

Jake dropped the pictures of Callie, Darcy, and a few other women on the table. "You used him in these photos?"

"Yes."

"How about this one?"

Jake dropped a copy of the photo of him and Darcy on the table. One Shamus had procured from Darcy's office safe. The picture of him and Darcy in an embrace glared up from the table.

"You came in with her and posed of your own free will," Melinda said, smirking.

He'd had enough. Jake made sure he had Melinda's full attention. "You should've tossed the gun after you killed Callie and Sal," Jake said, trying to provoke Melinda. "The pictures of me and Mrs. McGuire are doctored. This is not my torso, nor am I the same height as Mrs. McGuire."

"In what way are they supposed to be doctored?" Gantry asked.

"I don't pose for pictures, especially in my underwear and with another man's wife. Examine the torso of the man in the picture, Ms. Gantry, and you'll see there are no scars. Way before these pictures were taken I was wounded in the line of duty twice—recently and three years ago. Both left scars. And there are other telltale signs. I have a birthmark on my torso."

"Where are these scars located?" Gantry asked.

"Melinda, please tell your attorney where my scars are," Jake said.

"I don't kn…" Melinda stopped talking, folded her arms and sat back.

"Ms. Gantry, we need to establish the validity of the pictures. Please have your client answer the question."

Gantry and Melinda whispered back and forth. "She will supply that information at another time."

"Why? To give you time to look up my service record?"

"No."

"Let the record show that Melinda Mastrianni started to deny knowledge of the location of my scars before she refused to answer the question. Melinda, we've also stopped the pictures from being published by the paper. It's amazing what they won't print when they know a lawsuit will follow."

"Does the paper know the source?" Gantry asked.

"They didn't say," Jake said.

"Can we move on?"

"Melinda attempted to blackmail Mrs. McGuire with these pictures. Evidence will be available to counsel in discovery. Mrs. McGuire recorded her conversation with Melinda in the hotel room when Melinda demanded the blackmail money. The recording was taken into evidence at the scene and sealed in an evidence bag."

"Why then would she release the pictures to the press if she knew she'd get arrested?" Gantry asked.

"Do you have an answer, Melinda?" Jake leaned across the table, stared into Melinda's brown eyes.

Melinda squinted to shut him down. "You posed for them. Now your career will be ruined, you arrogant bastard," Melinda said.

"Arrogant? Me?" Jake quirked his brow, leaned back in his chair, and draped an arm over the back of Al's chair.

"Between your affair with McGuire and George Spaulding, you're done."

"Miss Mastrianni, I never had an affair with either George Spaulding or Mrs. McGuire," Jake said, giving Melinda a lopsided grin.

"I didn't mean George, you idiot. He's coming after you for setting him up for your sister's murder."

"Is that what George Spaulding told you, Miss Mastrianni?" Al Burke asked before Jake could.

"You'll have to wait and see to find out. Did you know, Jake, George is my new best friend? Wait until his interview hits the news."

"I'd like time to interview my client on this matter," Gantry said.

"Ms. Gantry, George Spaulding has nothing to do with this case. Who Melinda befriends is her business. George Spaulding is serving life for raping and killing my sister. It doesn't bode well for her character if her new best friend is another murderer," Jake said, the heat of his temper banging to come out.

"Murderer? Ha, he's going to get released with the new DNA tests, and he's coming after you and yours," Melinda said.

"Are you threatening me?" Jake asked.

"Lieutenant, I'm calling for a recess," Gantry said, banging her hand on the table.

"We've barely been at this for an hour—unless your client is in need of medical treatment, this interview will continue."

"I hate you!" Melinda screamed, her nostrils flaring.

He'd use her hate to hang her, although he didn't understand where it had come from. "Melinda, what gave you the idea to blackmail these women?"

"I never said I did."

"Mel," Jake said, switching to her high school nickname, "two people are dead, and one is in the hospital with grave wounds, thanks to you, so please explain how blackmail turned into murder."

"I didn't murder anyone. And you have no proof," Melinda said. "You know what I don't understand, Jake? Why the hell did you become a cop, a homicide detective, after what happened to your sister? You threw away a sports career, and for what—to deal with scum? It tells me the murder of Eva fascinates you."

God, I want to jump across the table and strangle her, Jake thought.

Instead, he clenched his hands together and rested them in his lap. He inhaled, careful not to express his hatred. He took a minute before he continued. "Melinda, let's get back on point. Why did you kill Sal Gallucci?" he asked in a quiet, controlled voice.

"I'm not confessing to anything. I'm innocent." Melinda also clenched her hands together.

"Well, you'll be locked up with many who claim the same thing. Good luck." He'd had enough for now and pushed his chair back as he stood. "This interview will continue at a later time."

"You bastard, you come back here and give me the respect I deserve," Melinda yelled.

"The thing is, Melinda, you don't deserve any. This interview has concluded and the tape is still running. Anything you say can and will be used against you." Jake stared hard and long at her.

Her shrill voice followed him out of the room and down the hallway—round one to him. He'd need to research her attorney and find a way around the minutiae to nail Melinda to the wall for her crimes. And then he never wanted to see her or hear her name again.

"When do you want to go back at her?" Al asked, tagging along after him.

"Let's give her time to talk to her attorney. In the meantime, get me everything you know about Carissa Gantry and bring it into my office. Stella, can you remain with the prisoner, or are you off shift?" Jake asked.

"No, I'm good, I'll hang," Fisher said.

"Let me know when the attorney wants to resume. I'll be in my office checking in with ballistics."

Chapter 29

At his desk Jake dialed Kraus's cell number. "What have you got?"

"Dunstan wasn't home, and Riverton called into work sick today. I've requested a warrant for their cell phones to see what tower they're pinging."

"Good thinking. Leave a uniform at their apartment. I want to know when they get home and if they leave give them a soft tail."

"I've ordered one already. I'm heading to Mrs. Dunstan's boyfriend's house."

"I forgot to ask him what his girlfriend's or wife's name is. Find out."

Smith's concern for Edy had seemed genuine, but was it an act? I never checked to see if he's married or engaged. Damn, I'm slipping.

"I'll call you later," Kraus said.

"I've got to take this call," Jake said and transferred over to the incoming. "What have you got, Louie?"

"There was nothing in the room. It was a meeting place only. But I hit the mother lode in her car. In the trunk was a blanket with blood, lots of blood," Louie said. "I sent it over to the lab with a rush request. Jake, the lab boys are starting to hate us. You get anything back from ballistics?"

"Not yet, but it's early—I was about to call them. Burke and I did the initial interview with Melinda and her lawyer. Do you know Carissa Gantry?"

"I had one case where she defended my suspect. She's precise and goes for the jugular."

"Did she win the case?"

"No, my evidence was pristine, but that didn't stop her from attacking me on the stand. An inexperienced cop might've blown it. She's also expensive. How is Melinda affording her?"

"Good question. I'll dig into it, but I bet her mother helped her out."

"Has Kraus dug up anything on Edy Dunstan?" Louie asked.

"No. When are you coming in?"

"I'm on my way. See you in twenty."

Jake crossed off items that Kraus handled on the Dunstan case, then started his research on Gantry. He hit Google first, moving on to social media next to get a step up on how to deal with her in interrogations. As he studied her Twitter posts, his cell phone rang.

"Lieutenant, a ransom note was delivered a few minutes ago," Ed Rockford said.

Now we're getting somewhere, Jake thought, picking up on the stress in Rockford's voice.

"Mr. Rockford, I'll be right there."

"No, don't come here, they said if they see cops, they'll kill her."

"How do you want to handle this?"

"I'm going to give them the money."

"How much?"

"Half a million," Rockford said.

"I can deliver it for you."

"No, Edy's life's more important than the money."

"You have no guarantees they won't kill her once they have the money."

Rockford has to understand it's stupid for him to deliver it personally. How can I make him understand?

"I'll make sure she's at the exchange or no deal."

"The FBI will have to be called in, now that there is a ransom note."

"No FBI, no cops. Please, Lieutenant, I only called to make sure you stayed away," Rockford said.

"How long will it take for you to get ahold of such a large amount?"

"A day."

"I'll give you a day to think this over, but I'm going to continue my investigation on my end, and follow procedure and notify the FBI. I'll ask them to stay back, but I can't guarantee they will. Hopefully, I find her first."

He'd call the FBI after he discussed it with Shamus. What Rockford didn't understand was once he paid, there'd be no reason to keep Edy alive.

"I hope so too, Lieutenant."

"One more thing, Mr. Rockford. If you go in there alone, what's to say they won't take you out also?"

"I'll have my security not far away."

"The same security you hired to protect Edy?" Jake asked.

"That was low, Lieutenant."

"I want you to consider every angle."

Rockford hung up on him.

* * * *

By the time Jake was ready to reinterview Melinda, Louie had returned to the station. Al Burke had given him his research into Gantry and Jake combined it with his own. She'd tried armed robbery suspects with some success, but this would be her first murder client. Gantry's partner, on the other hand, had experience in murder trials.

Jake updated Louie on the first interview as his friend helped himself to a cup of coffee and plopped down in the chair in front of his desk. McGuire hadn't come back after leaving for the hospital to see Darcy. The commissioner had gone home after the first round of questioning. When he and Louie finished up with Melinda he'd have to update Todd to try to explain why Callie had been murdered.

"I want you to take the lead," Jake said.

"Why?" Louie blew on his coffee to cool it off.

"It will annoy her. I want her to feel unimportant, especially to me. It will set off her temper and maybe she'll mess up and blurt out something incriminating."

"What if she brings up George Spaulding again?"

"I'm counting on it. I'm going to let whatever she says roll off of me. You'll ask her why she's so focused on an old crime when she's in deep shit here. Then push the angle harder. The more she tries to get my attention the more she won't. I might even leave the room to piss her off."

"It's your call."

"It is," Jake said, happy with the plan. "Let's move."

"Give me a minute to finish my coffee. You've had me hopping all day," Louie said.

Jake noticed for the first time how tired his friend looked.

"Bring it with you."

"No."

Louie's stubborn streak irked him at times, but Jake waited patiently while Louie enjoyed his coffee.

"I think you're wrong, allowing her to run the interview, if it goes the way you think," Louie said.

"Why?"

"You have tells when you're upset, and I don't see how you'll steer her into a confession."

"She's the one who sent the photos and notes to me. I want to get it on the record. It goes to personality and state of mind. It can also be construed as threatening a police officer. I need to pile on the charges. When she's convicted and sentenced it should be for life, nothing less."

Louie finished off his coffee and stood.

"Let's head out," Jake said.

They'd reached the door to the interview room. Louie went in first.

"Well, I see you brought your stooge along," Melinda said. Her attorney put a hand on Melinda's right arm to silence her.

Louie switched on the recorder and read the information into the record. Jake took a seat to Louie's left and ignored Melinda. Louie sat directly across from Melinda, opened his file, and rearranged a few pieces of paper. Melinda's attorney sat to her right. Melinda locked eyes with him and started tapping her fingers.

"Melinda, I'd like to go through a few points from your earlier interview," Louie said. "It says here you've denied the charges of murder and blackmail. How do you explain the large amount of Sal Gallucci's blood in your kitchen?"

Jake hadn't informed Carissa Gantry that the test for typing the blood found in Melinda's kitchen had come back. It was a match to Sal Gallucci. They'd waited for the DNA matching. His mother had sent in a sample of her blood for the test. The expressions on Melinda's and Gantry's faces warmed his heart.

"Why wasn't I informed?" Gantry asked.

"You just were," Louie said. "The DNA test isn't complete, but Sal's mother was happy to supply a sample of her own for the test and comparison."

"Is this how you want to handle it?" Gantry asked. "My client has told me Jake Carrington sexually assaulted her when he came to her home alone to question her."

"If that's a fact, why didn't she report it?" Louie countered.

"He's a cop, who'd believe her?" Gantry asked as Melinda stared at Jake.

The tenuous hold he had on his temper almost escaped his grip. Jake kept his face blank and had to fight to keep it that way throughout the interview. Though it killed him, Jake stayed quiet, his eyes drilling holes through Melinda.

"We take allegations against police officers seriously and investigate them fully. I will tell you, there'll be more charges if this is a stall tactic, Ms. Gantry," Louie said.

It hung out there for a second or two. Melinda whispered into Gantry's ear. Louie let it go back and forth for a minute or two. Jake folded his hands on the table. Time was up and Jake was about to speak when Louie asked, "Are we ready to continue?"

"My client has decided to withdraw the allegations," Gantry said.

Of course she did, because they're a damn lie, Jake thought, wanting to punch something. Someone knocked on the door, interrupting the session. Jake's chair screeched when he shoved it away from the table, the noise piercing his ears. Standing, he looked through the window in the door and caught Detective Al Burke waving a paper in front of him. Jake left the room.

"What've you got?" Jake asked.

"The ballistics report," Detective Burke said. "It's conclusive. The gun you took from Melinda in Middlebury—its striations are an exact match on the bullets that killed both Callie Burke and Sal Gallucci."

Jake looked it over and grinned. "We got her." Switching it up, he asked, "Do you have plans tonight?"

Burke pulled his double chin back and stared at Jake as if he'd grown a third eye. "What's up?"

"I'm stalling to make her nervous. Keep looking over my shoulder at the suspect and scowl at her every few seconds through the window. Shake your head, then walk away in a huff."

"Your game," Al said.

"It is."

Five minutes later, Al walked away. Jake stepped back into the interview room. Louie announced his arrival for the record. Jake handed Louie the report and waited as Louie read it, then read it again.

"Melinda Mastrianni, you are under arrest for the murder of Callie Blake and Sal Gallucci. Your rights have been read to you. If you'd like them read again, I will," Louie said while Jake remained quiet.

"What the hell's going on? Tell them they can't do this to me!" Melinda shouted at her attorney and banged her right hand on the table.

Louie handed the attorney the report. Gantry spoke to Melinda in a soft voice. Whatever she said quieted her client down.

"I'll make you a copy but I'll need the original back," Louie said, leaning across the table to take the papers back from Gantry.

"We'll be adding more charges once the handwriting samples are compared to hers and verified. From what I understand, Mrs. McGuire has filed charges against Melinda for assault and attempted extortion," Louie concluded.

Outside the room, Officer Stella Fisher started to escort Melinda back to the holding cell. Melinda's attorney stayed behind to gather up her papers, giving Jake the perfect opportunity to ask Melinda a question he'd been mulling over: "Why did you choose the police chief's wife? You had to know the whole force would come after you."

"Is the recorder off?"

"I'm not sure." He didn't bother to tell her he could still use what she said if someone else heard her.

Melinda leaned toward him and whispered, "Sal said Blake had political ambitions and we assumed he would never let photos be released to the public. If the bimbo hadn't punched me, she'd still be alive."

Her heavy, pungent cologne clogged his throat. "You picked up the money, and killed Callie," Jake said, hoping Louie was still in earshot of the conversation.

"Like I'd let that dimwit Sal take what belonged to me," Melinda said, her voice barely audible.

"What about Darcy McGuire?"

"She's loaded, but I didn't realize until it was too late that her husband was also a cop. Sal picked the women. With each victim we were going to raise the stakes."

"I thought your business was doing well, Melinda." Jake wanted to keep her talking.

"Not enough to get me out of all the debt Tony left me. The way things were going I'd be a hundred before I was out from under it. Sal promised this would be quick and dirty."

Jake heard high heels clicking on the slate floor behind him.

"Melinda, shut up right now," Gantry said. "Did you inform my client you could use what she says against her?"

"I did," Jake said. He didn't clarify that he'd told her in the interview room, not here. "Take her away, Officer."

"You did not, you bastard," Melinda said.

Officer Fisher tugged Melinda's arm to lead her down the hall, but Melinda had to get the last word and refused to go quietly.

"You're going to get what you deserve. I sent George's interview and pictures to the national press."

He waited until she was out of earshot. "I guess the storm is coming, one way or another, with Spaulding. There's no way to avoid it with the new DNA tests, and now Melinda's contribution adds to the mix," Jake said. "I'm tired. I'm tired of Melinda. I'm tired of George, and I'm tired of the whole thing coming back to bite me in the ass at unexpected times. I've got to find closure before I go nuts."

"We'll deal with it when the time comes," Louie said, patting him on the back.

"One closed, one more open. We need to find Edy." Jake inhaled, giving Melinda one last thought before he shoved her and Spaulding from his head. Edy Dunstan needed him at his best if he was going to find her alive. "Let's check in with Al and Kraus, see if they've gotten anything new for us."

"We need to inform the commissioner and Shamus of the results," Louie said.

"You take Shamus, I'll go tell Todd."

* * * *

It took an hour to answer all of Todd's questions. Jake understood and hadn't rushed him. Though a killer had been put behind bars—justice served—it wouldn't ease the pain of losing Callie. And each day of Todd's life he'd wonder if he could have done something different that would have prevented her death. Survivor's guilt took a piece of you each and every waking hour you outlived your loved one. Jake understood more than he wanted to admit.

If only...is a dangerous game. One I can't win. Nor will Todd.

He tucked his morose thoughts away for another time as he drove back to the station. Jake centered all his thoughts on Edy Dunstan and nothing else. He went straight to Al's desk when he entered the bullpen.

"Anything?" Jake asked without preamble.

"I've caught up with Dunstan and Riverton. They dined at Spartan's down the street from their apartment. The waitress said they spent an hour there. The timeline fits with Dunstan and Riverton leaving work. What now?"

"How about Linden Smith?" Jake asked.

"I haven't connected with him yet. I left him three voice messages in the last two hours."

"I'll take Louie and do an onsite visit. Do a BOLO to locate Smith's car and stress no action needed when it's sighted. Keep on it and contact me when you hear back from Smith."

Jake walked to Louie's desk. "We're going to Smith's house, but give me five."

"Smith? What'd he do?"

"Nothing I know about, but I want to reinterview him. Dunstan and his girlfriend haven't done anything out of the ordinary, which is suspicious in and of itself. I want to see what, if anything, Smith's up to, and if he has a wife, or a girlfriend besides Edy."

"Dunstan could've hired someone to keep a watch on Edy while he goes about his normal life," Louie said.

"My thoughts exactly." Jake rubbed the back of his neck, where all the day's stress had settled. "Her time is running out."

"We're doing everything we can, Jake."

"It's not enough if she dies, is it?"

He walked away from Louie, took five to regroup, and made notes in Callie's file on his visit with Todd before writing *Solved* on it. Though the trial could bring in new evidence, for now, it was done.

Jake reviewed the Dunstan case file and his interview notes on Dunstan, Riverton, and Smith. Nothing popped out. What had he missed? Dunstan, Riverton, and Smith tumbled through his head as he tapped his fingers on the desk. Half a million dollars in ransom. Of Cedric, Rosie, and Linden, who needed it most, and was it even about the money? Could the motive be control? But over what? Questions he had no answers to irritated him. Jake slipped on his jacket, loaded the files into his briefcase, and strode out to Louie's desk.

Louie sat on the corner of his desk, his tie loose and his files beside him. "Ready?" Louie asked.

"Yep, we'll hit Cedric and Rosie first." A thought struck Jake. He walked to Al's desk. "Al, do you have Smith's cell phone number?"

"Yeah, I have it right here." Al jotted it down for him.

"Good. Call me if anything new comes in on either case."

"You already gave Gunner those instructions. Why have Al duplicate the work?" Louie said.

"It's worth duplicating efforts if it saves Edy Dunstan. I don't want to miss anything." Jake hoped Louie brought it. The meds had muddled his brain.

Jake and Louie drove into the parking lot at Cedric's apartment and parked the car. "The gray car is Rosie's. I don't see Cedric's black one."

He stepped from the car and strolled around the parking lot, hunting up Cedric's vehicle. Why hadn't the officer on duty reported Dunstan had gone out again?

"Louie, check in with the OOD," Jake said.

Louie walked and talked as they approached the lobby. "He's on a dinner break."

"You're kidding me, right?"

"No, I'm not. No one was available to cover him. He got permission to pick up his dinner. He claims he wasn't gone more than fifteen minutes."

"Lovely. That's plenty of time for Dunstan to have ditched his tail. What the hell is the matter with people?"

"It's not the officer's fault. He did check in," Louie said.

"It's called common sense." Jake waved away Louie's next comment. He jabbed the elevator button hard. "Get on the horn and explain to the idiots in dispatch and the officer on duty that before they give permission for an officer to leave their post on one of my suspects, they are to check in with me first."

"Got it. Calm down, Jake. We'll find her," Louie said, taking his phone from his pocket.

A couple minutes later, Jake knocked hard on the door to 5C.

"What the hell do you want?" Rosie Riverton shouted through the door.

"Open up, Ms. Riverton," Jake ordered.

"Not until you tell me why you're here."

"Fine, but all your neighbors will realize you and Cedric are suspects in a kidnapping," Jake said loud enough to be heard down the hallway.

The door opened a few inches. Riverton blocked the opening with her body as she peered around it.

"We haven't done anything. Why do you keep bothering us?" Riverton asked.

"Where is Cedric?"

"He went to the store to pick up dinner."

"You dined out. You're having dinner again?" Jake asked.

"Cedric was right. You've got someone following us. I can't believe this." Rosie tried to shove the door closed, but Jake leaned his weight against it.

"Ms. Riverton, the hours are ticking away on Mrs. Dunstan. If you have any information, this is the time to tell me before you're arrested as an accessory to kidnapping and false imprisonment."

"We didn't do anything, I swear."

"Where was Cedric on Sunday night?"

"How would I know? I was out with friends. I'm done talking to you. Call my lawyer with your questions," Riverton said.

Jake removed his foot from the opening. Rosie slammed the door in their faces.

"What do you think?" Jake asked.

"She almost has me convinced," Louie said.

"Almost?"

"Yeah. Her left eye twitched when she claimed she wasn't involved."

"Let's go down to the parking lot and wait for Cedric to arrive."

"Jake, are we barking up the wrong tree? If not Cedric, who else should we be looking at?"

"We're looking at everyone. I have Al doing a search on the people Edy spoke with at the ball last week. We've cleared her maid and her father's housekeeper. I'm waiting on a few more items to come back to clear Smith. Edy Dunstan doesn't have a lot of close friends or people in her life. She has a tier of people she deals with through her charities. I'm stumped, though I believe it's one of the people in her small circle—husband, lover, servant, or all three. I can't see her father for this. *She's led a lonely life, isolated from most.* Jake decided not to voice his thought. The little bit he'd learned about Edy Dunstan and Ed Rockford pointed to a domineering father who had tried to control every aspect of his daughter's life.

"I never had the father in the mix," Louie said.

"I did, though he's been cleared." They'd reached the lobby doors. Jake stopped and pointed to a set of headlights pulling into the parking lot. "Let's see who gets out of the car."

Cedric Dunstan emerged from the car, then opened the door behind the driver's seat. He lifted a bag out and walked to the building. Jake and Louie backed up into the lobby and waited.

"What the hell do you want?" Cedric demanded, mirroring Rosie's response.

"Where were you?" Jake asked. Rosie had to have called him and clued him in to their presence.

"Out, and it's none of your damn business."

"Your wife's in danger, which makes you our business. Where were you?" Jake repeated.

Dunstan nudged his grocery bag forward. "Shopping."

"Why shop now, after you'd already eaten out?" Louie asked.

"We needed things," Cedric said. "Is that all?"

"No. Where is she, Cedric?" Jake closed the space between him and Dunstan.

"I told you before and I'll tell you again. I had nothing to do with her disappearance. I want you to find her safe, to end this once and for all."

Jake noted how Cedric avoided Edy's name each time he spoke to him. "Edy's time is running out, Cedric. You don't have an inkling who'd want to snatch her?"

"I don't. I hope you find her well, but she and I are through. She made that clear in our last meeting. Now if you'll excuse me, this bag is getting heavy." Dunstan turned away from them and walked to the elevator.

Jake waited for the elevator doors to close. "Did you get a look inside the bag?"

"No, he held it at an odd angle," Louie said.

"Let's go."

In the parking lot, Jake located the officer who had left his post, and read him the riot act. He wondered if Dunstan, after learning the officer was away, had taken off to check up on Edy.

Damn, a missed opportunity that might've led to Edy's whereabouts.

Chapter 30

The burning in Jake's stomach continued on his drive home and got worse as he climbed the stairs into his foyer. Inside, he toyed with the pill bottle in his pocket. He snapped the cap off and swallowed two pills and rinsed them down with a glass of water before he went into his bedroom and tumbled into bed next to Mia, still wearing his clothes. He landed on top of the covers and fell into a deep sleep despite the pain.

Groggy, he tried to shake off the heaviness of sleep nine hours later. The room spun when he sat up. *Damn meds.* He gave his body a few minutes to adjust to the light-headedness before he tried standing, and started for the shower.

"Well, good morning, sleepyhead," Mia said from the doorway.

"What time it is?" he asked through the cobwebs clogging his mind.

"It's after nine."

"Shit, I've got to get going. Why didn't you wake me?"

"You came in after midnight, Jake. Look at you. You're as pale as a ghost. I thought after you found Callie's killer you'd take time off and see the doctor."

"Mia, Edy's still missing. Do you want me to leave her out there on her own?"

"No, but I want you to take care of yourself. You'll be no good to anyone if you wind up back in the hospital."

"I promise I won't."

Mia turned and walked out of the bedroom without a word. Jake followed her to the living room and plopped down beside her on the couch. She had her arms folded across her chest as she stared at the television.

"I'll call the doctor today, but I can't stop being who I am," Jake said.

"I'm not asking you to. All I want is for you to take care of yourself. Being here the last few weeks, I realize you come last in your life. It's an unhealthy attitude."

"Today, I'll call the doctor first thing." He considered swallowing another pain pill to get ahead of the pain before he jumped in the shower, but he didn't dare take one in front of her.

"It's after nine, call now," Mia demanded, handing him the portable phone, and eyed him until he acted.

It was a no-win situation. He dialed, talked to the nurse, and made the appointment. "I'll be there in thirty." Jake hung up.

Jake called Louie after his shower and gave him his ETA and didn't bother to explain why he'd be late. The last thing he needed or wanted this morning was Louie ribbing him about his domestic situation.

* * * *

A half hour later, Jake sat on the exam table in Doctor Joel Kettleton's office and listened to Joel's harangue with half an ear.

"Jake, you've got a minor infection. If you keep at it, it will be a full-blown one. I stressed stomach wounds are the worst. You need to be home resting, not exerting yourself until you drop. Your job is stressful. It's not conducive to healing," the doctor said, his sandy hair styled and sprayed in place, his pale eyes concerned. Kettleton and he had gone to high school together. "You're running a low-grade fever. I'm serious about resting."

"I had no choice when the commissioner's wife was murdered. He called me back himself. And now a woman is fighting for her life..."

"Jake, doesn't the WPD have other detectives?"

"You don't understand—"

"I do. Remember, I've known you for years. You're a driven man and I respect your devotion to the job, but your health is more important," Kettleton chided.

"I promise to slow down after we rescue the victim. In the meantime, I need you to refill my pain meds," Jake said, looking around while his feet dangled off the hard exam table, the blood pressure cuff still attached to his arm. He wanted to climb out the tiny window to escape Kettleton's lecture.

"Hmm!"

"What?"

"I'm tempted not to refill it if the pain would slow you down."

"Doc, I only take half of a pill, or a whole, maybe once a day, if that. It takes the edge off."

"What time did you get home last night?"

It sucked when you were friends with your doctor, who knew you better than you knew yourself.

"Late," Jake said.

"How late?"

"It doesn't matter…" The doctor folded his arms across his chest and waited him out—Jake scowled. "Midnight."

"I'll fill the prescription one more time, but I'm also adding an antibiotic to combat the infection. I'm only going to do this if you promise me you'll work no later than eight each night."

Jake really needed the pills. He hadn't been able to function without them this past week. "I promise."

"And just so you know, I'll be contacting Louie and Mia with the same instructions," Kettleton said.

"What happened to patient confidentiality?" Jake asked, understanding he'd lost this round.

"You appointed Mia your health care advocate in the hospital, or don't you remember that?"

"How do I revoke it?"

"When this episode is done I'll tell you. The woman cares for you, Jake."

"I'm aware. I promise not to work past eight. Are we done?"

"Yes."

It irked him how long the doctor took to read him the riot act. Jake didn't get to the station until a little before eleven. When he got back to his desk, he called his attorney to revoke the power of attorney for his health care before he did another thing. He had to have been drugged to sign his rights away.

"Where were you?" Louie plopped into one of the chairs in front of Jake's desk.

"None of your business. What've you got for me? Anything new?"

"No, Edy Dunstan has disappeared off the face of the earth. Dunstan and his mistress haven't gone anywhere today. I'm telling you, if it's them, there has to be a third person involved," Louie said.

"I agree, but who? Outside of Riverton, Dunstan only has golf buddies and business associates. I don't see any of them helping with something like this. There are no other close relationships for him. We've verified Rosie's alibi for earlier in the evening, but she left her friends before seven thirty, which gave her plenty of time to kidnap or assist in the kidnapping. Did Smith get in touch with us yet?"

"He called in about an hour ago and apologized. He left his phone home yesterday and didn't get in until late. He'll be at work all day if we want to meet and talk there."

"Set up an appointment for twelve thirty at his bank."

Louie got up, walked to the door, and turned to face him. "You're not going to tell me where you were?"

"No."

Louie stepped out, stepped back in. "Did you call Mia and tell her what Joel said?"

"If you knew where I was, why did you ask?"

"I wanted to see if you'd tell me. Call her, she's worried about you."

All the poking around the doctor had done had aggravated his belly and worsened his mood. Jake tilted the bottle and shook a pill out. He eyed it, and then put it back.

* * * *

Jake and Louie walked into the Sandars Bank on East Main Street at one o'clock, where Smith was the branch manager. Smith hadn't been willing to give up his lunch break even for Edy's sake. As far as Jake could see, Smith held the position of middle management. Would dating Edy get him a job at her family's bank instead of here, raising his position in the world? Smith had a little bit of money, but with Edy he'd be a rich man. Was it a motive for kidnapping? *Christ, an argument was motive in some people's eyes*, Jake thought.

He spotted Smith behind the counter, talking to one of the tellers. Smith waved but finished up his conversation before he came out to greet them.

"Do you have news?" he asked.

"No, we have a couple more questions for you, Mr. Smith. Is there somewhere private we can talk?" Louie asked.

"My office, this way," Smith said.

They followed Smith into a nine-by-nine office with a window looking out onto the parking lot. Smith sat with his back to it. Jake and Louie took the seats in front of the desk.

"Mr. Smith, do you have a wife or girlfriend?" Jake asked.

"Why? How is that relevant?" Smith drummed his fingers on the desk.

"Everything is important in a kidnapping or murder case."

"You think Edy's dead?" He shot out of his chair.

"No, sit and please answer the question."

"I date on and off, nothing serious," Linden said.

"Anyone in particular?" Louie interjected.

"There's been one woman more than others for a year. We're friends."

"Why isn't it serious? A year's a long time."

"It's comfortable, and when we need a date we take each other to work functions. I wasn't ready for a long-term relationship until Edy came along. We clicked on our first date."

Jake bet that Edy's millions played a factor in Smith's decision.

"Is that the reason you were seeing Edy?" Louie asked.

"Edy and I are serious. I'm going to marry her. I couldn't take her to functions while she was married to another man. It wouldn't look right."

"Who's the other woman?" Jake asked.

Smith stared Jake down, folded his hands on his desk.

"I need the name and number, Mr. Smith."

A second of hesitation, then Smith reached for his cell phone and wrote down the information. It struck Jake as odd that Linden had to look up his girlfriend's number. Within days he'd had Mia's number memorized.

"If Edy didn't want to get remarried, what would you lose?"

"Nothing."

"Thanks for your time," Louie said.

Outside in the car, Jake scribbled notes in his pad. Louie did the same.

"Impressions?" Jake asked.

"He seemed annoyed he had to hand over his information, but…"

"Yeah, but—he had nothing to gain, unless it's all about the money. I still think the kidnapping goes deeper. You?"

"I agree," Louie said.

* * * *

Smith's girlfriend worked in a shoe store at the mall. She agreed to speak with them on her break. They strolled around the mall, killing fifteen minutes before they met up with Freya Pelham.

"Have you bought Mia a thank-you gift?" Louie asked.

"Why would I do that?"

"You're a grumpy patient, and she deserves a gold star for putting up with you these last few weeks," Louie said, popping inside a lingerie store. "How about this?" He held up a pair of red bikini panties.

"Will you get the hell out of there? I'm not buying her underwear or anything else," Jake said.

"Your loss, they'd have benefited you too." Louie shrugged.

"It's time, let's go meet with Freya."

Jake steered Louie away from the store. He spotted Freya—from the description she gave him when they spoke on the phone—sitting alone in the food court. He walked up.

"Freya Pelham?"

"Yes." The petite woman had her black hair pulled back in a ponytail, her makeup minimal. Jake guessed her to be in her late twenties.

"I'm Lieutenant Carrington and this is Sergeant Romanelli. May we sit?"

"Yes. Like I said on the phone, I don't know how I can help you." Freya kept folding and unfolding her hands.

"Are you nervous, Miss Pelham?" Jake asked.

Jake took in his surroundings and assessed the customers hanging around the tables in the food court. Mothers weary of chasing children sat with a cup of coffee or soda while the kids ate fries. A couple of kids cutting school sat at the far end of the area and horsed around with each other.

"I am. I've never been interviewed by the police for anything before."

"We only have a few questions, then we'll be out of your hair," Louie reassured her in his fatherly tone.

"Okay, fire away."

"Are you dating Linden Smith?" Jake asked.

Freya glanced off to her left. Her eyes fixed on the pizza counter. "Yes," she said in a low voice.

"For how long?" Louie asked. A child of indeterminate age scurried by, screaming and laughing like a hyena at the top of his lungs as his mother chased him.

"About six months," she said before adding, "we're not serious or anything."

"What's a normal date for the two of you?" Jake asked.

"Dinner and movie, sometimes he takes me to work functions."

"Do you know Edy Dunstan?" Jake continued.

"No, I never met her. Linden dates her, but that's it."

"And you don't mind?" Louie questioned.

"No, as I said, we're not serious."

Something was off with her answers. Jake decided to nudge her. "If down the road we find Linden is involved in Edy's kidnapping, and you lied to us, that will make you an accessory after the fact, Miss Pelham."

"I didn't lie…" She wrung her hands. "What if I didn't date him? Is that a lie?"

"Why would you say you did when you didn't?"

"I need something to drink," Freya said, quickly standing and walking away from them.

He latched his eyes on Freya's retreating back and made sure she didn't call anyone.

"Interesting," Jake said.

"Yeah, I think Smith put her up to this," Louie said.

Jake would give her another minute. If she didn't return to the table, he'd finish their questions at the food counter. Freya returned with her soda in hand.

"Do you want to change your story?" Jake asked.

"No, but Linden is really into Edy, and there's also another woman he's involved with. I don't know her name, but she calls him all the time when we're out. Oh, and Linden said that Edy's husband beats her. It's why she's getting a divorce."

Jake stared Freya down, gauging her answer. Neither Edy or her father had mentioned domestic abuse.

"Are you positive of your information, Miss Pelham?" Louie asked.

"It's what Linden told me. I never witnessed it, if that's what you're asking."

* * * *

They finished up their interview with Pelham and left her sitting there in the food court staring at her cell phone. In the parking lot, Jake didn't put the key in the ignition right away. He sat pondering Pelham's answers. Louie did the same. Jake called Benita first.

"Benita, this is Lieutenant Carrington. Did Cedric ever hit or beat Edy?"

"Oh God no, her father would've had him arrested," Benita said with her thick accent.

"You're sure?" Jake asked.

"Yes. I've been with them now for fifteen years and never witnessed any such thing."

"Thanks, Benita."

Jake called Ed Rockford next. "Mr. Rockford, Jake Carrington here. Did Cedric ever raise a hand to Edy?"

"No, he knew I'd kill him if he did."

"Thanks," Jake said, ready to hang up.

"Are you any closer to finding her?"

"I'm not sure. What time is the money drop?"

"In four hours, around dusk in Hamilton Park...Please don't be there, Jake."

"I'm hoping to find her before you drop off the funds. I'll ask you again. I'd be happy to act as the go-between."

"If it wasn't Edy's life hanging in the balance, I'd let you. But I'm not playing games with my daughter's life."

Rockford hung up.

Chapter 31

Footsteps overhead echoed through her prison. She must've dozed off. Hunger hit Edy hard as her stomach growled. It was the only sound in the darkness and echoed in her ears. Would they release her now? She squinted toward the window, trying to determine if it was night or day. Her heart jumped, pounding against her ribs. Would they let her out?

The door on the other side of the room creaked open, the hinges squeaking as a flashlight scanned the room. Edy assumed it was night, but found it hard to judge time. Had it been days or weeks since they took her? The light landed on her, blinding her to the person holding it. *Not one but two people this time, like the night they grabbed me.*

"Not so high and mighty now, are you, princess?" a woman asked gleefully.

"Shut up," a familiar voice barked. One she couldn't quite place. *It's a different voice from the last man who brought me food*, Edy thought.

"Listen, I've had it with you bossing me around. I'll talk when I want to," the woman snapped.

"You fool, if she gets out of here, she'll be able to identify you." His voice had a weird accent, as if he were trying to disguise it.

Think, Edy, think. You know this voice. No matter how much she tried, she couldn't say who it was. The rusty twang was throwing her off.

"Where's your flashlight?"

"Here," the woman said.

"Well, keep it on her face."

"I don't see why you're feeding her," the woman said.

"Because we're not going to kill her unless her old man doesn't pay up," the man said in an impatient tone.

Edy forced her eyes to focus as she squinted against the light shining in her eyes. The man's build was lanky, taller than the last one. She felt a thud as the tray hit the bed. Without thinking it through, she latched on to the tray with her free hand, dumped its contents, and swung out with all her might, hitting her target hard.

"You bitch, you'll pay for this," the man said, without the twang.

The voice froze her in place for a second. A second too long—the man reached out and punched her. *Why?* Was her last thought before slipping into an unconscious state.

* * * *

"Freya lied," Jake said turning the key in the ignition.

"I figured. She couldn't look us in the eye," Louie agreed. "It's after four now. Smith's bank is closed."

"I'll give him a call. I want another meeting."

Jake's call went into voicemail. He left his message and tapped his fingers on the steering wheel of his department-issued sedan.

He called the main switchboard for the bank but got a recording. "We're close enough. I want to drive by his bank and see if his car is there," Jake said pulling out of the parking lot of the mall.

"I wasn't looking at Smith," Louie said.

"Me either, and I'm still not one hundred percent sure we should switch up our suspect, but…"

"Yeah, but…" Louie repeated as Jake pulled into the bank's parking lot.

Smith's car wasn't in the parking lot, but something pinged deep in Jake's head, fleeing as quickly as it had floated in.

"Let's head back to the mall and question Freya again."

They caught her at the cash register ringing up a customer.

"Freya, have someone else wait on your customer. You need to be honest with us. If I don't like your answers, we'll be taking you downtown to the police station for further questioning. Do you understand?" Jake asked.

"Yes," she said, ignoring her coworker's inquiring glance.

"Well?"

"Ellen, finish ringing up this customer, please."

They moved to the back of the store. "Linden put me up to it. I never dated him. I'm engaged to his friend Bobby. I've never met Linden's real girlfriend, but she's not Edy. He kept her on the down-low. You don't really believe he'd kidnap Edy do you?" Freya's brown eyes opened wide in shock.

"It's looking more like it every minute. Where is he?"

"How the hell should I know? As I said, I don't date him."

"Where's your fiancé? I'll need his name, phone number, where he works, and his hours."

"Bobby didn't do anything," Freya whined.

"Now, Miss Pelham," Jake demanded. "When we leave, do not call either Bobby or Linden. If you do call, you'll be arrested for interfering in an investigation. Do you understand?"

"Yes."

They left Pelham at work, her fellow employees gawking at them, and made their way to the car. Louie wrote down everything she'd told them before he placed a call to Bobby Roderick. Jake steered the car across town toward Roderick's house.

"He'll see us now at his apartment. He just got home from work. Drive toward the east end, his place is right off of Meriden Road," Louie said.

Jake put a call in to the officer on duty watching over Dunstan. "Officer Vincenzo, has Dunstan or Riverton left the apartment today?"

"Riverton left about a half hour ago and I followed her. I notified dispatch, and they supplied a tail to relieve me so I could head back to my surveillance on the apartment. Last he reported in, she went inside the Sandars Bank on East Main Street."

"How long ago did they report that?" Jake asked.

"About twenty minutes ago. Dispatch said you were notified, sir," Officer Vincenzo said in a defensive tone.

It'd accomplish nothing for him to chastise the uniform again. Jake inhaled, got control of his temper, and thanked the officer. The minute he hung up he checked his cell phone voicemail. Nothing. He called Al Burke at the station.

"Al, I'm driving. Do me a favor and check my office phone for voice messages." Jake said before Al could greet him.

"Sure," Al said. "Just hold on."

"What's up?" Louie asked.

Flowery music filled his ears as he waited for Al to get back to him. Jake filled Louie in while he waited.

Al's voice returned. "There's a message from dispatch reporting in on the Riverton woman."

It wouldn't do any good to blow up at the messenger. "Thanks, Al."

Jake hung up and decided it was something Shamus would have to deal with it. He didn't trust himself to talk to dispatch directly after they had two screw-ups in two days.

"Idiots," Louie muttered.

Jake had gone a block before he made a U-turn and drove back, lost in thought. The single car in the bank lot should've triggered a faster reaction.

Damn it, I'm losing it.

"Was she withdrawing money, or meeting with Smith?" Jake asked. "This adds a new angle to the investigation. Let's drive around the building again. The OOD didn't report her leaving the bank."

Riverton's car was parked under a tree in the far corner of the lot. He and Louie climbed from their vehicle and checked the bank doors. Locked. Jake held a hand to the glass as he peered inside. No one came into view.

Jake called Rockford. "Mr. Rockford, I know Sandars is not your bank, but do you have the president's name and number?"

"Yes, why?"

"I can't say right now, but I'll fill you in when I can. It's important."

Rockford gave it to him. Louie called John McKenzie, president of Sandars, and explained the circumstances. He agreed to meet them immediately.

"I didn't see this coming," Jake said.

"Me either. You think Riverton and Smith are an item?"

"It's looking that way. Call Roderick again, and ask him to meet us here now."

Twenty minutes passed before Louie pointed out a red Mercedes pulling into the lot. Jake assessed the driver as he exited the car. Middle-aged, his hair going gray at the temples, he wore an impeccable blue suit. He approached them with sure steps.

"I'm John McKenzie. Officers, would you like to go into more detail now?"

"It's Lieutenant and Sergeant, Mr. McKenzie. I'm sorry, all I can tell you is I need to see if Mr. Smith and a certain customer are still inside," Jake said.

McKenzie walked briskly to the door, unlocked it, and turned off the alarm after notifying the security company.

Jake and Louie searched the place while McKenzie waited in the lobby. No one was there.

"Mr. McKenzie, do you have your tellers' phone numbers? We need to ask one of them if Smith left with anyone and if they left through an employee entrance."

McKenzie made the calls, and confirmed Smith left with a woman who matched Riverton's description. The employee entrance located in the rear of the building shielded Riverton's tail from spotting her when she left the building.

"Lieutenant, does this have anything to do with Edy Dunstan?"

Jake made a decision. McKenzie had gone out of his way to help. "Yes."

"I hope you find her."

"So do we, Mr. McKenzie, so do we."

In the car Jake slammed his hand on the dashboard. "For God's sake, I never even considered him a suspect, Louie. Now Edy might die. Call Officer Vincenzo and have him bring Dunstan to the station."

"Why Dunstan?" Louie asked.

"He's a world-class cheater. He had to know Riverton was cheating on him."

* * * *

McKenzie pulled out of the lot as Roderick drove in. "Louie, call for a patrol car. I believe we'll be arresting Roderick shortly."

Jake approached Roderick's car with his badge visible. Louie sidled up to the other side of the car.

"License and registration," Jake said.

Roderick handed them over without a word. Jake studied the license. It matched Roderick. Black hair, brown eyes, five eleven, and it also had his current address listed.

"Do you know why you were asked here, Mr. Roderick?"

"Freya told me you were questioning her about Linden Smith. Why?" Roderick asked.

"Mr. Roderick, where is your friend Linden? And where is he holding Edy Dunstan?"

"How the hell should I know?" Roderick pushed Jake's hand off his door.

Jake thrust open the door and he and Louie muscled Roderick from his car and slammed his back up against it. Jake switched off the engine and palmed the keys while Louie restrained Roderick.

Roderick didn't deny Smith had the Dunstan woman. That hadn't gotten past Jake. "You're going to jail until you tell us. If you helped Smith, you'll be charged along with him. Where is Edy Dunstan?"

"I'm telling you, I don't know," Roderick yelled. "First you pick on my fiancée and now me. Why?"

"Smith gave me Freya's name. He said he was dating her and Edy."

Let him mull that over.

Jake pointed to the patrol officer who had driven into the lot. "Take him downtown and hold him."

* * * *

"I'm telling you, you're wrong, Lieutenant. Rosie would never cheat on me," Cedric Dunstan said when Jake walked into the interview room a half hour later.

"Cedric, I don't have time to dick around." Jake banged his hand on the table in interview room 3.

"I'm not. I'd know if she was."

"Then where did she take off to today?"

"She said she had errands to run. I expect her home by six," Cedric said.

Boy, people are clueless, Jake thought, *or they don't want to know. Which is it for Cedric?*

"Cedric, I'm going to explain this one more time. Rosie met with Linden Smith at the Sandars Bank today. She left her car in their lot and took off with him. Where would they go?"

Cedric Dunstan's mouth drooped. "It can't be…"

"It is, Cedric. I think she and Smith abducted Edy. I need you to rack your brain and tell me where they'd keep her."

"I've not a clue. Smith lives in an apartment and Rosie lives with me," Cedric said, his voice strained as Jake saw the realization finally sink in.

Riverton had used him to get to Edy. Was Riverton really pregnant? He'd need to find out, and if so, whose kid was it?

He wasn't going to get anything else from Dunstan. He and Louie left him sitting in the room as they made their way to interview room 1. Next up, they'd go at Bobby Roderick. Jake notified holding to bring the prisoner up to the room.

Jake watched as Roderick was escorted into the room. A half hour in a holding cell had unglued him.

Jake took the seat to the left. Louie sat directly in front of Roderick. Beforehand they had decided Louie would go at him softly, before Jake went on the attack.

Louie started right in on Bobby. "Bobby, we need to find Linden. You've been friends with him most of your life. Where would he hold Mrs. Dunstan?"

"I'm telling you, I don't know," Roderick said.

"The way things are looking right now, Linden threw your fiancée into the mix, along with you. If he's such a friend, why would he do that?"

"I can't say…Freya's innocent."

"And you?" Louie asked.

Roderick sat in silence.

"I can't help you or Freya if you don't talk to me. Why should either one of you go down for something Linden did?" Louie asked.

Roderick rested his head on his arms against the table. Louie tapped him on the head to get his attention.

"Kidnapping is a federal charge that comes with a life sentence. Is that what you want for yourself and Freya?"

Jake watched as Louie kept hitting Roderick's weak spot. Freya meant everything to Bobby.

"Freya didn't do anything. And when I see Linden I'm going to punch him out for throwing her name into this." Once Roderick started talking, he didn't stop. "Linden promised me a large sum of money to bring food to the woman. He didn't give me her name. He said it was part of their sex game. Like that book that came out last year on bondage."

"Where did you bring the food?"

"It's a foreclosure home on Cedar Lake Avenue, number 10. The houses on each side of it are also owned by the bank," Roderick said. "Linden said it was the perfect spot for their adventure. No one would bother them."

"You listen to the news?" Jake asked.

"Yes."

"And you never made the connection to the kidnapped woman?" Jake quirked his brow as he stared Roderick down.

"I...I...started to wonder, but Linden wouldn't answer my questions."

"Did you know he was dating Rosie Riverton?" Louie asked.

"Yes, but he didn't want anyone else to know."

"Did you know she's living with Mrs. Dunstan's soon-to-be ex-husband?"

"No, I swear. If I did I would've called the police right away. Linden told me the woman would offer me money and beg to be released. He also told me she was into humiliation. It turned her on, so I ignored her pleas. My God, what have I done?" Roderick wiped his runny nose on the sleeve of his shirt.

Jake left Louie to finish up with Roderick and gathered a team to save Edy Dunstan. Louie caught up with him fifteen minutes later after turning Roderick over to the officer in charge. He'd stay locked up until they sorted it all out.

Jake held up a hand when Louie walked into his office, and continued to speak into his phone.

"Mr. Rockford, I believe we've found her. I've got a team together and we're leaving in five to rescue her. I wanted to give you a heads-up before we took off. This is important. I need you to follow through with the ransom. Make a bag filled with paper with bundles of money on top. This way if the kidnappers look inside they'll think they're all set. If they get past us, we'll grab them when they meet up with you. My men will be a block away from the park."

"How will I know if you found her and she's safe?" Rockford asked.

"On your way to the park, I want you to stop at the convenience store on the corner of East Main Street and Meriden Road. Go to the last aisle. An officer will be there in plain clothes to give you a radio. It will be preset to a channel which connects you to me. But don't contact or speak over the channel. When the kidnappers approach you, click it five times and help will be there in seconds."

"Okay, but how will I know Edy's safe?" Rockford repeated.

"One of the officers will inform you. I need to keep the airwaves clear." Jake hung up.

"Does he realize we don't have her yet?" Louie asked.

"Yes. I hope he doesn't jump the gun before we pull her from the house," Jake said. "Let's get this done."

God, I pray she's safe or all this has been for nothing.

Chapter 32

It took time to set up the operations. Jake had to contact the city's building inspector to get a copy of the blueprints to 10 Cedar Lake. Then he had to line up his team. Two and a half hours later, Jake parked at the top of Cedar Lake Avenue. He wasn't risking Riverton or Smith spotting them. He handed out everyone's assignments. The first team would circle around back on the street adjacent to the rear of the house. The second team would come from the right side of the house off Daley Street, and the third team would come at it from the left. He and Louie were going in the front door. Roderick had given Louie the lockbox combination.

After two tries, Louie opened the lockbox, grabbed the key and unlocked the front door. The smell of mildew hit them in the face. The house looked as if it had been closed up for years.

Cobwebs around the door and stairs stuck to their clothing. "Christ, I hate spiders," Louie whispered, pushing the cobwebs away with his sleeve to avoid to touching them.

Jake plowed through them without a thought. He pointed upstairs to the officer who had accompanied them inside. While the young cop quietly made his way up, they searched for the door leading down to the basement. He and Louie had studied the blueprints before leading a team into the place. *If no remodeling was done, the door should be in the kitchen. Let's hope it is.* He crossed his fingers as he and Louie stepped into the kitchen.

The stench hit them first. Dirty dishes rotted in the sink, and the refrigerator door hung open, crowded with spoiled food. The window curtains were a dingy brown. Jake assumed at one time they'd been yellow. Filthy pots and pans covered the stove in the corner by the back door. Something scurried across the floor. He swept the room with his eyes. Two doors to his left matched the plan. One was for a pantry, the second the basement.

Jake made his way over to the doors, his feet sticking to the grimy wood floor, which squeaked with each step, announcing their arrival. Jake hoped the sound didn't carry to the basement. He held up one finger, then two, and on the count of three he opened the door, flicked on his flashlight, and went down the steps first. Louie followed, his flashlight illuminating the area more.

Each step creaked when he put his weight on it, though Jake treaded carefully. A woman's piercing scream cut through the darkness. Jake rushed down the rest of the stairs, caution and his quiet approach gone. He shoved through more cobwebs and ignored the scurry of rodents scratching the concrete as he navigated into the room at the back of the basement. He stopped short to assess the situation and Louie slammed into his back.

"I got him, you take her," Jake said as he vaulted into the room.

The smell of human waste and urine smacked him in the face. Rosie Riverton was launching an attack on Edy with her fists as Edy tried to protect herself with one arm despite being handcuffed to the bed railing. When Edy blocked one of Rosie's punches, Rosie tugged on her hair. Edy screamed as her arm twisted in the cuff. Meanwhile, Linden Smith was trying to pull Rosie off Edy.

"You son of bitch, why?" Edy screamed, reaching around Rosie to swing at Smith's head. He ducked.

"Why? You've got to be kidding. You treat everyone as if they're your servants, no wonder your husband left you. And FYI, Edy, I don't like to be used," Smith said.

"Used? You used me and she used Cedric for what—money, you bastard?"

"Why is it people with money speak of it with disdain?" Linden shot back.

"Just knock her out again," Rosie shouted, slapping Edy open-handed. Edy's head lolled back.

It all happened in a split second. Jake assessed the scene while latching on to Linden's shoulders. Jake tossed him to Louie and fought to break Rosie's grip on Edy's hair, dropping his flashlight in the struggle. As he bent to retrieve it, a fist connected with his jaw. Pissed, Jake came up swinging. Rosie was no lady, and he'd had his share of entitled people.

As Jake straightened to his full height, Rosie elbowed him in the stomach, hitting his infected wound. It knocked the air from his lungs. He wanted nothing more than to wrap his hands around her scrawny neck and snap it in two.

Someone pushed him off to the side. Jake almost punched the person until he realized it was Louie. He'd lost track of Louie in the fight.

"Jesus, Mary, and Joseph, watch who you're pushing around, Louie," Jake hissed out.

"If I left you to your own accord she'd have won." Louie slapped the cuffs on Rosie's wrists and signaled for the two officers who had rushed into the room.

"Take this one to the wagon and then get the medics down here right away. We've got two patients," Louie said, directing the uniforms.

"One patient," Jake said, trying to hold it together.

Louie ignored him and turned his attention to Edy. "Mrs. Dunstan, help is on its way. Are you able to walk?"

"I think so. It's so filthy down here," Edy said, looking embarrassed.

The place smelled of urine, vomit, and mildew. Jake figured most of the mess was from Edy and though he'd never tell her, Edy stank. Riverton and Smith hadn't even extended the most common of courtesies, such as a place to bathe or a place to relieve herself. She'd been treated like a caged animal.

"We're going to get you out of here soon. Your father's been so worried. Hang in there," Louie said quietly. Jake composed himself as he leaned against the wall and waited for his breathing to return to normal. He struggled to meet Louie's stare head-on.

There is no way I'm leaving a crime scene on a gurney—yet again.

* * * *

Louie was torn between giving Jake a hand or letting him suffer in silence. Compassion won out. He walked to Jake and offered him a hand.

"You're a stubborn bastard, but you're in no condition to dictate to me if you'll be seen or not. I've taken over the scene, and as officer in charge, I say you'll be seen by the medics. Got it?" Louie demanded, shoving down his temper.

"Got it," Jake said.

"Now drape a damn arm around my shoulders and I'll get you upstairs."

"I can do it on my own." Jake started to limp away from him.

Louie had no choice but to watch as Jake's pride got in the way. The medics determined Jake had to go to the hospital. Louie waited until the ambulance pulled away before he went back in and processed the crime scene.

Smith and Riverton were inhuman, to make Edy sit in her own dirt. Where the hell did these cretins come from? Louie wondered. *How the hell did they develop into these uncaring, selfish individuals who took and took until there wasn't anything left?*

Two hours later, he left the mess to the crime scene techs and called Mia's cell. "Mia, it's Louie. Is Jake home or still at the hospital?"

"He's been admitted. Doctor Kettleton wasn't taking no for an answer."

Louie heard the smile in her voice and had to smile himself. Not many could get Jake to do something he didn't want to, but Joel was tougher than Jake.

"I bet he's ornery."

"You have no idea, but Joel Kettleton is my new favorite person," Mia said.

"I'm on my way there," Louie said.

"I'm outside his room waiting on the doctor to finish up with him. When you get here, come up to room 223. I have to go, here comes Joel."

Mia disconnected the call. He'd have to wait to find out what the good doctor had to say.

* * * *

Before Jake could talk to Mia, Edy stopped in his room to thank him. She bought along her father and a big fruit basket.

"We're so grateful to Jake and the sergeant for rescuing Edy," Rockford said.

"Yes, thank you, Jake. I would've been here sooner, but I had to get cleaned up. The nurse gave me her clothes to go home in."

"How are you doing, Edy?" Jake asked.

"I'm healing, and the doctor on duty gave me the name of a professional to speak with after I finish up with the police. The doctor said it would help me deal with the betrayals from Cedric and Linden."

"I'm glad to hear it."

Maybe I should speak to one, Jake thought.

Edy and Rockford didn't stay long. They left to let him rest. Jake eyed Mia and waited for her to fill him in on her conversation with Joel. Maybe it was time to change doctors.

"Well?" Jake said as Mia came into the room.

"What?"

"What did Joel say?" Jake asked.

Mia settled on the edge of his bed. "He said after a week of rest you should be back to normal."

"What else?"

"Jake, he told me he said the same things to you. Why the third degree?"

"I'm not staying here."

"You don't have to. Joel's setting it up for you to go into rehab at Green Willows. It's a lovely place and a quiet rehab center. You won't be able to work there," Mia said with emphasis on the *won't*.

"Mia—"

"Jake...you will go and you'll not say a word. You should've seen yourself when the ambulance brought you in. That's twice in a month's time I got the call."

"It was an elbow to the stomach, that's all."

Mia pushed up and turned her back to him. Jake reached for her hand. She shook it loose.

"Mia, it's a mild infection, and of course my belly's going to be a bit sensitive, but I can't stop my life because of it."

"You're not stopping anything. One week is not going to kill you." She sat on the bed, took his hand. "Besides, you promised me one week after this case was solved, so instead of going away, you spend it at Green Willows."

He spied Louie in the doorway to his room, grinning from ear to ear. Jake decided to table the subject until later.

"I owe you one, Romanelli," Jake said.

"Shut up and listen to the lady. She knows what she's talking about. And if you don't go on your own accord, I'll hogtie you to the bed and get you there one way or another, you stubborn ass," Louie said.

Well, they told me, didn't they? Jake closed his eyes to shut them both out and resigned himself to a week of forced rest.

At least he'd gotten a win this time around. Edy Dunstan was safe and back home with her father. In the end, that's what really mattered.

Acknowledgments

To Michaela Hamilton and Shannon Plackis, my editors at Kensington, for their wonderful advice and guidance with each story—thank you. And a special thanks to my beta readers Cathy Hopkins, Gerri Brousseau, and Lee Theroux; and to Apieling Pictures' Brenda Piel, photographer, for the wonderful author picture.

Sneak Peek

In case you missed the book that launched the Jake Carrington thrillers, keep reading to enjoy the first chapter of...

ALL THE DEADLY LIES

Now available from Lyrical Underground,
an imprint of Kensington Publishing Corp.

Chapter 1

"Sergeant, in my office, please." Captain Shamus McGuire stood at attention in his doorway, all six-feet-four inches of him. His steel-gray hair cut to military precision focused one's attention on his matching gray eyes.

Homicide Sergeant Jake Carrington of the Wilkesbury Police Department looked across his joined desk to his partner, and lifelong friend Louie Romanelli and shrugged. Louie threw him a questioning look as he adjusted his tie and started to rise from his chair.

"Just Jake, Louie," the captain said as he turned into his office.

Jake picked up their latest case file to update the captain and walked in to join McGuire.

"Take a seat, Jake." The captain pointed to one of the two institutional-gray ones in front of his desk. He took off his glasses and massaged his forehead.

Though Jake preferred to stand, he took the less beat-up seat on the right. The room was a monument to the man, all spit and polish. Sparse furnishing with a few awards and medals hung on the walls. Paperwork in precise piles, a picture of his family, the standard computer and phone were all he had on his desk. McGuire's appearance and stance spoke of his military background and warned his cops he took no crap from them. It wasn't like him to stall but that's exactly what he was doing at the moment. McGuire turned his smoky eyes on him. Jake went on alert. Something was up, something big.

"Captain?" Instincts had Jake bracing for what came next.

"Spaulding's coming up for parole again. And this time he's requesting a DNA test before he comes before the board." Jake's stomach curdled.

McGuire continued, "He's also requesting the DNA samples from your sister's crime scene be tested against his sample."

"What bullshit, Shamus."

Jake jumped up, roamed the office. His mouth went dry. Deep down he was afraid the old samples somehow wouldn't match and would set Eva's killer free. This new development would split his attention. What could Spaulding gain from this maneuver? To catch a killer, you had to get inside his head. Did Spaulding assume the system would release him if he got a new trial?

He looked out the window and studied the downtown area as he ran every scenario through his mind. This was his town, though imperfect as it was. He and Eva had been born here of immigrant parents. Its one hundred thousand residents depended on him and those who had come before him to protect it.

Outside of his tour of military duty overseas he didn't venture far from it, a good city, though down on its luck since all the manufacturing jobs went overseas. Wilkesbury recently had the distinguished honor to be named one of the top five saddest rust belt cities. And it's the one that was farthest south of the belt. In its glory days, nothing could touch Wilkesbury. Most of the crime in the city came from the twenty percent of the Wilkesburians living under the national poverty level. The city had its mix of people, businesses, homeless, shoppers, and kids. More kids claimed the downtown area since UConn had put a branch right across the street from the station. Today some of the kids wore shorts to celebrate the hot weather. Last week it was in the forties. Today the temperatures hit the seventies. *New England, you gotta love it*, he thought.

Clearing his mind, he focused on The Palace Marquee. Next month Johnny Mathis would be here for two days. He thought it a monument to the citizens of Wilkesbury when private citizens and businesses raised the money to save the Palace. It had been closed for eighteen years. The last performer had been Tony Bennett in 1987. Bennett had opened the newly restored theater in 2004 and it was still going strong. Jake loved the old theater. It brought back good memories from his childhood. The grand old theater done in the tradition of the Met was a step back in time. Since it had been refurbished it drew some big-name performers and plays. *It's about time we got something decent in the downtown area,* he thought. Murders were down in recent years but overall crime continued. Eva's death was the reason he became a cop instead of going on to play pro ball after college.

Turning from the window, he walked back to stand in front of Shamus's desk. "I'm sorry, I didn't hear the last part," Jake said.

"The sperm gathered at the time of the autopsy was preserved, and with new technology he has the right to ask for the testing."

"When will it happen? I want to be there through the whole process from collection to testing to make sure there aren't any switch-ups." *What a way to start a Monday.*

"It hasn't been granted yet. His lawyer is working on the request," McGuire stated.

"When will it happen?" Jake rubbed his temples where a headache was forming.

"The board acts in their own time. I'd say toward the end of the month. I'm behind you, as is the entire department, Jake, to make sure Eva gets justice."

Jake paced the room. Seventeen years and it seemed like yesterday. "When they took him out after the trial, Spaulding whispered to me he'd done it and enjoyed every moment of it," Jake said. It was a moment in time he would never forget.

There were nights after the trial he dreamed up ways of killing Spaulding, making him suffer as much, if not more, than Eva had. Even today, when his moral code screamed there was no justification for taking a life, he understood deep down in his soul that, if given the chance, he'd remove George Spaulding from the face of this Earth and not look back. Captain McGuire's voice floated back into his head. Jake felt shame standing in front of Shamus with thoughts of murder in his head. If he did kill, what would separate him from the ones he hunted every day of his life?

"As a cop, you and I both understand the evidence is what convicts, along with a smart prosecutor. Spaulding's lawyer has petitioned the court. Even if the DNA isn't a match, it wouldn't get him an immediate release. There was other evidence putting him at the crime scene. And there was an eyewitness who saw him push Eva into his car. All it will get him is a new trial. If I remember this right, all of the evidence pointed to him. Have faith, Jake."

"Faith? Is that what I should tell Eva? Oh wait. I can't. Because she's dead!"

The captain ignored his outburst. "If he goes to trial I promise we'll reopen the case and work it along with our current files. But, you can't touch the file when we do."

"That's bullshit."

"No, it's not. If we want the chain of evidence to remain pure you can't touch it. I'll respect and appoint whoever you want to work it," McGuire said.

"Louie."

"It can't be him either." McGuire held up his hands before Jake could interrupt him. "He's too close to you."

"What's not to say any of the men in my department aren't too close to me?"

"Whoever you pick will have a state trooper working with him."

"You don't trust your own men?" Aggrieved, Jake threw up his hands. "Do you want answers?"

"Shamus, I already got my answer. I've no doubt Spaulding is guilty," Jake said.

"Then this is the best way to handle it. When we catch the killer, it will ensure a conviction," Shamus said.

Jake pushed a hand through his hair. The air thinned, cutting off his next breath. "I need to get out of here."

He rushed from McGuire's office. At his desk Jake grabbed his car keys and ignored Louie's questions. He didn't trust himself to speak. The pit of his stomach burned. What if the DNA didn't match Spaulding's? Damn, he wanted to punch something. No, not something. He wanted to punch out Spaulding.

I swear if they release him—I'll—I'll kill him.

"Jake, wait up." Louie Romanelli followed him out of the bullpen.

"Not now." Jake kept walking.

Louie caught up to him and grabbed his arm as he would a suspect and twirled him around. If he wanted to, Jake could've decked him. They were evenly matched in height and weight. Instead, he stood rigid. "Talk to me," Louie said.

"Give me a couple of hours to pull myself together. We'll meet at my house later if you can. In the meantime, work the Wagner case. I'd hate not to give the Wagners the answers they need." He didn't bother to mention the case was so similar to Eva's that he too needed the closure.

"Tell me what's wrong. Did McGuire fire you?" Louie's olive complexion whitened as he asked the question. His dark eyes searched Jake's face for an answer.

Leave it to Louie. For the first time in over a half hour, he laughed. "No, I'm not fired. Spaulding's up for parole again and has requested new testing."

He stared down his friend as Louie processed the information. If it wasn't for Louie and his family during the weeks and months that followed Eva's death, he wouldn't be standing here today.

How different we are, Jake thought. Louie, married for seventeen years to his grade-school sweetheart, now had three kids. He, on the other hand, liked being single. Side by side, though they matched each other in height, his skin tone paled next to Louie's dark Italian coloring.

"Shit."

"Go back to work. I'll talk to you later."

Jake walked away with his head down and his mind spinning out in every direction. No matter what Shamus said, he owed it to Eva to find the answers.

It's my fault she died.

* * * *

Louie checked the time. It was gonna be a tall order keeping Jake focused if Spaulding was released. McGuire beckoned him from his doorway as Louie reached for the Wagner file.

"Stay with Jake, he needs a friend right now."

"Cap, I'm meeting him at his house in a couple of hours. You want to fill me in?"

"Spaulding will come in front of the board sometime in late summer or early fall. The test results could make it sooner. It will depend on the lab's current and backlog caseloads," McGuire said.

"I got that from Jake. What aren't you telling me?" Louie asked.

"Spaulding's sure the results will clear him. He wants a new trial, an acquittal, this way he won't ever be tried again for the crime."

"It doesn't mean he'll get it." Louie ran a hand through his hair as he outlined the possibilities of Spaulding being set free.

"No, it doesn't. But a lot of prisoners have gone free with no DNA match, no matter what the other evidence against them was. Lawyers are now holding court in the press."

"If the case is reopened, who are you going to appoint to the case?"

"I'm not jumping the gun, but if it comes to it, Burke and Kraus."

* * * *

This time of day the bullpen came alive with activity. Criminals locked to chairs complained of their innocence or wrestled to free themselves. Some spit or let loose other bodily functions as revenge for getting caught. Victims cried, reliving their horror as they gave their accounts of events. Nervous witnesses sat waiting their turns to speak. In the midst of all the activities, Louie tried to concentrate on the Wagner file, but kept coming back to Jake and that horrible time in their lives.

Since they were ten, he and Jake had been as close as brothers. In fact, he was closer to Jake than to his own brother. Their lives had become a nightmare when Eva had been killed. Nothing he'd done had helped Jake deal with the tragedy. The only thing he had been able to do was be there for him. The helpless feeling overwhelmed him again. One event had changed many lives. What was he going to say to Jake?

Maybe I should ask Sophia to come with me? Nah, Jake would feel like we're ganging up on him.

Louie picked up the Wagner file. A thick one with no answers, little evidence, and statements on how wonderful and perfect Shanna was. If they didn't catch a break soon, Shanna Wagner's case would go into the unsolved file. A shadow fell over his desk as he studied the file. Looking up, Louie bit back a curse. *Not her again.* The petite brunette with the sloe eyes stood with hand on hip, waiting on him to look up at her. *Chloe Wagner, the bane of Jake's existence,* Louie thought.

Thank God Jake didn't have to deal with her in his current state of mind. Louie looked around the bullpen as the noise level lowered to a hum. *There's no one nosier than a cop.* Chloe's frequent visits had become louder and more accusing since Jake had dropped her. Louie wondered if the woman had ever cared about her sister. *Oh well, deal with it.*

"How can I help you, Ms. Wagner?"

"I need answers. My parents need answers. When are we going to get them?"

"Your sister's case is being worked every day. But we need new evidence, something to lead us in a new direction. Everything we've investigated has led to dead ends."

"My family's torn apart. My mother checks up on me several times a day to make sure I'm okay. My father walks around in a fog, like he's lost. I'm positive they're heading toward a divorce. You say you can't do anything else? That's a load of crap. You expect your answer will make me go away? Well, it won't. I'll go over your head, Detective," she shouted. The other detectives in the bullpen came to attention and went on alert. Action or gossip, it didn't matter to the detectives as long as it got their adrenaline going.

"Take a seat, Ms. Wagner." Louie pointed to the single torn-up chair on the side of his desk.

Chloe Wagner didn't resemble her sister in looks, personality, or activities. Her five-foot-two-inch frame carried one hundred five pounds. Her almond-shaped eyes, along with her hair, were brown, offsetting a round face and full lips, and all of it wrapped in a bossy, possessive nature.

Louie could see her appeal until she opened her mouth. Her personality would be a turnoff for any man, but a man like Jake, with commitment phobia—it had sent him running. He'd dumped her within a month, but for some reason, this one wouldn't let go. It would have been amusing if she wasn't hounding the entire department. Louie understood deep down that Chloe could ruin Jake's career. He never should've dated her while the investigation was going on, but Jake had ignored the rules. The decision seemed to be coming back to bite Jake on the ass ever since. Though they cleared her, Chloe was still a suspect.

Louie repeated himself. Maybe this time it would get through. "Ms. Wagner, we explained it all last week. We're working the file. Shanna is not forgotten." He picked up the file and held it out with Shanna's name facing Chloe. "We haven't given up."

"It's been over two months since she was found."

"We'll be interviewing everyone again. In the heat of the moment people sometimes forget the details. Once they calm down they remember more." He scribbled a number on his pad. A number he and Jake had given her every time she showed up there. "Here's the number to the station's switchboard if you have any further questions."

Chloe was a dog with a bone. "If I don't get answers soon, I'll be going over your heads!" she shouted. She didn't take the paper from his hand but lowered her voice. "Where's Jake?"

"He's out on another case. What else can I do for you?"

"Why's he not returning my phone calls?"

Her anger directed at Jake belonged to the killer. "I have no idea. You'll need to discuss it with him."

He stood, dismissing her as he started to walk her toward the door. "I would if he'd answer his freakin' phone," Chloe said in a huff.

"I don't get involved in his personal life, Ms. Wagner. I'll tell him you stopped by."

* * * *

Before he headed home, Jake walked around the downtown area hoping the distraction would clear his head. The weather for April suited him. It was said, if you didn't like the weather in New England, you only had to wait five minutes for it to change. *And that was no folktale*, he thought. The sixty-degree temperatures were a gift this time of year. Last week there was frost, this week heat. A mild breeze ruffled his auburn hair, the promise of summer in the air. *I was looking forward to summer and the outdoor activities until McGuire dropped his damn bomb.* He passed the new modern courthouse on Meadow Street. Smokers puffed away outside the building. The courthouse stood out against the nineteen-thirties architecture of the other municipal buildings lining the street. The size of the city suited him. One hundred thousand-plus residents made it a city, but kept the small-town attitudes and feelings alive.

His lanky stride ate up the sidewalk as he headed down Grand Street toward the federal building, which housed the main post office and other federal divisions. *Son of a gun, it isn't my day.* As he walked past city hall, Wilkesbury's idiot mayor, along with his entourage, stepped in front of him.

The Honorable John Velky sucked in his gut and puffed out his chest like he always did when he met up with him. Jake found it amusing most days. The mayor, with his styled brown hair and expensive suits, was a true politician. He kissed babies one moment and overtaxed their parents the next. Jake had never voted for him.

"You don't have anything better to do then stroll around town, Lieutenant?" Mayor Velky asked.

"Good morning, Mayor." It took all his control to be polite, as he tried to walk away. *Today isn't a good day to get in a pissing match with the mayor. It might cost me my career.*

Jake studied the quote over the doors of city hall as he tuned out the mayor. *Quid Aere Perennius.* The meaning was something you were taught in local schools. His father, as an immigrant and Wilkesbury cop, had him and Eva studying the history of Wilkesbury, "The Brass Capital of the World" in its heyday. Translated from Latin it meant, "What is More Lasting Than Brass?" He forced his attention back to the mayor.

"I'll be at the station this week in discussions with the commissioner," Mayor Velky said before walking away, leaving Jake baffled. He watched Velky jump into the back of the town car. *It takes all kinds*, he thought. His mind drifted back to Eva. A girl he would never see beyond her fifteen years, thanks to Spaulding.

* * * *

At home, Jake rummaged through his basement, searching for his father's records. *Why now?* He couldn't get the question out of his head. What did Spaulding and his lawyer hope to achieve with the new testing? Every couple of years he was subjected to this torment. And every couple of years he gathered his strength to face down the parole board with his gruesome evidence. The pictures of the crime scene, along with Eva's bruised and bloody body, gave them many reasons to deny Spaulding's request. His father had kept a copy of Eva's case file at home since he wasn't allowed to work it. The other detectives made sure he had every bit of evidence he needed. It was one of their own who'd been victimized. Nobody messed with a cop's family and got away with it. *Except maybe this time*, he thought as he rubbed his throbbing head. Had George Spaulding found a way to cheat the system? It couldn't be true after seventeen years that they had imprisoned the wrong man. If it was true, then who had killed his sister Eva? Jake couldn't wrap his mind around it.

No, it was George.

The fifth box he opened was dedicated to her case. On top, his father had marked it one of five. After hunting down the other boxes, he brought them upstairs and placed them in his office. The first box he opened sent him right back to hell and his first visit to the morgue. It was the year he had lost his innocence.

A buzzing rang out in his ears from the fluorescent lights overhead. The starkness of the corridor as their footsteps echoed in the silence created the crescendo of a day gone horribly wrong. The buzzing grew louder as they approached the door. The medical examiner, Doctor Ed Jerome, put his hand up to stop them.

Taking a deep breath, Doc Jerome said, "James, you've done this a hundred times, but this is different. I can make the identification for you."

"No, I need to do this, Ed," Captain James Carrington said.

"Okay. Why doesn't Jake wait out here?" Doctor Jerome offered, giving him an out.

He spoke up, his voice louder than intended. "I'm going in." He said it with such force it brooked no argument.

Ed pushed open the door.

On the table lay a body covered with a white sheet. Ed's assistants had set the victim up for viewing. There was no way to hide the odor of death, though they tried to camouflage it with disinfectant, air fresheners, and Clorox. "The house of death" is what the cops called it.

Jake inhaled as he looked to his father for support. His father, a tall man, who Jake favored in height only, squared his shoulders and nodded to the M.E.

"Show me," James demanded.

Doc Jerome pulled back the sheet to reveal a girl in her mid-teens, black and blue from head to toe, the violent trauma of death etched in her horrified expression. Fright forever pasted on her face.

"Was she raped?" James asked, while tears escaped his eyes.

"Yes," Doc Jerome said.

Neither man paid attention to Jake's weeping at their side. He couldn't stop as he viewed his younger sister. With a gentle caress, he touched her forehead, her cheek, then kissed her good-bye on the lips.

He turned away in grief, saw both his anger and his pain reflected in his father's face. His father's fists clenched, his shoulders racked with heavy sobs as he viewed the broken body of his daughter. Jake understood he looked with a father's eye, not a cop's.

"My baby," James cried.

Jake listened every night at dinner when his father spoke of his cases. It was something distant, stories that didn't touch his life. Until now.

The buzzing in his ears increased. Time and space slipped by, then someone held a glass of water to his lips. The stress of the situation had overtaken him—he'd collapsed on the floor.

"I'm sorry, Jake. I shouldn't have brought you here." James hugged him, crushing him to his chest.

"I'm fine, Dad. When you catch the bastard, I'm going to kill him for what he did to Eva. You need to know I'll do it."

It was the first time he'd ever cursed in front of his father.

It took every ounce of strength within him to pull himself out of the memory. A fist squeezed his heart. He couldn't do this alone. God, he needed a drink. No, he needed Louie.

After a couple of hours, Jake decided to go back to work. Until a new trial came to fruition, he'd continue to line up the info on the case if and when they needed the ammunition to get a second conviction on Spaulding. He'd have it ready. Tonight, he would lay out a strategy and organize the files as he would for any other case he worked.

* * * *

News traveled fast in a cop shop. Among curious glances thrown his way, or comments of support from his detectives in the bullpen, Jake ignored them all. He took a seat at his desk across from Louie. His friend eyeballed him but didn't comment, which Jake found out of character for him. The Wagner file he wanted to review wasn't in his desk drawer.

"You got the Wagner file?"

"Yes." Louie gathered the papers spread across his desk, placed them back in the file, closed it and handed the bulk of it to Jake.

As he took the file from Louie, Jake studied his partner and his messy desk. The finicky Louie didn't match up with how he maintained his area. His suits pressed, his pants creased to razor sharpness, along with his precisely knotted tie and styled black hair, were at odds with the mess on his desk.

He wondered how Louie worked with all the clutter. Jake kept a phone and computer on his desk. All his files were in the desk drawer, alphabetized for easy access. Louie had all his files on top, an in-and-out box, an empty coffee cup and this morning's wrapper from his breakfast sandwich. *A cluttered desk would clog up my mind*, Jake thought as he opened the file. Pushing Eva's case to the back burner, he tried to concentrate on Shanna's.

"Are you free tonight to throw a couple of things around?"

"Yep."

"We'll do it at my house after we get out of here. I'm going to suggest to McGuire that Burke and Kraus work Eva's case if Spaulding gets a new trial," Jake said.

"I agree."

"I'll need to tell him. And I don't care what he said. I need to be in on the briefing. I'll be right back."

Jake got up and walked into McGuire's office without knocking. "Shamus, give the case to Burke and Kraus. When the time comes, I'd like to be in on the initial meeting in case they have questions."

"I'll need them to come at it with fresh eyes, Jake, not with your preconceived notions."

"I'm not going to offer personal opinions. The file will speak for itself. No one is more familiar with it than me."

McGuire checked his calendar. "We might as well get ahead of this. Set it up in Conference Room One for three o'clock on Wednesday afternoon. I want to refamiliarize myself with the file and also give Burke and Kraus time to do the same. And Jake? I'm still in charge here." Jake took the mild slap on the wrist without comment.

After reserving the conference room, he left it up to the captain to speak with Burke and Kraus. All day he tried to keep his mind off Eva's case while he dug into Shanna Wagner's file and rearranged the contents to coincide with the timeline as they understood it.

"I'll let you catch up before I give you my thoughts on this." Louie scratched his head. "Chloe Wagner stopped in to see you."

"Shit." Jake blew out a breath.

"Yeah, she asked a few questions about her sister, but she seemed more concerned about you ignoring her calls."

He'd been an idiot to date her in the first place. Right from the beginning, he handled her wrong and now he was paying for it. Never before had he disregarded a regulation. *Ha, the one time I do and it's a catastrophe.* An indiscretion like this could cost him his career. He'd been flattered by the way she had pursued him. Her pretty girl-next-door looks fooled him. No matter where he turned, restaurants, bars, the grocery store, Chloe was there. Alarms should've sounded. What a fool he'd been. On the second date, she had insisted on bringing dinner to his house. Before he had a chance to open the cartons of takeout she was on him. He should've kicked her out then. Instead he took what she had to offer. Afterward when they lounged in bed, Chloe had started to talk of the future. She stressed how they both had dealt with death at an early age and understood it was important to live for today because there might not be a tomorrow. Before she had finished her sentence, he had her dressed and out the door. She had scared the living hell out of him. No way had he led her on about commitments and forever.

When she called the next day, he ended the relationship over the phone. In hindsight, maybe he should've done it after a third date, not the morning after, but the woman had shopped for a damn ring, for God's sake. After he broke it off, he decided to keep a journal of the times she had showed up at a place where he was dining or drinking. It went from flattering to creepy, fast. She seemed to have arrived at a place even before he made plans to be there. "Cripes, dating her was a mistake. What did you tell her?"

"I told her I don't get involved in your personal affairs."

"Oh please! I can't get you out of my personal life. There's something off with her. Did you feel it?"

"No," Louie said, wiping the grin off his face.

"Well I did, when I was with her. We should have taken a closer look at her sooner."

"You can't miss what's not there, Jake."

"I'm hoping we did. Otherwise we have nothing. Let's put everyone back on the suspect list and start over."

With fresh eyes, Jake studied the crime scene photos first. Once or twice he caught himself comparing them to Eva's wounds. It was difficult, but he forced himself to remain in the present. Such brutality in most cases meant the victim knew her killer. Somewhere along the line, Shanna had pissed off someone and paid the ultimate price. The question was who had she angered? *Rage,* Jake thought. The crime scene photos exhibited uncontrollable rage.

Everyone they had interviewed stated Shanna was well liked with no enemies. An ambitious woman, she was first in her class, a scholarship athlete like himself, and she had held down a job while attending college. Had she set off a competitor? Could her achievements be the foundation for jealousy? Eliminate her, eliminate the rivalry? Shanna had interned with an accounting firm who had offered her a job a year before she'd even graduated.

No steady relationships. Shanna had dated one person in the six-month period prior to her death. He was another accountant at the firm where she had interned. According to her family she hadn't dated often because she had been goal orientated. Maybe it was a guy she turned down and his ego couldn't handle it. But it seemed farfetched.

"Do you remember this Cavilla guy? The one she dated," Jake said.

"Yeah, he seemed a little old for her. Why?"

"The answers lie in the rage; this kind of violence suggests a scorned lover or wanna-be lover to me."

"We looked at him but nothing popped," Louie said.

"We did, but let's relook at his alibi."

"Got something?"

"No."

Jake dug around in the file until he unearthed the information on the boyfriend. Mark Cavilla, at five-nine, weighed about one hundred fifty pounds. He had black hair, black eyes, and a black temper to go with it.

"Your notes say his answers seemed rehearsed at the time. What else do you remember about him?"

"His statement seemed off and he had an attitude right from the beginning," Louie stated.

"He was alibied by the bartender at a bar less than two miles from the scene. I always believed the killer was a local guy since she was dumped in town even though she was supposed to be up at school in Storrs at the time of the killing. It's a long way to travel to dump a body unless you're familiar with the area and that particular construction site. They picked well. No one would be around a construction site at night. I want to re-interview the bartender before too much time goes by. Okay, what else...?" Jake's head snapped up.

A couple of his detectives were going at it. Amused, Jake listened in. He didn't do anything about them. These things tended to work themselves out if left alone.

"What was I going to say?"

"Christ, Carrington, can't you read without your lips moving? I'm trying to concentrate here," Burke yelled.

Al Burke had his moments. A detective in the department for over ten years, he'd seen it all. Fifteen years a cop and his face showed it. He wouldn't consider him attractive, with his hard eyes, the stomach the size of Jupiter, and a Rudolph-red nose from drinking. Jake figured Burke had a few more years on the job before it crushed him. The guy'd been divorced three times, and produced five children. A heavy drinker, he could turn on a dime, but his investigative skills were prime. He had no problems going through a door with Burke.

"Al, how'd you get the black eye?" Jake asked with a wide grin on his face. He knew, but he wanted Al to say it out loud.

"Shut up. Everyone, shut up," Burke said, walking toward the coffee machine.

"A ninety-year-old woman landed a punch when his guard was down," Kraus, Burke's partner, said.

"I'm warning you, Kraus. Shut up." Burke slammed down his coffee cup. "You guys don't know the half of it."

Laughing, Detective Gunther "Gunner" Kraus continued, "To his credit, Sarge, she was like a pit bull."

"I'll say mean." Burke took over the story as he yanked up his pants and tightened his belt. "Never mind like one, she was. I got away easy. You should have seen what she did to her poor husband. Carved him like a roast because he complained about her smoking. Her freakin' smoking? I thought those things were supposed to kill you. She's ninety freaking years old. What I saw today, she'll last another ten years, if a day. I feel sorry for her cellmate. Her poor sliced-up husband lived with the witch for seventy-five years. Me, I would have killed myself around year two."

"We can help. What's your choice of weapons, Al?" Louie threw in to bait him.

"Funny. I'm breaking my stitches on that one, Romanelli."

Movement to the side of Jake pulled him from the banter between his detectives. McGuire stood in his doorway with his arms folded over his chest as he listened in on the conversation.

"Jake, you got a minute?" Shamus asked.

"Sure, what's up?" Twice in one day, he hoped it was better news than this morning.

"We'll talk in my office." McGuire turned and walked in. Jake followed. "Shut the door."

"More bad news on Spaulding?"

"No. The board reviewed your request." *Lord Christ, the man has the best poker face I've ever seen.*

"What's their decision?" Jake braced himself for the news. The way this day was going, it couldn't be good.

"The chief and I feel you're not ready to sit at a desk handling administrative issues. We feel you and the citizens of Wilkesbury will be happier and better served with you on the streets with Louie," McGuire said.

With his stomach sinking to his knees, he asked, "Did the board review any other items on their agenda?"

McGuire stared him down for a second before he stuck out his hand. "Congratulations, Lieutenant! You've earned it, Jake. This division is yours, if you still want it."

"I do." He'd been apprehensive when he took the exam. If he passed he wasn't guaranteed homicide. The brass would put him where they felt he was needed. This was a gift.

"You're a credit to this department and the city. The ceremony will take place at the mayor's office on the twenty-fifth at noon. Congratulations again."

"Thank you, sir. I'm sure we'll go out for a couple of beers to celebrate. Join us?"

"I'd love to. Instead I'll be sitting in a hot, sweaty room, waiting for my child to dance, applauding like I'm at a Broadway show. Boys are much easier to raise than girls. Think of me when you lift your glass. I've never had a better officer on my team than you, Jake."

Those recitals could take hours. Louie once guilted him into one of Marisa's, and as her godfather, he'd had no choice but to say yes. Every year after that he made damn sure he had plans. He washed the horrific memory of it out of his head.

Ignoring Louie's finger tapping when he returned to his desk, Jake picked up the Wagner file and started to read.

"Okay, what gives? What did the captain want this time?"

"That's Lieutenant to you, Detective."

Louie jumped up. He pulled Jake into his arms for a hug instead of giving him a handshake. "Well this calls for a real celebration. Hey, Burke, Sergeant Carrington is now your Lieutenant. He's the head cheese of homicide. Hot damn!"

Louie threw a couple air punches. Jake hoped Louie's test results were positive this time around. It killed Louie when he'd failed the sergeant's test not once but twice. But maybe the third time around was the charm. He wondered why Louie's face didn't split in half with such a wide grin on it.

Cops swarmed Jake's desk from all divisions.

Louie tapped him on the shoulder. "Captain wants to see you again."

Jake broke away from the crowd. "Yeah, Cap?"

"The title comes with an office. Pick one out as soon as possible."

McGuire came around his desk with his briefcase in his hand. He patted Jake on the back, then turned off his office light and left.

How would this promotion affect the dynamics between him and Louie? *What a day. First the news about Spaulding and now he'd been promoted.* He couldn't figure out if he wanted to celebrate or punch someone out.

"This is great, because you're already coming to dinner. Oh, but weren't we going to review your files?"

"They can wait until tomorrow night, Louie. We cancel the celebration now, Burke would stone us."

"Okay, we celebrate and then have dinner with Sophia and the kids. I'll call her now. Have her make a great dessert." Louie's face gleamed.

"Thanks, Louie."

That night, when he got home, he'd try to get through the files on his own. The words his father had spoken to him on the day of his promotion to detective echoed in his head.

"With command comes great responsibility, son. Treat your officers the way you'd want to be treated." Then Captain James Carrington pinned the new gold shield onto Jake's dress uniform. Pride shone in his father's eyes as he saluted him. Days later his father died of a heart attack.

Jake felt his father had died of a broken heart.

With his father gone, Jake had one close relative this side of the ocean, his mother. The rest resided in Ireland, where his parents were from. She hated his job. He thought better of sharing his news with her.

Though unrelated, his mom felt his sister's death had resulted from her husband's job. Not logical. A spoiled kid had ruined their lives. Eva had turned him down. He had taken what he'd wanted anyway, punishing her for rejecting him.

Thoughts of his mother surged into his head and brought on the familiar guilt. Jake promised himself he'd visit her this week. Cripes, he hated walking into the nursing home. The odors assaulted his olfactory senses. He always held his breath until he reached his mother's room. The crying and begging from the residents as they reached out to him when he walked by tore at his heart. He tried not to rush by them. He hoped to God he never wound up there. In his opinion, a bullet to the head would be better.

His beautiful mother had brownish-red hair, cream-colored flawless skin, high cheekbones, and sad emerald eyes. She had forgotten how to live after Eva died. He got his height from his father, but his coloring from his mother. At five-six Maddie packed quite a punch when her temper flared. It wasn't something you wanted to be on the receiving end of. Now trapped in the past, his mother lay in bed all day, crying, telling stories about her Eva through her tears. Jake wondered why she hadn't run out of them.

We lost two people on the day Eva died. My mother blamed me. She blamed my father. She blamed the police, the school—and anyone else who popped into her head. . . Something snapped in her brain on the day Eva died. He didn't understand if she couldn't or wouldn't move forward. *A tight family unit, once happy—never the same after that day,* he thought. *We all loved each other, and were looking forward to the bright future ahead of us. Yes, I'll visit her tomorrow.*

Louie touched his arm, brought him back to the present. "Hey, you in there? Let's head out now." Louie grabbed his jacket off the back of his chair. "Oh, boss..."

"Funny, Louie. What?"

"First round's on me. I want everyone to know I'm playing up to the new boss. Got it?"

"Oh, Louie—rounds two, plus three and four, are also on you," Jake said shrugging into his jacket.

Maybe he'd take tonight off before he immersed himself in Eva's file. God, he'd need to get a boatload of courage before he ran through it all.

www.ingramcontent.com/pod-product-compliance
Lightning Source LLC
Chambersburg PA
CBHW020609260626
47157CB00003B/930